"I don't ha[ve] ... in having a husband."

He took a step nearer. "Yes, you do."

Something about the way Jack looked at her—something about the way warmth seeped from his chest to hers, kindling a new kind of heat between them—made Grace's heart stutter. Her breath caught and held, too. She didn't know what to make of the sensation. Discomfited but resolute, she stepped forward. It wouldn't do to let herself be cowed by a mere male like Jack Murphy.

The heat between them flared higher.

"I don't need a man for anything," she announced.

His lips turned up. Parted. Even his teeth were nice. She'd never had such a close-up view of them before. For the first time ever, Grace caught herself approving of his clean shave.

"Darlin', if you believe that," he said, "then you need a man for certain. You need a man real soon."

* * *

The Rascal
Harlequin® Historical #825—November 2006

The Rascal

Lisa Plumley

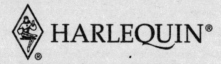

HARLEQUIN®

TORONTO • NEW YORK • LONDON
AMSTERDAM • PARIS • SYDNEY • HAMBURG
STOCKHOLM • ATHENS • TOKYO • MILAN • MADRID
PRAGUE • WARSAW • BUDAPEST • AUCKLAND

ISBN-13: 978-0-373-29425-1
ISBN-10: 0-373-29425-5

THE RASCAL

This edition published by arrangement with Harlequin Books S.A.

® and TM are trademarks of the publisher. Trademarks indicated with ® are registered in the United States Patent and Trademark Office, the Canadian Trade Marks Office and in other countries.

www.eHarlequin.com

Printed in U.S.A.

Available from Harlequin® Historical and
LISA PLUMLEY

The Drifter #605
The Matchmaker #674
The Scoundrel #797
The Rascal #825

**DON'T MISS THESE OTHER
NOVELS AVAILABLE NOW:**

#823 MISTLETOE KISSES
Elizabeth Rolls, Deborah Hale, Diane Gaston

#824 INDISCRETIONS
Gail Ranstrom

#826 THE DEFIANT MISTRESS
Claire Thornton

Please address questions and book requests to:
Harlequin Reader Service
U.S.: 3010 Walden Ave., P.O. Box 1325, Buffalo, NY 14269
Canadian: P.O. Box 609, Fort Erie, Ont. L2A 5X3

To my husband, John, with love

Chapter One

November 1881
Boston, Massachusetts

If Jack Murphy had to face down another giggling, giddy woman baring herself in nothing but a corset and drawers, he knew he was going to go completely barmy.

Eight times in three days was simply too much for any man. Even one so appreciative of the female form as Jack considered himself to be. Ordinarily, he enjoyed women of all kinds, in all sorts of diverse arrays. In the satiny embrace of an evening gown. In the close-fitting hug of an afternoon dress. Or in the altogether, as God—and right-thinking males—preferred.

But now, gazing in dismay at the widow Marjorie Lancaster's curvaceous form, adorned with its telltale gussets and lacings and froth of lacy trim, Jack felt his…er, enthusiasm wane.

Given his yen for intellectual pursuits, he couldn't help but analyze the situation. The only explanation he could discern was simple. As experiments went, his accidental foray into ladies' unmentionables had turned out disastrously.

Not merely because of the aforementioned women, all of whom had waylaid him—one being so bold as to strike in his offices at Boston College—to make clear their admiring status of his sartorial "gifts." But also because, thanks to his unwelcome notoriety, he could scarcely leave home without inspiring gossip and speculation—or inciting women to clamor for samples and, in the case of the brashest, to offer him further "insight" into their most intimate clothing needs.

It was true that Jack—a professor by training but an inveterate inventor otherwise—had accidentally created the city's most scandalous ladies' undergarments. But that didn't mean he wanted his whole life turned wrong side up. He refused to stand for it. Which was why he'd come here, determined to enjoy at least one aspect of his day…and his night.

Marjorie wriggled on her bedroom's red velvet settee, trying another seductive pose. Her silky dressing gown slid further askew, improving his view of her unmentionables.

Her damned, trouble-causing, all too familiar—

"Jack? Is something wrong?"

Her question drew him to her bewildered frown, then to the alluring pout of her lips. Misgivings assailed him. It wasn't Marjorie's fault that he'd had such a turnaround in his fortunes—nor that he'd been forced to evade several representatives of the Jordan Marsh department store on the way here. They'd been veritable pests of late, ever since the news of his chance invention had gotten round.

"Nothing I can't manage," he told Marjorie.

At least that much was true, Jack assured himself as he crossed the room, doffing his suit coat in the lamplight. He tossed it to a nearby chair, then loosened his necktie and collar as well. At the end of a long day, all a man wanted was to be comfortable. And maybe, in isolated instances, to be comforted. Which was the other reason he'd come to Marjorie's.

"Because if you want to talk about things," she went on, "I'm certainly willing to listen. I know a man like you doesn't require assurance, but perhaps we should catch up on events. Ever since I returned from Philadelphia—"

"Shhh. No talking." Kneeling at the edge of the settee, Jack took her face in his hands. He surveyed her familiar features, her dimpled chin, her experienced demeanor. They'd dallied together for years now, whenever either of them felt lonely. "No talking," he repeated sternly, "and no thinking."

He kissed her, hungry for exactly that.

Marjorie's guffaw disturbed the moment. She leaned back, nearly succeeding in drawing his attention to her damnable undergarments again. Deliberately, Jack concentrated on her face. He didn't see what was so funny—and that was with his Irishman's good humor to aid him, too.

"*You?* 'No thinking'?" Her eyes shone with utterly unsuppressed mirth. "That will be the day. Aside from which, you haven't said a single thing about my new lingerie. We may have been friends for a long time now, but that doesn't excuse you from common courtesy. Let's start over, shall we?"

Agreeably, Jack nodded. He reached for his cuff, preparing to shed his shirt. The sooner he could be naked, the sooner he could forget the travails of the day. The sooner he could persuade Marjorie to shed her underclothes, as well.

She modeled them for him, gracefully spreading her arms to show off her garments' most outrageous features. Her expression told him she expected admiration and commentary. Banter, just as they'd always shared. But after a full day spent debating, dodging specious "investors," and finally moving his things out of his now-*former* offices at Boston College, even blarney-tongued Jack didn't have the will to oblige.

"Those things will look superb on the floor." He kissed her again, reaching for the nearest set of lacings. Their innovative design was woefully well known to him. He tugged them free with his usual ease. "After I take them off you."

"You rascal!" Giggling, Marjorie slapped his hand away. "There'll be no removing anything till you've fully appreciated the extraordinary effects of this bodice. It's positively revolutionary, wouldn't you say so?"

No, he wouldn't. Jack tightened his lips, not wanting to ponder the garments that had inadvertently wrecked his life and his livelihood. But apparently Marjorie didn't realize she was wearing one of his own "revolutionary" designs. She'd been in Philadelphia when all the trouble had started, so she couldn't have known what an entanglement those undergarments had turned out to be.

Neither could Jack, else he'd never have drawn them in the first place. He'd created them—a modification of the typical feminine undergarments—as a lark, performed while naked and sated and inspired. He'd never realized his scandalous schematic would go any farther than his notepad and pencil.

Unfortunately for him, it had. Disastrously.

He looked away, profoundly unwilling to discuss it. He would finish undressing, he would take Marjorie in his arms and he would forget his current predicament. He'd be damned if he wouldn't. After the week he'd had, he needed solace.

But Marjorie wasn't offering solace, and she wasn't settling for his *not* admiring her ensemble either. With her customary assurance, she tipped his chin in the desired direction. Her bejeweled fingers gleamed in the lamplight, adding to the luxuriousness of their surroundings.

Since taking over as proprietress of her late husband's bookshop, Marjorie had done well for herself. Her jewelry proclaimed as much, as did her well-appointed town house.

"Pay attention," she urged playfully. "Otherwise you'll fail to notice how cunningly this lace frames my…"

Trailing off, Marjorie paused. As though getting her first truly good look at him, she peered into his face more closely. In reply, Jack raised his eyebrows and went on unfastening his shirt cuff, giving her his best carefree expression—the one every Irishman kept at the ready. But Marjorie wasn't swayed. She merely went on studying him.

No, no, no. He had, typically, not chosen a cotton-brained woman to pass his nights with. Just at that moment, with his longtime paramour's astute gaze pinned on him, Jack sorely regretted it. Why couldn't his tastes in women fall toward silly bits of skirt with no ambition, no sense and no interest in anything beyond their own stylish bonnets?

"Well, now. This is a twist." Marjorie's eyes met his. She gestured to her clothing. "I thought you'd be pleased. I had to pay a pretty penny for these fripperies. There's scarcely a set to be had in all of the city, you know."

"I know." But he wished he didn't.

She watched him unwaveringly. Damn it.

"Something else has happened, hasn't it?"

"Yes." Jack tried out a wolfish smile. "I've let nearly eight minutes pass without getting you out of those clothes."

She wriggled out of reach. "Shall we talk about it?"

His smile faded. He didn't want to talk. Didn't want to think, didn't want to remember. Instead Jack pushed his attention to Marjorie's bounteous bosom. He waited for the usual spark of interest to overtake him.

It was a wondrous bosom, uplifted to a perfect degree by her corset's ingeniously stitched seams and its heretofore untried design elements. It was further augmented by the cleverly hidden horsehair-padded—

Blast it. He was doing it again. Ruminating on the structural elements of corsetry when he had a perfectly proportioned woman to divert his attention. What was wrong with him?

"I heard rumors about some shocking design you'd created." Marjorie touched his sleeve. "I discounted them at the time, of course. But Mrs. Parker had it from Mrs. McIntire that the college might request your resignation. Is that what's the matter? What's diverted your attention from…me?"

She gestured elaborately, indicating her seductive attire. Jack frowned, resolutely not glancing at those incriminating undergarments. Doggedly, he unfastened his other cuff.

"Or have they already? Have they asked you to leave?" Marjorie tilted her head in concern. "Oh, Jack. I'm so sorry."

Her soft voice knifed through him, making him feel even more pitiful than he had when he'd arrived. Leaving his shirt unbuttoned and his cuffs loose, he knelt to remove his shoes.

"No worries, darlin'," he managed huskily. What the hell was wrong with his voice? Jack cleared his throat. "Till I take another position—" *if there were any to be had for him* "—I'll have more free time for myself. More free time for you."

His teasing tone did not have its desired effect.

"But how could the college do this to you?" Marjorie persisted. "You've enjoyed your professorship there for ages. You've done remarkably well for yourself. Surely your invention, whatever it was, was not so shocking as all that."

"Well…"

Wryly, Jack recalled the past few weeks. Ever since his four sisters had found his schematics, taken them and had samples made up to market, his life had turned into a fool's bonanza of shilling salesmen, outraged faculty members and women clamoring to show him his own handiwork. He'd never have guessed there were so many females interested in newfangled corsetry with all its attendant horns and bells and whistles.

Glancing at Marjorie, Jack shook his head. "It's a ridiculous imbroglio, not worth discussing further."

"But if it's cost you your position—"

He slanted her a quelling look, then lifted her hand for a kiss. Her fingers curled around his in response. Fondly, Jack gazed at her—and for a moment, relented. Marjorie deserved the truth. "It turns out my talent for undressing women has brought on a knack for dressing them, as well. I can't believe you didn't guess…given the present circumstances."

Wanting to make light of the whole mess, he raised his eyebrow toward her ensemble. For a moment, Marjorie merely seemed perplexed. Then, finally catching the direction of his gaze, she widened her eyes. She slapped her hands over herself.

"*This?*" she breathed, caressing her corsetry. "Truly?"

With a shrug, Jack nodded. He hadn't come here to unburden his troubles on her. But she would learn of them soon enough, he reasoned, and as the inspiration for his designs…

"Those drawings were just a diversion!" she protested. "Just a way to pass the time between our…oh, my."

Mouth agape, she glanced in astonishment from her undergarments to Jack, then back again. He nearly regretted confiding in her…until, in the next moment, Marjorie recognized the significance of their situation.

"*I* am the model for the city's most faddish new dress!"

"You needn't sound so thrilled with the fact," he noted. "As you pointed out, it's cost me my position."

"I know. And I'm sorry for it. Truly, I am." Her gentle squeeze reassured him. "But still…isn't it exhilarating? I've inspired a sensation! And all thanks to your genius."

Her sparkling eyes and flushed cheeks made him grin. The widow Marjorie Lancaster was hardly a girl, to become boundlessly excited like this. But seeing her this way, so enthusiastic and pleased, almost erased Jack's displeasure over the whole mess. Almost.

He dragged his braces from his shoulders, still intent on his original plan. He'd come here to forget his troubles, and that's what he intended on accomplishing. With Marjorie's help, of course. If he could only persuade her to undress...

"Honestly, Jack. This isn't so awful." Marjorie levered upward on her settee and wrapped her dressing gown around herself, apparently settling in for a businesslike discussion of this new development. "There's a potential fortune to be made here! You're the darling of fashionable eastern women now—"

He quirked his lips. "Purely involuntarily, I assure you."

"—and perhaps, especially with your teaching position forfeit, you should take advantage of that."

"No." The last thing Jack wanted was to prove himself the "sissified corsetry creator" his more sober colleagues at Boston College had sneeringly accused him of being. He refused to consider the incident any further, much less embrace it. "And that's enough talking for now."

"You shouldn't be too hasty," she opined. "After all, I've learned a great deal about the world of commerce since taking over the bookshop, and it's only wise for you to—"

"Enough," he growled and descended upon her at last.

Marjorie's words ended in a shriek, then a lusty giggle. The settee groaned beneath their combined weight, but Jack knew it would hold. It had done so many times before. Clad only in his britches and unbuttoned shirt, he cupped Marjorie's head in his hand and kissed her again.

"Quiet now," he warned, shoving all thoughts of business and colleges and corsets from his mind. "Otherwise I won't have the concentration to ravish you properly."

Marjorie scoffed, more than wise to his ways by now. "You always have concentration aplenty. Perhaps too much, especially when it comes to—"

Jack silenced her complimentary chattering with another

kiss. He didn't need to be told of his prowess in bed, particularly by the very woman with whom he'd soon be demonstrating that selfsame skill. Groaning with the need to lose himself in comfort, in familiarity, in a woman's welcoming embrace, he slid his hand lower.

Marjorie squealed in delight.

He grinned. Ah. This was better. This was right. This was the perfect way to force his troublesome day from his mind. Jack relaxed a fraction, enjoying the sweet smell of her hair, the sensuous entanglement of their bodies…the lacy froth of the undergarments that had wrecked his entire existence.

Damnation. Remembrance and regret stilled his hand, but Jack refused to acquiesce so easily. He caressed Marjorie again—and encountered another handful of undergarments.

He closed his eyes, pushed to the limit by this damnable intrusion. He wanted to appreciate undergarments as adornments for the female form, just as he'd always done before. Not as the unwitting instruments of his downfall. But he couldn't.

This was serious. Would he never be able to undress a woman freely again? Would he always be reminded of his lost livelihood when he tried?

One of life's profoundest pleasures was being with a woman. Jack wasn't sure he could survive without it. Yet from here on, it would be his own damned fault if he had to.

The moments lengthened, he rasping for breath and Marjorie squirming subtly beneath him.

At last, she craned her neck. "Jack…?"

The disappointment in her innocent query gutted him.

"Shhh. It's fine." He kissed her again, hoping to buoy himself and recapture the moment. Somehow though, everything felt skewed. Wrong. "I'm fine. *I'm fine.*"

A pause. "You know, it's all right if you'd rather…oh, I

don't know. Discuss business, perhaps?" Her chirpy tone belied their intimate position. "I've been having a few ideas about your dilemma. And about potential financing. And about how to inform women of your marvelous creations."

Jack groaned. "You've had time to contemplate all that?"

Affably, Marjorie nodded. She regarded him expectantly.

Jack's spirits plummeted. Circumstances were more dire than he'd thought. Of a certain, he was losing his touch. He had set out to seduce a woman and had only succeeded in igniting her business instincts. What was the matter with him?

Carefully releasing her, he sat up.

"Oh, Jack." Marjorie grabbed his arm. "I'm sorry! I didn't mean to upset you. It's only that I got to thinking—"

"It's all right." He managed a smile, then patted her knee for reassurance. "My mind works overmuch, too. I can't stop it. We have that in common."

He tried for a light tone to leaven the statement, so she wouldn't guess how much the fact of it bothered him. Here he was, inches away from a willing woman, and his thoughts were crowded not with her myriad charms, but with his new notoriety, his lost teaching position and the peace of mind he might never savor again.

Thrusting his hand through his hair, Jack considered the situation. He could not go to work. His professorship was as lost to him as his good reputation was. He could not go home, at least not without facing bold female admirers, scheming opportunists and his meddlesome sisters' visits to explain their participation in the whole debacle.

He certainly could not linger overlong with Marjorie. Their lives were independent and always had been, by a mutual agreement that had forever suited them both.

But now… As much as Jack yearned to deny it, as much as he'd endeavored to escape it, one thing seemed evident.

His life would never be the same again.

"Don't worry. Everything will be fine." Wrapping her arms around him, Marjorie hugged him to her. "You're not the only man who's had trouble being intimate."

"I do *not* have trouble being intimate." He gritted his teeth. "I'd show you, except…ah, hell."

His throat tightened. His eyes burned. All at once, Jack felt like bawling. He'd never been weak. He'd been strong. Accomplished. Proud. But now his whole life was in shambles, and there was no immediate way out.

Not now that seducing Marjorie had failed him.

"I understand." This time, Marjorie patted his knee in a commiserating fashion. "I do."

Jack wished *he* did. But he refused to admit as much aloud. He was an educated and discerning man. An inventive man. Yet right now he did not understand. Anything. And he hated it.

Marjorie's insightful look softened. "Don't worry. You need time to get used to things, that's all. Then you'll feel like yourself again."

Frowning, Jack prayed she was right. With the discipline and attentiveness that had characterized his dual vocations as academic and inventor, he studied her dressing gown's embroidered silk. Despite his efforts, frustration swamped him.

There was only one thing left to be said. But before Jack could muster the apology Marjorie deserved, she hugged him close once more. She released him, then examined him cheerfully.

"I'm only sorry you didn't offer me an investment opportunity in these unmentionables of yours," she teased as they sat side by side on the settee, old friends regardless. "If you become rich and famous from them—"

"I'm already *in*famous."

"—I'll certainly wish I could benefit. Trust me, Jack."

Marjorie swept her hand toward her middle. "I've never worn anything more comfortable or ingenious—or flattering—in my entire life."

He slanted her a dubious glance. But her faith in him lifted his mood all the same. Marjorie did not discuss money and investments casually. She meant what she said.

"Those undergarments aren't meant for comfort," he reminded her with a devilish grin. "They're meant for easy removal. Not to mention a few more…shocking purposes. I'd be glad to explain them in detail, if you've forgotten."

She put her fingers to his lips, shaking her head at his offer. Her eyes sparkled, doubtless reflecting the renewed glint in his own.

"There's no need. Besides, however inconvenient this may be right now, remember—you're only 'infamous' here in Boston."

"This is where my home is."

Marjorie waved her hand carelessly. "You can always go somewhere else for a while. As it happens, my friends in Philadelphia might host you." Her smile turned keen. "Some of us relish a good scandal now and then, you know."

Regrettably, Jack wasn't one of them.

"Scandal is more enjoyable when it doesn't bankrupt you."

"Pshaw. You must have savings. Investments of your own or a nest egg of some kind." Sounding unconcerned, Marjorie pushed to her feet. She padded to the opposite end of the bedroom, her dressing gown fluttering richly in her wake, then lifted a decanter. "Whiskey? To help you think on it?"

Jack gazed at the amber liquid, mostly unseeing. "Thank you." Prodded by habitual chivalry, he rose. "I'll pour."

Their hands met over the uncapped decanter's neck. Jack wasn't sure what was wrong with him, but a shot of Old Orchard couldn't hurt, he reasoned. The liquor's unmistakable tang rose to meet him, clearing his head.

Solving his predicament would require something drastic, he determined as he downed his first swig. It would require wit and inventiveness and hard work. It would require courage. It would require, as all things did, certain and pure inspiration.

All the better, Jack told himself as he poured another whiskey. He had all those qualities and more. And inspiration had always come easily to him, whether he wanted it to or not. Witnessing Marjorie in her finery was proof enough of that.

"Mmm. You look better already." Marjorie sashayed nearer, seeming pleased. "Have you found a solution so soon?"

Jack examined his glass. "I have," he was surprised to hear himself say. "And you will never believe what it is."

Chapter Two

Fourteen months later
Morrow Creek, northern Arizona Territory

"Ale," came a voice from the other side of the bar.

Glancing up, Jack slung his barkeep's towel over his shoulder. He stifled a grin. The big man who took a seat before him was a favorite among all his saloon's customers.

Blacksmith Daniel McCabe was renowned for his abilities to swing a hammer, seduce a lady, or hold his liquor. Some of those talents had been stifled, of course, since his marriage to schoolteacher Sarah Crabtree a few months ago. But enough raw edges remained that Jack found Daniel eminently imitable.

Which was one reason he was happy to see him now.

Not to put too blunt a face on it, Jack still needed tutelage on becoming a proper western roustabout. Once he'd mastered that, he reasoned as he pulled the ale, he would fit in perfectly among his new friends and neighbors. McCabe just might be the man to offer him—however unwittingly—a few necessary tips.

Anticipating exactly that, Jack slung the ale across the bar in a practiced arc.

McCabe nodded. "Much obliged."

Jack only grunted. Grunting had proven surprisingly useful during his first few months in the west, saving him more than once from accidental lapses into professorial lecturing or elaborate speech.

After wiping up a splash of spilled mescal, Jack pocketed the blacksmith's coin. Being a saloonkeeper was not making him wealthy. But it did offer him peace of mind. Thanks to his troubles in Boston, that seemed far more valuable these days.

When he'd first come to Morrow Creek more than a year ago, intending to prove himself more man than "sissified corsetry creator," he'd expected to be exposed right away for the academic he really was. Or possibly for the scandalous, whispered-about inventor he'd unintentionally become.

Surprisingly, things hadn't turned out that way.

In the west, it seemed, people saw a man for who he was—not who he used to be. They looked no further than the present. So to Jack's satisfaction, everyone had accepted him as the taciturn Irish saloonkeeper he'd professed himself to be. And he'd immediately taken to the northern reaches of the territory itself, with its mountain ranges and deep ponderosa pine forests and boundless opportunities. So he'd contacted a land agent, arranged for the lease of a new saloon property—setting it as far away from his old life in Boston as possible—and begun anew.

It had cost him plenty, to be sure, Jack mused as he served up a mescal to a sun-browned cowboy. All his savings. All his close contact with his family and friends. Everything he'd once held dear.

But now he had a new life in Morrow Creek, with his past a close-held secret and his unwanted notoriety securely be-

hind him. If he could turn his saloon into a profitable ven
ture, in fact, he'd be well on his way to having everything h
needed.

All in all, life was simple. Peaceful. And that was exactl
the way Jack liked it. He'd staked everything on an existenc
filled with not much more than hopes of a rousing goo
time, a bit of coin to rub together and a few willing wome
who weren't wearing his radical undergarments. Thes
days, when end came to end, all Jack wanted was to mak
his saloon a success…and to prove, to himself more tha
anyone else, that he would be master of his fate from her
on out.

He didn't ever want to be at the mercy of public opinion—
or the subject of public excitement—ever again.

To that purpose, Jack filled his days with serving up whis
key and lager, and his nights with rowdy meetings of the Mor
row Creek Men's Club. He kept to himself, not talkin
overmuch or getting too close to anyone. It was all for th
best, he reasoned. He couldn't let anyone really know him
Otherwise they'd uncover his secret past, and his quiet lif
would be set akilter all over again.

So he hid away his books in his solitary rooms at the rea
of the saloon, tossed away his suits and neckties for shirts an
britches, and answered most inquiries with a grunt or a joke—
both designed to keep folks securely at their distance.

"Hey, Murphy. How come you can't play the piano?" th
cowboy across the bar whined, tipping up his hat. "The saloo
I was in up round Kansas City had a piano and dancing girl
and even a little monkey what would bring you peanuts for
penny. How come you don't have ent'tainment like that?"

"Quit yer caterwauling, Perkins." The blustery rejoinde
came from the gambling tables across the saloon's sawdus
covered floor, where several men wagered their newly as

sayed mine earnings. "You're just fed up 'cause you already lost on this here faro game."

Several other patrons agreed, offering good-natured guffaws. Someone suggested Perkins hog-tie them a dancing girl himself and bring her inside.

"Now, now." Jack spread his hands, palms down, gesturing for order. "There won't be any women in my place, hogtied or not." He couldn't help but display his Irishman's grin, nor hide the mischievous glint in his eye. "Leastwise not till I get my boardinghouse rooms set up upstairs."

"When's that gonna be, anyhow?" A grizzled miner peered up from his cards. "Me and some of the other fellas could sorely use someplace to stay in town 'sides the Lorndorff. It's damned near picked my pockets clean already."

There were nods all around. Demand was high for affordable lodging space, especially with the railroad stopping weekly.

"I'm working on it." Jack pulled another lager, its yeasty aroma teasing his nose. "I've run across a few…difficulties."

Thinking of those difficulties, he shot a beleaguered look toward the top floor of his leased space. For the umpteenth time, he wished he'd had the necessary funds to secure the entire building for his own use. Unfortunately, when he'd arrived, his meager savings hadn't spread that far.

Because of that, Jack was stuck with a neighboring tenant directly above him. And unless he convinced his fellow leaseholder to surrender the space to him on payments he could afford—now that his saloon was doing moderate business— his plans for expansion would have to wait.

"You let me know whenever you're ready to get those boardinghouse rooms started, Murphy," Marcus Copeland said. The local lumber mill owner had joined McCabe while Jack had been slinging mescal to the cowboy, and now sat with his ledger books spread, as usual, directly in front of him. "I'll give you the lumber you need to finish those rooms for a good price."

"Hey!" the blacksmith protested, elbowing him. "That ain't what you told me when I wanted to buy supplies for Lillian and Lyman's new house, out near the general store. You didn't say a blasted thing about 'a good price.'"

"That's because your sister and her husband can afford to pay full cost," Copeland pointed out reasonably, his voice tinged with humor. It wasn't for nothing he was known as the most frugal-minded man in the territory. "They don't need a good price. But Murphy here…he does, and we both know it."

McCabe tilted his head. "Yep. I guess so. On account of the 'Grace factor,' I reckon. He surely does."

Blandly, he gave Jack a mournful look.

His supposed pity was a shameless sham—underlain through and through with a born joker's appreciation for good humor—and Jack knew it. Everyone in town considered his ongoing feud with Grace Crabtree to be a riotous joke.

Today Jack was having none of it.

"Quit jawing, the both of you," he commanded. "Else I might decide to charge you both full price for your liquor from here on out. To make up for the 'nag factor.'"

He raised his brows, challenging his friends to disagree.

Both men chortled, not the least intimidated.

"You wouldn't dare." Lazily, McCabe dropped his flat-brimmed hat to the bar. "You'd lose your two best customers."

Copeland merely examined him, a knowing gleam in his eye. "You'll have to own up to it sooner or later, Murphy. Grace wants something from you, and it's useless fighting a Crabtree woman when she's got her mind set on something. I ought to know." He cast his eyes heavenward, probably thinking of his wife, Molly, a celebrated baker and a Crabtree woman herself. "And Grace is the most set-minded Crab-tree of them all."

"Amen to that." McCabe lifted his ale and quaffed.

Jack frowned, not wanting to discuss the "Grace factor" with them. Or anyone. Grace Crabtree—his aforementioned upstairs neighbor—had proved problematic nearly from his first day in town. He didn't need her two brothers-in-law, both of them idiotically surrendered to marriage already, to remind him of that. As far as Jack was concerned, their marriages alone proved their lack of appropriate mental faculties.

Not that he intended to explain as much. Coming out with a phrase like *appropriate mental faculties* would peg him as a man who was more than he seemed, for certain.

"It's not my fault you're both shackled with wives," he said instead, deepening his brogue for effect. "Just because you two have to kowtow to females doesn't mean I should start humoring Grace Crabtree. Now does it?"

Mouths quirked, his friends exchanged knowing looks.

"She'll picket your saloon if you don't," Copeland warned.

"Or lead her ladies' auxiliary members in an organized protest," McCabe added cheerfully. "Remember what happened to Nickerson's Book Depot and News Emporium when Ned decided not to stock that highfalutin lady author's book Grace wanted?"

"Jane Austen," Copeland put in agreeably. "Molly told me the whole story. It was a Jane Austen book."

Much as Jack appreciated knowing at least one other person in town who possessed a familiarity with literature beyond Beadle's fantastical dime novels, he did not want to discuss Grace Crabtree and her radical, interfering ways. Nor did he want to join his friends in gleefully predicting his saloon's further troubles. Why could no one understand that?

Hoping to distance himself from the conversation, he

swiped his towel over the bar, then dusted the gilded frame of his famous above-the-bar oil painting, as well. Its enormous canvas depicted a scantily clad water nymph. He'd affectionately nicknamed her Colleen, and her risqué image lent a popular allure to his saloon—one Jack felt rightly pleased with.

No "sissified corsetry creator" would hang a painting like that one. He felt damned certain of that. It had been the first thing he'd purchased upon settling in Morrow Creek.

"Right. Jane Austen," McCabe agreed, nodding. He sounded utterly unrepentant in needling Jack. As usual. "Remember how Deputy Winston had to unchain Grace from the news depot's hitching post and haul her off to the sheriff's office?"

Both men laughed. Copeland hoisted his customary sarsaparilla for another swig, and McCabe finished his ale.

It was easy for them to make fun, Jack groused. They weren't saddled with a rabble-rousing female who spent most of her days within shouting distance. He was. And the longer he stayed in the territory, the more problematic Grace became.

At the end of the bar, the cowboy rose. He tossed down a pair of coins, then tucked his hat on his head, situating it just so. His grimy fingernails told the tale of many days on the trail, as did his bedraggled, mud-splattered clothes.

"Well, I'm off to Miss Adelaide's for a bath and a haircut. And maybe a mite more entertainment." He chewed his plug tobacco, then aimed a stream of juice toward the spittoon. "If I can lasso me one of them dancing girls, I'll bring her out your way, Murphy."

His cronies shouted ribald endorsement of the idea.

The cowboy chuckled. He held up a weathered hand in good-bye, prompting Jack to offer a matching wave.

Some days, Jack considered, he missed his old life of educating and learning and philosophizing. Other days, like today, he felt satisfied merely to have a pint at his elbow, a few customers to keep a roof over his head and an afternoon without bossy Grace Crabtree nagging him about something.

He didn't know where his aggravating upstairs neighbor was right now, it occurred to him. But he hoped it was far away. And he hoped she stayed there for a while, too.

The cowboy sauntered out, his spurs ringing on the floor. For an instant, the jangle of passing wagons and the overall bustle of town whirled in through the doorway, then subsided. The saloon settled into its usual rhythm of slapping cards, murmuring men and clinking billiards.

"Now there's a man who's truly free." Jack shook his head wonderingly. "*That's* what I came out west for."

His wistful announcement fell on deaf ears.

"Well, you're not getting it," McCabe declared in his usual prosaic fashion. He gave a wink, then stepped away from the bar. "Not till you cope with Grace Crabtree, that is."

"Damnation, McCabe." Why did the man have to ruin Jack's one moment of peaceful contemplation? "Stop yapping already."

"He's right." Copeland jerked a thumb at the blacksmith, then set to work gathering up his ledgers. "Mark my words, Murphy. Never underestimate a Crabtree woman. Not unless you want to be the one who ends up hog-tied."

Jack scoffed. "You're both daft. I can handle Grace Crabtree. That's all I've done since I got here, isn't it?"

His friends all but split their ribs with laughing.

Jack's frown deepened. He slapped his towel on the bar. "You two are damned know-it-alls anyway. What makes you think—"

"Handling her?" McCabe interrupted.

"Is that what you're calling it?" Plainly out of his head with hilarity, Copeland swabbed a tear from his eye. He smacked his hand genially on the bar, then made ready to leave. "That's a good one, Murphy. Good luck with that tactic."

"Let us know how it turns out." McCabe guffawed again.

"I've practically got her subdued!" Jack protested.

And only half exaggeratedly, too.

But his friends merely laughed louder, then strolled from the saloon with their heads bent—doubtless to share another jest at Jack's expense. He didn't know exactly when, it occurred to him, he'd become such a source of amusement to the men in town.

Whenever it had happened, Jack didn't like it one bit. Although Copeland and McCabe's teasing was all in good fun, it still smacked of his experiences in Boston—the same experiences that had made him leave for the west.

It was time to put a stop to it. Once and for all.

The next time he saw Grace Crabtree, Jack vowed, he would lay down the law in no uncertain terms. He would show her that no woman gave orders to a rough-and-ready man like himself—even a self-made rough-and-ready man like himself. Grace didn't need to know his newly rugged persona was still progressing.

Hell, neither did anyone else.

Confidently, Jack grabbed a plug of tobacco from the stock for sale behind the bar. He stuffed it in his mouth, both hands propped manfully on the polished wood. Deliberately, he sucked the tobacco's papery, strongly flavored mass against his cheek.

Ugh. Grimacing, Jack spat it out. The sorry truth was, he just wasn't a tobacco-chewing man. No matter how hard he tried to cultivate the popular habit.

But he was not a quitting man either. Narrowing his eyes, Jack considered the packets of cheroots and Mexican cigarillos stocked nearby. There was more than one way to develop a manly aura, he reasoned. With enough tobacco stuffed in his pockets, he'd smell as masculine as the heartiest western roughneck.

Feeling assured, Jack rammed three cheroots in the pocket of his britches, then sauntered to the end of the bar with his big boots ringing, ready to greet his next adventure.

As far as anyone could remember, only two women had ever been confined to the Morrow Creek town jail. One was Ruby Pemberton, an angelic-looking female who'd earned notoriety by smuggling mining camp gold in her bustle. The other was Grace Crabtree. Folks claimed it was only fitting the two of them wound up locked up together one clear January afternoon, awaiting the arrival of the beleaguered sheriff.

But Grace knew better. "Fitting" had nothing to do with it. Serendipity did. Determined to make the most of her good fortune, Grace spent an enjoyable afternoon sharing exploits with Mrs. Pemberton. She emerged from her scandalous sojourn a little wiser than she'd been before—and vastly more entertained, too.

Not that her two sisters, Molly and Sarah, strictly agreed.

They launched their first salvos outside the jailhouse, while Grace was still pulling on her gloves and practical winter hat—procured through mail-order, extremely cozy and likely not the least bit stylish—in preparation for the snowy trek home.

"Honestly, Grace." Molly, the youngest of them all, shook her head as they trooped toward Main Street. "I don't know what gets into you sometimes. It's as though you want to be the subject of unending gossip in town!"

"Posh." Grace scoffed. "Mrs. Pemberton was fascinating. Do you know she would have succeeded flawlessly if only one blundering miner hadn't pinched her during her getaway?"

Neither of her sisters seemed suitably impressed.

"Be that as it may, you ought to be more discerning," said Sarah, the middle sister. "All of Morrow Creek is up in arms about Mrs. Pemberton's exploits. Her notoriety is all my students—and their parents—can talk about."

Molly nodded. "People say she's a boldfaced thief."

"So?" Grace marched onward, firm in her convictions. "People usually peg me for some variant of 'uppity female,' and I consider them heartily wrong in those opinions, too."

Both her sisters sighed.

"You did just come from the jailhouse, Grace," Molly said.

"A mere misunderstanding about my latest protest march," Grace assured her sister. "Now that it's over with, I have a great deal to accomplish. Beginning with returning this book to the practical library of the Social Equality Sisterhood."

"Now? This minute?" Sarah eyed Grace's suffrage text with dismay, then followed as Grace swerved in her desired direction. "We promised we'd bring you directly home."

"Of course now. I'm the presiding officer!" Grace said. "Not to mention an inaugural member of the Sisterhood. It's my duty to present a good example to my local chapter."

Both her sisters exchanged knowing glances—puzzling knowing glances—as they continued toward the small library building.

"Er, speaking of the Social Equality Sisterhood—"

"And all your other clubs," Molly said. "We think—"

"We think you might want to consider readdressing your efforts toward other activities." Sarah bit her lip. "Soon."

Perplexed, Grace glanced at them. "What are you talking about? Everyone is counting on me." At her sisters' dubious faces, Grace enumerated the ways. "There is the Ladies' Aid Society to think of, the Morrow Creek Bicycling Association, the Ornithology Club *and* my work on behalf of female suffrage. Not to mention my efforts with the women's baseball league."

"See?" Sarah urged. "You're stretched too thinly."

Grace shook her head. "Nonsense. I enjoy all of it."

Demonstrating as much, Grace lifted her chin and tromped down the street at her typical no-nonsense pace. Thanks to her single petticoat, simple woolen skirt and tucked-in shirtwaist—all worn beneath her coat and scarf—she could move much faster than her stylishly outfitted younger sisters with all their flounces and frills and fancy Louis-heeled shoes. Her toes felt toasty warm, too—a prime benefit of the comfortable men's shoes she'd adopted for wintertime practicality's sake.

Molly hurried to keep up, then aimed a despairing glance at those selfsame brogans. "Perhaps if you didn't expend all your energies on causes and clubs and rabble-rousing—"

"—you'd have a bit to spare for finding a husband." Sarah gave Grace a pointed look. "I can testify to the truth of it myself. A love match is possible…with a little work."

Grace snorted, offering a dismissive wave. "You two sound exactly like Mama. I don't *need* a husband. I don't *want* a husband. Heaven forbid I should actually *search* for a husband. What kind of ninny would do such a thing?"

"One who didn't want to wind up all alone." Molly gazed at her with utmost seriousness. "With no one but her fellow suffragists and bird-watchers for company."

Solemnly, Sarah looked on. "We worry about you, Grace."

With an instant denial already on her lips, Grace paused. Something in her sisters' tone troubled her. Caught unprepared by it, she stared back. The moment stretched between them, fraught with earnestness and puffs of frigid air.

"Don't be ridiculous." Resolutely, Grace shook off her sisters' concern. They didn't understand her, and that was that. "I'm fine. I like suffragists and bird watchers."

"There is more to life than frenzied activity," Molly said.

"There is love!" Sarah agreed, her eyes shining. "And laughter. And so, so much more. Don't you want to—"

"No, I most certainly do not!" Grace flailed her arms impatiently as she strode onward. They'd wasted enough time on this nonsense. "Both of you, married less than a year, and already you're proselytizing on behalf of wedded bliss. Well, I'll have none of it. I'm a spinster, and I like it."

"Honestly?" Molly stopped beside the shuttered mercantile, catching hold of Grace's coat sleeve. "You truly don't mind?"

Sarah gazed on silently, looking troubled.

For an instant—only that—Grace actually wondered if she did mind. If her sisters were right, and there were good things to be said about matrimony. If love, true love, could honestly be found with a little effort.

After all, her parents had provided all three sisters with the opportunity to wait for true love, rather than be married for expediency or social convention's sake. Fiona and Adam Crabtree were intelligent people. Surely they would not have allowed for such an eventuality if it weren't a feasible one.

Would they?

Well, she simply wouldn't allow herself to wonder about that, Grace decided. So what if she participated in various activities and clubs and rallies? So what if she found comfort in reading and painting picket signs and joining her fellow association members for an invigorating bicycling outing? Those things kept her engaged. They kept her busy.

They kept her from feeling lonely.

I truly don't mind perched on the tip of her tongue, waiting to be said. But somehow, as Grace looked at her sisters' expectant faces, she simply could not come out with it.

"It will only take a minute to return this," she declared instead, hoisting her book—a fine text by the renowned activist Heddy Neibermayer—in her gloved palm.

Then she hurried inside the library of the Social Equality Sisterhood...uncomfortably aware of Molly and Sarah's skeptical gazes following her all the while.

Chapter Three

As one of only four typesetters at her father's successful newspaper, the *Pioneer Press*, Grace valued punctuality. She valued accuracy and speed. She valued, more than anything else, dedication to the task at hand. Which was why it bothered her so much to arrive at her desk a day later— on time—only to find no one else in evidence at the typesetters' office.

Grumpily, she surveyed the silent workroom.

It could not be, Grace assured herself as she shed her coat to the rack by the door, that she was still unsettled by her sisters' questioning yesterday. After all, she had been a spinster for a long time now. She enjoyed the freedom spinsterhood afforded her. She relished the liberty to come and go and do as she pleased. She most assuredly did *not* want a husband.

But sometimes…

Sometimes, when catching glimpses of her newly wedded sisters' shining faces, Grace did speculate. She did ponder her own solitary state and wonder why she hadn't even been afforded the opportunity to refuse a man's offer of marriage. At least then her status as an old maid would have seemed a deliberate choice—rather than a public denunciation of her womanly allure.

On the other hand, Grace decided with a brisk stride to her waiting desk, she didn't give a fig about womanly allure. It was utter nonsense, designed to keep women tightly laced and compliant, too breathless or addle-headed to cause a fuss.

Furthermore, if she were bound to a husband, she would not be available to carry on the Crabtree family legacy—the *Pioneer Press*. And that was what she most wanted to do, for her father's sake and her own.

To be sure, Grace had only begun her radical life of picketing and reading and overall rabble-rousing to impress her papa. He, more than any man she'd known, was an original freethinker of the highest quality. No doubt Adam Crabtree, at least, appreciated his daughter's unique talents.

Even if some others in town did not.

Because of that, Grace expected to hear—any day now—that her father had appointed her to succeed him as editor of the newspaper. No one else was a more natural or fitting choice. Everyone in Morrow Creek knew her papa planned to retire soon, and although no official announcement had been forthcoming yet, Grace felt positive the outcome would favor her.

She could scarcely wait to make the *Pioneer Press* her own. Leading its advance toward the next century would be her crowning achievement, Grace knew, effectively silencing everyone who'd doubted her nontraditional ways.

Savoring the notion, she hooked her finger in her tray of metal type pieces to draw it nearer, then considered the various newspaper articles that awaited her. She pursed her mouth. What she needed were a suitable headline and an appropriate position below the masthead. With both items finally decided, she next set to work choosing letters to fit her composing stick, then slid each line on the waiting galley tray.

Hers was a painstaking and deliberate job, requiring precise fingers, excellent vision and a superior grasp of both grammar and showmanship. That was why Grace was proud to do it—and why she was dismayed to find herself alone in the offices fifteen minutes later. Lizzie still hadn't arrived.

That wasn't like Lizzie at all. Although lately…

Squinting, Grace peered through the frosted window glass. The sun had warmed the square pane just enough to allow a view of the street beyond and the timber-framed buildings that bordered it on the opposite side. Just as she'd hoped, she spied a bundled Lizzie tromping from the direction of the Lorndorff Hotel, which stood near her family's small house.

A wintry breeze, pine fresh and invigorating, swept into the office along with Lizzie and a hearty dose of Arizona Territory sunlight. Breathing hard from exertion, she unwound her scarf as she pushed the door shut with her other hand.

"Thank goodness! I was wondering about you."

"I'm so sorry, Grace!" Lizzie's guilty gaze swerved to meet hers. "Truly, I am. I didn't mean to be late, but I had another long night of it last night, and I overslept. It's got to do with me and Alonzo—"

"Don't give it a second thought." Grace didn't want a lengthy discourse on Lizzie's fiancé. The two had been engaged for a mere three months, and in Grace's opinion were making a tremendous mistake in marrying so young. "I'm nearly finished with the front page of the next edition, so if you'd like to start working on page two, that would be excellent."

Lizzie took her place at the stool beside Grace. Then she stared forlornly at her type case, her shoulders hunched. She didn't select a single letter.

"Lizzie? What's the matter?"

"I'm awfully sorry." Again, Lizzie's pleading gaze met hers. "I'd meant to tell you this sooner, but I didn't have the courage." She drew in a deep breath. "The fact of the matter is…I'm quitting the *Pioneer Press*."

"Quitting?" Grace gaped. "Why? You're an excellent typesetter, one of the finest I've trained."

"I know. And I do enjoy my work here ever so much." Nervously, Lizzie sifted hand-cast type through her fingers, jumbling the contents of her wooden tray rather than meet Grace's gaze. "But after my wedding next month—"

"Ah." Suddenly, Grace understood. "Your wedding. Is that all that's worrying you? Don't trouble yourself any further." Relieved, Grace patted Lizzie's shoulder. "My father will allow you to keep working here. He's very progressive."

"I know that." Lizzie transferred her gaze from her type tray to her fancy high-buttoned shoes, watching melting snow drip from their encrusted heels. "It's Alonzo. He doesn't want his wife to be employed. He says it's not fitting, especially at your father's, er…"

"My father's…what?" Grace urged. "Out with it, Lizzie. Be brave. Bravery is the mark of a strong woman, you know."

"His, um, rather radical newspaper." Cringing, Lizzie cast her a sideways glance. "I'm sorry. Please don't be cross with me. I know you pretend to be indifferent to marriage—"

"Pretend?"

"—and seeing as how you haven't any beaux of your own—"

"*Beaux?*" Grace could only gawp.

"—I couldn't expect you to…" Lizzie bit her lip. "Oh Grace! It's only that I love Alonzo so very dearly—"

Suddenly caught up in her favorite topic, Lizzie rattled on, extolling the virtues of her future bridegroom with a gleam in her eye. Grace couldn't bear to listen. Now she was losing one of her best typesetters—one of her friends!—to the addle-headed state of marriage. It saddened her greatly.

"What is it about matrimony that makes mush of women's minds?" Grace demanded. "I honestly don't understand it."

She also didn't understand how she would cope without her friend by her side. Without the stories and confidences they shared, her workday would seem dreary indeed.

"Oh, Grace." Lizzie's face shone, bearing a marked resemblance to her sisters' countenances of late. "I guess… I don't suppose you would understand, would you?"

Grace crossed her arms, supremely discomfited. It wasn't like her to show an excess of emotion, but she couldn't help feeling as though she were…missing something somehow.

With an expression alarmingly akin to pity, Lizzie examined her. She leaned nearer and patted Grace's shoulder.

"But if you're very fortunate, and if you try *very* hard to find nicer shoes—" her gaze skittered to Grace's prized, sensible footwear "—then maybe someday you'll snare a man of your own. Just keep hoping!"

Before Grace could refute that outrageous advice, Lizzie hopped down from her typesetter's stool. Then she sashayed happily toward the door that divided their workplace from the newspaper offices proper, doubtless to tender her official resignation—and, inadvertently, to leave Grace behind.

As usual.

With her heart pounding wildly, Grace approached the closed door of her father's office. This was it. The moment she'd waited for. The moment when Adam Crabtree would turn over the day-to-day management of the *Pioneer Press* to the next generation of capable Crabtrees.

To her.

Confidently, she rapped on the door. Her papa's jolly voice rang out, offering her admission.

An instant later, Grace found herself standing amid piled

newspapers and amassed volumes of books and bookshelves and an enormous desk covered with every aspect of an editor's responsibilities. Articles. Pencils. Drawings. Newly submitted advertisements. Assorted India rubbers.

The whole lot of it felt like home. It felt like everything she'd worked toward for so long. And looking at it now stimulated feelings in Grace she'd scarcely experienced before—a mishmash of belonging and protectiveness and anticipation. With the accoutrements of this position at her disposal, she could accomplish so much! She could make her father proud.

Adam peered up at her, pausing his fingers against his tall Remington Type Writer machine. There were no others like it in town. Her father was nothing if not an innovator.

"You asked to see me, Papa?"

"Yes, I did." Sighing, he removed the spectacles he used for close work, then rubbed the bridge of his nose. "Why don't you sit down, Grace?"

"I'm fine standing." In fact, she felt as though her renowned oversize shoes might not be adequate to keep her feet on the ground. That was how fraught with eagerness she was. "Thank you all the same."

"Very well. Have it your way." His smile flashed. "After all, you usually do."

Grace smiled back. "That's something I share with you."

"Yes. Fine." Clearing his throat, Adam looked to the open doorway. "Perhaps you'll want to close the door?"

"Oh! Of course." He wouldn't want to let anyone in the exterior offices be privy to their conversation. It was a monumental one, after all. Nearly dizzy with hopefulness, Grace fairly skipped to the door. She shut it. "There. Now…exactly what did you want to see me about?"

"It's about the newspaper. As you know, your mother has been after me for some time to retire. To let 'a young buck' take over the running of the *Pioneer Press,* so we can get on with our golden years. Naturally enough, it's been difficult for me to hold her off for as long as I have. Your mother is a very determined woman."

He broke off, fondness suffusing his face.

For her part, Grace concentrated fiercely on being still. She needed to demonstrate her utmost maturity. That would make her papa feel better about handing over the newspaper to her care. She clasped her fingers and waited.

"Also I would like to indulge my artistic ambitions a bit, if I could find the time. I've been putting them off for years. And, well…" He cleared his throat again, then peered up at her. An uncommon unease seemed to have gripped him. "The end of the story is this. A new editor is on his way here. I just received his wire today. He's on the westbound train, set—"

The floorboards waved beneath Grace's feet. Her ears rang, and a hollowness gripped her belly, even as her papa went on talking in his solid, familiar voice. Surely he hadn't just implied that *someone else* was coming to take over the newspaper?

She must have heard him wrong.

"…very capable man," her papa was saying, "direct from New York University. He'll bring something new to the *Pioneer Press,* an outside perspective we've been lacking for too long." He broke off abruptly, brow furrowed. "Are you sure you wouldn't rather sit down? You look a bit pale."

Not for anything would Grace have moved from that spot. She did have her pride to consider. At this moment, in fact, it might be all she had to consider.

"I'm sorry. Did you say…" Grace shook her head. "Exactly whom have you appointed the next editor?"

"Thomas Walsh. Fine man. Best credentials."

"Oh. I understand." Woozily, Grace realized she did not. And perhaps she never would. She clenched her fists more tightly. "But Papa, I'd always believed you might allow me to—"

Unshed tears squeezed her throat, obliterating everything else she'd meant to say. Grace could not believe that now, now when it most mattered to her future, she would succumb to feminine weakness. What was wrong with her?

"That I might—" she tried again. "You see, I've spent so much time—" Again, frustratingly, her voice failed her.

"I know, Grace. I know." All at once, her papa seemed surpassingly weary. "But it's not to be. I have to at least try Mr. Walsh first. You must understand, I built this newspaper with my bare hands, up from a single printing press assembled beneath an oak near the town square. As admiring as I am of your capabilities, I simply can't afford to risk the reputation of—"

"I see." She felt rooted to the spot, numb with disbelief.

"I'm not sure you do." Her papa rose from behind his desk, his gray brows drawn together with concern. He pulled her into his arms for a gruff hug. "See now. I love you, Grace Abigail. I won't have you looking so unhappy. Someday you'll realize—"

But all Grace could realize was that her dreams had been dashed, and her hopes for carrying on the family legacy stymied. Without them to sustain her, she wasn't sure what to do. But she could not stay there, that was for certain.

Desperately, she drew in a quavering breath. She stepped out of her father's embrace, her skirts swishing.

"I…I understand. That's fine, Papa," she managed to say. "I know you must do what you think is right. As for myself, I really must get back to the typesetting room."

Grace offered a feeble gesture in that direction, praying her papa wouldn't notice the way her hand trembled…the way her voice shook and her eyes burned. She could bear up under this disappointment, she vowed. She could and she would.

Somehow.

Her papa gave her a grave look. Something in his solemn eyes made her wonder if he'd guessed how distressed she truly felt. But then Adam Crabtree only released another sigh and nodded.

"We'll talk later," he promised, patting her arm.

"Yes." She gulped another sob. "Later."

Then Grace sighted the doorknob through watery eyes, wrenched it open and set herself free…free to a world that had suddenly emptied for her in a very real way.

For the first time in her life, Grace had no plan to assist her, no grand scheme to take her from one point to another. She had only movement. Striding with ever-larger steps, she left the *Pioneer Press* offices behind her, her oversize shoes squeaking clumsily against the slushy snow.

All around her, the streets of Morrow Creek teemed with activity. Local farmers' wives shopped at the mercantile. Miners rode through with mules close behind, carrying supplies for hardy winter surveying. Teams of horses pulled wagons freshly equipped with sleigh runners for the season, gouging deep tracks in the street. Before long, springtime would be here, and even more townspeople would venture out.

Moving briskly, Grace jerked her head high and pretended to be on a very urgent mission. She narrowed all her efforts to putting one foot in front of the other, deliberately not thinking about anything other than where to go next. Returning to the newspaper offices was unthinkable. Knowing they would soon be under the management of a stranger—

Swerving, Grace sent her thoughts in a new direction.

Home. She could go home and deal with this disappointment in private. But her mama would be there, doubtless previously informed of her papa's decision, and she would want to talk the whole issue to pieces. Sympathy, to Fiona Crabtree, meant a nice pot of tea and a marathon session of chattering. And commiserating. And chattering some more. To Grace, the thought of it was simply unbearable.

Almost by rote, she found her feet carrying her in the opposite direction, toward the building she used for meeting-room space for her various clubs and activities. *Yes,* Grace thought in relief as its false-fronted facade and two-story solidness loomed ahead, smoke puffing merrily from the chimneys. *I'll go there and cope with all of this privately.*

Even as she veered in that direction, she could scarcely contain her disappointment. Her confusion. Her rising—and strangely comforting—sense of righteous indignation.

Thomas Walsh indeed!

Grace could not believe this was happening. Now after all her hard work! After all her hopes and dreams.

By the time she drew near enough to read the cursed sign promoting her neighbor Jack Murphy's downstairs saloon, she was riled up fair to fuming. How dare her papa hire a replacement? Especially one nobody knew? It was outrageous!

Chances were excellent, she assured herself, that the unknown Mr. Walsh had no notion at all of what he was getting into. Eastern men from the States often traveled to the territory, prodded by tales of adventure they culled from silly dime novels and fantastical periodical articles penned by irresponsible journalists.

Once Mr. Walsh realized he would be a simple editor of a simple newspaper in a simple small town, Grace brooded, he would probably give up. Exactly as befitted the ill-spelling, unoriginal, tabloid-reading opportunist he indisputably was.

Conjuring up his many potential faults—an activity she found invigoratingly consoling—Grace stomped her way toward the snowy steps that led to her upstairs rooms. Thomas

Walsh was probably incapable of editing at all, she fumed. They'd be fortunate if he could struggle through one of Sarah's prized McGuffey Readers. He probably dressed poorly, enjoyed stinky cheroots and believed Nast's cartoons to be the pinnacle of political sophistication.

Still seething, Grace caught the handrail and brought her heavy shoe to bear on the first step. Then the next. And another, moving as fast as frustration could carry her.

All her life, doing something—being active—had kept her from feeling anything she didn't want to feel. Now although the best she could manage was to move steadily upward toward her solitary rooms, she remained steadfastly at it.

Suddenly, her man-size shoe failed to find purchase on the icy stair. Right in the midst of a silent discourse on Thomas Walsh's evident inability to comprehend familial loyalty, Grace plummeted down the slippery steps to the ground.

And wound up on her hands and knees in the snow.

Startled by her new position, Grace realized she'd need a moment before she could move. At the least, she'd had the wind knocked out of her. Trembling, she took stock of her situation.

Her left knee stung fiercely, wet with snow melting through her skirts. Her elbow ached. Her ankle felt bruised. One of her mismatched gloves was abraded, too. She stared unthinkingly at its unraveled knit, the sight somehow terribly affecting.

It used to be such a serviceable glove, she mused. Now look at it. Useful for nothing and without a mate besides.

The swish of saloon doors interrupted her reverie.

Heavy footfalls came next, undoubtedly from someone who possessed untraitorous footwear. An enormous pair of boots entered her field of vision, packing down the snow in a gigantic clump. Then a large masculine hand descended, palm up and bare of any gloves at all.

"It's been awhile since a woman fell at my feet," came a disturbingly familiar Irish brogue. "Although I haven't forgotten what a kindhearted a gesture it is. Much appreciated, too." His teasing tone seemed warm enough to melt the snow. "Come on now, let's get you up."

Jack Murphy. Grace had time only to recognize his voice, discern the inevitable humor within it, then attempt to refuse his proffered help before he pulled her to her feet. She arose clinging to his burly arm. With dignity, she wrenched loose.

"I was not falling at your feet!"

The rascal only raised his brows toward the woman-size indentation marking the snow near his boots. He shrugged.

With that simple gesture, Grace had a target for her ire at last. He was a big one, too. A glare was too good for the hardheaded Irishman who bedeviled her daily by refusing to move his saloon, she decided. Even if he had just come to her assistance.

Already Jack Murphy had cost her heaven only knew how many club members—women who were too afraid to pass by the drunks and troublemakers who frequented his saloon in order to attend her meetings and rallies.

What's more, the barkeep—a former Bostonian, Grace was given to understand—was far too interested in joviality. The man scarcely had the sense to use his time wisely or well, all the while costing Grace the unmolested use of her leased property. She'd done all she could to get him to move and leave her in peace, but the man seemed to hold the addled belief that it was she who lay at fault in their dispute.

"Ah." Mr. Murphy shook his head, probably catching sight of her mulish expression. "If I'd known it was you thudding down the stairs and causing all that ruckus, I might have left you here. You and the frosty air probably get along just fine."

"As do you and your frivolous whiskey. Good day."

Grace raised her hand in farewell, intending to leave him

hulking there in his typical brutish fashion while she nursed her disappointments in private. She'd no more taken a single step than Mr. Murphy grabbed her wrist.

"You're hurt," he nearly growled. "Come inside."

Evidently he'd caught sight of her abused glove. Refusing to meet his gaze or even contemplate his dark-haired, devilish-eyed countenance for a single moment, Grace yanked free.

Or tried to. Jack Murphy held fast with surprising force.

Grace frowned. As a rule, they tried to avoid each other. Although given their proximity, doing so had not been an easy endeavor thus far.

"I have clean towels inside," he said, "along with a bolt of tequila for the pain. Come with me."

"Mr. Murphy, I will not!" she exclaimed, scandalized.

He towed her forward anyway. "Will not enter my saloon? Or enjoy a snort of tequila?" After glancing both ways, he entered the saloon with Grace in his grasp. "I would think a free-spirited suffragette like yourself would savor both."

The doors swung shut behind them, sealing her inside a murky world smelling of liquor, cigar smoke and masculinity.

"The respectful term is suffragist," Grace rebutted automatically, limping slightly due to her knee injury. "Referring properly to persons of either gender who advocate the natural right of women to vote. I'd prefer it if you—"

"Bunch of twaddle." Incredibly, Murphy shook his head.

Incensed, Grace found the strength to hobble faster, determined to keep up with him all the way to the bar. She spared an incredulous glance at the bawdy painting hanging above it, then centered her attention on Jack Murphy. The man was impossible. Aggravating. And, from all evidence acquired during their first year's acquaintance, possibly simpleminded.

Of course, she supposed reluctantly, his features could be considered handsome. Regular. Manly. Possessing a certain rugged charm, even. If one liked that sort of thing. But strictly if the person doing the considering were female, susceptible and not Grace Crabtree.

All at once, the pressure on her hand increased.

"Ouch!" she cried. "What are you doing?"

"Removing this splinter." He eyeballed a shard of wooden handrail with satisfaction, pinching its newly liberated length between blunt fingertips. "There's another one, if you'll—"

"I will not!"

Mr. Murphy lowered his shoulders—a certain sign, she'd learned during their acquaintance, that he was attempting to summon patience against his indisputably uncivilized nature.

She doubted it worked.

"Hold still," he commanded.

Biting her lip, Grace did. Grudgingly. She hated to admit weakness and loathed even more following rules she had not set down herself. But Murphy was, after all, only trying to help.

Also, practically speaking, she couldn't perform the delicate maneuver herself. Not easily at least.

She watched at first, wincing as he poked at her palm with a barkeeper's instrument of some sort. He was adept with his hands, she was surprised to note—probably owing to his talent for pouring whiskey and scooping up the profits. Then Grace realized what other distractions lay nearby, quite apart from Jack Murphy's blunt fingertips, and decided to take advantage of her unprecedented admittance to that most sacred of all men's establishments: the saloon.

Swiveling her head, she examined her surroundings unabashedly. Only a few patrons sat at the tables nearby. Two played dice at the bar. A pair gambled at faro near the billiards table—Sheriff Caffey's favorite lounging spot.

"There." Jack Murphy's rumbling voice interrupted her interested inspection. His tone seemed tinged with…something almost kindhearted. He went on holding her hand, very nearly cradling it in his. "Better now?"

Grace stared, transfixed, as he stroked his thumb over her palm. Tingles radiated from the place he touched, banishing the chilliness she'd felt before. She wouldn't have credited him with so much agility, much less so much sweetness.

She made the mistake of looking into his face.

His level gaze met hers, vividly blue and filled with an unprecedented quantity of concern. Concern unlike anything she'd experienced all day. Concern that ran very contrary to the dream-crushing reality of the morning she'd spent so far.

Horrifyingly, Grace felt her chin wobble. Then her throat tightened. And instant later, tears prickled her eyes, defying her staunchest efforts to hold them back.

No, no, no. She could not cry in front of Jack Murphy!

She'd made it all this way. She could wait for the privacy of her rooms upstairs. She had to remember her goals.

His brow creased in obvious confusion. Unwillingly, Grace noted that the gesture lessened his ridiculous good looks not in the least.

"Is it your knee?" he asked. "Tell me where it hurts."

The scoundrel softened his voice. *Softened his voice!*

Why had he chosen now to become considerate? Jack Murphy's unexpected kindness affected her all the more. For some reason, she couldn't take a single step…couldn't leave this peculiar, unlikely circle of comfort he'd created.

With growing alarm, Grace felt a tear fall.

"It's not—" she choked out. "I simply— It's because—"

"That's it," Mr. Murphy announced, shoving her behind the bar. "I'm having a look at your injured knee."

"No!" she shrieked, but it was already too late.

The next thing Grace knew, he'd knelt before her, hoisting her skirts in a decidedly unpolished—but effective—

manner. Cool air struck her ankle. Then her calf. Determinedly, Jack Murphy shoved her ice-frosted skirts higher, his shoulder keeping her steady in her ignoble position between him and the bar.

Grace could scarcely breathe, much less move. Shock held her pinned to the spot, as did the scandalous heat of Murphy's body. She couldn't remember the last time anyone had rendered her motionless *and* speechless—Jack Murphy or no.

"Hmm," the rascal mused, suddenly pausing in his efforts. He tilted his head, his gaze pinned unmistakably on her feet. "I own those same shoes."

Chapter Four

"I refuse to discuss footwear with you!" Grace said.

Then she walloped Jack with her heavy skirts, effectively ending his doctoring of her wounded knee and also deafening him to the sharp-tongued tirade that followed.

For that, he was grateful. Because, frankly, no woman had ever mastered the art of speaking her mind quite as effectively as bossy Grace Crabtree, and Jack had already endured more than his fair share of her opinions. He was sorry he'd brought her inside. Sorry he'd heard her falling down the stairs and gone to investigate. Sorry, most of all, he'd seen her cry.

It had made her seem almost…vulnerable.

Which was clearly a trick of some kind. Because Jack knew a less vulnerable woman had never been born than Grace Crabtree.

He caught hold of her flailing arms, dodged one more soggy woolen wallop, then peered into her face. "Better now?"

Sometimes females needed to express their more hysterical impulses. Any man who'd spent more than a few hours' time with a woman knew that. Ordinarily, Jack kept himself well out of the way. This time… Well, this time he didn't know how he'd gotten caught in the middle of things. He didn't much like it.

"I'm fine." Grace sniffled. She narrowed her gaze. "I don't know what you mean by being so kind, Mr. Murphy, but rest assured, I don't credit it for a minute. You're up to something, I know it. And I won't be swayed by this pretense of decency."

He nodded. "I'd better work on my pretenses."

"I won't be lulled by your agreeableness either!"

He endeavored to scowl.

"There you go again! It's positively unnatural."

Jack shrugged, knowing he would lose in this situation no matter what. Grace's declaration of skepticism was unconvincing in the extreme—especially accompanied, as it was, by a wobbling chin and teary eyes. Her admonition lacked punch to be sure. But he didn't want to say so. She seemed dangerously close to all-out bawling again.

At the realization, uncertainty swamped him. Jack wanted to help somehow, but a gentlemanly display of good manners and concern would hardly help matters. Or bolster his rough-and-ready image. Instead he resorted to his usual tactic.

He grunted. The all-purpose sound earned him a roll of the eyes and a disdainful sniff, which seemed—blessedly—a lot more in keeping with the Grace Crabtree he knew.

Heartened, he produced a handkerchief. After a small tussle, she accepted it, then swabbed indelicately at her face.

Whoever had originally claimed women looked beautiful when they cried had obviously never seen Grace Crabtree do it. Her eyes streamed, her lips trembled like a trout and her putty-colored hair straggled from its knot to join the whole mess.

"This is a very clean handkerchief," she managed to say, twisting it in her fingers. Despite her efforts, tears welled in her eyes and threatened to spill over. "Is it Irish linen?"

Watching her struggle for composure, Jack felt horrified. And strangely hurt. As though he shared her distress somehow.

The notion was too bizarre to credit.

"How should I know?" He did know, because in the days when he'd enjoyed genteel things, he'd ordered that handkerchief himself from a fine Boston seamstress. "It's yours now."

Grace's red-rimmed eyes widened. "Oh." She clutched the limp linen as though it were a square of embroidered gold leaf, then promptly burst into tears. Loud, caterwauling tears.

To his knowledge, Grace Crabtree had never cried before. She was well on her way to making up for lost time now.

Hell. So much for kindness.

"Stop that blubbering," Jack demanded, gesturing manfully outward. "Else you'll scare away my customers."

Several already stared at them, their lagers ignored. Apparently, his patrons had been content to ignore the woman in their midst—until she'd reached the level of a bawling calf.

"I'm not blubbering! I never cry. If you would just quit being so...so considerate." From her, it sounded a perfectly vile accusation. As though sensing the irrationality in that, Grace shoved ineffectually at his chest. "Just leave me alone."

Jack considered it. "I would, but your man-shoes are crushing my toes."

Her eyes flared. Whoever had adjudged women the gentler sex had gotten that wrong, too, Jack decided. Else they'd never met Grace Crabtree. She was an odd one. He knew it was true, because usually women liked his jests.

Pointedly, Grace shifted her feet two inches to the left.

"There. Do you know, I quite like it here," she announced, plainly rallying as she offered a sweeping glance at his gaping patrons. With her practiced orator's voice, she said to the room at large, "In fact, now that I'm inside this vaunted male sanctuary, I may never leave!"

Several gasps sounded. Grumbles of discontent were heard. Frowning, Jack grunted at her. Very, very loudly.

Obliviously, Grace flung her arms outward, almost smacking him in the nose. "I may stay for the Morrow Creek Men's Club meetings," she added, clearly gaining momentum and fervor, "and have my say there, too. I may have a whiskey! Why not?"

"Calm down." Consternation deepened Jack's brogue. His shoulders tightened. "You're not thinking clearly."

"Ah, you're worried now, aren't you?" Grace's eyes gleamed dangerously. "You should be! After all, I have nothing better to do—" her voice wavered, then broke "—now."

Now? That pitiful-sounding word niggled at him, as did Grace's brokenhearted admission. She looked a fright and sounded it, too. If he could only figure out what *now* meant...

Abruptly, Jack quit puzzling over that nonsensical statement. He was done with analyzing things. The plain fact was, Grace was the busiest person he knew—the busiest person *anyone* knew. She had plenty to do besides invade his saloon.

On the other hand, he mused, she had never hesitated to launch one of her outrageous plans either. He should send someone for Sheriff Caffey, just for preparedness' sake. Then show her the door. Decisively.

"Now?" Jack found himself repeating instead.

She nodded forlornly.

Which didn't help him decipher things in the least, although the gesture did—against all reason—rouse his sympathy. He peered closer, then touched her hand. "What do you mean?"

Her gaze skittered to his hand atop her ruined glove.

All at once, Grace's whole face crumpled. Her shoulders did, too. Clearly she'd finally been overcome by her heavy coat, her mannish shirtwaist and the cumbersome weight of her obstinacy.

Either that or she wasn't accustomed to simple courtesy. Jack wasn't sure which. But he was sure of one thing: trying to make sense of Grace Crabtree was the height of foolishness.

Despite that fact though, Jack held fast, concernedly squeezing her hand. He'd known Grace for over a year now. She was the person he wrangled with most in town. That gave them a bond of sorts. He didn't like to see her so downtrodden.

"Don't you have protesting to do?" he asked gruffly.

Grace shook her head, tendrils of hair sticking to her blotchy cheeks. She looked woefully pathetic and a little lost.

"Somebody else to pester?" he tried. "Work to do?"

At that, she heaved a tremulous sigh. Her whole chest shuddered beneath the exhalation, setting her shirtwaist aflutter. At least as much as the starchiness of it would allow, that is. Not many women looked as sensible on a daily basis as Grace did, and today was no exception. Aside from her tears.

They oughtn't fool him, Jack knew. All appearances to the contrary, those tears did not magically make Grace Crabtree delicate or sensitive. She was still the same woman who had surreptitiously plastered a hand-painted CLOSED sign on his saloon's entryway just two months ago, in outright defiance of his open-for-business status. It had taken him weeks to regain his former level of patronage.

"Well, yes. I do have typesetting to do," Grace allowed, surreptitiously swiping at her cheek. "But I have half a mind to leave all the work to the new editor my father hired."

"Hmm." Jack didn't think it was much like Grace to ignore work, but he'd already gotten in collar deep this morning. He didn't want to tempt fate. "Maybe you ought to leave it."

"I should!" Her face brightened, taking on a distinct glow. "After all, that odious Thomas Walsh can learn for himself what it takes to run the *Pioneer Press* from top to bottom."

"Top to bottom," Jack agreed. He adopted his best rugged

stance, contemplated a manly grunt, then frowned instead. He didn't want to overplay his hand. "I reckon."

Grace's thoughtful gaze lit on him. "You know, you're not so bad, Mr. Murphy."

"Neither are you, Miss Crabtree."

"Why, you're almost intelligent!"

"And you're not quite as disagreeable as I thought." Jack leaned against the bar and crossed his arms, nodding. Now that things seemed settled, however nonsensically, he felt better. Relief loosened his chest—and perhaps unwisely, his tongue. "Adam hired a new editor, you say?"

Grace nodded.

Jack considered that. "You want to know something funny?"

"Most certainly. If you feel yourself capable of wit."

He couldn't help but grin. Now that her fighting spirit was restored, Grace seemed herself again for certain. She'd be out of his saloon lickety-split. For the first time since coming to the territory, Jack felt a hero just for helping her.

"I almost had the idea Adam would give you the newspaper to manage," he confided. "It's the most radical in the territory, after all. And you're…you." He chuckled. "I guess you just might have had the gumption to take on the job."

The silence that came next felt ominous. Even underlaid, as it was, by jovially clinking glasses and the resumed billiards game in the corner of the saloon. Nearby, dice clattered.

"I would have." Grace's voice sounded as stiff as her high-necked shirtwaist. "If I'd been allowed to. Apparently though, my papa believes an outsider would do a better job."

She shook out her skirts, then lifted her chin higher. The moment of camaraderie they'd shared—however briefly and improbably—vanished like so much mescal delivered to a table of thirsty miners. Jack could scarcely keep up.

Was she going to start bawling again?

"Well, now." He made his voice soothing, to prevent any further outbursts. "That's good news, isn't it? Now you'll have more time for other things, like…uh, getting hitched."

Her brow arched. "'Hitched'?"

"Yep." That sounded an appropriately western term to him, and it was the first feminine goal that had come to mind. "You can fulfill every woman's dream and get yourself a husband."

"A husband?" Her cheeks reddened. "Why, you—"

"A fancy dress, a big fluffy cake, a preacher to announce you man and wife," Jack elaborated, stricken all at once with the rightness of it. He nodded. "If you could only find a man who'd have you, you could finally get married."

Grace opened and closed her mouth. She gawked. She blinked. She even appeared to consider the idea for an instant.

"Ha! *You* get married!" she cried.

With that outrageous rebuttal, Grace shouldered her way past him, her clodhopper shoes slapping briskly across the floorboards. Even though he was happy to see her go, Jack couldn't help but reflect that a husband would make her wear decent shoes. A husband would make her wear a proper dress instead of those suffragette dress-reform getups she favored. A husband would…

He would make her stay away from Jack's saloon.

The solution to all Jack's troubles dropped clean on him. He had to find Grace Crabtree a husband.

"I mean it," he protested, following her. "Wait."

Typically contrary, she shoved through the saloon doors instead. Jack followed, pursued by ribald jests from his amused patrons and temporarily blinded by the sunlight sparkling from the slushy snow. By the time he sighted Grace again, she was about to ascend the stairs to her meeting rooms

Her damned meeting rooms. They were usually packed to the rafters with prissy protesters and radical women and off-putting officers of some ladies' club or another, all of whom disrupted his business and his customers' enjoyment of their libations.

Jack had had just about all he could take of Grace and her meeting rooms. If she had a husband, he told himself, she'd have to quit them. No reasonable man would allow his wife to continue with her wild pursuits—especially pestering her neighbor. Him.

Her stomping feet hastened upward.

She was getting away.

"Wait!" he called again.

Huffily, Grace halted. She wheeled around on the stairs, sending chunks of snow pinging toward his knees, regarding him with a demeanor likely to give a man frostbite.

"Well?" she prompted. "What is it? Because I won't allow you inside my meeting rooms, and that's a promise."

Undaunted, Jack offered up his best Irishman's smile—the one that had always proven nigh irresistible. This was no time, he reasoned, to worry about cracks in his new-minted ruggedness.

"I'm going to find you a husband," he announced.

She seemed stunned by his largesse. "Mr. Murphy, I can assure you that I do not want a husband."

"Plenty of men come into my saloon." He raised his arms expansively. "One of them is bound to be willing."

"'Willing'?" She seemed gobsmacked by the very notion. "This is not about 'willing' or 'plenty.' It's simply—"

"Come along now, Miss Crabtree." Another smile for good measure seemed right to him. He leaned casually on the railing. "There's no need to be shy. We're neighbors, after all. If you're doubting I can find you a suitable man—"

She hooted with laughter.

"—you shouldn't be," Jack finished patiently. "I can be very resourceful when I have to be."

"Oh?" Her lips quirked. "Is that so?"

Now he'd seen every side of Grace Crabtree—dubious, weepy and downright foolish included. But with his solution well in sight, Jack was of no mind to quit now…or to let her needling get to him the way it usually did.

"It is," he told her, his typical good cheer returning despite her recalcitrance. "You just wait and see. I'll find you a husband faster than you can say 'I do.'"

Grace regarded him dryly. She raised her brow. "I do."

"See now?" Jack winked at her. "I'm right pleased to hear you practicing that. Afore I'm through, you'll be saying those words and meaning them."

She rolled her eyes. "That will be the day, Jack Murphy."

It *would* be the day, Jack told himself as he watched her clomp up the steps, then disappear. It would be a very fine day indeed when he finally got Grace Crabtree safely wed and away from his saloon. After all, how problematic a task could it be?

Especially for an inventive man like him?

Whistling with hope for the first time in months, Jack turned on the stairs and headed back to his saloon. He had a husband to snare and a wedding to expedite—and the sooner, the better, to be sure.

Chapter Five

Grace first noticed something askew two days later, while leaving her meeting rooms on her way to the *Pioneer Press* offices. She'd decided to continue with her typesetting work. Her papa would need someone to help watch over the Crabtrees' interests at the newspaper for some time to come, Thomas Walsh or no, and Grace considered herself ideal for the task. No one else understood the inner workings, the philosophy, the mission of the *Pioneer Press* as well as she did.

No one else, to be plain, cared as much.

But on that late January afternoon, as she clattered downstairs and strode past Jack Murphy's saloon, something peculiar happened. All the men assembled on the boardwalk outside—most of them bundled against the cold into pungent woolen lumps—lifted their hats to her. In unison.

"Afternoon, ma'am," said the boldest.

Grace, profoundly unused to being the center of any man's attention save the sheriff and Deputy Winston, ignored them at first. Her mind filled with headlines and typestyles, she kept going through the drifting snow.

"Nice day, ain't it?" another male called.

She glanced around. Oddly enough, no other woman stood nearby. She frowned in puzzlement. This was odd.

"Salutations." The third man bared a shy smile.

Grace stopped, staring at them. The first man gripped his hat in grimy hands, politely keeping it at elbow height. He nodded, seeming distinctly—and curiously—eager.

"'Salutations,'" the second man mimicked, nudging his compatriot. "Humph. Shut up, Arbus, you damned show-off." He shifted his gaze. "Uh, pardon my language, ma'am."

"Yer both making us look bad," the first man complained. "Hush up and try to look civilized. I'm hankering for some corn bread and mebbe a clean shirt, and I aim to get 'em."

"Quit bossing us around, George. This ain't the mill."

"What do you know? You never been this close to a woman without being all likkered up."

Grace raised her brows. Jack Murphy's clientele was something to behold, that was for certain.

"I know a highbrow woman like that one—" astonishingly, the third man's sideways chin jerk indicated Grace "—don't want to scrub your stinky drawers." He guffawed. "Do you, ma'am?"

As though that were a reasonable question, the trio peered at her interestedly. Grace blanched.

Then recovered.

"Laundry is a menial endeavor whereby mankind strives to enslave woman by chaining her to a washboard with a never-ending quantity of labor," she proclaimed. "In my estimation, if you soil it, you should wash it, or an equitable division of household tasks should be agreed upon."

The men gaped, hands going limp on their hats.

"In other words, gentlemen, I suggest you take yourselves off to the mercantile, buy a set of washboards and learn to appreciate womankind." Grace flung her knitted scarf over her shoulder with a flourish. "Good day."

Cheerfully, she continued on her way. The simple truth was, Grace loved an opportunity to enlighten people. Therefore, a new spring to her step existed as she proceeded through town, anticipating a lovely outbreak of washboard purchases at Jedediah Hofer's mercantile that very afternoon.

The next oddity occurred a mere day later. Beset with the accoutrements of her latest project, Grace tramped through the snow toward her meeting rooms. Although spring hadn't yet arrived in Morrow Creek, soon it would be time for her annual petition to have her women's baseball league added to the town's burgeoning team roster. After being defeated last year, this time Grace intended to be prepared.

Fortunately, it had occurred to her that she possessed an unappreciated secret weapon. Since Grace believed in using whatever advantages worked to egalitarianism's benefit, however meager or unexpected, that realization had cheered her immensely. There was nothing more satisfying than fighting for a worthy cause, she'd found.

Furthermore, although she knew that some of the townspeople were resistant to the notion of sportswomen, Grace considered female activity wholly natural and perfectly fitting. Women were strong, determined and every bit as capable as men were. Perhaps more in some instances. Her bicycling and ornithology clubs—where women greatly outnumbered men—were proof of that.

Grace had discovered that every hand-stitched, regulation weight horsehide baseball intended for use by the local men's teams was produced not by the players but by gentle-seeming women. At least a few of whom enjoyed vigorous sports activity themselves. And all of whom had agreed, upon

Grace's request, to forestall further baseball production until their demands for equality were met.

There was a tiny hitch in her plan though. Grace had to ensure that the town's store of existing baseballs was secured before the springtime thaw, when practices began. Otherwise her efforts would come to naught. Also she didn't want anyone to know what she was up to. Surprise was a mighty advantage in some instances. So, made awkward by her burden but more than capable of handling it, Grace kept going, her breath puffing in the frigid wintertime air.

"There she is!" came a sudden cry from the saloon steps.

Two men bolted upright and ran toward her. Grace stopped in confusion, her gloved hands wrapped securely around her burlap sack. The baseballs inside shifted with her abrupt stop, clattering in a heavy mass against her coat-covered back, where she'd slung the bulk of the bag.

"Let me help you, ma'am!" one man panted.

Amused onlookers watched as both men bore down upon Grace. If she had been the belle of every ball, she could not have been more the center of attention in that moment. Stunned, she saw the first man shove the second. He slipped and fell with a whoosh in the snow, then scrambled to his feet.

"That's too heavy for a little woman like yourself," he yelled, drawing the attention of more passing townspeople.

"Here, hand that over, ma'am," cried the second man.

Hearty chuckles could be heard nearby, rising over the clinking of harnesses and the snorts of horses. In a town the size of Morrow Creek, interesting events did not occur every day. Not even when Grace Crabtree was involved. She took an ineffectual step backward, unsure how to react.

The men reached her almost simultaneously, each one vying to capture the neck of her bag. They nearly had to jump to do so. Since Grace was almost a head taller than either of her supposed rescuers, she had a difficult time keeping a straight face. Supposing that patting them on the head would be patronizing, she pushed her arm out to ward off further assistance instead.

"I can manage just fine," she said. "Thank you kindly."

Her mama had always taught her that polite persistence yielded the best results. It was a philosophy Fiona Crabtree practiced with unusual efficiency in the Crabtree household, whether dealing with the family's new Grahamite vegetarian diet, their regular games of charades, or a simple debate at the dinner table.

Determinedly, Grace edged forward, doing her best to ignore the onlookers. Although she didn't mind having all eyes on her for the sake of a protest march or a worthy cause, when it came to her ordinary existence, she felt uncomfortable with undue attention. She was, for a habitual freethinker and avowed suffragist, a very private person.

One of the men grabbed her bag.

So did the other.

The wrestling match that followed, Grace realized, would probably be talked about in Morrow Creek for months—and not proudly by Fiona Crabtree in particular. But she couldn't surrender her burden—not without endangering the prospects for her women's baseball team. And she was far too stubborn to relent when others were counting on her.

"No, thank you," she insisted with a grunt. "Let go."

"You heard her, Jim," one man said. "Leave off."

"You leave off. I'm helpin' a lady who needs assistance."

"I'm helping."

"No, me." Yank. "Give it over, ma'am. You're too weak."

Considering that Grace had prevailed over two wiry men already, she figured she wasn't so very weak after all.

"Actually, gentlemen," she said as she maintained her sensibly gloved grip, "insofar as strength is concerned, if either of you spent as much time in industrious nature trekking or respectable work as you do bragging, blustering and swilling pints at the saloon, you might have a reasoned argument."

Their hands went slack. So did their mouths.

"As it is, you gentlemen are sorely in need of physical and mental conditioning." Grace took advantage of their inattention to wrest control of her bag, thereby proving her theory. "I suggest Indian clubs for corporeal agility, daily outings for healthful fresh air and plenty of cod-liver oil—two generous spoonfuls at daybreak—for proper bowel functioning. Both the Indian clubs and the cod-liver oil can be obtained for a reasonable price at Jedediah Hofer's mercantile."

They dropped the bag, clearly aghast.

"Please be sure to tell Mr. Hofer that Grace Crabtree sent you. Neighborly collaboration is the heart of any community."

Feeling victorious, Grace shouldered her bag more securely. Leaving the duo behind, she marched down the street, satisfied she'd done another good deed in enlightening the local menfolk. She'd nearly achieved her mama's courteous example, too.

Sometimes it wasn't easy growing up as the eldest daughter in a family as famously progressive as hers. A family made up of unique individuals and original talents—Molly's for baking, Papa's for horticulture and journalism, Sarah's for teaching and Mama's for nigh-invisible persuasion. Not to mention the overall abundance of poetry writing, musicianship, needlework, whittling, painting and popcorn making.

Moving onward, she congratulated herself on her charitable reply to her latest would-be helpers. And on her quick thinking, too. It wasn't until she'd passed the bulk of the spectators, nearly rounded the corner to her meeting rooms and spied the lean form of Jack Murphy lingering outside his saloon that she entertained second thoughts about the matter.

Despite the brisk weather, Murphy lounged as comfortably as a cat in a patch of sunlight, wearing plain trousers, a woolen vest and a white shirt. The whole assembly, she noticed, displayed entirely too much musculature for decent company.

Catching her watching him, he lifted his hat to her. He winked scandalously. "I will say one thing." He angled his head toward the still head-scratching men she'd left in her wake. "You're a handful of woman, Grace Crabtree."

"And you are a thoroughly predictable male, Mr. Murphy."

He smiled as though he enjoyed sparring with her. Perhaps the daft man did. She'd never met anyone more all-out contrary than Jack Murphy, that was for certain. Their ongoing property dispute was proof of that. Why wouldn't he just move?

"That's five good candidates down, too." Sighing, he stared down...at shoes identical to her own. Drat the man! "I might have known just any husband wouldn't do in your case."

Grace yanked her gaze from his all-too-familiar footwear to find Murphy shaking his head with mock sorrow. In a rush, the reasons behind her sudden appeal to the opposite gender became entirely clear. The truth struck her with almost as much impact as that dastardly Jack Murphy's sparkling blue eyes did.

She jerked her chin higher. Find her a husband, would he? There was no chance of that!

Despite Molly and Sarah's apparent happiness with their marriages, Grace remained skeptical. Any institution that required a woman to forfeit her name, parade about in her most impractical attire, procure a wedding cake and kowtow to a man simply had to be counterproductive to female happiness.

"I might have known you'd try to make good on your offer." She stepped nearer, despite the danger of their matching shoes becoming too noticeable. "And I do mean 'try.'"

He scratched his shoulder contemplatively. Squinted. Locked eyes with her again, giving her full benefit of his dazzling Irishman's gaze. Against all reason, Grace held her breath.

Had she pushed him too far? Would he abandon his efforts now? The notion left her strangely bereft. Without Jack Murphy to enliven—er, *disrupt*—her days—

He interrupted her untoward thought with a chuckle.

"'Try'? I don't know about that." Behind him, the raucous saloon carried on its debauchery, even at midday. No wonder she wanted it relocated somewhere more suitable. "I came mighty close to succeeding with Arbus, over there."

Was he mad? The man had discussed his drawers in public!

"On the contrary," Grace disagreed, absently shifting her baseballs. "But please don't let your failures till this point distress you. I realize you may feel discouraged right now."

He offered a bland look. "I'll try to keep a level head."

"Yes, you most certainly should."

With some surprise, Grace realized that she enjoyed their bantering, too…which explained why she'd lingered so long already. Especially when she had work to do, and contraband baseballs to conceal in some safe place upstairs. Oddly enough, though, arguing with Jack Murphy felt invigorating. It gave her an opportunity to hold her own—to feel bonded, in a way, with someone who didn't fear her, pity her or find her incomprehensible. That was a rarity in Morrow Creek.

She arched her brows. "It's not a personal failing of yours. You must feel assured of that. Scientifically speaking, men simply aren't very adept at the intricacies of relations."

She gave him a sham commiserating tsk-tsk.

Which affected Jack Murphy not at all.

"You, Miss Crabtree, have no idea what I'm adept at."

That was ridiculous. "I most certainly—"

"No idea." He looked smug...and not in the least deterred. Which was extremely odd. "No idea a'tall."

The oaf. "Of course I do. You're adept at pulling whiskeys, causing trouble and, of course, wasting my time."

He only smiled more widely—even knowingly—at her.

Something in his rascally demeanor made Grace pause. It wasn't often that people flummoxed her. Surely this one man—however aggravating—hadn't managed that feat?

No. It wasn't possible. She knew what he was up to—marrying her off like some pathetic old maid. It should have been simple to detect from the first. Because truth be told, Jack Murphy was as charming as a field of daisies...and approximately as skilled at subterfuge. That much was plain. Like most of his gender, Grace reminded herself, he was an open book to the discerning female, ripe for page turning and easy interpretation.

The only real mystery was why she hadn't detected his ham-fisted attempts to hurl marriageable men her way— exactly as he'd offered to do—until today.

But now that she had, she was having none of it.

"Proving that I'm right, I find my time being wasted right now." She hefted her bag of baseballs with her best amateur batter's grip, then nodded in dismissal. "Good day, Mr. Murphy."

"Miss Crabtree."

His brogue sounded more devilish than ever. His seemingly polite tip of his hat carried a roguish charge, too. He was clearly out to needle her in any way possible.

But not if she bested him first.

Leaving him behind, Grace headed upstairs to plot the most sensible reprisal she could think of. Her grand exit was spoiled only in that Jack Murphy did not follow her progress all the way upward as she'd hoped. Instead he reentered his saloon with a jovial "Drinks on the barkeep!", leaving his patron's rowdy "Hurrahs!" ringing in her ears all the way upstairs.

* * *

The only thing more challenging than keeping up with her myriad clubs, activities, organizations and interests, Grace learned a short while later, was being forced to juggle several ridiculously dogged suitors, each one intent on becoming the husband she'd never wanted.

"Thank you for your offer," Grace told a shaggy bull-whacker on her way from the jail, "but I wouldn't care to 'hunker down' with you in a wifely manner. However, now that I've made your acquaintance, I would like to recommend that you visit the mercantile for a razor and strop." She examined the man's gnarled, windblown beard. "I daresay using them faithfully might improve your prospects with other, more malleable women."

He scratched his head. "More what?"

"Malleable." Seeing his puzzled frown, she added, "Agreeable. Agreeable women."

"Not so prickly as you, you mean?"

"That's right." Grace smiled brightly at him. It wasn't his fault Jack Murphy had misled him. "Remember, just tell Mr. Hofer that Grace Crabtree sent you. He'll take care of you very well."

The disappointed man shouldered his whip, then trudged away in his high boots, kicking aside snow with every step.

"This may come as a surprise to you," Grace cheerfully informed another hopeful lumber-mill worker later, doing her best to maintain her mama's principles of courtesy and kindness, "but I am not interested in becoming your 'bountiful bride.' Good luck with your next invitation, however. And do drop by the mercantile for some castile soap—perhaps a dozen cakes or so?"

The worker looked bewildered, but nodded nonetheless. Encouraged, Grace continued. "Mr. Hofer stocks a powerful brand that just might improve your chances of appealing to the ladies. Particularly if you also purchase some laundry soap, dishwashing powder and cleanser and use them all."

He boggled. "All that? On myself? I'll go plumb raw!"

She offered a heartening smile. "I mean that you should use those items on your clothes, your floors and your dishes," she clarified. "And the castile soap on your person. No woman can resist a man who keeps an orderly household and hygienic appearance—most particularly, the orderly household."

"Ah. I will. Thank you muchly, ma'am."

Beneficently, Grace waved off the aromatic young man with the trailing end of her scarf, careful to keep her distance. She hadn't progressed more than fifty yards, though, before being beset by another proposal of marriage. How did truly alluring women manage it? Grace wondered.

Gritting her teeth as she listened to her fifth prospective suitor of the day, she found new sympathy for her sister Molly. Molly, naturally beautiful and vivacious, had always struggled to turn away unwanted beaux—men interested more in the heft of her bosom than in the weight of her thoughts.

"Thank you, no," she interrupted the butcher's apprentice, a scrawny boy less robust than Grace herself. She doubted he even had whiskers to shave yet. "I'm afraid I'm finished with entertaining marriage offers for today. However, there is a lovely young lady working at the mercantile who might enjoy your company, if you'd care to make her acquaintance while purchasing an item or two. I believe you two might suit."

"Is she pretty?"

Grace lifted her chin. "She has a very beautiful character, and that is more important than mere loveliness."

Looking glum, the young man headed toward Main Street. Having accomplished that bit of matchmaking—a family hobby she hadn't much indulged in till now—Grace hurried to the sanctity of the *Pioneer Press* offices. The abhorrent and doubtless underqualified Thomas Walsh had yet to arrive on the eastern train, and until he showed his pointy-nosed face, Grace wanted to accomplish a few more changes in the editorial content of the newspaper. Her papa had granted her unprecedented leniency of late, probably owing to his discomfort with the whole Walsh debacle, and she meant to take advantage.

Blissfully, Grace shut the door behind her. The warmth and familiarity of the typesetters' office quickly enveloped her.

Ah. No one would dare to bother her here.

She unwound her scarf and tugged off her gloves, dropping both to her desk beside her box of type, her composing stick and her special revolving inkstand. Feeling markedly relieved, Grace sat on her chair and closed her eyes, not even bothering to remove her coat. In a minute she would…after she recovered from her trying after-lunch trek between the jailhouse and here.

"Uh, Miss Crabtree?"

Grace sighed. Apparently, her moment of peacefulness was already at an end. She reluctantly opened her eyes to find Barney Bartleson waiting on the other side of her desk, his ink-stained apron a near match for his ink-smudged hands.

He blinked rapidly, looking ill at ease. As one of her father's printing press operators, he generally seemed more comfortable with equipment than with people.

"What is it, Mr. Bartleson?" Grace kept her voice gentle, so as not to startle her meek colleague. "Is there something wrong with the printing press?"

"No, ma'am. It's fine. It's only—" He gulped, looked out the window, then shifted from foot to foot. "You see, I'm nearly twenty-five now, plenty old enough to…uh…"

He faltered and stopped. Ruddiness bloomed from his collar to his haphazard hairline. He stared at the floor.

"Well, what I mean to say is that I sure could use me a wife, and if you're amenable to the prospect of becoming *Mrs.* Bartleson, then, uh, perhaps we could, er…"

"Mr. Bartleson. Is this a proposal of marriage?"

He brightened. "Yes, ma'am. I guess it is."

"A proposal of marriage here, at my workplace?"

"I reckon so." He shrank back a little, hands twisting in his apron. "Ma'am, I hate to pester, but…is that a yes?"

"No, Mr. Bartleson, it is not." Suddenly feeling pushed to her limits, Grace grabbed her gloves. She yanked them on with aggravated jerks, then wound her scarf around her neck. "I'm sorry, but this simply won't do. I've had enough."

"But…" He blinked at her. "You never leave your desk before the evening edition is set. You never leave when there's work to be done." He seemed flummoxed. "You never even leave when someone else's work is still to be done. Where are you going?"

Grace paused with the office door open. She felt a little like the warrior goddess Athena, off to fight a great battle— and a lot like a beleaguered spinster suffragist, off to skirmish with a certain blue-eyed Irish prankster.

"I'm going to end this nonsense," she informed Barney crisply, "once and for all."

Then she pulled on her practical hat and set out for Jack Murphy's saloon, every hasty step bringing her closer to improvising a plan of retribution unlike anything Morrow Creek had ever seen.

Chapter Six

"You don't say? A whole performing troupe?" Daniel Mc-Cabe whistled, his muscular blacksmith's frame filling more than his due allotment of space at Jack's saloon. He hefted his ginger beer for another lunchtime swig. "Not just dancing girls like you had in here last year?"

"A whole troupe," Jack confirmed. He'd been corresponding by post with the entertainers for months now, but he still hadn't entirely convinced them to stop in Morrow Creek on their way west to San Francisco. "Acrobats and all."

Daniel nodded in approval. "That ought to cost you a pretty penny. I reckon it'll be worth it though."

"Yep," Jack agreed. Although it occurred to him that if he didn't get Grace Crabtree safely wed before the troupe arrived, she'd probably stage another one of her protests and ruin all his plans. "I hear the Birdcage in Tombstone hired a troupe, and their profits were—"

"Hmmph," Harry interrupted from nearby. The older man had been the first person Jack hired in Morrow Creek, and he typically felt he deserved a say in things. "A whole troupe oughta pack this place up right tight. Don't have room on that itty-bitty stage for a whole 'troupe' plus customers, too."

Dolefully, the man shouldered his way down the bar behind Jack. He slid a plate of beans with bacon across the polished wood to a waiting cowboy. The corn bread on the plate wobbled precipitously—as Harry's food was wont to do— then settled.

Working from the small kitchen in Jack's quarters out back, Harry kept customers supplied with what he called "basic victuals." Jack figured Harry's simple meals kept men tipping back whiskeys instead of leaving to eat someplace else, and that meant more business for him. There was some profit to be made from the food, too, even if it was barely edible. It turned out that so long as the grub didn't stink, smoke or scuttle away, bachelors weren't picky.

Harry also doubled as Jack's backup barkeep, for those rare occasions when Jack couldn't serve himself. It didn't happen often. All Jack had in Morrow Creek—hell, all Jack had in the whole world—was his saloon. He never saw much reason to leave it. Despite Marcus Copeland's needling that he'd grow himself clean into place behind the bar like a massive ponderosa pine and never be able to get free.

"The customers won't be onstage." Jack grinned, sharing a fun-loving glance with McCabe. "They'll be at their tables buying twice as much liquor as usual. At least that's my hope."

He needed the money, too, if he were to keep the place afloat. He'd already sunk most of his funds into payments collected by a land agent on behalf of his landlord. Leasing operated differently in the territory than in Boston—which was how Jack had come to share the property in the first place. Despite the obstacles presented by Grace Crabtree, he hoped to buy the whole caboodle someday and make his new life complete.

"Bunch o' dang fool nonsense if you ask me," Harry grumbled. He wiped his hands on his grimy apron, then shuffled toward the saloon's back room again. "Jest don't expect me to feed all them trapeze monkeys and whatnot, 'cause I ain't."

Daniel watched the man leave, then regarded Jack with his usual carefree grin—an expression that had grown even more expansive since his marriage to Sarah. "Looks like you're the one stuck with feeding those trapeze monkeys, Murphy."

Jack shrugged and grabbed his polishing cloth.

"One of these days, Harry's going to take over this place," Daniel opined. "You ought to show him who's boss."

"Right." Jack tucked his cloth into the next glass, cleaning it with a practiced motion. The gesture made his pocketed cigarillos sway, emitting the rich scent of tobacco. "I should show him who's boss, the way you do with your wife whenever she wants you to bring home some ribbons or lace from the mercantile?"

The blacksmith's face turned ruddy. "It was only that one time. Just one damned basketful."

"But you looked right purty with all that pink on."

"I wasn't wearing it. I was carrying it."

Jack plucked another glass. He gave a noncommittal grunt.

"What the hell does that mean?" Daniel demanded.

With a shrug, Jack arced his cloth inside the glass. Secretly, he felt downright pleased with himself. His grunts must be getting better—manlier—if Daniel took them to mean something. He affected a casual demeanor. "Only that a man shouldn't let a women push him around."

Daniel eyeballed him with all the skepticism borne of their yearlong friendship. "Fine. Soon as you get yourself a woman, I guess you can try out that philosophy. Until then, you can just keep your addle-headed opinions to—"

The saloon's doors slammed open, interrupting him in

mid-sentence. Daniel glanced to the entryway in surprise. Jack double checked the position of his customary under-the-bar pistol. Anybody stomping into a saloon that way was looking for trouble, plain and simple.

"Jack Murphy, I've had just about enough of you!"

Grace Crabtree. And she was definitely looking for trouble. Jack blanched. "Miss Crabtree, get out of here."

Naturally enough, she kept coming instead. Jack couldn't in good conscience fire a warning shot to keep her at a safe distance either—more's the pity. Actually using his Colt would have solidified his rugged western image nicely. Reluctantly, he eased his hand away from his pistol.

With her usual vitality, Grace strode fearlessly into the saloon's midday gloom. Her shoes thumped forward in as unladylike a fashion as they always did, and her whole face shone with a fervor Jack might have mistaken for enthusiasm in anyone else. With Grace Crabtree, though, a man never knew.

Despite everything, Jack found himself admiring that about her. Most women simply didn't possess his uppity neighbor's audacity, her unpredictability, her intelligence. Those were rare qualities—qualities to be appreciated. Not that he'd admit as much to anyone in Morrow Creek, Jack assured himself.

He'd rather kiss a trapeze monkey.

Grace marched right behind the bar as if she owned the place, her scarf trailing behind her like a banner. Every man paused with his whiskey or mescal halfway to his lips, snooping unabashedly. Several frowned. More than a few rose in their seats, apparently prepared to oust the female in their midst. After the debacle of the other day, when Jack had rescued Grace and wound up with her occupying his saloon for the better part of an hour, his patrons were right to be wary.

Grace cast a scathing glance toward Jack's over-the-bar oil

painting—his most prized artwork—in which his beloved Colleen cavorted in all her saucy water-nymph's glory. If looks were matches, his barkeep's pride and joy would doubtless be aflame twice over. Jack stepped protectively toward it, meeting Grace at the middle of the bar.

He caught her arm. "You cannot be in here again."

"It's too late." She wrenched loose with surprising vigor, then regarded him triumphantly. "I already am."

"All my customers will rebel." Reasonably, Jack nudged his chin toward his irate patrons. "I can't be responsible for—"

"I'm not leaving until you hear me out."

Behind her back, he shooed his customers to their tables, making sure they knew not to come any closer. To her face, he presented his most no-nonsense demeanor. "I'll listen outside."

He tried towing her that way. Undaunted, Grace wriggled from his grasp. She stood her ground, blocking the way with her hideous reformer's bonnet trembling—probably from the sheer force of its ugliness—then planted her feet. She regarded him with an expression chockablock with stubbornness.

"You'll listen right here and right now, if you please."

He didn't please. For an instant, Jack experienced a distinct sense of commiseration with Sheriff Caffey and Deputy Winston. How many times had those poor men interrupted Grace in the midst of a protest, a strike, a long parade of picketing? Staring down at her determined, upturned face, he knew exactly how out of their depths those lawmen must have felt.

Those men, however, didn't possess Jack's famous charm. He tried a smile. "Come on now, darlin'."

Her eyebrow rose at his use of the endearment, but Jack pressed on anyway. It wasn't like him to be deterred easily. Grace must have learned that by now. "Won't you be more comfortable outside with a nice sarsaparilla?"

"It's snowy outside. I don't want a sarsaparilla."

Jack gestured to Harry, who'd come out at the first sign of commotion. Daniel McCabe watched interestedly, too.

"Harry, bring Miss Crabtree a nice hot cup of tea. No sugar. I reckon she's sweet enough already."

Her snort could be heard all the way to the faro tables.

Jack smiled more widely, appallingly conscious of his audience. If he'd been able to be himself—with all his talents for handling women—he'd have dispatched Grace long ago. But with a goodly portion of Morrow Creek watching, he couldn't risk it. The last thing he wanted was to be discovered for his past.

"Harry?" he nudged. "Is the kettle on?"

"I heard ya' the first time." Complaining, Harry headed for the back room, clearly reluctant to miss the spectacle.

"No, thank you," Grace called after him, hands on her hips. She gave Jack a pointed stare, ignoring McCabe's presence as easily as she did the rest of the customers. "I won't be needing anything from Mr. Murphy except his acquiescence."

"Hmmph." Daniel sounded as though he were stifling a guffaw, the damned knucklehead. "I'm not sure he's got any."

Grace didn't so much as glance at her brother-in-law. "Kindly stay out of this, Daniel."

"Yes, ma'am."

He didn't sound contrite in the least. Quite possibly, that was why Grace swiveled her gaze to center fully on him.

"Shouldn't you be at the blacksmith's shop?" She spied his mostly empty plate of beans and bacon, and her eyes narrowed still further. "I happen to know Sarah makes you a wonderful homemade lunch every day. What are you doing eating here?"

"Sarah's lunch has vegetables in it." He grimaced. "Carro—"

Grace's barbed look stopped him flat.

"That's it." Daniel grabbed his hat. He breezed past Jack with his hand raised in farewell. "You're on your own, Murphy."

With a sinking feeling, Jack watched his friend amble outside in jovial defeat, his long winter coat trailing. Chairs scraped and empty glasses hit tables, then several other men followed. A few made their displeasure known with over-the-shoulder glares.

Clearly too irate to notice, Grace turned her attention to Jack again. She may have been two heads shorter and a whole lot skinnier, but she possessed uncommon pluck. Or gall. Or just plain doggedness. Jack wasn't quite sure what to label it. He only knew he wanted her gone.

He crossed his arms. "You're ruining my business."

"You're ruining my peaceful existence." Grace jabbed him in the chest. "Stop sending husbands my way."

Ah. So his plan was working. Jack sucked in a deep breath to keep from smiling outright. "Tempted by a few of them, are you? Well, I might have known. Truth be told, you always looked like the marrying kind to me."

"Perhaps," Grace observed, "you need spectacles."

"Listen." Jack cocked his head, cupping one palm to his ear. "I can almost hear those wedding bells chiming already."

Grace rolled her eyes. "Or an extra-large ear trumpet."

"Oh, I don't know about that." Jack caught himself admiring the slender curve of her hips, proof positive that what he really needed was a dose of common sense. She'd obviously driven him daft at last. He dragged his gaze from the dowdy lengths of her practical skirts to meet her eyes. "I've never known a woman who didn't want to be married, all my sisters included."

At that moment, Harry groused his way past the array of whiskey bottles behind Jack. He clunked a watery cup of tea on the bar, prompting Jack to wonder exactly where he'd procured a fancy china teacup. After all, Jack had outfitted his saloon in a deliberately rustic manner—all the better to suit his new nonprofessorial life…and his paltry funds.

"I put in eight spoons of sugar," Harry announced.

Grace met his gimlet gaze with unexpected courtesy. "It looks lovely, thank you. Very kind of you."

Grizzled old Harry actually blushed. Jack goggled as his secondary barkeep and his primary female adversary exchanged pleasantries behind the bar. Then Grace turned to Jack again, catching him frowning in confusion.

"You have sisters? I didn't know that. That's very interesting. Very interesting indeed. How many sisters?"

He wasn't going to answer, Jack told himself. He wasn't. He wanted her out this time, and that was that. He wouldn't be lulled into further conversation. He was no Harry, eager to be caught flat-footed by Grace's dubious feminine wiles. Instead he offered his best rugged frown and watched Harry shuffle down the bar to serve a lager to the cowboy, determined to the last.

"Four," he said.

Grace smiled, obviously pleased.

Damnation. He'd been driven to it, Jack knew. Driven to it by…something he couldn't put his finger on. Maybe it was the uncommon brightness in Grace's expression. It confused him, which was peculiar in itself. Generally, nothing confused him. But Grace rarely looked at anything that way—short of radical texts, her sister Molly's cinnamon buns and her newfangled bicycling apparatus.

"Four sisters." She steepled her hands, then took a contemplative step nearer. "Hmm. What do you know?"

Hell. He'd accidentally given her more personal information in mere minutes than he'd given the rest of Morrow Creek in an entire year and a half. And he'd actually entertained thoughts about her hips, too. Her bony, in-his-way, aggravating hips.

What was wrong with him? Determined not to wreck his taciturn reputation any further, Jack clamped his mouth shut. He recrossed his arms for good measure, too.

Grace still regarded him with that exasperating sense of enlightenment. Her mouth quirked. He couldn't believe he was noticing her mouth at all. He needed a whiskey. Or a good slap.

"Tell me, Jack." She pursed her lips. "What would you think if one of your sisters, simply to protect her reputation and her sanity, was forced to enter a saloon this way?"

"I would think she should leave." In a moment of sheer honesty, Jack gazed at her squarely. "Please, Grace. Just behave like a regular woman for once."

Her eyes widened. Her mouth opened. Her throat worked, undoubtedly conjuring up a scathing reply—perhaps in answer to the fact that he'd inadvertently called her by her first name instead of the appropriately proper Miss Crabtree. Jack tended to think of her as Grace, he realized. Just Grace.

That was curious. In light of their disagreements…

"I'll wait at the stairs to my meeting rooms for precisely five minutes," she informed him starchily. "After that, I'm enlisting the aid of the Social Equality Sisterhood. My local chapter is very effective, as you may recall. I believe we still have those picket signs from last year, when we shut down your place for a spell. Consider yourself forewarned, Mr. Murphy."

With that dire pronouncement, Grace wheeled on her clunky shoes, flung her scarf over her shoulder, and left his saloon.

Afternoon sunshine poured over Main Street, melting the icicles strung from Jack Murphy's saloon eaves. They dripped steadily on the water barrel outside, fooled by the unseasonable warmth into believing springtime had nearly arrived. Knowing better, Grace crossed her arms over herself and shivered. She jerked her chin upward, willing herself not to cry.

She never cried over anything.

With the exception of her sisters' weddings, naturally, which she'd explained as ire over the patriarchal institution of marriage. And the first time she'd successfully pedaled her bicycle and remained upright, certainly, but that had been easily hidden behind her bicycling goggles. And the day she'd learned about her father's decision regarding editorship of the newspaper, of course, but that aberration had clearly been brought on by Jack Murphy's peculiar brand of kindness afterward.

Perhaps the alcohol fumes inside his saloon affected her strangely, Grace mused. Or the sight of his provocative behind-the-bar painting offended her eyes just that strongly. She wasn't sure how to explain it, but she still felt a sob lodged in her chest. It stuck there with all the force of Molly's early and misbegotten attempts at snickerdoodle cookies, refusing to budge. The plain fact was, ever since Grace had first set foot in Jack Murphy's saloon, she hadn't felt like herself…and the effect didn't appear to be abating either.

It was worrisome. In fact, Grace admitted privately, she hadn't quite felt like herself ever since meeting him over a year ago. She'd felt, at times, variously fluttery and girlish and unacceptably interested in Jack's comings and goings. Not that she'd mentioned as much to anyone, even Molly and Sarah. Now, particularly on the heels of his mean-spirited comment, Grace meant to never mention anything favorable about Jack to anyone at all.

Just behave like a regular woman for once.

Wounded despite her resolve to ignore such foolishness, Grace hugged herself tighter. She was a woman like any other! Perhaps a little more active, more prone to books and causes and clubs, but a woman all the same. Why couldn't Jack see that?

She didn't care, Grace told herself, straightening determinedly in her sheltered area to the side of the saloon. She didn't. Jack was a loutish ne'er-do-well without a single industrious thought in his head. He meant nothing to her save an obstacle to the efficient operation of her many ladies' groups.

But the heavy footfalls that sounded next on the boardwalk—and her quickening heartbeat in response to them—made her declaration a lie. She did care, else she wouldn't have recognized that those footsteps belonged to Jack Murphy. She wouldn't have felt glad he'd followed her outside after all.

Miserably, Grace realized she would have known the unique cadence of his footsteps anywhere. Late at night, Jack often wandered his saloon downstairs while she planned new suffragist campaigns upstairs. Both she and Jack, it seemed, led solitary lives…divided only by some beams and a few planks of lumber.

And, of course, by their ongoing property dispute.

Funny, that she'd think of him as Jack, Grace considered idly. Mr. Murphy would have been more proper, and yet…

Dismissing the thought, she steeled her expression into determination—the same tactic she used when facing any battle. Then she hurriedly whisked her palms over her cheeks, bit her lip and fluffed out her rumpled skirts.

She'd just realized her error when Jack rounded the corner.

She froze in midfluff, her gloved hands buried in her skirts' sensible fabric. What was she doing? *Primping?* Grace Crabtree primped for no man, especially one who galled her so. Besides, she possessed no vanity at all. Leastwise as far as Jack Murphy was concerned. It wasn't practical or commendable.

To hide her mistake, she spoke first. "How did all those men know to recognize me?" she demanded. "To propose to me?"

Lazily, Jack lifted his gaze from her clenched fists. He seemed lost in thought for a moment, but recovered rapidly. In a heartbeat, he returned to the burly Irishman she knew, wrapped in a wool coat and an air of forthright male certainty.

"I told them to look for the plainest, most fast-walking, fast-talking woman they'd ever seen," he said.

Abashed, Grace stared at her shoes. And her gray skirts. And her haphazardly gloved hands. Her gloves didn't match, it was true, but they still kept her cozy. Was she really that plain? The plainest woman in town, identifiable on sight?

"I told them to follow any signs of trouble, and they'd find you," Jack continued.

Considering, Grace wiggled her toes. The motion made not a dent in the solid leather upper of her shoe. Perhaps…

"I told them if they spied a woman who looked capable of outrunning, outtalking and outthinking them, that was you."

All at once, the pressure in Grace's chest eased. She lifted her head, beaming. "You do understand me!"

Jack seemed perplexed. His frown marred his good looks not at all. Neither did his obvious reluctance to speak injure his appeal. Which made not a lick of sense to Grace, who had always dismissed laconism as feeblemindedness and expected herself to prefer a man of elocution, grace and courtesy.

Instead Jack Murphy grunted. He crossed his arms.

Grace tried to feel disgusted. Or aggravated. Or at least a little less admiring of the timbre of his brogue, the width of his shoulders, the certainty of his stance. She failed.

They stood that way, identically situated with their bodies bundled and wrapped and protected, facing one another. It struck Grace that she and Jack Murphy might well be equally stubborn.

"This will make everything so much easier," she announced firmly. *Outrunning, outtalking, outthinking.* Those were qualities she prized in herself, to be sure. Apparently, Jack valued them as well. "You may have already noticed that I never back down from a challenge. As I always say, anything worth having is worth fighting for."

He shrugged. His shoulders still looked wide.

"So you may as well quit now," she added.

He exhaled. His mouth was nicely shaped, too.

Not that Grace cared about physicality, she reminded herself staunchly. She was an aficionado of the intellect, the heart and the soul. Not of masculine lips, however intriguingly formed. Perhaps all the marriage proposals she'd sustained had affected her ability to behave normally.

"Because," she stated, a little too loudly, "I don't have any interest in having a husband."

He took a step nearer. "Yes, you do."

Something about the way Jack looked at her—something about the way warmth seeped from his chest to hers, kindling a new kind of heat between them—made Grace's heart stutter. Her breath caught and held, too. She didn't know what to make of the sensation. After all, she was eminently fit, having practiced a variety of outdoor activities for years. Bicycling, baseball, ornithology, Indian club exercises… Discomfited but resolute, she stepped forward, too. It wouldn't do to let herself be cowed by a mere male like Jack Murphy.

The heat between them flared higher.

"I don't need a man for anything," she announced.

His lips turned up. Parted. Even his teeth were nice. She'd never had such a close-up view of them before. For the first time ever, Grace caught herself approving of his clean shave.

"Darlin', if you believe that," he said, "then you need a man for certain. You need a man real soon."

Grace snapped to herself again. Jack's conviction—and something more, something intriguing in the rasp of his voice—almost stopped her. But she soldiered on anyway. "I don't want a man. Please stop sending them to me."

There. That ought to do it.

"Well, now." Jack scratched his forehead thoughtfully, tilting up the rim of his black winter hat. His eyes sparkled. "I guess I could do that."

"Very well. See that you do." Sanity had been restored, even if she'd had to endure a momentary lapse into indecorous ogling to achieve it. Satisfied, Grace hitched up her skirts.

"Except for the reward and all."

His words ended her victorious retreat. Slowly, Grace turned back, her skirts fluttering lower. "What reward?"

"The one I offered for marrying you."

Disbelieving, Grace stared. How had she ever found Jack Murphy tolerable, even for an instant? Even for as long as it took to be lulled by his big, strong demeanor, his ready smile, his too-teasing voice?

Two words were all she could manage civilly. "Explain yourself."

"Any man who successfully marries you gets free drinks in my saloon for a year." Generously, Jack spread his arms. He possessed two heartily unlikable dimples. "It was supposed to be for a month, but I didn't have very many takers, so—"

"You beast!" Furiously, Grace walloped him with her scarf. "You're auctioning me off like a—a—a cow?"

She'd never heard of anything more mortifying.

His low chuckle drove her mad. "I wouldn't go that far. It's more akin to a reward than an auction. But if you think it would be quicker for you to just get up onstage…"

"Arrgh!" Infuriated, Grace paced. She was never at a loss for words, but this time…she was.

"Come on now. Don't be this way," Jack urged. "Those free drinks are going to cost me plenty, you know. This isn't cheap, but I reckon it'll be worth it in the end. To both of us."

Was that his notion of an apology? She couldn't even speak, she felt so embarrassed. Snow squished beneath her shoes as she went on tramping it down in enraged, unsatisfying circles. Beyond them walked curious passersby carrying packages. Some rattled past in sleighs, their breaths puffing in the cold.

Grace hoped none of them could overhear this indignity. Including the horses.

"I thought you would at least admire the initiative involved," Jack went on, sounding absurdly reasonable. "It was—"

"Initiative? I can't believe you even comprehend the word," Grace sputtered, flinging her arm outward. She quit pacing long enough to glare at him. "You oafish, self-concerned—"

"You ought to be happy. All you have to do is say yes."

"—uncultured excuse for a human being!"

With a shrug, Jack leaned against the stair rail.

He issued an indifferent sound, then lifted his burly arm and scratched underneath it.

Grace recoiled. All the man did was grunt, scratch and— inexplicably, given that he did not partake of it—smell richly of tobacco. He obviously had no sense of decorum or civility or acceptable behavior. Any man who would raffle her to the most successful marriage bidder was clearly lacking in intelligence as well. Had all that whiskey pickled his brain?

"If you were the least bit civilized," she began, staring in aggravation at the hard line of his jaw, the unseemly size of his muscles, the rough disorder of his clothes, "you would realize exactly how inappropriate your efforts are."

He grunted. "Don't care." Settling more comfortably against the stair rail—almost as though he were enjoying himself—he smiled in a way that put both dimples to scandalous advantage. "You won't either, after I snag you a husband or two."

Now he meant to get her more than one! Gaping at him, Grace finally understood the depths to which he was willing to sink. She'd never met anyone she couldn't influence, but this time…this time her back was against the wall. Even her threat to enlist the valiant ladies of the Social Equality Sisterhood hadn't made an impression. Jack was just that loutish.

And exactly that swaggering.

If only she could make him see reason, Grace fumed. But how? How did a person go about instilling sensibility in a man like him? A man who saw nothing wrong with marrying the town spinster to the thirstiest, most penny-pinching drunkard?

Then it occurred to her. Like magic, as she examined his big uncouth hands and handsome oafish face, Grace realized the truth. All she had to do was civilize Jack! It was as plain as castile soap meeting dirt. Surely once she had properly improved and shaped and enlightened her problematically burly neighbor, he would appreciate how sensible it would be to leave her in peace—and to leave her free of husbandly candidates, too.

Why, he might even go further, Grace reasoned excitedly. With her expert tutelage, Jack might finally see the sense in segregating his saloon from her meeting rooms—and all her difficulties would be solved!

It was obvious. Elegant. Perfect.

She couldn't believe she hadn't realized it before. Now that she had, it was as though he'd presented her the solution with both hands—however mucky they might have been with tobacco, tequila and temerity. Surely once Jack Murphy was fully transformed into a broad-minded egalitarian thinker, he would be bound to see reason—her reason—at long last. It was brilliant!

Craftily, she scrutinized him. Oblivious to her racing thoughts, he watched the passersby, probably plotting to snare her yet another hairy, smelly, or gangly potential husband.

Yes, Grace decided. Yes indeed. All the raw materials of a proper gentleman were there, albeit in terribly rough form. All she had to do was exert the correct persuasion with Jack, make available the appropriate influences…manage the whole endeavor with cleverness and patience and zeal. Which shouldn't be too terribly difficult, she reminded herself. After all, cleverness, patience and zeal were her specialties!

Nothing could stop her now. With all the enthusiasm she could muster, she would turn Jack Murphy into a reasonable and quick-witted man—and accomplish that feat long before he could produce a marriageable suitor for her. It was faultless.

"What's the matter with you?" He frowned anew, studying her face. "You look strange, all of a sudden."

"Nothing at all." She widened her eyes with deliberate guilelessness—a gesture she'd never before attempted. She feared it was a poor fit for her. "In fact, I've never felt better."

Another grunt. "I don't trust that smile of yours."

"That's quite all right, Mr. Murphy. Your trust isn't necessary—only your cooperation."

Then Grace patted his arm, straightened her hat and left him behind to begin her improving program straightaway. She had a man to enlighten and a saloon relocation to finagle—and the sooner, the better, to be sure.

Chapter Seven

"Oh, Lizzie!" Molly exclaimed, as chatty and exuberant as always. "What a beautiful wedding! I daresay I've never seen a lovelier bride. And your gown is absolutely exquisite."

She brushed Lizzie's sleeve with her fingertips, her mouth open in a circle of awe. Among all the women gathered around the new bride, Grace's younger sister was by far the most effusive in her admiration, but then she'd always possessed an eye for fashion. Even now, while preparing for her and Marcus's first child, Molly managed to appear effortlessly stylish.

Unlike a certain Crabtree woman who might be mentioned...

With an unaccustomed sense of self-consciousness, Grace peered at her own dress. Constructed of sturdy forest-green wool with plain white trim at the collar and cuffs, it was the fanciest item she owned. Unfortunately, it was also the itchiest, and it restricted movement in a most unreasonable manner. For anyone other than her friend Lizzie, Grace would never have appeared in public wearing it. Given the festive occasion, though, she'd decided to loosen her practical outlook.

She already regretted it though, especially feeling, as she

did, foolishly trussed up…like a prickly green chicken surrounded by finer-garbed peacocks. Grace's only consolation was that her skirts and stiff bodice and voluminous petticoats seemed to have bewildered her would-be suitors.

Doubtless they didn't recognize her, because none of the marriage proposals she'd grown accustomed to had been forthcoming. Their lack was almost enough to induce Grace into tight-laced gowns every day. Almost. But not quite.

She did, after all, have her reputation to consider. People looked up to her, especially the members of her various clubs. As a woman who'd advocated female dress reform on several occasions, Grace didn't feel right abandoning her views for the sake of looking pretty—or dodging her specious "beaux" either.

Despite the absence of fresh marriage proposals though, Grace noted plenty of frivolity in the air. All around her, the wedding reception proceeded in merry fashion. The Stotts had opened their home to most of Morrow Creek, it seemed, and their small living room and parlor were packed with well-wishers.

A trio of musicians played in the corner, competing with the hum of conversation and laughter. People milled to all sides of Grace, enjoying the refreshments the bride's family had provided—some of them baked by Molly herself.

Reminded of her sister, Grace glanced up. Molly still chattered about lace trim and embroidery, fascinated by both. Feeling much less comfortable with the subject matter, Grace excused herself. She made her way through the parlor and arrived in a safe corner, clutching her cup of cider. She watched the partygoers, fervently wishing she had something useful to do. She should have volunteered to take charge of…something.

Grace was not good at leisure. Possibly because she'd deliberately avoided it, preferring activity to feeling alone.

Unlike the rest of her family, she was far from adept at social occasions, unless they involved picketing, and heartily preferred a nice protest march to a frivolous dance.

Usually, Sarah kept her company at such events, the two of them identical wallflowers. But today Sarah was smiling on the arm of her new husband, Daniel. She wouldn't be joining Grace to discuss a novel or decipher a metagram or meet a poetry recitation challenge—to name just a few of their favorite pastimes. Sarah wouldn't be helping Grace hide her awkwardness.

Several moments ticked past, fraught with merriness Grace didn't know how to take part in. From across the room, she spied her papa, having no such trouble at all. Clad in his best suit, Adam Crabtree beamed with joviality. He and Grace had spoken again about the newspaper's editorship and had reached an understanding of late. Grace still felt less than elated about Thomas Walsh coming, but she understood the reasoning behind it.

As she watched, her papa caught her mama's hand. The two of them danced to the fiddle music, Fiona laughing as they dodged parlor furniture and other partygoers. It was so like her parents, Grace considered with a fond smile, to be the first ones to dance. Doubtless they'd be the last to quit as well.

Scratching the back of her neck—an impulse spurred by her itchy gown—Grace craned to see Lizzie again. The new bride conferred excitedly with her husband, rising on tiptoes. She blushed as he whispered something in her ear. Their faces shone with joy, bringing a pang to Grace's heart. As happy as she was for her friend, she still felt…a little left behind.

Which was nonsense, Grace assured herself. Honestly. If she'd wanted a husband, she'd had plenty of offers to choose from lately! She was alone of her own choice. An unmarried woman of her own volition. Independent and proud and indisputably busy—especially with her plan to civilize Jack Murphy added to her already-burgeoning list of duties. No woman truly required more. The speeches and writings of Grace's own personal suffragist heroine, Heddy Neibermayer, assured her of that.

With that recollection in mind, Grace put down her cider and made herself stroll the perimeter of the party, determined to make the best of things. She still felt lonely. But considering Heddy's example, she decided that the very best remedy would be useful activity.

Perhaps she could seek out a few of her fellow ornithologists or women's baseball league members and discuss their springtime fund-raisers. Or buttonhole Sheriff Caffey and engage him in a debate about appointing female officers to the town government. Or track down Jack Murphy and pair him with someone suitably enriching…someone who might put forward her refining plan without delay. Like a minister. Or a lady artist.

So caught up was she in her thoughts of a downstairs neighbor who neither grunted nor scratched, Grace barely noticed when a gentleman stepped into her path. Until it was too late.

"Oh, I'm terribly sorry!" Embarrassed to have blundered straight into the man, Grace cursed her shoes. At Molly's urging, she'd abandoned her favorite men's brogans—the pair identical to Jack's—in favor of delicate slippers. She had no notion how other women managed to move adroitly in the things. "I didn't see you there. Please excuse me."

"On the contrary," he said. "It's my fault entirely. I can't imagine how I could have missed such a vision of loveliness as yourself."

Oh, dear. She'd stumbled upon another potential suitor. This time, her ladylike disguise hadn't deterred him at all. In fact, to judge by his eager tone, her itchy gown may have functioned as an incentive. Just one more reason not to wear it.

Resigned to deflecting yet another unwanted proposal, Grace glanced up. Past a fancy waistcoat, past a snowy shirt and velvety necktie, higher and higher until she reached an unfamiliar face. At the sight, her prepared refusal stuck in her throat. No man in Morrow Creek was this tall—save her brothers-in-law—and even well-suited Marcus Copeland didn't possess the same kind of dapper elegance the stranger did.

Wearing a broad smile, he extended his hand. "Please forgive me. I fear I haven't quite found my land legs after having departed the train."

Invigorated and relieved, Grace accepted his handshake. He wasn't another bumpkin eager to win free liquor. He only wanted to exchange small talk. That she could manage. "I haven't had the pleasure myself, but I hear the rocking along the tracks is akin to being aboard a schooner."

"Indeed it is." He produced a lacy handkerchief and mopped his forehead. His eyes were kind behind his spectacles, his face youthful. "With fewer pirates, however, I'm delighted to say."

Instantly, she liked him. It wasn't often an unfamiliar person came to Morrow Creek, but this man was the epitome of culture and sophistication.

His educated speech and spruce dress reminded her of a drawing from one of Molly's periodical magazines…magically come to life with stylish lines and sophisticated banter. She didn't doubt he had many interesting stories to tell. She felt flattered that he'd selected her to share them with.

"Then let me be among the first to welcome you safely from your journey." Grace found herself smiling boldly. This must be one of Lizzie's far-flung relatives or a relation of the groom. She had definitely underestimated the caliber of her fellow wedding guests. "I am Grace Crabtree."

"Grace Crabtree?" The glimmer in his eyes suggested he'd heard of her. Likely Lizzie had written him about their work as typesetters. "Then I am doubly glad to make your acquaintance."

Proving his words, the man swept into a bow the likes of which Grace had never seen, making her laugh. When he straightened, his stylish hair flopped to his forehead in a most endearing fashion.

"I am Thomas Walsh," he said. "Your new editor."

So long as the smooth-talking knuck with the sissy clothes and the overfriendly manner and the spectacles as big as teacups merely shook hands with Grace, Jack figured he could stand it. But the instant he actually lifted her hand to his mouth and kissed it, the moment she laughed with very un-Gracelike glee, Jack knew he had to do something.

Clearly, Grace was out of her depth. Never mind that the man had cheeks like a chipmunk's and an overbite to match. He was obviously up to no good, and Grace—innocent, confounding Grace—was ill prepared to cope. She needed Jack to extricate her whether she realized it or not.

Determinedly, he strode across the room. Several times partygoers stopped to talk with him, partially blocking his view. The music swung into another quickly fiddled tune, making it impossible for him to eavesdrop on Grace's conversation.

Hell. Was she still simpering and smiling at that pretentious twit? Or was she swooning, as she'd nearly done a few minutes ago? Jack didn't know.

Getting free to go to her was a matter of a few hearty stomps, several manly grunts and—in one urgent instance—a gruff shove between two railroaders. Damnation! He had developed a rowdiness a real mountain man would have been proud of.

Suddenly, he broke loose between two cider-sipping ladies in old-fashioned wide gowns and spied her. Grace was staring up into the unknown man's face, her eyes wide with what looked like speechless ardor. Had he actually struck her dumb? Jack wouldn't have thought it possible. He hurried closer.

And nearly collided with them both.

Grace glanced up, startled. Her gaze swung from the stranger to Jack and back again. He realized—astonishingly—that he was nearly panting. Apparently, the trek across the room had been more strenuous than he'd reckoned on. Also the strategy he'd counted on devising when he got there hadn't quite caught up with him yet. What the hell was he doing?

"Mr. Murphy." Grace looked dazzled. "Please meet—"

"You promised me this dance," Jack blurted.

She wrinkled her brow. "I did?"

Momentarily befuddled by her appearance, he didn't answer right away. Up close, there was something different about her. Her gown? Her hair? He'd almost decided it was her hair—possibly those loose, unschoolmarmlike tendrils she sported so atypically—when Jack realized it was her expression. He'd never seen Grace appear less than one hundred percent certain about anything. Particularly anything relating to him.

Dismissing the aberration as the chipmunk's influence, Jack stuck out his hand, palm facing.

"You did," he lied. "I remember it distinctly."

"You do?"

Jack nodded. Vigorously. Now that he'd embroiled himself, he meant to act to the fullest. The stranger looked on, doubtless disgruntled at the possibility of having the sole object of his attentions taken from him. The man opened his mouth to object, displaying those monstrous teeth. Jack decided he looked more donkey than chipmunk.

Still hesitating, Grace puckered her lips. Just this once, Jack prayed she would not be her usual contrary self.

"Indeed, I did. I'd entirely forgotten our dance."

In a haze of relief, Jack felt her hand slip to his. He wasn't sure how they arrived at the area cleared for dancing. Once there he pulled her in his arms and let instinct take over. Years of faculty mixers and Boston society events had prepared him for moments like this, but Grace had experienced no such training. She surprised him by stepping nimbly into place.

"Don't look so astonished," she admonished him as they turned. "I happen to excel at all things corporeal. I'm terribly agile and very fit. It's because of all that protest marching, you see. And what is dancing, I ask you, if not another physical endeavor, meant to improve the heart and strengthen the limbs?"

Jack mustered up his best manly expression. "Dancing is an excuse to hold a woman close." For good measure, he held her tighter, trying not to think of how well she fit in his arms. This was Grace Crabtree, he reminded himself. The thorn in his side since his arrival in town. "Nothing more."

"Nothing more? Nonsense. Dancing is an exercise in coordination, in music appreciation and in social interaction. Really, Mr. Murphy. You must broaden your thinking."

"I already have." He'd broadened his thinking to include the notion of his troublesome neighbor looking feminine and behaving gracefully, for one. She hadn't even waved a single suffragette banner beneath his nose. "You'd be amazed at what I'm thinking right now."

"Excellent!" Bracingly, Grace executed another turn, smiling up into his face. "Next thing you know, you'll be a fully refined gentleman. Won't that be wonderful?"

Her cheeks flushed prettily. Her eyes sparkled, too. No wonder the donkey had pounced, Jack realized. He didn't know she was really a passel of problems in disguise.

Not waiting for his reply, Grace continued on. "I must say, I was surprised by your invitation to dance."

Jack was, too. He still felt mystified at what had come over him when he'd glimpsed Grace with the stranger. Wasn't a match for her what he'd wanted? Then why interrupt what had looked to be a promising flirtation with the donkey, spectacles and all?

"But I'm not displeased." She glanced at their joined hands as though taken aback by the union. "Your invitation may have been a bit...unpolished, but your dancing is competent."

He bit his cheek to hide a grin. "Thank you. Yours is less toe-crushing than I'd feared."

"Almost a compliment! We are well matched today."

"Your new friend doesn't think so." Jack turned them both so Grace could view the donkey glowering at them from beside a parlor chair. "Who is he?"

A curious expression flitted over her face. For an instant, Grace seemed almost entranced...provoking him all the more.

She lifted her chin. "The *Pioneer Press*'s new editor."

Ah. That explained everything—except the sense of relief Jack experienced. "No wonder he slobbered all over you."

"What?" Looking appalled, Grace transferred her attention to Jack. He couldn't say he missed the dreamy contemplation she'd displayed when looking at her new editor. "He did not slobber all over me," she informed him.

Jack arched his brow. "Looked that way to me."

"That's because you're—unlike me, you—oh, never mind." She sighed. "Mr. Walsh is sophisticated. You wouldn't understand."

Jack hmmphed. "Not much mystery to a slobbery kiss." He offered her an overly solicitous gaze, ducking his head to do so. "Do you want to borrow my handkerchief?"

Her reply was a glower well-matched to the donkey's.

"I'm surprised you could take my hand," Jack added, "seeing as how yours was probably slimy from that kiss." He pretended to examine his hand. "Maybe I need my handkerchief."

"Mr. Murphy. That is enough."

Grinning, he spun her round. "It's not nearly enough."

It wouldn't be either. Not until he got her duly wed.

The fiddles picked up tempo, separating him and Grace for part of the dance. When next she returned to his arms, she'd recovered her fighting spirit—and Jack had recovered his equilibrium. She was only Grace…Grace who had bedeviled him nearly from the start. He could handle her and would.

"I had a reason for asking you to dance," he said.

"Oh?" Grace's gaze sparkled mischievously. "And what was that? A compelling urge to match shoes again? I'm sorry to disappoint you, but I'm not able to indulge you today."

Daringly, she flashed him a glimpse of slipper.

Caught off guard by her lightheartedness, Jack laughed. Then he spun her around, meeting her playful mood with one of his own. Still smiling, he laid his cheek against her hair. "Ah, Grace. You have no notion how you've indulged me already."

They slowed in their dancing. With near fondness, he inhaled the fragrance surrounding her…a unique blend of castile soap, oil paint and stubbornness. He couldn't fathom why it made him feel so contented. Having such difficulty pulling himself away from her was foolish in the extreme.

"Indulged you? I've done no such thing!" she protested.

But she had, Jack realized. Mysteriously so. Around them, other partygoers danced and talked and feasted on cakes and cider, but for him—of a sudden—there was only Grace. Just Grace. She made him feel oddly at home in his skin. Perhaps, he reasoned, someone had liquored the cider. He'd lay odds that Daniel McCabe was the rascally culprit.

There was no other excuse for the way he felt, Jack told himself—all free and happy and improbably drawn to the most splintery spinster in Morrow Creek.

He definitely needed to avoid spirits in the future.

Doggedly, he rallied. "The reason I asked you to dance is to tell you to leave off." He attempted to look stern. "I know what you're up to, and I won't have it."

"Why, Jack! I can't imagine what you mean."

At Grace's shameless—and boundlessly overplayed—innocence, he couldn't help but smile more widely. Foolish as it was, her use of his given name warmed him through, too. Either that or he'd simply danced too much in the overcrowded room.

"Ask your friend, the poet." He maneuvered them toward the parlor corner, intent on having his say as privately as possible. "The one who sneaked into my saloon yesterday, ready to 'improve' me with his poetry readings."

Grace widened her eyes. "Oh? Did you enjoy them?"

Hell. His intuition had been correct. She *had* set that damned poet upon him.

"Enjoy them? Can't say," he told her matter-of-factly. "By the time my customers quit buying him Old Orchard, your poet—"

"My poet? I'm sure I don't grasp your meaning."

"—couldn't see well enough to read."

"Oh. Poor Cedric." Squinting worriedly into the crowd of revelers, Grace gave a distressed sound. "He's so talented, too."

"Almost as talented as that bird watcher I met the day before at the apothecary." Jack frowned. "She wouldn't let me buy my bottle of bay rum hair tonic until I learned all about the wonders of the dark-hooded, red-backed Junco."

Grace's smirk was telling. "Truly? How fascinating."

Damnable female. He couldn't even manage a grunt.

"I have long considered the *Junco hyemalis dorsalis* a most thrilling species of sparrow," she nattered on. Her gaze met his with all appearance of earnestness. "They're active this time of year. The Junco is a migratory bird, you know."

"I wish I didn't." Unfortunately, her bird-watcher friend had seen to the contrary. He could still hear her chirping.

"They have lovely white tail feathers," Grace continued.

She looked awfully pleased with herself. How she managed to dance so lightly with the weight of all that meddling on her shoulders, Jack didn't know.

"Most ornithologists of my acquaintance can identify all varieties of Junco upon sight," she informed him. "Easy as pie."

"Hmm. Some rarities are like that." He gave her a shrewd look. "Pretty obvious once you know what you're looking for."

For instance, once Jack had started noticing the pale-faced intellectuals and motley artists and rabid reformers coming out of the woodwork, he'd immediately discerned a pattern. Every one of them had been intent on enlightening him on subjects ranging from tea drinking to Celestial philosophy to the bards of the Renaissance. The whole lot of them, he'd bet, had one particular rabble-rouser to thank for their inspiration.

"Whatever you're up to," he said, "it's not going to work."

"On the contrary." Grace studied his shirt collar, then lifted her gaze to his face. "It's already working."

Eager to refute her claim, Jack was nonetheless unsure how. Because he still didn't grasp what Grace was playing at. Was she reacting to his attempts to get her wed? Attempting to retaliate, after a fashion? Even for her, that was nonsensical.

Left with no option that wouldn't endanger his new rugged persona, Jack was forced to grunt. As negatively as possible.

Undaunted, Grace nodded. "It occurs to me I've never seen you dance before. Dancing is awfully...civilized, isn't it?"

Her impish expression galled him.

So did his own response to it. How could he enjoy sparring with her, even while she drove him daft? And what exactly did she mean by emphasizing *civilized* that way? Had Grace somehow guessed the secret of his past life in Boston?

Chilled, Jack had to acknowledge it was possible. Grace was more erudite than most. Her interests ranged far and wide. She might have read about his professorship. She might even have blundered onto his infamous corsetry creation… and meant to dangle it in front of his face, newfangled laces and all.

Unwarranted, a vision of Grace attired in nothing but a tight corset and some clever embellishments burst into his mind. She crooked her finger, beckoned him nearer…and smiled seductively. He almost shook with the vividness of it.

"Look," she said. "You've popped one of your braces loose."

Grace's voice cleared his head, returning Jack to the wedding-day swirl of revelers, music and laughter. He frowned.

"See?" She indicated his shirtfront, where one of the braces meant to hold up his trousers drooped ineffectually. "Here. I'll move sideways so no one can see while you mend it."

With no maidenly modesty at all, she shielded him, pretending to admire a painting on the Stotts' parlor wall.

Revelers danced past them, whooping with laughter. No one paid any mind to the goings-on in their corner. Hastily, Jack repaired the metal fastening—only to find that Grace had turned to examine his actions with scholarly interest.

"Wait a minute." She squinted. "I've never seen braces like those before. Not even in the dress reform pamphlets. Are they—"

They were his own design, Jack realized belatedly. He should have known her perceptiveness would cause trouble.

"—some newfangled version from the east?"

She stared at him artlessly, awaiting his reply.

Was she baiting him? Right then and there, Jack vowed to be as *un*civil and as *un*cooperative as possible, especially when Grace was around. If she wanted him civilized, he promised himself silently, he'd be as rough and ready as any lumberjack or railroader. Possibly more. All the better to throw her off the trail to his past and safeguard his new life in the west.

He crossed his arms. "If you want a man's britches to patch up, you ought to take on one of those husbands I've been sending your way."

That proved exactly as diverting as he'd hoped.

"Husbands? Most of them are barely able to stand upright!"

"Well, now." Jack summoned up his best satisfied look. "That'll make mending their britches especially tricky, won't it? But I do know how you appreciate a challenge."

Grace crossed her arms, evidently struck speechless. What the bespectacled donkey couldn't do, Jack clearly could.

"No need to thank me." He held up both palms, warding off her supposed gratitude. "It's my pleasure to help a neighbor."

Just then, another partygoer ambled past. He glanced at Grace, then at Jack, then back at Grace again. He stopped.

"Tarnation! If you ain't that marrying gal!"

Grace ground her teeth. She cast Jack an accusatory glance.

"Yessir." Jack slapped the man on the shoulder, drawing him nearer with his friendliest barkeep's manner. "This is Grace Crabtree. Finest mender of britches in all the territory."

Grace stomped his toe. Her slipper made not a dent.

"You don't say?" The man grinned, then rubbed his nose with enthusiasm. He left a trail of spice cake on his cheek, adding to the dirt and smudged tobacco already there. "I guess I could use me some patched-up britches sometime."

"Then this is your gal." Jack did his best to ignore Grace's murderous look. He felt reasonably certain his hair was on fire all the same. "You probably didn't recognize her without her man-shoes on."

"Hmm. Well, I sure didn't rec'nize her until I saw you two standin' together, Murphy. That there's a plain fact."

The man looked Grace up and down, clearly considering.

"If you ask me to open my mouth and show my teeth like a packhorse," Grace informed him, "I'll kick like one, too."

He guffawed, elbowing Jack. "Feisty, ain't she?"

"That she is," Jack agreed mildly. "That she is."

"All right." The man exhaled, treating them to a blustery dose of liquored cider. Creakily, he began bending on one knee.

Looking horrified, Grace grabbed his shoulder. "No! The answer is no. No no no! Please don't go any further."

"But I want them free drinks Murphy's got," he objected, hunkering awkwardly in place. His bushy brows drew together. "I reckon you seem presentable enough. A mite skinny, but—"

"No." She shuddered. "I'm afraid it's quite impossible."

The man glanced to Jack. Jack shook his head.

"I ain't askin' twice," the man warned.

"I understand." Humbly, Grace clasped her hands.

"She'll try to bear up under the disappointment," Jack said, deepening his brogue. "Better luck with your next wife."

"Hmmph. I ain't too sure I want one. Now." He eyeballed Grace. "Thanks kindly, Murphy. I'll be by your place later."

"I'll be there." Harry was minding the saloon now.

Raising his hand in farewell, Grace's latest suitor shuffled away, grumbling all the way to the cake table. She watched him leave with an expression of pure relief.

Jack edged nearer, close enough to catch a whiff of her castile soap. He waited patiently until she met his gaze.

"Miss Crabtree, I just don't understand you."

"I should think that would be patently obvious."

"So I'm wondering if you'd help me out."

Her raised brows indicated she might, however reluctantly.

"Just tell me… Exactly how picky do you plan to be?" Manfully, Jack stifled a grin. Then he spread both arms wide. "After all, that one even had most of his teeth."

Chapter Eight

A week later, Grace found herself still mulling over Jack Murphy's outrageous matchmaking. Not that she intended to indulge in such folly. It was simply that everywhere she went, there were reminders of his meddling. Potential suitors approached her in the street, after church and even within the frilly confines of the millinery shop.

Only the *Pioneer Press* offices were safe.

Relishing the predictable orderliness of the newspaper's clippings-covered walls, clattering press runs and inky smells, Grace dragged her tray of type closer. She'd considered quitting once Thomas Walsh had arrived. But after working with him a while, she was glad she hadn't behaved rashly. The man had an eye for logical columns, an ear for liberal news and a mind for radical causes that nearly matched her own. Because of those fine qualities, he and Grace had formed a rapid camaraderie.

"Miss Crabtree, this is brilliant!" Mr. Walsh strode into the typesetters' office with his coattails flapping. His spectacles slanted askew. He righted them impatiently. "An absolutely galvanizing piece of work. You've done it again."

"Thank you, Mr. Walsh." Given their like-mindedness, there was no need for polite modesty between them, a reality Grace found refreshing. "I'd hoped you would think so when I wrote the article. The issue of poor nutrition among children is so important. It must be addressed, and quickly, too."

The editor agreed, nodding in that thoughtful way he had. As they conversed further, Grace idly examined Mr. Walsh. For a handsome man—and one who cut an especially fine figure in his suits and stylish hair—he stirred none of the giddy feelings she experienced in Jack Murphy's company.

It was peculiar, yet undeniably convenient. Without her emotions to assail her, Grace could concentrate fully on making the most of the *Pioneer Press* and her part within it. So long as she felt free to contribute, she realized, she did not regret losing the editorship to Mr. Walsh. Likely, without the additional struggle of convincing the townspeople of her good intentions, she could actually achieve more.

"You'll set this for tomorrow's edition then?"

At Mr. Walsh's inquiry, Grace started. She had, she was appalled to realize, drifted into a reverie involving Jack Murphy's surprising skill at dancing. She recalled the devilish way he'd regarded her while goading that near-toothless codger into proposing marriage. At the memory, Grace frowned.

She could not go on this way.

"Indeed I will." She accepted the article with a brisk nod.

Mr. Walsh bowed. "I'm indebted to you, ma'am."

Grace watched him depart for his office—the same office Adam Crabtree had relished leaving, given his jubilant manner upon packing his belongings. She leaned her head in her hand and sighed. Now that her workday duties were settled, all that remained were her private troubles to deal with. Beginning with one particularly pesky Irishman…and ending, Grace felt certain, with her eventual triumph.

* * *

At Molly's small bakeshop later, Grace drew her plate nearer, savoring the cinnamon bun she'd selected. Among all the women in Morrow Creek, her sister by was far the finest baker, even if it had taken her awhile to develop her skills. Now Molly had turned from a flibbertigibbet of a girl to a respected businesswoman in her own right, thereby proving Grace's long-standing opinion that there was nothing in the world a Crabtree woman couldn't accomplish if only she put her mind to it.

Which brought Grace very neatly to the topic at hand.

"I can't see any way around it." She watched her sister shape cookies and place them on her waiting baking sheets. The whole maneuver was mystifying, and did not appear very gratifying, but Molly seemed to enjoy it. "I'm simply going to have to civilize Jack Murphy myself."

Molly frowned, but didn't stop in her work. "Are you sure that's a good idea? You never know what will happen when you meddle with a man. Believe me." She smiled, doubtless thinking of her premarital travails with lumber mill owner Marcus Copeland. "I've had a quantity of experience in the matter, and I can't say I'd recommend taking that kind of wrangling upon yourself. Not even you can predict how a man will react."

"I most certainly can!" Grace disagreed. "Men are boundlessly predictable." She ignored her sister's skeptical twist of the lips. Obviously Molly had never considered the matter at length. "Besides, you can't convince me you would do things differently with Marcus. I won't believe it."

"Differently? No." Molly's smile widened. "Things did turn out wonderfully in the end, as you know." She patted her belly. "But this feud of yours with Jack Murphy…it's different." Momentarily abandoning her waiting dough, she offered a straightforward look. "Honestly, Grace. You two will be leasing that building together for some time to come. Can't you just cooperate with him? It would be so much easier."

"Easier for Jack, perhaps, but not for me."

"Ah." Molly waggled her brows. "It's 'Jack' now, is it? Well, that's very interesting. Very, very interesting."

"Mr. Murphy," Grace substituted hastily. She tore off another bite of cinnamon roll, forcing her attention to its spicy sweetness rather than her inadvertent slip of the tongue. "Membership in all of my clubs is down by a third, and the decline is directly relatable to his saloon. Women are afraid to come near it. The place is too rowdy by far."

"Saloons often are." With a shrug, Molly sprinkled sugar on her unbaked cookies. She surveyed the effect critically, then added a little more. "Have you considered that perhaps the men downstairs are louder because they're trying to drown out the sounds of your women's choral group upstairs?"

"Why would they? We sound wonderful!" Indignantly, Grace straightened on her fancy ironwork stool, letting her skirts swing freely over her brogan shoes. "I'll have you know, we're bringing much-needed culture to this town."

Molly quirked her lips, decrying that claim without a single word. When had frivolous Molly, youngest of all the sisters, become so sensible? So savvy to an ostensibly innocent statement? Serenely, she slid her baking sheets into the warm waiting ovens. When she returned to the work counter, her gaze was knowing beneath her fashionably curled bangs.

"And you've never, not even once, encouraged your fellow singers to—shall we say—put forth a little extra effort?"

Grace chewed her next bite of cinnamon bun with more defiance than she might have otherwise. She didn't answer.

"You've never," her sister continued tirelessly, "sung your melodies a little louder than strictly necessary?"

Grace reached for her cup of tea. She sipped delicately, then raised her chin. "There is nothing wrong with enthusiasm."

Molly laughed. Shaking her head, she wiped her hands on her apron. Flour dusted the rug underfoot and snowed onto her gingham skirts, too. With a moue of distress, Molly shook them out. Grace half suspected that her sister had decorated the entire bakeshop in a similarly froufrou manner—from the floral wallpapered walls to the trim blue wainscoting—to purposely coordinate with her wardrobe.

"You can't fool me, Grace. I know you too well." Eyes sparkling, Molly went to her bakery shelves. She put one hand to the small of her back, then reached to the row of napkin-lined baskets waiting to be outfitted with cookies or lemon-raisin pies. "Never mind that I'm the youngest." She puffed, red-faced. "I've gained a great deal of experience over the past year."

"I daresay you'll gain more experience yet." Eyeing her sister's expanding waistline, Grace hurried from her chair to help take down the baskets Molly sought. "Once the baby arrives, I mean." She paused, her own troubles momentarily forgotten as she considered what lay ahead. Soberly, she met her sister's gaze. "Moll… Are you afraid?"

"Of the baby coming? Pish posh." Molly waved away the notion. "I'm looking forward to it. I hope he—"

"Or she!"

"—looks exactly like Marcus."

An adorable little boy skipped into Grace's imagination, dark haired and chubby-cheeked…and bearing a marked resemblance to Jack Murphy. Her imaginary self stood near the pair of them, beaming contentedly, without a single protest banner or picket sign in sight.

Egads. What was wrong with her? She never daydreamed, much less about sentimental pap like children and husbands.

Clearly, the endless parade of potential bridegrooms had affected her for the worse. Grace resolutely returned her attention to Molly.

"Although I do miss some of my favorite dresses already," her sister was saying. "I'll admit that much, however silly it may be of me. Mama promised to help make new gowns that will fit for the duration, and Cook will be helping out with some of the baking duties here at the shop. She hasn't as much to do at home now, you know, with Sarah and me both gone…."

She nattered on cheerfully while Grace plunked more baskets on the work counter, trying to ignore the pang she felt at Molly's mention of their steadily emptying household. Once the Crabtree home had been filled with chatter and cozy dinners and games of chess and reading aloud. Now it was lacking in all but the quietest murmurs and her parents' occasional jests. Things weren't the same at all. And they never would be again.

Suddenly, silence descended.

Molly put her arm around Grace's shoulders. She gave a squeeze. "I'm sorry. That was thoughtless of me. I don't know what got into me, to be running on that way."

Grace shrugged, plopping down one basket and lining the rest up neatly. She would not think about how alone she sometimes felt without her two sisters nearby. It wasn't as if Molly and Sarah had left the territory or even the town. But their lives were full of other things now—other people—and Grace found it harder than ever to overlook her own loneliness.

She drew in a deep breath, then produced a smile.

"Nonsense," she said briskly. "It's good of you to offer Cook something useful to do. Every woman needs to feel productive, to give her life meaning and purpose. That's what Heddy Neibermayer wrote about so brilliantly last month in her article in *The Suffrage Gazette*. It was—"

"Every person needs to feel loved," Molly interrupted softly. She contemplated her array of baskets, then seemed to come to a decision. She lifted her gaze to meet Grace's directly. "You need to feel loved, Grace. Do you think that maybe, if you spent a little less time with your clubs and such, that you might find—"

"But my clubs are all I have!" Grace cried.

Molly's pitying look was more than she'd bargained on.

"What I mean to say," she rejoined carefully, taking her seat at the counter again as an excuse not to meet Molly's sympathetic gaze, "is that they are important to me." She fussed with her coat, all the better to seem composed, then jerked her chin higher. "I won't allow Jack Murphy to ruin them. As soon as I make him see reason, everything will be solved. You'll see."

Her sister sighed. "When it comes to this disagreement between the two of you, did it ever occur to you that perhaps you're a part of the problem?"

Rebelliously, Grace bit into her cinnamon bun. She refused to dignify that statement with a response. She was the beleaguered party, not Jack. Overloud singing or not.

"Whether you'll admit it or not, you know I'm right." Molly surveyed the bakery, hands on her hips as though deciding what task to take on next. It was nearly time for the shop to open. "Perhaps this time you'll need to bend a bit."

Ha. Only if Jack did so first.

"I'm already bending," Grace informed her sister. She'd bent to consider Jack a man with attractive lips, for one. She'd bent to admire his voice and his shoulders and his hands. She'd bent to try dancing with him, too! But she would be as likely to confess enjoying it as she would be to take up watercolor painting or knitting tea cosies. "I'm personally involving myself in my civilizing project, for one."

Not that she'd had much choice in the matter. Jack had discerned what she was up to with alarming rapidity. Grace didn't have time to waste sending him more poets and artists and reputability-bestowing bastions of the community. For utmost efficiency, she'd decided to take matters in her own hands.

"I don't know about this project of yours. Civilizing?" Molly shook her head. "I've met Mr. Murphy, remember? He's a smidgen rough, and a saloonkeeper besides. You may have bitten off more than you can chew this time."

"Pshaw. That will never happen." Grace rummaged in the rucksack she used for ornithology expeditions, pushed aside her specialty spyglass, then proudly withdrew her planning journal. "Look. I've made a list of the necessary steps."

"You have? This I simply must see." Wearing an eager grin, her sister leaned nearer. "Step one, reasoned debate. Step two, active protest. Step three…repeat steps one and two."

She glanced up, stricken.

"What's the matter?" Defensively, Grace turned the journal to face herself. It still looked exactly as she remembered it—exactly as it had after her feverish strategizing session in her meeting rooms last night. "As plans go, this one is simple and clear. And this strategy has proven very effective."

"Certainly. When encouraging Ned Nickerson to order Jane Austen novels for his Book Depot and News Emporium, perhaps," Molly exclaimed, wide-eyed, "but not when dealing with a man!"

Affronted, Grace closed her journal. Her sister had been wed mere months. Yet already she was an expert on persons of the male persuasion? Nonsense. Grace knew better.

"Sarah appreciated it," she said crisply.

Of course, her other sister hadn't fully absorbed the plan. Sarah had been writing an arithmetic lesson, overseeing a student's examination and giving instructions to her new teaching apprentice when Grace had arrived at the schoolhouse earlier. So a verbal overview had had to suffice.

Grace supposed it was possible that she'd exaggerated the merits and complexity of her three-step civilizing scheme when describing it. She was a fairly skilled orator, after all, having studied all the great speeches of Susan B. Anthony, Heddy Neibermayer and Elizabeth Cady Stanton in detail.

Molly blinked. "Do you truly intend to debate Mr. Murphy?"

"Well… I may try a strike instead," Grace confided, feeling prodded into defending herself. Surely once Molly realized how indomitable her plan truly was, she would see its usefulness. With relish, Grace spread her arms wide, envisioning the scene. "Else chain myself to his bar rail. That's proved excellent in the past. He certainly won't be able to ignore me."

She lifted her chin, already imagining herself tutoring an appreciative Jack Murphy. A refined Jack Murphy. A fully civilized Jack Murphy who had her to thank for enriching his thinking…who gazed at her with adoration and gratitude and respect. What her ornithology friends and fellow poets hadn't been able to accomplish, Grace vowed, she would. It would be wonderful. Absolutely, marvelously, wonderful.

"Grace!"

"What?"

Molly opened her mouth. Closed it again. Opened it, as though she didn't know quite where to begin. "Do you honestly believe that's the civilized way to approach things?"

Wrenched from her musings, Grace stood silent. She didn't want to admit it, but worry niggled at her. Exactly as did, these days, her helplessness at coping with Jack Murphy and the feelings he engendered in her.

"Fine. Never mind." Grace shoved her journal back into her rucksack. Clearly, Molly didn't properly appreciate innovation. "I'm sorry I showed you anything. I'm off to the newspaper."

She got to her feet in one swift movement.

"Oh, horsefeathers! I've done it again. Wait a minute," Molly urged, hurrying around the work counter to stop her. "I'm sorry, Grace. Truly, I am. It's only that… Well, sometimes I forget exactly how different we are."

Her sister's gaze held Grace steady. For an instant, only that, she felt herself relent. How could she not, when bright-eyed, endlessly optimistic Molly urged her to?

It was exactly akin to their childhood days, when the three Crabtree sisters had been inseparable. Certainly Grace had been the leader then. Sarah had been the organizer. But Molly…Molly had kept them all together through their inevitable squabbles. She had kept them together in every way.

Grace looked away. "Please don't tell anyone."

Molly didn't ask what she meant. Doubtless she didn't have to. The truth must have been written on Grace's face, she knew, ready for anyone who truly understood her to see it.

"He's not like anyone else," she admitted quietly.

She cast a pleading glance in Molly's direction. It was as close as Grace had ever come to asking for help. With her breath held, she waited for her sister to make a joke, to roll her eyes, to turn away. Turning away would be worst of all.

When Grace had been ten years old, she recalled, a mere slip of a girl with dirty knees and tumbled hair, she'd once gotten stuck in a tree too big for safe climbing. When Sarah and Molly had happened upon her, so lofty and so scared, she'd boastfully announced that she'd decided to live there amid the branches. She'd even sent both sisters home for a blanket and pillow for the night. It had seemed a far better plan than admitting weakness.

It had been Molly who had refused to entertain talk of tree-top camping. She'd shimmied up the sticky pine trunk to coax Grace down instead, her eyes huge through the whole upward journey, and they'd all gone home together. No one save the sisters had ever known.

And Grace had never been happier to touch solid ground.

"Well," Molly said staunchly, returning Grace to the present with her eager demeanor. "That's perfect then, isn't it? Because you're not like anyone else either."

It was so like Molly to ladle on the kindness just when things had turned their most troublesome. No wonder Grace had felt drawn to come here. Awash with gratefulness and more than her fair share of memories, she hid her smile behind her thick knitted scarf. She suspected Molly saw though, because she smiled back more widely than ever before.

Then she clapped her hands. "Let's get to it, shall we?"

"Get to what?" Grace asked. "Surely you don't mean…"

"Exactly." Molly beamed, bubbling over with eagerness. "It's all settled, isn't it? I'm going to help you devise a plan for dealing with Jack Murphy!"

A wintry breeze followed Jack down one of Morrow Creek's wide streets, carrying along with it the usual scents of horse traffic, wet woolens, new-milled lumber and swaying pine trees. Appreciatively, he inhaled. It wasn't often he left his saloon this way. Maybe that was why he welcomed the crush of snow beneath his boots, the bite of frost on his tongue, the bustle of townspeople moving past.

Just beyond Morrow Creek, the ponderosa pines and scrub oak climbed the face of the nearby mountain, nearly touching the cloudless sky. Closer in, the false-fronted buildings hunkered in rough rows. Wagons equipped with sleigh runners cut paths everywhere, taking people about their business.

Jack had heard his patrons talk of how the town was growing—had heard them exclaim over its expansion since the railroad had come in. Old-timers criticized the crowding at meetings of the Morrow Creek Men's Club, complaining that so many buildings shut out the view and choked out sociability and brought in all the wrong elements. But to Jack, the place still felt open, chockablock with kindliness and possibility.

More so than Boston had in the end, to be sure.

Carrying on his chores, he veered toward the small row of houses near the railroad tracks, where the rail workers lived. He dropped his dirty washing with the laundress he employed there, offering her a smile and a hearty thank-you. Next he ambled to the cobbler and left his spare boots to be soled.

Then, heart kicking in anticipation, he strode to the west end of town where the stagecoach station stood. It was always his last stop on these journeys, and his hammering heartbeat told the reason why. The building was humble but busy, with horsemen arriving, a drummer departing and several travelers waiting for passage. At the threshold, Jack paused to knock clean his snow-encrusted boots, earning himself a few peculiar looks in the process.

Damnation. In all his keenness, he'd forgotten where he was. Scowling for good measure, he slammed his boot extra hard on the doorstep, as befit a real western man, then galumphed inside. He made sure to keep his shoulders broad, his chest out, his manner swaggering.

There was no telling who he'd see here, and he couldn't afford to appear overly fastidious. If he didn't make his entrance convincing, he'd have to stride carelessly through a bit of far worse street leavings just to make his mark.

He tipped his hat to some waiting ladies, then bellied up to the counter. On the opposite side, the station clerk glanced up. His greeting was the same it was every week.

"Afternoon, Murphy. Nice weather we're having."

Jack grunted. "Fine enough."

"I guess you'll be wanting these then." The clerk shoved a twine-wrapped packet of letters across the counter. "Been waitin' a couple of days for you."

Jack would swear his hands dampened beneath his thick leather gloves. It was always this way when he came to collect his mail. One part anticipation, one part fear and one part hopefulness that the saloon plans he'd been working toward would come to pass before he went plumb bust from expenses.

He nodded, then snatched up the bundle. "Mighty obliged."

"Yep." Already occupied with his next duty, the clerk didn't glance up. "See you next week."

Outside, Jack fisted his letters and kept walking. The first note was a solicitation to buy parts for his own still, courtesy of a drummer he'd met some time back. The second was a mail-order flyer about a new hair tonic that, in a pinch, also cured dyspepsia and doubled as a bar cleaner. The last bore patently familiar handwriting in a fancy curled script.

Beneath his breath, Jack swore. He shoved the rest of his mail in his coat pocket, clutching the final letter. Ladies swept past in twos and threes, chattering as they shopped. Men lumbered onward on foot and on horseback, going about their dealings. None of them glanced his way. Still, Jack debated opening the third letter.

He should wait until he reached his private rooms behind the saloon. Prudence would be most sensible. If someone saw the postmark on that letter, they might ask questions. They might wonder, and rightly so, why a simple saloonkeeper received so much mail at all, much less every week.

Jack had attempted to disguise that incongruity by sending away for every mail-order pamphlet and patent-remedy leaflet he'd ever heard of. He'd hoped to detract from telling letters like this one. Letters that ought to be kept private. And yet...

Carefully, he smoothed the envelope. Memories rushed to him, filled with laughter and gossip and all varieties of perfume. Rose. Lavender water. Lily of the Valley. Fondness swept through him, taking his breath away. Damnation.

This letter wasn't what he'd expected to find today. He'd expected word from the Excelsior Performing Troupe and its management. He'd anticipated that they'd answer his last letter with a decision to detour to Morrow Creek for a series of performances after all—performances that could well ensure his saloon's successful future and reputation.

Instead he'd gotten this. This handful of memories.

Releasing his pent-up breath, Jack raised his hand to his mouth. He bit the tip of his glove, tugging it off and tasting burnished leather. With tingling fingers, he opened the letter. Another burst of sweet fragrance struck him, tugging at the remembrances he usually tamped down and safeguarded.

Dearest Jack, he read. **Surprise! You probably didn't think you would hear from us again so soon, but Corinne excels at finding post offices everywhere we stop. We wish she were as skilled at leaving some of her possessions behind! She has consumed all the space in our satchels again. They're overstuffed so much we might well upset the train car soon.**

Helplessly, Jack smiled. Merely gazing at those neatly penned lines made him feel at home. Also lonelier than ever. Why this? Why today? He hadn't even had time to prepare, the way he usually did, for a letter like this one.

Below the first paragraph, the ink had smudged. As clear as day, a new ink color and a different looped handwriting began.

Don't listen to her! it read. **I need all those things**

because Arleen, Glenna and Nealie never bring
enough of their own. One of us has to be prepared, and you know it's always me.

A crease in the paper came next, culminating in several
smoothed-out folds. Jack could easily imagine the tussle that
writing this letter had produced. The chatter, the laughter, the
grabbing and jostling to be next with the pen. He'd experienced all of it himself, many times. But he'd never thought he
would miss any of it…not so much that he ached with its lack.

Frowning anew, both warmed and bereft at once, he
went on.

We wish you would come home to Boston again,
came a bolder handwriting, marked with heavy strokes and
flourishes. We promise the furor has died down,
Jack! Even if it hadn't, Nealie has a plan to make everything right. Only Arleen is looking over my
shoulder, shrieking that I mustn't tell, so I won't.

Jack didn't wonder at Glenna's mulish tone. Although she
was loath to admit it, his youngest sister had always been the
worst at keeping a secret. Any secret. Although she had managed to do so, most notably and regrettably, at least once—
when she'd spirited away his schematics and had them made
into those disastrous corsetry samples. It only went to show
that women—even well-intentioned ones—couldn't be trusted
not to make everything worse. He was better off away from
them.

All the same, Jack touched his fingertips to the words, imagining the scene. All four of his sisters, arguing for the use
of the paper, the ink, the best spot at whatever desk they'd
managed to find. The Murphy girls were unrelenting when
they thought they were right—which was, admittedly, most
of the time.

You'll never guess where we're headed next, he

read. Nealie says it's our duty, and I guess she's right. But she always says things like that, in that virtuous, bossy tone of hers, so however can a person be sure? Anyway, please keep a lookout for Indians. And if you see one, kindly ask him for his inscription. I would treasure it always and always. If only I could keep it out of Corinne's hands, because you know she'd just sell it for a profit someplace and miser all the money, else spend it on boring old necessities like coal oil.

He guffawed. That came from Arleen, who had their eldest sister pegged, to be certain. There wasn't anything Corinne wasn't willing to do to make sure her loved ones were provided for—including squirreling away their savings whether they approved or not. His was a bossy brood, but a special one.

His exposed fingers growing chilled, Jack turned over the letter. Every inch of the paper was covered in writing to maximize the postage cost, and where there weren't any sentences, there were squiggly pencil drawings. Those came courtesy of Glenna, who had never met a person or place she didn't yearn to capture on paper.

Do write back to us soon, he read, grinning at the multiple underlines beneath the word *soon*. Otherwise we will spread the word that you have joined the circus and wed the bearded lady—

He laughed. "Bearded lady?"

"Yes," someone agreed from nearby, sounding amused. "I hear they stay quite warm in wintertime."

At the sound of that voice, Jack jerked his head up. Grace Crabtree stood before him, looking unaccountably pert in a way he couldn't explain. She peered interestedly at his handful of scribbled-upon, creased and ink-blotted memories from home

Hastily, he rammed the letter in his pocket. He needed a diversion. An explanation. A bolster for his manly persona and an excuse for his lack of self-possession all at once.

Especially if Grace suspected, as he thought she might, who he really was and where he'd really come from. And why.

"It's a gambling device," he declared loudly. "I get solicitations for them. Being a saloonkeeper and all."

Her eyebrows rose. Her gaze remained jammed on his pocket.

"You wouldn't be familiar with it, seein' as how you don't spend much time wagering." Manfully, he spread his legs and plucked his braces with his thumbs, adopting the western pose he'd observed. "A bearded lady is akin to a dice cage, only—"

"Hairier?" she supplied, lips quirked.

"Exactly. Hairier. Hence the name. Yessir, that's it."

"Hmm." Grace pondered that for a minute.

Hellfire. He was caught. Snared by his own inability to lie convincingly. Any minute now, Grace would pin him with one of her measuring looks, point out some logical inconsistency and refuse to leave him alone till he confessed the whole truth. She'd probably muster up a whole protest, too, complete with banners and some of that caterwauling choral music she favored.

Jack wanted to groan aloud. But Grace only went on thinking, allowing him far too much time to admire the roses in her cheeks and the all-over vibrancy of her appearance. She looked especially pretty today, he thought. Softer somehow.

The lacy scarf pinned at her throat made her bosom appear particularly generous. He'd never noticed that before. Most likely he wouldn't have noticed today, except for the damnable strain he felt. Clearly, his mind had enacted a desperate bid to distract him from his letter-reading mistake.

Jack was so busy gawking and so chagrined to have been

caught reading something so potentially revealing in public that he did not react quickly enough when Grace finally moved. With no warning at all, she thrust a napkin-lined basket upward, nearly poking him in the nose.

"Would you like one?"

Jack hesitated, utterly flummoxed that she hadn't pursued the question of the "bearded lady" any further. A lack of curiosity was distinctly unusual in his neighbor. "One what?"

"A dried-apple fritter. One of my sister's specialties."

Grace flipped back the napkin, presenting a tidy row of sugar-dusted pastries. She smiled, too. The surprise of it fairly bedazzled him. Who would have thought tetchy Grace Crabtree could look so fetching? Not the man who'd unsuccessfully paired her with so many potential suitors, that was for certain.

He squinted. "What's wrong with them?"

Her smile dimmed. "Nothing's wrong with them."

"Then why give one to me?" Decisively, Jack covered the fritters again. "Likely they're sugared-up fried bricks. Or dynamite in apple-covered packages." He gave her a quelling look. "Are you on your way to bust a protester out of jail?"

Grace looked affronted. "Of course not!"

"Then what's wrong with you?"

She drew in a fortifying breath. "If you truly must know, I've come to ask you to walk me home, Mr. Murphy. I knew you would be here today, just as I've noticed you tend to be every week at this time—"

He attempted, unsuccessfully, to break into that stunning announcement. Grace was having none of it. She mowed onward.

"—and so I determined to waylay you. The fritters are an inducement, and as such, I made particularly certain they are delicious. I may be new at these things, but I am not an idiot." Moving stiffly—as though she'd practiced the maneuver, however ridiculous a notion that was—Grace crooked her elbow. "Now, Mr. Murphy, I would be most flattered if you would agree to escort me home. It's just that way, if you please."

More befuddled than ever, Jack stared at her. She kept one elbow bent for his use in accompanying her, and the other in place to offer the fritters. She pointed her chin homeward. If she'd suddenly burst into mooing, he could not have been more astonished. Was Grace Crabtree…courting him?

"If you'd kindly take my arm instead of standing there gawking like a trout," she instructed, "I would be eternally grateful, sir. People are staring."

Indeed they were, Jack realized. The sight of his apparent standoff with the town's most implacable spinster had begun to draw a crowd.

"Doubtless they expect fisticuffs at this point," Grace observed. Her gaze met his and held. Astoundingly, she smiled more widely, as though amused by the idea. "Shall we oblige?"

Jack guffawed. He simply couldn't help it. In the moment between her bizarre invitation and her jest, Grace had become the woman he expected again. It was that woman—not the one who had sweetly offered baked goods and inexplicably refused to call him out on his tall tales—whom he wanted to walk with.

"It's my practice," Jack grumbled, "never to oblige anybody anytime. No matter what kind of goodies they've got."

Then he relieved Grace of her basket, took her arm and guided them both toward the end of town where the Crabtree household lay…thereby proving himself a paltry liar all over again, but caring not quite as much as he knew he ought to.

A mouthful of tasty apple fritter, he found, helped the retraction go down quite nicely. So, he discovered further, did

Grace's answering laughter. And before Jack knew quite what had hit him, he found himself struggling with a near fascination with prickly Grace Crabtree—fancy bosom, bossy notions, tetchiness and all.

Chapter Nine

❦

Once Jack came to terms with the notion of seeing Grace Crabtree peaceably for a change, he realized it made a great deal of sense. How better to discover exactly what qualities she enjoyed in a potential husband, he reasoned, than to spend time with her? To talk with her and observe her and perhaps even woo her a little, all for the sake of ensuring her eventual wedded bliss—and his own saloon-bound happiness?

He would question her, he would learn her preferences and priorities, and then he would deliver them to her—in the form of an ideal husband candidate. One whom Grace could not refuse. It was an augmentation to his plan that couldn't fail. In fact, Jack almost wished he'd struck upon the idea of such enhanced togetherness himself.

Not that his approval was strictly necessary to the proceedings, as it turned out. Because from the day of their dried-apple fritter incident onward, Grace simply didn't let up.

She was there when Jack stepped outside to sweep his saloon stoop in the mornings, smiling with a cinnamon bun or a jar of jam for a gift. She was there when he paid calls through town, falling easily into step with him between the butcher's and the laundress's, chatting about politics and news and literature.

She was there when he ate dinner upon occasion at the Lorndorff Hotel, ready to question him about knives and forks and deportment. There when he emerged from Miss Adelaide's bath house establishment with a fresh haircut and shave, eager to applaud his new "refined" appearance. She was there when he broke up fights at his place, prepared to applaud his efforts.

"My!" she exclaimed as he hauled a particularly disorderly patron onto the street one night. "He's a big one, isn't he?"

"You shouldn't be here, Grace." Breathing hard, Jack dumped the man into position against the porch railing. The knucklehead was as big as he was, but heavier. He gave him a nudge. "Stay put."

"Whatever you say, Captain," the man slurred. "I never meant to cause no ruckus." He wavered. "Only the other miners and me, we had ourselves a disss—" A blink. "Disagreement."

"Er, if I might intervene?" Grace stepped closer, tilting her head as she examined the man. She wrinkled her nose. "Would you mind terribly putting him out back or to the side instead?" She gestured past the stairs leading to her meeting rooms. Her hopeful gaze lit upon him. "I'm expecting the ladies for our women's baseball league organizational meeting any moment now. We'd be most appreciative if you could assist us."

She'd demanded he do the same before. Many times. But on this night, somehow, Grace's request felt different.

Jack shrugged. "Easily done." He squared his shoulders, then grabbed the man by the collar and dragged him around to a suitably sheltered corner. After getting the man settled, he brushed off his hands, only to find that Grace had followed him. Manfully, Jack broadened his chest. "That's done. Anything else?"

She glanced ponderingly down at the man. Loud snores issued from his direction. Apparently moving him had proved much gentler to his disposition than the seven bolts of tequila had.

"Won't he get cold?" she asked.

"I'll make sure he gets back to his boardinghouse."

"Then I think that will do," Grace murmured. She girded her courage. "Except, of course, for this one little thing."

Then she grabbed Jack's shoulder for balance, raised herself on tiptoes and kissed him. Full on the mouth.

It was the briefest of contacts, lasting only moments. But for Jack, shocked into place by the tenderness of the gesture, the warm softness of her lips, the whirl of pleasure that shot through him, it felt much longer. Much, much longer.

He stared as she lowered again, her face a study in shadow and moonlight. Their breath puffed between them, visible in the wintry cold, coming more quickly than ever before.

"Thank you kindly," she added, almost demurely.

It wasn't until Grace excused herself and walked away, her practical skirts swooshing beneath her bulky coat and ugly hat, that Jack fully realized what had just happened. Grace Crabtree had kissed him. Grace Crabtree had kissed him... and he'd liked it.

He raised his hand to his mouth, still staring.

Tarnation. This was a development he hadn't reckoned on at all. And he had no notion how to cope with it either.

Puffing with exertion, Grace tightened her grip on her wooden sled's tow rope. She'd bundled herself so thoroughly against the cold afternoon that she could scarcely see through the opening between her wrapped scarf and her knit hat. Simply identifying Sarah beside her, towing an identical sled, required turning her head and shoulders all the way to the right.

Snow sprinkled Grace's coat and Sarah's. It filled in their footsteps and drifted into their faces, making them both blink with wet eyelashes. Nevertheless, they continued upward, scrambling their way up the track that had been cleared for their ascent.

Morrow Creek had enjoyed slightly warmer weather until recently, when a cold snap had put the lie to rumors that spring was on its way. Like Grace and Sarah, the citizens of the town dealt with that handily enough, though, by heading to the foothills to the south, where the sloping curves offered ideal conditions for winter fun. Not a person, young or old, was impervious to the lure of a fast run down the snowy hillside.

Proving as much, people of every age and description gathered around them, similarly bundled and wrapped. Alone or in twos and threes, they flew past on sleds. They rode improvised carriers like pickle-barrel lids or burlap flour sacks. They clumped together on toboggans, chattering and whooping as they zoomed by, all decorum thrown literally to the wind.

Grace could not imagine why she had never devised a club dedicated to this activity. After all, it was enjoyable, physically enriching and equality minded—much as birdwatching or snowshoeing were. Simply devising a more appropriate official attire would consume a great deal of time, keeping her occupied for days. As it was, her woolen winter skirts were snowy, laden with ice clumps at the hems. They crackled against her laced boots, swinging again and again with her forceful strides.

"Look, there's Daniel." Sarah waved to her husband, who lugged beneath his burly arm a sled equipped with wicked-looking runners. Doubtless he'd designed it specially in his blacksmith's shop for exactly this occasion. "And Eli, too."

The small boy beside Daniel—shorter and skinnier but with identical dark hair and posture—waved both arms, making his coat flap crazily. His grin shone all the way across the hill. At nearly nine years old, Eli was Daniel's only nephew. He was one of Sarah's most mischievous students at the schoolhouse, too.

"He looks fit to burst a button." Grace smiled, waving also. "As though he can't wait to start sliding down the slope."

"Sledding is one of Eli's favorite activities." Sarah gazed at the boy fondly. She blew a kiss, which he pretended not to see, instead frowning fiercely at his mittens. "He and Daniel have been inseparable, even since Lillian and Lyman came back."

For a time, Eli's mother and her new husband had left Eli in Daniel's care. Not long after, he and Sarah had married. In a sense, those two males—one tall and one small—had brought Grace's sister more happiness than she'd ever known before.

Now, both males tromped merrily through the snow, searching for an ideal spot to try out their sled. Or at least Daniel searched. Little Eli busily copied his uncle down to the last gesture, scowling at the drifts and peering at the horizon.

Still climbing, Grace watched the distant pair wistfully. "Well, it just goes to show, I guess. You simply can't underestimate the power of love."

Happily, she tugged her sled upward. At the end of its rope, the painted wood and metal jostled over bumps and dips with every step. Just a few more feet and she'd be at the top, ready for a thrilling ride down the slope. Despite her interest in civility and equality, Grace found she truly enjoyed a brisk—

She stopped, sensing something was wrong. Sarah was nowhere to be seen. Confused, Grace swiveled—only to find her sister a good two yards back, gaping at her in plain disbelief.

"What's the matter? Is your sled stuck?" Setting the soles of her boots against the snow with practiced agility, Grace maneuvered her way downward again. She arrived breathlessly beside Sarah, who still hadn't moved. "Give me the rope. I'll help you tug it free. I'm stronger than you anyway."

Not even that sisterly jibe earned a proper reply.

Sarah blinked. "Did you just say, 'the power of love'?"

Had she? Abashed, Grace gazed across the hill again. She wished a tobogganer would careen nearby, forcing them to move—and handily changing the subject in the process.

"I may have done, yes," she admitted. "What of it?"

Sarah still gaped. "What in the world has come over you?"

Uncomfortably, Grace fidgeted. She felt as awkward as a woman trussed into a brand-new corset—who had just discovered she'd stepped on an anthill. Perhaps Sarah would simply give up.

"Does this have to do with you and Mr. Murphy?" Sarah demanded, finally snapping to herself again. In direct contradiction to Grace's hopes, this was her sister's best schoolmarm's tone, and it brooked no nonsense. "Are you—"

Grace had no desire to learn the rest of that question.

"Let's just say that Molly's methods proved surprisingly effective." Particularly her tutorial on how to capture a man's attention with the tiniest kiss. Grace fisted her tow rope and pulled, heading uphill again. "And leave it at that, shall we?"

Grace wanted to. Else she'd be unable to sled properly. Instead she'd spend all her time daydreaming—as she had shamelessly done for the past few days—lost in recollections of that kiss she'd shared with Jack. That single, magical kiss.

Her heart had pounded so, it was as if she'd snowshoed ten miles beforehand, and her hands had trembled when she'd first touched his brawny shoulder. It had felt like hot stone beneath her fingertips, so broad and strong. And his mouth! However brief their kiss had been, Grace had had ample time to savor the shocking warmth of his lips, the husky sound of surprise he'd made, the light-headed sensation she'd experienced…

But she'd determined not to daydream today.

Until now, she'd been doing quite well.

"No, we shan't leave it at that!" Sarah hastened upward, too. She met Grace's every step with a vigorous one of her own, displaying the tomboyish qualities that had always been unique to her. "I want to know every last detail. Give me a complete reporting of what's happened between you two so far, and don't leave anything out."

Impatiently, Sarah waited, one hand on her hip.

"Hmm. If you ever tire of teaching school, you might find a position at the *Pioneer Press*," Grace teased, reaching the top at last. She surveyed the scene below them, where sporting friends and neighbors sped over the packed snow-and in some cases, tumbled comically. She rewrapped her scarf. "You would likely make an excellent journalist. I shall alert Mr. Walsh straightaway as to your investigative potential. He's really quite capable, you know, and has remarkable plans for the newspaper."

"I can't believe it! Now you're being coy?"

"Nonsense." Grace lowered her eyelashes as Molly had demonstrated, attempting her best modest demeanor. "I'm not."

Stomping closer, Sarah dropped her tow rope. "I never thought I would see the day. My suffragist sister is a full-blown coquette. No wonder I've seen so little of you lately."

Grace shrugged and situated her sled. The runners creaked and the red-painted boards peeled at the edges, but she and her sled had seen many adventures together. Just contemplating taking her seat upon it made her feel carefree again.

Apparently recognizing an imminent escape when it was nearly upon her, Sarah dragged her sled in place as well. They sat side by side on them as they had so many times before, carefully tucking in their skirts with gloved hands before hoisting both feet to their separate metal yokes for steering.

"Wait." Sarah peered dramatically, going so far as to lean closer. Her freckled face was barely visible above her bright red scarf, but her dubious expression was plain all the same. "I know you confided your plan to me, but… Mr. Murphy is not just another project to you, is he?"

"Of course he is."

"No, he's not. I know you, Grace. If he were a project like any other of yours—and that project were proceeding as successfully as your face suggests right now—"

Hurriedly, Grace clamped down on her dreamy grin.

"—then you wouldn't be able to resist crowing about it!" Sarah sucked in a revelatory breath, charging onward with evident glee. "You'd be telling me forward and back how very civilized you've made the saloonkeeper, exactly according to your plan. How terribly cultured he is these days, and how—"

"Jack did purchase a volume of sonnets at Nickerson's Book Depot and News Emporium yesterday," Grace pointed out in her own defense. She wiggled on her sled, getting comfortably situated. "When I caught him, he claimed it was a gift for a prostitute."

Sarah gasped, wide eyed. "No!"

"Indeed. No," Grace opined, shaking her head. "I happen to know that Mr. Murphy does not visit women of ill repute. He's far too busy for that. For instance, on Mondays he receives his liquor and lager order from Jedediah Hofer's mercantile. On Tuesdays he hosts the Morrow Creek Men's Club meeting. On Wednesdays he collects his mail, regular as clockwork—and an impressive bundle he gets, too! On Thursday he generally—"

Seeing Sarah's peculiar expression, Grace broke off. "What's the matter with you?" she asked.

"Nothing. It's simply that I've never seen you smitten with a man before. It's quite remarkable."

Grace scoffed. "Stop it."

"I'm trying my best to memorize your expression," Sarah added, her face screwed up with the apparent effort required. "For posterity's sake. This is a monumental event, you know. My sister is in love. With a scandalous saloonkeeper!"

"Hush." Urgently, Grace glanced around to learn if they'd been overheard. She fixed her boots more firmly upon her sled. They'd delayed their descent long enough. "Let's go."

"Daniel was resistant, too, you know," Sarah confided, pointing out her husband and Eli again—this time at the bottom of the hill. Hampered by no such dillydallying as Grace and Sarah had employed, they must have finished their latest boisterous run. "Almost all the way to the end, he tried not to fall. But when it's love, there's no fighting it. Not truly."

Stubbornly, Grace kept silent. She felt Sarah's gaze pinned expectantly upon her, and wasn't sure what to say. Making confidences—like making compromises—did not come easily to her.

"Mr. Murphy does have his charming moments," Grace finally admitted. Casting her gaze skyward, she inhaled deeply. This broad-mindedness project of hers had affected more than its target, to be sure. "For instance, his vocabulary has improved dramatically—at least when he's around me. I'm awfully proud of that. And his appreciation for art and music show no bounds."

At least they didn't, she'd observed, when the art consisted of his bawdy over-the-bar painting and the music entailed dancing girls to go with it. But those were temporary pockets of resistance, only to be expected. With a little concentrated effort, Grace felt certain she could overcome them.

"He is a lively conversationalist, too. He blusters about politics like any other man, but I believe I am teaching him to become more discerning in his opinions."

"Of that I have no doubt," Sarah said wryly. "None of us is safe from your opinion making."

"I'm sure Jack's become more enlightened already." Grace recalled his innovatively designed braces—the pair he'd worn to Lizzie's wedding. "I didn't realize it before, but his potential was there all along. I believe Jack may have an interest in dress reform, too. You should see the way he looks at my gowns these days, as though admiring their design."

"I'd guess he's admiring more than their design. He's admiring the woman inside them."

Grace rolled her eyes. "Don't be silly. He still hasn't quit tossing potential husbands my way. The latest was an inveterate gambler whose notion of courtship consisted of showing me his gold tooth." She shuddered. "They become easier and easier to turn down, I must say."

Sarah twisted on her sled. "Maybe that's because you've already found the man you're interested in," she suggested teasingly. "And his name is Jack Murphy."

"Really? Let's see if you still believe that nonsense at the bottom of the hill," Grace said. Then, grinning, she gave her sister a shove and sent her flying down ahead of her.

Outfitted in his meanest boots and darkest hat, Jack stood at the counter of the *Pioneer Press* offices. Although it was early in the afternoon, the place was deserted—strangely so. He heard the press running somewhere distant, but all the desks were vacant. A sideways glance to the open door of the typesetting office told him even Grace was absent from her duties. If he hadn't known better, he'd have sworn it was a holiday. One nobody had seen fit to tell him about.

Impatiently, he slapped his palm on the call bell again.

"Sorry, so sorry. I'm coming!" came a voice from a rear office. A door opened and shut, then Thomas Walsh—the donkey himself—appeared at the other end of the room. He hastened across with a harried look, wearing a coat and hat, distractedly pushing his prissy spectacles higher on his nose. He'd clearly been on his way out. "What can I do for you, sir?"

"I'm here to place an advertisement."

"Very well." Walsh plucked a pencil from its holder, then surveyed Jack. His brow furrowed. "Shall we plan it together?"

"Together?"

"Yes. Indeed." Another sweeping glance, this one taking in Jack's rough coat, his stubbled jaw and his gloved hands. "Many of our advertisers prefer assistance when writing out an advertisement. Some of them aren't strictly familiar with—"

"I can write, if that's what you mean." Tersely, Jack withdrew his customary saloon-advertising copy from his pocket and slapped it on the counter. "It's all right here."

He should have been pleased. Evidently his new western persona was so convincing that Walsh believed him to be both uncouth and uneducated, incapable of writing a simple saloon advertisement. But for some reason, Jack found Walsh's helpful attitude irksome. He scowled.

"Very good!" By all appearances oblivious to Jack's lack of neighborliness, Walsh picked up the paper. Hastily, he examined it. "This all seems to be in order." His cheerful expression met Jack's frown. "How would you like to pay?"

"On account. Jack Murphy."

"Ah. That's right, you're Mr. Murphy." The man nodded. "We met briefly, didn't we? I'm afraid I didn't recognize you without your dancing shoes on." He gave a broad, winking grin.

Jack frowned more deeply. He didn't want to think about the Stotts' wedding party, when he'd made a spectacle of himself by whisking Grace away from Walsh and dancing with her.

"All the same," Walsh said cheerfully, "this is an occasion, isn't it? Since then I've heard all about you."

Jack stifled a groan. Heaven only knew what fabrications Grace had shared with Walsh and her fellow newspaper workers. Wanting this whole endeavor over with, Jack grunted.

As usual, the uncivilized sound served him well. Prodded by its lack of friendliness, Walsh didn't shilly-shally in finishing their transaction.

"Anyway, be that as it may." Hurriedly, Walsh scribbled a note on the paper, then tucked it securely in place below the counter. "I'll make sure this runs as appropriate, Mr. Murphy. Here at the *Pioneer Press*, we strive to please both our advertisers and our readers. The public deserves no less."

Another grunt. They came easier and easier.

"I'll just see you to the door, shall I?" With a cultured sweep of his arm, Walsh indicated the exit. He hastened that way, his fancy clothes distinctly out of place in the homespun office. "I was just on my way to the hill outside of town for a little sledding party," he confided with an air of excitement, his chipmunk cheeks puffed. "You may have noticed that we're a bit short-staffed today, but as the new editor, I feel it's important to demonstrate an understanding of local customs. I agreed to indulge everyone."

Outside on the steps, Walsh produced a set of keys. He locked the door securely, then turned with an anticipatory expression. Eager to be gone, Jack raised his hand.

"Much obliged to you," he said in farewell.

He'd only managed three snowy steps before Walsh spoke.

"Er, Mr. Murphy? Just one moment please."

Reluctantly, Jack turned back. Since seeing Grace fawn all over the man at the Stotts' wedding party, he was not eager to spend more time in Walsh's presence. For the life of him, he refused to believe this was the kind of man Grace preferred.

"You wouldn't happen to know the way to the correct hill, would you?" In clear bewilderment, Walsh shielded his bespectacled eyes with his gaudily gloved hand. He surveyed the terrain surrounding them, moving past the sparsely populated street and closed businesses. "I believe that when she extended the invitation to join her there, Miss Crabtree forgot I'm new to town."

Miss Crabtree. In a flash, Jack discovered a keen interest in sledding parties. Mustering a hearty smile, he tromped in Walsh's direction. He slapped the man on his scrawny back.

"Hell, I'm headed that way now. I'll show you."

Ill-equipped for sledding but determined to last the duration all the same, Jack reached the crest of the hill. Despite the sun breaking through the clouds, soft snowflakes dampened his face and dusted his coat. He wasn't dressed for a long stint in the snow, but he would rather roll downhill buck naked than admit as much to his companion.

Beside him, Thomas Walsh clapped his hands. "Marvelous! Just look at all the people, would you?"

The hillside was jam packed. People of every description swooped down the snowy trails, and others lugged their sleds upward for new runs. Jack only cared to identify one woman though. She ought to be easy to spot, he reasoned.

Doubtless Grace had devised some outlandish getup for sledding in or had gathered an entire club for the purpose of organizing the activity. He didn't doubt he'd find her surrounded by eager ladies, all of them possibly singing a rousing tune about equality for sporting women.

"I certainly wish Mr. Crabtree had alerted me to this seasonal activity when I accepted the newspaper position," Walsh went on, studying the scene eagerly. "If I had known such opportunities existed here in the territory, I'd have had my toboggan shipped on the train."

"That's bad luck to be sure." Still searching for Grace, Jack

gave his jaw a manly scratch. Finally what Walsh had said
registered. He glanced sideways. *"You're* a sportsman?"

He even managed not to guffaw upon saying it. Damnation!
After all his hard work in erasing the professor from his per
sona, Jack began to suspect Grace's "civilizing" lessons were
taking hold. How else to explain his interest in being polite to
the man who—for all intents and purposes—was his rival?

On the other hand, if a highbrow man like Walsh earned
Grace's favor and wound up wedded to her, he would probably
encourage her to keep her meeting space. Clearly, the two of
them needed to be kept apart. Jack couldn't stand the risk.

For the sake of his saloon, of course.

"Indeed." Walsh nodded. "I am a sportsman of the highest
caliber. Championship tobogganer of the New York Univer
sity team, yet useless without the proper accoutrements of my
sport." He offered a resigned grin. "It's a shame, isn't it?"

Championship tobogganer?

Jack frowned. "Damned shame."

He devoutly hoped Grace cared nothing for athleticism.

"Ah. There is Miss Crabtree now!" Walsh waved exuber
antly, making his high-buttoned velvet coat sway to and fro.
He clapped his free hand on his bowler to hold it steady.
"Woo-hoo! Miss Crabtree. Over here!"

Jack looked. For some reason, the sight of Grace tromping
toward them, pink-cheeked and high-spirited, took his breath
away. Here in the outdoors, she seemed surprisingly happy.

Evidently she'd been here for quite some time. A large
patch of snow clung to her coat sleeve. Another adorned her
scarf, both of them telling the tale, no doubt, of a few brac
ing tumbles in the snowdrifts.

She reached them with her skirts ice-spangled, her hair
springing from its confinement and her gloved hand firmly
grasping the tow rope of her sled. The thing was a woeful af

fair, with one dented runner and a paltry coat of red paint. But it was clear by the careful way she tugged the wrecked length of it that Grace was fond of it.

As respectability-minded as Grace seemed to be, it occurred to Jack, she was not concerned overmuch with appearances. Especially for their own sake. That battered sled proved as much, as did Grace's hearty strides. She acted as she pleased and cared for whatever she wished—no matter how weather-beaten or out of place. For that—and more—he admired her.

"Mr. Walsh! I'm so glad you came." She beamed up at the man, exhibiting a distinct lack of formality. She squeezed his skinny, overdressed arm in a jolly manner. "Did you get the evening edition on the press and finished early after all?"

"I did." Proudly, Walsh puffed up in his froufrou coat. "All the better to experience this spectacular occasion. It's exactly as you described, Miss Crabtree. As I've mentioned before, you have a particular eye for the telling detail."

Grace actually appeared to blush. "You're too kind."

"Not at all. The newspaper is fortunate you've decided to stay on in the typesetter's office. We'd be sorely lacking without your special expertise."

"Nonsense." Her breath puffing in the chill, Grace waved away the notion. "I merely enjoy watching you bring my father's newspaper in a bold new direction. I certainly didn't expect the two of us to be so harmonious in our approaches."

"Pshaw. You flatter me!" Walsh preened.

Grace shook her head, still beaming at him. "It's a great relief for me to have met you, and now to have worked with you, too. My father chose very wisely when he chose you as editor."

Their mutual admiration made Jack's jaw ache. Fully fed up with it, he stepped closer. The motion drew Grace's attention exactly as he'd hoped. She glanced up, plainly startled out of her conversation.

"Oh, Jack! You're here, too. What a surprise."

Her warm smile settled on him, offering surprisingly little comfort. Too? He was here, too? Disgruntled, Jack nodded.

"I didn't realize you and Mr. Walsh knew one another so well."

"Mr. Murphy is an advertiser with the *Pioneer Press*," Walsh piped up. "He kindly offered to show me the way to the hill."

"He did?" Speculatively, Grace examined him. There was something amused in her expression—something knowing. Or maybe that was simply the glow of outdoor activity making her seem so exuberant. "That's very polite of Mr. Murphy. Almost civilized. Even open-minded. Wouldn't you agree, Mr. Walsh?"

"Certainly, I would. Yes indeed. Most civilized."

They both regarded him, grinning like loons. Jack felt uncomfortably like a child who'd learned, at long last, to tie his own shoes or shovel his own mouthful of mush without leaving most of it slopped on the table. He scowled anew.

Why had he come here again?

Before he could reason it out, Grace turned briskly to her newfound editor friend. She examined the snow-covered ground to the sides and back of him. "But Mr. Walsh, this is truly a tragedy. I see you don't have a sled!"

Walsh spread his arms. "Regrettably, that's true. I thought I would visit for the camaraderie, though, and perhaps watch for a while. It's no trouble."

"But that won't be enjoyable. Or very healthful in this cold air. Here. You must take my sled!" Grace tugged the tow rope, bringing her derelict sled closer. "I insist."

"Oh, I couldn't," Walsh demurred. "What will you use?"

Grace pondered the question for less time than Jack would

have liked. She bit her lip, calling to mind the single, tantalizing kiss they'd enjoyed. Jack couldn't help but wish for another, longer version. Simply for comparison's sake.

Or for diversion from these galling circumstances.

"We'll share, of course," she announced. "Both of us."

Walsh brightened. "Truly? That's so kind of you."

"I'm sure we'll fit." Grace gestured to her sled. "We'll simply have to scrunch up tight, that's all."

They beamed at each other like lovesick beavers. At once, Jack unhappily imagined the two of them ensconced on Grace's dilapidated sled—Walsh with his arms around Grace from his steering position in the back, Grace laughingly allowing him to guide them both downhill…downhill toward a union Jack obviously could not allow.

What would happen with his saloon then, if both of these radicalizers fell into marriage together?

There was nothing for it. There was only one way, Jack knew, to securely capture Grace's attention for his own.

He cleared his throat, then pulled his black hat over his eyes. Striving for as gruff a manner as possible, he turned to Grace. "Actually…I was hoping you would teach me how to sled."

Grace's eyes widened. "Truly? You don't know how?"

It pained Jack greatly to shake his head. "Never learned," he lied, "much to my regret. It's a sore gap in my education."

"Oh. Well then." She turned to Walsh, frowning with apparent regret. "I'm afraid my first duty must be to instruct poor Mr. Murphy. You do understand, don't you?"

"Of course." Walsh grasped his sissy coat lapels. "You must do all you can to help those less refined than you. It's your obligation as a woman of importance in the community."

Neither of them so much as glanced at Jack. He would have earned more attention were he one of Harry's trapeze monkeys.

"I knew you would understand." Grace fluttered her eye-lashes, then offered another squeeze to Walsh's arm. "You're ever so courteous, as always. Thank you for your kindness."

"My kindness pales in comparison with yours, Miss Crab-tree. Clearly, your willingness to help Mr. Murphy suggests that much, doesn't it? It's not often a lady will go to such lengths."

Stifling a groan, Jack ignored the rest of Walsh's nattering. Instead he shoved his gaze to the people milling around them—hauling sleds and wooden barrel lids, laughing and talking—and tried to seem brusque. In need of sledding instruction. And unabashed by their discussing him as though he were lacking in both wits and hearing. Less refined. Hell.

He didn't know how Grace could swallow such twaddle. Surely she was a fine woman. A woman of intelligence and humor and remarkable achievements. But to suggest so boldly that the whole community needed her? Jack knew he needed her most of all.

Beside him, Grace and Walsh laughed merrily.

Suddenly, the answer to his troubles appeared. Marcus Copeland stepped over the rise in the hill, accompanied by his wife, Molly. The two of them pulled an enormous toboggan, crafted of fine-honed boards doubtless culled from Marcus's successful lumber mill at the edge of town.

Spying them, Jack raised his hand in salute. "I see your sister and brother-in-law are headed this way, Miss Crabtree."

She and Walsh glanced in that direction—Walsh more cheerfully than Jack would have expected of a man who'd just been denied an opportunity to "scrunch up tight" with Grace.

"Their toboggan looks equipped for carrying three, I reckon," Jack added. "You're in luck, Walsh."

"Perfect!" Grace exclaimed. "Mr. Walsh, let me make the arrangements posthaste. I'll take care of everything."

She hurried away, moving with her usual no-nonsense strides, leaving her sled behind. Jack glanced at its pathetic construction, its well-worn runners, its frayed rope.

"It's terribly neighborly of you to take my place with Miss Crabtree." Walsh offered Jack a handshake—one that felt surprisingly sturdy—and a good-natured grin. "I couldn't think of a single way out of getting on that contraption. I'm most grateful, Murphy. You're a far braver man than I am."

He offered a single shuddering glance at Grace's rickety sled. Then he left to join Grace and her family, holding his bowler with both hands, clearly unaccustomed to wilderness living but mustering the pluck to tackle it all the same.

Grudgingly, Jack found himself respecting the man. He knew firsthand how difficult it was to head west, away from everything familiar and citified and predictable. Doing so required a brand of bravery not everyone possessed. For all he knew, he and Thomas Walsh had many things in common.

But Jack did not want one of them to be Grace Crabtree.

Intending to ensure exactly that, Jack tromped toward their small gathering. Sarah and Daniel and Eli had joined the assemblage, too, during those few moments when Jack had been watching Walsh take his leave. Everyone gestured happily, chattering in that animated way everybody associated with the Crabtrees eventually seemed to adopt.

Jack had something beyond conversation in mind for him and Grace—something much more intimate. Much more enlightening. And, ideally, much more enjoyable. It was time to make good on his claim of needing sledding instruction…and, more than likely, to gather a bit more information about Grace's courtship preferences while he was at it.

Oddly enough, he could hardly wait.

Chapter Ten

～～～～～

"All right then." Briskly, Grace trooped back to Jack's position at the top of the hillside, having handily matched up Mr. Walsh with Molly and Sarah and all the rest of her family and dispatched them toward their own fun. "Let's get your lessons started, shall we?"

With her limbs tingling from the exertion she'd expended already, Grace hauled her sled into position. She toed it more in line with the track she'd already followed for several runs, then glanced up. Jack was being strangely silent. Jack was…

He was following the progress of Mr. Walsh's group with narrowed eyes, his whole expression stone-faced and surprisingly stubbled. Perhaps he'd missed his morning shave. That was no reason to appear so fearsome though.

She nudged him, aiming for his ribs but accidentally encountering his belly instead. It felt every bit as solid as the rest of him. Warm, too, even through the layers of his rugged coat and shirt. Startled, Grace snatched her elbow away.

He glanced down. Instantly, his whole demeanor softened. Had his eyes always been so blue? So clear? At that moment, Grace couldn't be sure. But she did feel pulled into their depths, drawn to wondering what he was thinking about…or whom.

He blinked, and the spell was broken.

Grace started. What was the matter with her? She acted as though Jack's plain black hat were positively mesmerizing— or else the man beneath it might be.

"We'll begin with a survey of the parts of the sled," she announced, doing her best to carry on with her plan despite her preoccupied state. In as businesslike a fashion as she could muster, she strode a circle around their vehicle. "These are the runners, specially curved to bite into the snow for improved steering. This is the body of the sled, sized for one or two." Another glance at him. "We will be a tight fit, I fear. You're quite a bit bigger than Mr. Walsh."

At her mentioning it, Jack actually appeared to glow. She must have imagined the effect though, for with his next breath he seemed as unaffected as ever. Now that she thought of it, size wasn't the only difference between Jack and Thomas Walsh, Grace mused. Jack was bigger, it was true, but he was also tougher, stronger and somehow more compelling.

Why that should be, Grace didn't know. Surely Mr. Walsh was the more cultured, the more enlightened, of the pair. She'd noticed those differences in the two men straightaway. But as interesting and skilled and professionally accomplished as she considered Mr. Walsh to be, particularly after working very amiably with the new editor for weeks now, she still found Jack twice as thrilling. Especially when she kissed him.

Dreamily, Grace contemplated his jawline. Perhaps next time she would touch him there…sample the texture of his skin and the harshness of his whiskers. Would they feel soft? Or bristly?

And what of that hollow at his throat? It drew her eye, the only bit of exposed skin visible above his coat collar. Likely it led to even more fascinating areas below—areas she'd never glimpsed on a man, but suddenly felt boundlessly intrigued by.

Jack nodded. "I am much bigger."

"Yes." Desperately, Grace cleared her throat. "Nonetheless, we will endeavor to make this lesson work, tight fit or no." She indicated the pointed front of the sled, where the tow rope dangled. "This plane is meant to cut into snowdrifts. Also the mechanism beneath offers rudimentary steering capabilities—"

"Let's get on with the doing of it." Jack's voice was husky, his brogue deepened. "You know I'm not much for talking."

"Oh. Very well then." He sounded impatient. Inexplicably disappointed, Grace regarded her sled blankly. She'd rather been looking forward to spending a bit more time with Jack than this—to enjoying his company without feeling pressed for a suitable excuse. "I suppose if you'll just take your place then—"

Instead Jack grabbed her sled by its body. He hoisted it easily under his arm, then pointed his chin toward a distant trail, all the way at the edge of the cleared hillside.

"That looks like a good spot."

"But that area is not even improved!" Grace protested. "It's positively wild over there, with all sorts of obstacles. That's why no one is sledding down that portion of the hill." Otherwise its privacy would doubtless have lured young lovers, perennially interested in enjoying courtship without their neighbors eavesdropping. She and Jack were—of course—too sensible for such shenanigans. More's the pity. "It's probably got bumps and buried rocks and trees—"

"Sounds interesting. Let's go." Jack trudged that way, clearly expecting her to follow him.

She didn't, of course. Overbearing man. What made

him think he could lead this endeavor? Grace was the one with the knowledge and experience, she reminded herself staunchly.

Stubbornly, she remained in place, watching Jack stride across the hilltop. He carried her heavy sled as though it weighed nothing, his shoulders marching effortlessly toward the ponderosa pines bordering the wilder section of the hill.

It seemed he meant to guide their lesson—something she should have expected but hadn't. It would be just like the two of them to battle over this encounter, too.

As Jack passed by, people of all sorts stopped their activities to glance at him, Grace noticed with surprise. Young and old, they smiled at the saloonkeeper as though pleased merely to be in his presence. It was a phenomenon she'd never noticed before. But to be honest, she understood how they felt.

Of late, she'd experienced a very similar sensation. The more time they spent together, the more intriguing she found him—which was something she definitely had not reckoned on.

While Grace considered that dilemma, Jack kept going, neatly making off with her prized sled.

"Wait!" she called, waving her arm.

He paused, then turned with easy athleticism. She'd swear she caught a wolfish smile on his face, but it jogged up and down as she hastened to catch up, and Grace couldn't be certain.

"For an avowed student," she announced, panting as she reached him, "you don't seem very interested in listening to your teacher. I would have asked Sarah for advice, had I known I'd be enlisted to wrangle with such an unruly learner."

Jack gave a careless sound. "I am interested in listening to you. I want to know everything you have to say."

Surely he was placating her. Grace harrumphed.

"I want to know everything that's in your mind." Startlingly, he touched her temple with his gloved hand, smoothing a wayward tendril of hair. His gaze met hers. "I promise I will, after today."

Unexpectedly affected, Grace stilled. Warmth skated over her forehead, then receded. Jack smiled at her. His touch was as light as a feather—but markedly more rousing. As absurd as it sounded, she felt as if her whole person blushed.

"Nonsense," Grace blustered. "I am a very private person. No one is privy to everything that's in my mind."

He winked at her. "That's because no one has asked the right questions. Yet."

Wholly unable to devise a response, Grace stared at him. Right questions? What were those? She was so lost in wondering that she scarcely noticed when a group of people passed by—until one of them stopped. Pulled from her reverie, Grace recognized Alma Potter, one of the members of her weekly literature group.

"Why, Grace! That is you. Wherever have you been?"

"Hello, Alma," Grace began. "I don't—"

"You haven't been to a meeting in weeks!" Alma carried on. She gave Grace a shrewd look. "Don't tell me you've shirked in reading the book selection. I won't believe it."

Pinned by her friend's observation, Grace heartily wished for a diversion. Another rogue tobogganer, perhaps, or some assistance from Jack. A gentleman would have sensed her predicament and offered some distraction. But Jack only stood there, looking amused, waiting to see what she'd say.

The truth was—however loath Grace felt to admit it—that she'd quit attending a select few of her clubs and activities lately, pushed to it by the need to divide her time between Jack and the newspaper. Simply put, Grace had been forced to prioritize. She hadn't realized until just this minute what the order of her priorities suggested.

That she'd rather spend time with Jack than with the members of her longtime clubs—more than a few of which she'd founded herself in a bid to stave off loneliness.

Grace gestured awkwardly. "I'm afraid you've pegged it, Alma," she prevaricated, even though she'd read the group's selection twice over in preceding years. Admitting as much certainly wouldn't squeeze her out of her current predicament. "I'm woefully behind with my reading. I didn't want to say so."

"Hmm. I never thought I'd see the day." Alma looked Grace over once more, clearly taken aback. Then she gave her a warmhearted pat to the shoulder. "Don't trouble yourself though. You can catch up, can't you?"

"Indeed," Grace agreed, relieved. "I suppose I must." But strangely, she felt less interested than ever before in losing herself in chitchat, even with regard to great literature. "I do hope the meetings have been going well?"

"Fine, fine." Alma glanced backward, locating her companions. "We've all pulled together to organize things. Sally Cooper has your spare keys, of course, so we're able to conduct meetings as usual. In only a *slightly* less organized fashion."

Grace smiled at the compliment, remembering entrusting her friend—in case of an emergency—with the auxiliary keys to her leased space and the responsibility that came with them. For the first time, she felt glad to have relieved herself of both.

However temporarily.

"But it's certainly not the same without you." Alma waved to her fellow sledders, then offered an apologetic smile. "I really must be off, but I hope I see you next week!"

Grace said her goodbyes, then turned to face Jack again.

He watched her interestedly…and with far too much perceptiveness in his gaze. "You've missed your meetings?"

"Only a few." Hastily, Grace regrouped. It wouldn't do for Jack to realize exactly how much she'd drifted from her customary routine. "Now then. Once we're actually situated upon the sled, ready to proceed downhill—"

"I'll take my position first." Nonplussed by the snow-covered trail ahead of them, Jack dropped her sled. A moment's stretching of his strong legs and broad arms—then a firm grasp on the sled's body—brought him into place. Thus seated, he spread his knees, then gestured toward the sliver of wood visible between them. "Get on board."

Grace could no more follow his suggestion than she could sprout wings and fly away. She was too busy staring. His position was positively immodest! How did Jack sit there with such appearance of casualness? It was downright scandalous.

And strongly appealing, however much she wanted to deny it.

Grace stepped back. "You don't even know how to sled."

"I'm a quick study," he said.

"But I haven't even taught you anything yet."

"No matter." He should have looked incongruous there on her sled, a big man all hunkered atop it with scarcely room enough for his enormous feet. But for some reason, Jack didn't. Jack only looked...charming. "We'll learn as we go," he said.

He held out his hand. Skittishly, Grace studied it.

"You'll have to let me steer," she cautioned. "You don't possess the expertise for the task."

Unsurprisingly, he did not agree. Grace took a deep breath, then glanced to the area he'd indicated. Or at least she tried to. With his legs sprawled and his manner so casual, Jack all but stole her attention himself. His legs were muscular, filling out his everyday brown trousers in spectacular fashion. His chest looked broad enough to rest on like a pillowed headboard.

Suddenly, she yearned to do exactly that.

"I fully intend to steer," she announced instead, grandly raising her chin. "You're strictly a passenger on this sled."

"I heard you the first time. Get on. I'm cold."

Well now, Grace reasoned. That was no wonder, given the insufficient weight of his coat. It was the sort of garment a man would throw on to pay a quick call down the street, not to frolic in the snow. He wasn't wearing a scarf either. Clearly, Jack should have planned better. She'd have to mention such skills when offering him her upcoming broad-mindedness tutorials.

On the other hand, it would be positively unsociable to refuse him a bit of warmth, wouldn't it? That would prove contrary to all the enriching, enlightening and emancipating she'd attempted to accomplish in all this time with him.

With a final nervous glance to the scant inches of sled seating that were her destination, Grace carefully and bravely lowered herself into position. It was not a simple maneuver, with her skirts to arrange and her modesty to preserve.

This was not the first time she'd shared a sled ride with a man, of course. Such occasions were one of the few opportunities for both sexes to mingle, Grace knew, given that everyone tended to bundle up enough to make even the merest improprieties impossible. One glance around her reminded her of that. Just a short distance away, an entire toboggan full of men and women swept down the hill, its occupants whooping.

She was being ridiculous to quibble over a harmless sled ride with Jack Murphy. After all, she'd been alone with him before. If he'd intended to behave indecently, he'd have done so long ago. Besides, men usually did not experience untoward urges when in her company. Something about her seemed to stifle bawdy behavior, tamping down such masculine desires before they began.

Never before had Grace yearned to ignite them instead. At this moment she did. Foolishly.

Jack clearly could not discern as much. He merely put his mouth next to her ear and spoke in his usual straightforward manner. "Are you ready?"

Rolling her eyes at her own fancies, Grace grasped the tow rope, dragging it safely out of the way of the runners. She planted her feet in position, having learned through long practice which place afforded the best steering. She nodded.

As she'd expected, Jack put his arms around her next, cinching them tight at her middle. A long shiver ran through Grace, one that had nothing at all to do with the brisk temperatures. How did he make his chest so broad? His arms so strong? His touch so…rousing? Wrapped in his embrace—however practically motivated—she felt positively secure.

The very notion spooked her. "Stop. This—"

Jack didn't listen. Instead he brought his big feet around to crowd hers against the front of the sled, effectively taking control. He hugged her tighter, his knees and calves and burly thighs joining the effort as his limbs snuggled up to her skirts. He tucked his head against her shoulder, undoubtedly improving his view of their downhill track.

All of a sudden though, Grace cared nothing for the view. Instead she considered the soft tickle of his whiskers, right against her cheek. That unshaved area didn't feel bristly or at all as she'd expected. It actually felt rather nice and—

With a push and a whoosh, they set off.

Waaah! The whole world jostled past her, gaining speed. Snow sprayed from the runners, making her sputter. The cold air sped by, ruffling her unruly hair still further.

How had Jack developed so much impetus with a single push? He must be even stronger than he seemed. Grace yelped and grabbed the edges of the sled. Her gloved hands bit into the ragged wood, holding on for dear life.

"Hold on to me!" Jack instructed at a shout.

Grace shook her head. Suddenly his embrace didn't seem so very secure after all. Trees sped past, veering dangerously close. Determinedly, she tried to steer toward a more open area of the hillside, but it seemed Jack had control of their vehicle. With scarcely any effort at all, he maneuvered them straight down the path he'd selected.

A path that seemed far too risky to her.

Grace's heart pounded. Her hat slipped, as though trying to mate with her scarf and become one knitted unit. She could scarcely see, but she didn't dare release her grasp on the sled to straighten it. "We're too close to the trees!"

Jack hollered with delight, not hearing her. She'd never imagined he could be so uninhibited. Like a boy, he whooped the whole way over the next hillock. They soared, momentarily airborne, then came down with a thud that made her teeth rattle.

Their sled veered crazily. Expertly, Jack held her tighter and leaned them both sideways, righting them.

Grace shrieked, her eyes streaming with the cold air and the rowdiness of their ride. They kept going over one bump and the next, the sled runners scraping loudly against the snow. The bottom of the hillside loomed, curving onto a flatland.

With a start, Grace realized the other sledders to the side of them were mere specks in the distance. She couldn't glimpse anyone familiar. Somehow, she and Jack had veered even farther off track than she'd envisioned at the start. And they were coming precariously close to the trees again, too.

She couldn't stand it. Cursing her ice-clumped skirts for hampering her movement, Grace tried her best to steer with her booted feet. She pushed with all her might, but there was nothing for it. Jack had control of their sled and refused to relinquish it. They tussled for a few moment anyway, both of them shoving feetfirst in a wrestling match for authority.

"Damn it, Grace!" he said in her ear. "You're going to—"

She couldn't listen. "Watch out for those trees!"

"I see them." A sound of frustration. "Move your feet so I can keep us out of the way."

They zigzagged wildly, careening over bumps and icy patches. Intending to force them to the right—toward every one else on the hill—Grace stomped her foot hard on the sled's yoke. She encountered solid resistance and realized it was Jack's foot she'd bashed instead.

"Oh, I'm sorry!" she cried. "Are you all ri—"

She never finished her question. An instant later, Jack clutched her tighter, wrenched sideways…and they both tumbled off the sled. Everything turned white and jostling, caked in snow and movement as the hill rushed up to meet them.

The impact wasn't as alarming as Grace expected. Probably, she realized shortly, because she did not thud directly into the snowbank. Instead she landed atop Jack.

His whole body cushioned their fall. She encountered broad chest, warm knees and strong hands, all before painfully clonking foreheads with him. The impact reverberated through her skull, cushioned merely by her hat. She winced and yowled. Jack only grunted—as usual—then rolled her safely beneath him. Dazed, she required a moment to realize they were no longer careening downhill but had come to a stop.

They lay crookedly on the snow, both panting hard. To her left, pine trees rose valiantly, capped with white and bowed with the weight of their wintry coats. To her right, a drift shielded the rest of the hill from her vision. She saw nothing beyond Jack's black hat, which had landed askew in the snow, doubtless knocked aside in their fall.

Fearfully, Grace craned her head—just as her riderless sled zoomed between two trees. It crashed to a stop in a tangle of fallen oak branches some thirty yards away.

"See? I told you we'd crash in the trees!"

"We didn't crash in the trees." Jack directed his gaze from her sled's resting place to her, then raised himself on both elbows above her. He looked unfazed by their near collision. "No thanks to you, Miss Hundred-Pound Boots. I got us off that sled just in time. Now if you'd let me steer from the start—"

"Let you steer?" Incredulously, Grace regarded him. Aside from the obvious, was he intimating that she had gigantic feet? "You haven't the faintest notion how to steer!" she replied hotly. "That much is clear to everyone."

His mouth straightened. "I had a plan."

She scoffed. "A plan to kill us both?"

"Pshaw." Appearing downright invigorated by their ride now that he'd had a moment to recover, Jack brought his hand to rest on her shoulder. He grinned. "I heard you hollering. You were having fun until you decided to take over."

Stung, Grace hesitated. Had she been hollering? With glee?

"I don't generally have 'fun.' Ask anyone," she informed him to the contrary, not wanting to consider the matter of her potential rowdiness any further. "And I always take over."

"Not with me, you don't."

"Oh? Is that right?" Vigorously, Grace wiggled her legs, trying to get free. As it happened, she was pinned beneath Jack's tall frame and didn't manage much progress. The sensation wasn't wholly unlikable though—and no one could see them in their surprisingly sheltered spot—so she decided to rest awhile. To regain her strength for the trek to retrieve her sled. "Well, I'll have you know, you'll get no special treatment from me."

Jack audacious grin widened. Something about it made her belly flip-flop. He still touched her shoulder, his thumb now moving in slow circles over the bulk of her coat. Was he checking for injuries? The gentleness of the gesture was especially peculiar given the way she frowned at him. It was even stranger how his warmth—his touch—penetrated all the way through the thick wool.

"I was attempting to teach you a valuable skill." Grace hoped she sounded less stirred to his ears than her own. "I don't think you could have been a more recalcitrant student, however."

He arched his brow. "Recalcitrant?"

"Yes. It means headstrong. Obstinate. Unwilling to—"

"I know what it means. It describes us both."

Momentarily flummoxed, Grace stared at him. "I suppose you know that because of my broadening influence on your vocabulary. Well. That's wonderful, isn't it?"

She snatched at her scarf, trying to unwrap it where it had become pinned beneath her opposite shoulder. The center of its knit felt cold against her lips, frosted with iced-over breath. Her gloves made her clumsy though, and she couldn't seem to locate the correct end of it.

In answer, Jack only watched as she went on plucking at her scarf. He gave her a rather mysterious smile. "You have been a terrible influence on me," he countered. "Why else would I be here at the hill today, leaving poor Harry to tend bar?"

"I'm sure I don't know what you mean."

Another long look. "It's because I had to see you."

She stilled. Her heart pounded, and not from the exertion of their sled ride. Was that tenderness in his gaze? "Why?"

"Well…"

She held her breath, waiting as Jack appeared to consider the rest of his reply. Would he say something poetic? Something wonderful? All at once, and quite unreasonably, she wanted him to. Which was beyond silly.

They hadn't even discussed Elizabethan sonnets yet.

"I couldn't let you have the last word," Jack said.

Disappointed, Grace scoffed. "Don't talk nonsense."

She couldn't imagine what he meant. And that had definitely not been poetry from his lips. But the intent look on Jack's face certainly gave her pause all the same. No man had ever looked at her that way. Most likely, no man ever would again. It was just as well she didn't become accustomed to it.

"You might think it's nonsense," Jack said cheerfully. "But you'll listen all the same."

While he enjoyed the last word? Ha! That would be the day.

Stubbornly, Grace fiddled with the scarf at her neck, more briskly now. Were both trailing ends trapped beneath her? She should move to fetch them, to free herself, and yet…being caught beneath so much tall, strong man was rather pleasant.

Perhaps even healthful, given the chill in the air.

"It's most gentlemanly of you to keep us both so warm," she said demurely.

His grin quirked. "There's nothing gentlemanly about it." From somewhere, Jack emerged with the end of her scarf in his hand. He toyed with it, brushing its fringe against his cheek. Teasing her. "And you won't be changing the subject before I've said my piece. Don't you want to know what I have to say?"

"Of course. But yours still won't be the final word in the matter," Grace warned. "I might as well tell you, I've been known to stage a filibuster or two in my time, for a cause that's worthy of it. I've been known to talk and talk—"

"Shh." Carefully, Jack lifted her scarf. By degrees, its stiffened, tangled knit came away from her face and neck, admitting cold air. "You'll miss it."

"Nonsense. I'm excellent at paying attention."

"Good."

He lifted her scarf fully away, then turned his hand to wind the length of it around his broad palm. He fisted the ice-clumped knit, doubtless melting every bit of snow trapped inside as he tugged it free. It occurred to Grace, in a very uncharacteristic whimsical moment, that Jack Murphy might just be capable of melting all the snow surrounding them, if only he smiled at it.

"Ooh, that's cold." Grace touched her fingers to her mouth. It felt chilly to the touch. "I thought having my iced-over scarf gone would be better, but—"

"Try this," Jack said and kissed her.

In a single motion, he tugged her fingers away with his free hand and brought his mouth to hers. Shocking warmth struck Grace first, making her realize exactly how cold she had been until now. Then other sensations began, starting at her mouth—where Jack plied her with tiny, expert kisses—and traveling rapidly all through her. Helplessly, she curled her toes in her winter boots, scarcely able to withstand so much feeling. So much gentleness. So…much.

It was like nothing she'd experienced before.

If she were dreaming, she wanted never to wake up—at least until she discovered what lay at the end of this kiss.

Rumbling with a low moan, Jack raised his head. He looked pleased. Then, evidently changing his mind about stopping, he favored her with another, slower kiss. Grace knew she must be cross-eyed, so hazy did he look to her. She felt somehow limp and yet vigorous, lulled and yet unsatisfied. How it could be that a saloonkeeper kissed with such finesse and care, she didn't know. She only knew that his notion of kissing was much, much better than the paltry novice's attempt she'd made outside his saloon.

He gazed at her, his own glance looking as heavy-lidded as hers felt. Up close, his stubble was even more compellingly male. So were his lips. They smiled at her, as did all the rest of him. Logically, Grace knew that made no sense. But she felt it all the same and was unduly glad for it.

"That's much better, thank you," she said.

What was wrong with her voice? It sounded low and hoarse and somehow intimate. Appalled at the change, Grace tried again.

"Of course, that doesn't qualify as having the last word," she informed him, reviving a little, "seeing as how yours was an action and not a word at all. I don't think that counts."

Smiling for no reason she could discern, Jack pondered it. "Let me try again."

This time when his mouth met hers, it was with a little less gentleness and a lot more urgency. He cupped her cheek in his hand, his leather glove cold and smooth, and brought all the heat he'd mustered before back to her. He kissed her deeply, coaxed her mouth to open and kissed her more deeply still.

Surprised at the first deft sweep of his tongue, Grace stiffened. Never had she felt anything more invasive, more controlling, more... Ah. Suddenly, that intimate kiss became something new. Something she welcomed. Clutching his coat for balance, she squeezed her eyes shut and lost herself to Jack's greater experience. For the first time in her life, she let someone else take the lead—and astonishingly, she enjoyed it.

When their kiss ended, Grace did not want to open her eyes. She flopped her arms on the snowbank like a girl making snow angels and merely...luxuriated. She sighed. Nothing in her life had ever prepared her for a sensation like this.

Kissing. Who could have guessed it would be so wonderful? So compelling? So close?

"Now I've done it," Jack mused, laughter in his voice. "I've gone and made Grace Crabtree faint dead away with a kiss. I ought to have a statue of myself made to commemorate the occasion."

Grace roused herself enough to shove his chest. Her eyes flew open. "If you do, I'll tell everyone in town you used your tongue." Doubtless it was an eastern peculiarity, familiar among Bostonian rascals like Jack but mostly unknown in the territory. "Everyone will be horror-struck."

"Only until I tell them you liked it."

"You wouldn't!" Grace gasped. "You never—"

"I wouldn't," he agreed, then brought his thumb to sweep along her cheek, almost as though he cherished touching her. "If I did, I might never get to repeat it."

His next kiss felt even headier than the first few. Sweetly and surely, Jack lowered his mouth to hers in as leisurely a fashion as had ever been conceived. He seduced her with each kiss, each touch, each tender look. Hidden there in the snowdrifts, surrounded by nothing more than the wind in the trees and the very, very distant whoops of sledders, he took every notion Grace had of competency and hurled it aside with ease. In this at least, Jack was beyond expert.

"One area you don't require tutelage in is kissing," she confided. Feeling comfortable and cozy, Grace wiggled more firmly into position. She fingered Jack's coat buttons, daring to touch him even without the excuse of an eyes-closed kiss to hide her actions. "I'm happy to say you seem to have that skill mastered."

"I'm happy you think so."

"Even without me helping you."

"Ah." Another grin. She'd never seen so many from him

before. Never had he looked so devilish either. "You're an expert then?" he asked.

"Well, not an expert. Not exactly." Caught in her own bantering, Grace hedged, reluctant to seem less than wholly in command of…well, everything. "But I am in a fine position to evaluate your performance, and that's nearly as good. Although I daresay your chosen partner deserves a bit of the credit—"

"Oh, does she now?" Grinning more widely, Jack shook his head. He seemed to care nothing for his missing hat, nor the unruly shock of dark hair that fell over his brow, making him seem all the more rakish. "Does she truly?"

"Indeed." At his fond look, something inside Grace seemed to loosen. All at once, she felt nearly as though her heart expanded—nonsensical as it sounded. She found herself returning a smile of her own, helpless to prevent it. "Perhaps we are well matched in this kissing endeavor."

"Perhaps," he agreed. "Except that you keep talking."

"What?" She pretended to feel snubbed, but in truth Grace felt as light as air—as though she could accomplish anything. "There is nothing wrong with talking, I'll have you know. It is through talking—and writing and agitating and protesting—that real change happens. It is through talking that—"

His next kiss muffled her words, cutting off her breath. Swept up in the pleasure of Jack's arms, Jack's mouth, Jack's husky sound of enjoyment, Grace found she did not mind so very much. In fact, her newly curled toes told a tale of pure happiness.

She beamed at him. "You must quit making your point that way. I find I am quite helpless to argue against it."

"Good."

Another kiss, one so incredibly affecting that Grace arched upward, letting her neat ivory buttons smash against the bigger horn buttons on Jack's coat. Their bodies strained together, fraught with a need she could neither describe nor refute. It simply was, and for now, that was enough. Emboldened by her feelings, she grasped Jack's lapels, hoping to find purchase in a world that somehow had tilted since they'd left their sled.

If this was what it meant to surrender the final word, Grace thought dizzily, then she had been missing out on a great deal all these years. Thrilled, she kissed him back. Hers must have been an effective gesture, for she felt him shudder in response, his whole body shaking.

Jack drew back, giving her an admiring look. "Grace, you are a fast learner. I should have known."

Dismayed, Grace touched his mouth. "Your lips are blue!"

"It's nothing." Bundling deeper into his paltry coat, Jack hunkered lower. His teeth chattered. "So long as you're warm."

Sweet suffrage campaigns, Grace realized. He was shaking from cold, not passion!

Vigorously, she wriggled her arms and legs, truly meaning it this time. "We're getting up right now. You need a warm fire and a cup of hearty tea, in that order."

"Right now, all I n-n-n-need is you." He brought his mouth lower and kissed her ear.

Good heavens! While this new variety of kiss was unexpectedly delightful, the sound of his clattering teeth was not. Poor Jack. What was he thinking?

"Obviously I've kissed you senseless," Grace announced. She gave a mighty shove, dislodging Jack's mouth from her earlobe. His disappointed moan followed. "Get up. I'm taking you home."

His answering wink was scandalous. "I hope—"

"Just keep moving, if you please."

She supervised as he heaved reluctantly to his feet, then

got up herself. She marched to his hat. A quick brush and fluff, and it was as good as new. Readying herself to plunk it on his head, Grace fussed to rearrange his disarrayed hair. While those dark burnished locks held a certain appeal, especially given her remembrance of how they'd gotten that way, it wouldn't do for the two of them to return to town looking quite so...

Well, looking as though they'd been doing exactly what they'd been doing. And nearly freezing to death in the process.

Grace pushed back Jack's hair, then paused. "Oh, dear."

"What's the matter?"

Standing upright with him, even on tiptoes, Grace was struck by how much bigger and broader Jack was than she. But not even he was impervious to injury, it seemed.

"You're hurt." Gingerly, she touched his forehead, where a swollen area had already turned color with an impending bruise. "You have a goose egg the size of a gold nugget."

"I'll have it assayed when we get back to town."

She couldn't believe he would joke about this. "It must have happened when we collided while falling off the sled."

"Diving very purposely off the sled," Jack insisted. He raised his hand to his forehead, then winced when he located the bump there. "I was saving us from a far worse fall."

"I believe you might already be delusional." Worriedly, Grace peered at him. "Sometimes head injuries affect people strangely. I'd better get you home and send for Doctor Finney."

"I'm fine. I don't need a doctor."

"Stay here. I'll collect my sled and we'll be on our way."

"I don't need a doctor! It's just a bump."

Hands on her hips, Grace examined him. "You're having a visit from the doctor whether you like it or not." Strangely, she felt like weeping, mostly at the thought of there being something seriously wrong with him. It would be all her fault, too, for making him linger in the snow…kissing her! "I don't want anyone dead merely because I decided to try kissing."

"I won't be—try?" Jack hand stilled against his forehead. His expression perked up interestedly. "You mean you've never kissed a man before? Before me?"

He seemed pleased to learn that. Why Grace had admitted such a telling detail, she didn't know. She only knew that she had to get Jack someplace warm and secure, whether he cooperated in the activity or didn't. She simply couldn't bear the thought of him being injured, especially because of her.

"It wouldn't be polite to say," she prevaricated.

"Come on now." His smile urged her. "Nobody's listening."

"Well…" How did he tempt her so easily? "Let's just say your kisses are incomparable and leave it at that, shall we?"

Then she strode to the bramble of trees, ignoring his continued protests behind her. If Jack Murphy keeled over on the way home, Grace reasoned, she might well need her sled to tote him back to town. All six stubborn, stubbled, stupidly perceptive feet of him.

Chapter Eleven

Doctor Finney, elderly, white-haired and none too gentle with his instruments, gave Jack a thorough examination in Jack's quarters behind the saloon. He drew blood, muttered over the state of Jack's innards, inquired after any existing neuralgia, prescribed a daily dose of castor oil and generally poked and prodded in a wholly unpleasant way.

"Nobody's ever sent two runners for me before," the doctor said, persisting in making small talk as he peered at Jack's head. He probed at the swelling, nodding and making assessing sounds. "Much less seven of them, all shouting to come quick."

Jack winced, remembering his and Grace's hurried departure from the sledding hill and their eventful return to the streets of Morrow Creek. Given the way she'd hollered for people to let them pass, anyone would have thought Jack had sustained a dreadful injury—not a simple conk to the noggin.

"Miss Crabtree has quite a command of the newsboys employed by the *Pioneer Press*," he explained. "Most of them have worked with her and her father for a long time."

"Hmm. That reward couldn't have hurt either."

"No." Jack said nothing else. It still embarrassed him that Grace had volunteered a printing-press position working with Barney Bartleson for the newsboy who'd fetched the doctor the fastest, claiming it was a matter of life or death for "poor injured Mr. Murphy." He was a man, damn it, fully capable of determining his own condition! And then the way Grace had rambled on about his probable state of delirium…

"That gal must care something fierce for you," Doctor Finney went on, offering a knowing glance from beneath his shock of bushy white brows, "to have caused such a ruckus on your behalf. Hell, I had to threaten not to treat you, just to keep her decently out of this room."

His bedroom. Jack glanced at its meager furnishings, all visible from his grudging position on the bedside chair. The chair doubled as both his bureau and his bedside table. He'd had to move his washbasin, towel and pitcher from the seat for his examination.

"I daresay she's taken over your kitchen though. Hear her in there?" The doctor rummaged through his medical bag, pushing aside various bottled remedies, a book about animal husbandry, a flask of whiskey and a hefty bundle of bandages. "When I asked Miss Crabtree to make me a cup from that pot of tea she's brewing, she nearly took my head off." He chuckled. "If that's not love, I don't know what is."

Increasingly, Jack worried about the competency of his care. It was fortunate there wasn't anything truly wrong with him. He'd sustained far worse injuries while breaking up saloon brawls over the past year or so. He was only sorry Grace had glimpsed the swelling on his head and ended their time in the snow so soon. He would have gladly risked frostbite for more of her kisses.

Your kisses are incomparable, he remembered her saying. She'd been deliberately misleading him of course. He knew full well Grace was too inexperienced to have any basis for romantic comparison. Her very lack of bossiness while they'd kissed told him that. Not that Jack cared a whit. Despite everything, he grinned. There was no one else like his Grace. No one at all.

And there was no one as hardheaded as her either—in all definitions of the word. Doubtless she'd have coldcocked a weaker man with that cast-iron skull of hers. Jack would have to be sure old sawbones looked her over before taking his leave.

A sturdy knock issued at the door. "The tea is ready," Grace called. "I'm entering right now, so—"

"Leave us be!" Doctor Finney bellowed. He gave Jack a conspiratorial waggle of those astonishing eyebrows, man-to-man style. "My examination is not yet finished, Miss Crabtree. Furthermore, Mr. Murphy is plumb naked."

Jack gawked in protest, waving his hands wildly. Anyone could see he was still fully clothed. In fact, Grace had hauled an extra coat and a blanket from his bedside chest and forced him to wear both before they'd shooed her from the room. She'd been unreasonably concerned with his warming up promptly. She'd even laid a fire in the mostly unused grate, stomping about in that practical manner of hers to collect fuel and tinder.

The doctor ignored him. "Do you want him to catch his death of cold?" he shouted through the door. "In the end," Finney intoned dramatically, laying a hand over his heart, "his untimely demise will rest on your conscience, young lady."

A pause. Jack could almost hear Grace's skepticism, heartily at war with her determination to have control.

The doorknob turned. Then halted. Then returned to its usual position. In the end, apparently, caution won over.

"Make sure that fire is hot enough!" Grace commanded

through the door, her tone of authority clearly carrying. "It will need another log soon."

Doctor Finney rolled his eyes. He poked Jack's forehead, muttering something about the strident women of today.

After a few more seconds, Grace's footsteps sounded, moving away from the door. Jack pictured her striding around in his makeshift kitchen. Because it was strictly a bachelor affair, it was equipped with nothing more exotic than a stove, a worktable and a zinc basin. Plus thirty pounds of dried beans in a barrel and two sacks of cornmeal—the latter courtesy of Harry.

It gave him a surprisingly comfortable feeling to know that Grace was outside ready to care for him, Jack mused. It had been a long time since anyone had cared for him—certainly since before he'd left Boston. Jack had never imagined Grace Crabtree would be the one to do so. Hell, he'd never quite imagined she carried the softer side necessary to accomplish it.

But he'd glimpsed it today, out there in the snow.

Even now he felt her touch on him, tentative at first but growing increasingly bold. He remembered her fervent wiggles, her sweet moans of pleasure, her beautiful, tenderhearted smiles. He should have told her she looked beautiful, Jack realized with dismay. He should have told her that just lying there with her, even after a combative sled ride and its snow-flurried aftermath, made him feel frankly happy in a way he hadn't since coming to Morrow Creek to start his new life.

"I'd say you love her back," the doctor opined, as though their initial conversation had never ended. He nodded with conviction. "Because you look all walleyed and spooney, Murphy, and I'm poking the hell out of this contusion of yours."

Jack blinked. "Ouch!"

"There now. That's better. I was starting to wonder if you really were delirious, like Miss Crabtree said." Decisively, Doctor Finney stood. He closed his medical bag with a snap. "But you're not frostbit, and that's nothing but a little bump you've got there, son. Try not to smack headfirst into anybody else for the next few days, and you'll be right as rain."

Jack frowned at the doctor. He grunted by rote, feeling discomfited. He tried mightily to recall exactly what he'd been thinking to engender that sentimental look Finney had mentioned.

Grace Crabtree…beautiful?

Maybe he had gone delirious. Or maybe—just maybe—he'd finally woken up to the truth. Either way, Jack realized belatedly, he hadn't made much progress with his plan to discover Grace's courting preferences. He'd been too carried away with their downhill sled battle to think about it.

Although he had learned a great deal about how Grace preferred to be kissed, Jack reflected happily. The research involved in that matter had been downright pleasurable, too.

But he'd just been presented with a golden opportunity to learn more—to spend time alone with Grace without undue suspicion. He couldn't believe he hadn't realized it before. After all, any fool could see that Jack was running out of time to handpick Grace's husband, given the preposterous way she and Thomas Walsh had been carrying on with each other.

He had to do something. Now.

The doctor raised his hand in farewell, preparing to leave.

Jack bolted to his feet. "Wait. Before you go, there's one more thing I need from you."

Doing his best to appear less than robust, Jack meandered into the kitchen shortly after Doctor Finney departed. He put his hand to his brow to achieve a more feeble effect, then leaned against the doorjamb limply. He waited. Nothing.

Through the gap between his thumb and forefinger, he glimpsed Grace, fussing across the room. He knew she was unharmed—the doctor had informed him so. But it was still a relief to see her there...even if she was too preoccupied to notice Jack's very obvious injuries and come to his aid.

She picked up a pair of his cast-off mucky boots, which he'd dropped in their usual place—wherever Jack found himself when he came home. She frowned, then carried his boots to the door. Neatly, she set them there. Then frowned anew. Then arranged the pair perfectly perpendicular to the wall. With careful consideration, she toed them an inch to the left. Perfect.

His whole living area—all of it combined with his kitchen and sitting room—had been similarly set to order, Jack noticed. All his newspapers were stacked by the fireplace. His spare coat hung on its rarely used peg...arranged beside Grace's coat. They seemed peculiarly suited there together.

His rugs had both been straightened, Jack observed further. His table had been dusted. His dishes had been washed and put away, and his coffeepot had been scrubbed to within an inch of its graniteware life. Even the dried beans and cornmeal had been rearranged to fit with the rest of his foodstuffs—in, Jack suspected with a curious glance to the open shelves in his kitchen—alphabetical order. He should have guessed as much.

Still not noticing him, Grace strode to the single window overlooking the alleyway behind Jack's saloon. Her shoulders were straight, her hands neatly clasped behind her skirts, her manner as brisk as ever. Her hair, newly liberated from her knit cap, sprang from her updo in wild frizzy tendrils, all of them an ordinary color of brown that nonetheless made him smile.

Realizing his error, Jack hastily clamped down that smile. He attempted to look wounded instead. He gave a small groan.

Instantly, Grace turned. Her pale face and anxious expression almost gave him pause. Did she truly worry over him?

He'd never known her to be softhearted or especially sentimental. It was true that they'd shared something special there on the hillside, something a bit beyond the information gathering he needed to find her a husband…but then she was hurrying toward him, and Jack had no time to reconsider.

His new plan had been set, with Doctor Finney's help— however amused the man had been to give it. Jack had to see it through to the end. The matrimonial, saloon-saving end.

"Oh, Jack!" Grace touched him, squeezing her hands hastily over his shirt-covered shoulders and chest as though assuring herself he was truly going to survive. Her gaze skirted to his forehead. She gasped, covering her mouth. "Your head! You should sit down immediately. I can't believe you're up at all."

Her stern tone allowed no argument. Grace shepherded him toward a chair. He could see her trying not to gawk at his head. She nearly succeeded, in masterful fashion. Keeping one dutiful hand on his arm, Grace leaned sideways. A ladder-back chair scraped into position at the table. "Sit here and don't move."

Admitting a gusty sigh, Jack sank onto his seat.

"Wait here," Grace ordered. "I'll get your tea."

"I'm not thirsty," Jack protested.

He hated tea. After much bustling, pouring and upheaval, it arrived anyway. He regarded the procured cup with distaste.

Eagerly, Grace nudged it closer. "It's Mama's special restorative recipe. A combination of Pekoe tea, reconstituted valerian root, orange peel and castor oil." Ignoring the face Jack made, she urged, "Drink up. You'll feel better."

"I feel better already." He rallied, hoping she would forget about the devil's concoction she'd brewed. It smelled like toenails, but he didn't want to say so. It might set things off on the wrong foot. Literally. Instead he glanced around his scanty living quarters. "You've made it look so homey in here. Someday you'll make someone a wonderful wife."

It was Grace's turn to grimace. Wholeheartedly.

"Have you thought any more," Jack prodded, widening his eyes in what he hoped was an innocent fashion, "about finding a husband? Looking at all you've accomplished here, I have a feeling you just might be in a nesting mood."

He smiled encouragingly, hoping to get back on course. If he didn't find Grace a husband—a husband who would convince her to move her meeting rooms before the Excelsior Performing Troupe agreed to stop in Morrow Creek—there was no telling how his saloon would survive. His customers had begun staying away. Word of Grace's repeated intrusions—and her threatening looks at Colleen the water nymph—had gotten round.

"I am not a member of the *Junco hyemalis dorsalis* family, Jack. And you're not fooling me." Grace's gaze wandered to his head again. "You're trying to distract me, which is very kind, but it won't work. That's an extremely large bandage you've got there. Doctor Finney warned me you'd need extra care and watching over until it was meant to come off in a week or two—"

"I won't hear of you staying here," Jack interrupted, stepping neatly into the opening she'd provided, knowing she was exactly contrary enough to gobble at his bait. "Absolutely not."

"—and I assured him I would take charge of everything." Brightly, Grace took hold of his hand. She stroked his palm, then lifted her gaze to his. Her eyes shimmered with suppressed tears, astonishing him. "I'm so sorry you're hurt. I didn't realize the extent of your injury until I saw you just now. Your bandages are so huge! I've never seen the like. They're—"

"Bound to become a new fashion." He angled his head for her to admire, like a fashion plate in *Godey's*. "Even grooms might someday wear them to get marr—"

"Don't joke! Jack, you have six inches of bandages on your head. That's serious. Also you're behaving very strangely." She pursed her lips in evident concern. "I can tell from your babbling about marriage that you're still a little off-kilter."

He frowned. "It's the fumes from your 'tea' talking."

"Speaking of which—" Grace squeezed his hand once, then efficiently brought it to his cup. She wrapped his fingers around the warm width of it, threading them through the cup handle. "I want to see you drink every drop."

"I can't hear you." Jack cupped his free hand around the place where his ear should have been visible, had it not been obscured by the full contingent of unnecessary bandages he'd requested Doctor Finney embellish him with. "These blasted bandages have deafened me."

"I said," Grace shouted, "drink your tea!"

Not even exhibiting the cynicism he expected, she pantomimed lifting the cup to his mouth. This was going to be all too easy. Resigned to his fate, Jack did so. He didn't dare examine the contents first. The noxious odor alone nearly knocked him out of his seat.

Why was he doing this again?

A ruckus came through the walls, reminding him anew. His saloon. His new life. He had to find Grace Crabtree a husband and steer her away from the likes of citified Thomas Walsh at the same time. He had to find her a man who would oppose her meeting space and all her rabble-rousing activities alike.

"Harry is minding the saloon," Grace informed him, noticing his glance toward the adjoining wall and offering another gentle squeeze to his arm. "He's agreed to do so for as long as it takes for you to recover, so don't worry about that at all. You won't be going back to the saloon until you're well."

"No!" He hadn't counted on this. "I'm perfectly able—"

"I've taken care of everything, Jack," Grace assured him warmly. "Exactly as I intend to take care of you."

Her penetrating gaze slipped to his wobbling empty cup. Appallingly, she immediately hastened to the kettle to refill it. She wrapped his hand around his second dose of steaming tea, then nodded. "One isn't nearly enough, you know."

Manfully, Jack gulped, trying not to breathe. Instantly, his insides rebelled. Quite possibly, they turned inside out and upside down as well. He shuddered. One cup of that diabolical brew had been bad enough. Apparently, two cups taken together were downright lethal.

"Excellent." Grace beamed. "Only a few more cups to finish the pot, and then I'll make you more. It's a failsafe remedy, with my mama's assurance of effectiveness. She keeps up on all the latest news in wholesome living, you know. In the meantime, I want you to keep warm."

From somewhere, Grace had procured a thick woolen blanket. She proceeded to tuck its smothering width around him, fussing and fluttering. She fastened it securely in place with something, then regarded her work with satisfaction.

Jack glanced down. "A lady's brooch? Grace, no. I—"

"Shh." She laid her finger against his mouth, nimbly removing the spent cup from his hand as she did so. She smiled. Hers was such a beatific smile, Jack actually wondered if he had been drugged to be capable of thinking such a thing about his meddlesome upstairs neighbor. "No one will see you save me," she promised him, "and I think you look very handsome."

She thought he looked handsome?

She'd paid him a compliment?

"Now I know I'm delirious." He sat there for a minute. Or possibly more. Jack couldn't be certain, so discombobulated was he by this entire experience. He reconsidered things. "That tea is not as bad as I thought," he heard himself say.

Obligingly, Grace refilled his teacup. He drank almost gratefully, gazing at her over his cup's rim as he did so. There was something calming about having her care for him this way. Something sweet. Jack decided he quite liked it.

He held out his cup for more. It wavered. "When you quit wobbling that way, Grace, I wouldn't mind a bit more tea."

"Wobbling? Me?" Then she smiled. Both of her did. "I'm not wobbling, that's just the valerian root taking effect." Grace peered assessingly into his eyes. "Mama says it's capable of making even Molly be silent, which is quite a feat, I assure you." A moment's pause while Jack felt his head sway, then… "It's off to bed with you."

She took his arm, her touch surprisingly soothing. Her manner accepted no nay-saying. Jack found himself being led toward his bedroom, his girly pinned blanket trailing him like a blasted ball gown, with Grace beside him. She murmured something about coddling him in his present state, her voice soft.

He liked her voice soft. It reminded him of the way she'd felt when he'd kissed her. Soft all over…soft just for him. He liked soft Grace Crabtree. He liked her all over.

They reached his bedroom. For a fleeting moment, Jack's heartbeat leaped wildly. There would be more kissing now. He felt he could perform masterfully, all of a sudden. Despite his bleariness, he could make Grace happier than she'd ever been.

To be truthful, he had occasionally indulged in thoughts of having her here alone with him, he recalled as he shuffled in her wake with a roguish grin, eyeing her bedraggled skirts and shawl-wrapped shoulders. He had hoped she might let down her frazzled hair and practice her most liberated ways beneath his sheets. He'd always believed those fanciful thoughts were his alone, not shared by Grace. But now it seemed…

Dazedly, he leaned on her. "I know you're not really that liberated," he said to reassure her. "Not like I've dreamed."

She only smiled knowingly. "I believe I'll decrease the dose next time I brew up some healthful tea for you. I may have overestimated your size and vigor."

He thumped his chest. "I have plenty of size and vigor!"

"Yes, that's fine," she soothed. "Come right this way."

Aggravatingly unconvinced in the matter of his virility, Grace sat him down on his bed. She dropped to her knees, then gazed up at him. Belatedly aware of her suggestive position, Jack's whole body surged to alertness.

His head pounded. So did his loins. The activities Grace's pose brought to mind were thrillingly seductive and, in his befuddled condition, seemed distinctly possible.

His boot clunked to the floorboards. And another.

"See?" Jack tried, blinking against his disappointment. "You are wonderful at that maneuver. If your new husband were a lying-down drunk, you would be very qualified to care for him."

"Yes." Grace rolled her eyes, then tucked his wayward blanket more securely. She rose again, fluffing his pillow. "That's exactly what I want. A drunkard for a husband."

Her sarcastic tone made her true feelings known. Jack was not too addled to recognize that much. "Aha!" he bellowed, louder than he intended. "Then what do you want in a husband?"

Her considering look met his. Yes! This plan was proceeding apace, despite its rocky beginnings and his own bewildered state. Grace would confide in him, she would explain all her innermost desires to him, and then he would satisfy them with a proper husbandly candidate.

"Blah," she said confusingly. "Blah blah blah."

He may have overestimated his own ability to cajole Grace Crabtree, Jack realized with alarm. He may have bitten off more than he could chew. He may have made a mistake in drinking that damned tea of hers.

"Blah?" he repeated, perplexed.

A heartbeat later, Jack fell fast asleep.

"Hmm. For a scandalous saloonkeeper," Grace said, "you have a very faulty ability to withstand remedying compounds."

At the bracing sound of her voice, Jack roused himself. He blinked groggily, unsure where he was at first.

His initial assessment told him this place was too clean and too tidily arranged to be his own purposely rugged territorial lodgings. He'd deliberately strewn those with cast-off clothing, miscellaneous belongings, cigarillo stubs and empty liquor bottles—all the better to offer the correct nonprofessorial impression to anyone who visited them.

Grace's form came into view as she sat on his bed beside him, bathed in sunlight from his single window. Its wrinkled curtains had been flung open for the first time ever, revealing an expanse of slushy alleyway better left unobserved.

Ah. So he was in his bedroom.

He felt muddled, Jack reflected. Also smothered in what felt akin to a triple layer of woolly blankets, making him sweat. His mouth tasted of tree bark and oil slick and toenails.

A memory whacked him upside the head.

"You drugged me!" he accused, pointing. Or at least trying to point. His myriad blankets stifled his movements, making it necessary to burrow his way impatiently from beneath them. At such vigorous movement, something poked him. He slapped at his chest and discovered…a lady's brooch? Jack plucked at it in disbelief. "You dressed me like a damned churchgoing matron?"

Grace merely shrugged, carrying on with unwrapping something. A bar of soap. She placed it beside his newly full water pitcher and basin. "I always do exactly what's necessary, Jack. You know that. Now it's time for you to get cleaned up."

Completely astonished and hoping to muster the where-withal to understand what the hell was happening, Jack put his hand to his forehead. A thumb's width of bandages met his fingers.

His plan to spend time with Grace rushed back to him.

So did last night's misgivings about its implementation.

Oblivious to them, Grace held out a dripping cloth. "Here you are. All soaped up for you."

"I'm not a damned infant! I can soap it myself. Wash myself, too. When I choose to." Jack glared at her, attempting to enact a standoff. But he was overwarm. He grabbed the cloth and swiped it over his face. Eyes screwed shut against the stinging soapsuds, he shoved the cloth back for a rinse. He waggled his fingers for its return. He scrubbed again, blinded but grudgingly refreshed. "Did you pile more blankets on me last night while I was drugged?"

He opened his eyes on Grace's amused expression.

"What?" he snapped, gesturing for a towel.

"Nothing." She handed it over primly. She was not likely to be hired at Miss Adelaide's saucy bathhouse anytime soon.

Disgruntled, Jack scrubbed the towel over his face. It scraped over his whiskers and set his hair on end, performing its job admirably as usual. He flung it onto the bed, then met Grace's obviously stifled guffaw.

"What is the matter with you?" he demanded.

"You wash up like a little boy. It's adorable."

He didn't want to be adorable, Jack reminded himself. He wanted to be effective. In the clear light of day, he realized he couldn't shilly-shally around with kissing Grace Crabtree. He had to play matchmaker for her. Immediately and permanently.

One glimpse at his nearby trunk told him there might be a problem with that. Atop it at precise right angles sat a neatly folded blanket and pillow-items, judging by their pristine state, that had been recently employed by his bossy nursemaid.

"Did you stay here last night?"

"Of course." She plucked the towel from beside his blanket-covered hip, not behaving in nearly as tittering and blushing a fashion as a real western man might have warranted. She draped the towel over her arm, then rose with the pitcher and basin and cloth all in hand. Grace beamed at him. "I promised I would take care of you, Jack. How is your head this morning? Do you need more tea?"

He warded her off with both hands. "No tea. Lord knows what I did under its devil influence last night."

Grace laughed merrily. "You couldn't do a thing."

Which only bothered him all the more. For the first time since he truly had been a small boy, Jack felt discomfortingly out of control. Even vulnerable. He didn't like it.

"You have to leave," he said, casting his well-meant plan to the wind. He'd do without it. He got up, hoping that placing both feet—both bare feet?—on the floorboards would increase his authority. At least he was still dressed in his own damned clothes. "You have to go home right now. Your reputation might still be salvaged if you sneak out the back way. I'll show you."

"Oh, I'm not leaving." Looking carefree, Grace waved her arm. Her clothes were disheveled, clearly leftover from yesterday. But she'd managed to redo the tight knot of hair at her crown, giving her a stately air, and her skin glowed with cleanliness, too. "My whole family knows I'm here—in my meeting rooms at least. I sent them a message yesterday. They've long since given up on corralling me into acceptable behavior, you know." She pondered the matter cheerfully. "I believe it was my first few stints in Sheriff Caffey's jail that turned the tide."

Jack didn't know how she could be so blithe. Her attitude was disastrous to his plan, he realized. "No man will marry you with a ruined reputation," he warned. "You ought to—"

"No matter. I've done without a husband quite nicely all this time. Although I begin to believe I've missed out on some wondrous kissing." With a wink, Grace turned smartly, still carrying his washing implements. "Come along. I've made us breakfast. After that, I have a whole regimen of wholesome potions and remedies and exercises for you."

He stared. Clearly, Grace had taken over here. What had happened to his clever plan?

He ought to abandon it, Jack told himself. It had rapidly skedaddled sideways in a manner he hadn't predicted.

On the other hand, it probably wouldn't hurt to have breakfast before making any rash decisions. He ought to keep an eye on Grace, too.

Doggedly and blearily, Jack followed her swishing skirts into a suspiciously clean and unsticky kitchen.

Coffee perfumed the air, making him feel a bit more alert.

"I should consult with Doctor Finney first," he disagreed, cursing the day he'd devised this backfiring scheme to help get Grace married. "He might have other ideas, ideas that aren't—"

"Not to worry." Sunnily, Grace gestured toward a waiting chair. "I asked Doctor Finney about your treatment last night before he left. He's such a dear man. He agreed to everything I suggested as far as your convalescence is concerned."

Jack would just bet he had. Damn the man. The doctor had double-crossed him. Groaning anew, Jack sank onto his chair and put his head in his hands. Those hellfired bandages met his fingertips again, reminding him of the fix he'd gotten into.

He couldn't run his saloon. Couldn't relieve Harry of duty. Couldn't so much as wash himself without Grace Crabtree supervising every facet of his day.

What would she think if he simply tore off those bandages? If he confessed?

If he gave up his plan to get her wed altogether?

Doubtless Grace would sink in the heels of her blasted man-shoes and refuse even more obstinately to move her meeting rooms. Jack would not be able to bring his performing troupe to his saloon. Would not be able to regain his patronage or open the upstairs boardinghouse rooms he wanted. Would not be able to enjoy the new western life he'd worked so hard for.

This time, Jack was well and truly sunk—sunk by his own hand. For the next week at least, he was at Grace's mercy.

Heaven help him.

Chapter Twelve

For the next several days, Grace slept upstairs in her meeting room space, on a cot thoughtfully moved there by her papa and Marcus. She looked in on Jack frequently, bustling in to examine his bandages, deliver a meal or tidy up his messy bachelor rooms—she would swear they disordered themselves between visits while Jack slept. She added his chores to her itinerary, too, dropping by the butcher's, the post office and the laundress on the same schedule as Jack had done.

Not for anything would Grace have admitted knowing that schedule in advance, however. A woman did have to safeguard her pride. Even from a man who had wholeheartedly kissed her. Instead she dutifully pretended to concentrate as she wrote out the list of tasks Jack recited, going so far as to bite her lip in consternation as she struggled to enumerate every one.

It was, Grace decided afterward, a splendid performance.

Despite Jack's obvious—and maddening—skepticism.

Encouraged to do so by Mr. Walsh, Grace did carry on with her typesetting work at the *Pioneer Press* in the afternoons, but she abdicated most of her club and ladies' organization meetings for the time being. She persisted in working toward her various causes on her own, however, writing letters and devising schemes on behalf of the Morrow Creek women's baseball league. Spring was on its way, and she needed to be prepared.

All in all, her days were busy and satisfying. Grace found it fulfilling to be in charge of so many varied doings at once—so much so that she scarcely missed some of her more ancillary activities, such as her women's archery society and her Indian club exercise group. Perhaps Molly and Sarah had been correct. Perhaps she had overcommitted herself. Just a bit.

With that realization in mind, Grace decided to dedicate herself to a few select activities for the time being. Beginning with Jack…and his continued convalescence.

He was a difficult patient, to be sure. In fact, he possessed so much vigor, so much ability to gainsay her remedies and wrestle over the administering of them, that it was sometimes difficult to remember he had been injured at all. Grace even found him sneaking into the saloon to play billiards, snatch cheroots or supervise faro dealing with Harry. Once she caught him lugging in a store of firewood, too, looking astonishingly adept at hauling such a heavy load.

Without Doctor Finney's assurance that Jack required diligent care, Grace might have begun to doubt the necessity of her being there for him. Fortunately, she did have the doctor's blessing—and an able excuse for her presence, too.

Under those terms, Grace indulged her secret desire to be with Jack Murphy. Cloaked under cover of doing her usual good works, she cared for him as often as she could and removed every possible burden from his shoulders—something she felt uniquely equipped to do. Which was how she came to be striding toward Jack's saloon one clear February morning, with his mail in her satchel and her reformer's hat happily squashed on her head.

"Ho, there!" someone called from across the street, surprising her. "Miss Crabtree, over here!"

Half fearing another awkward marriage proposal—of which she'd had admittedly fewer lately—Grace turned. To her immense relief, Jedediah Hofer waved from beneath the awning of his busy mercantile, his ruddy complexion and white-blond hair in stark contrast with his dark suit.

Pleased to see him, she headed in that direction.

"How are you, Mr. Hofer? Business is brisk, I see."

"*Ja,* very brisk. So much that I've had to hire a second assistant!" Mr. Hofer beamed, gesturing toward the people still browsing the wares in his crammed store. Among them were several graying miners and a few cowboys, along with a dandified gambler. "That's why I wanted to call you over here. Grace…"

He paused, his face turning even redder than usual. His cheeks puffed alarmingly, too. Concerned, Grace stepped nearer. "Mr. Hofer, are you all right? You look—"

"Thank you!" He suddenly wrapped her in an impulsive bear hug, murmuring his gratitude all the while. "You have sent so many customers to me! I am in your debt."

"Oh! Well…" Muffled by his shoulder, Grace attempted to nod. This was a great deal of emotion. She wasn't sure she was equipped to cope with it politely. "Yes, I see. If you mean my potential husbands, I suppose I did send a few of them here."

"A few? No! No, there were many. And all of them bought things. Razors, soap, washboards. Readymade clothing. Sweets. Ribbons and cleansers and brooms and mops." Squeezing harder, Hofer laughed with pure joy. He patted her on the back. "You are a good woman, Miss Crabtree. Perhaps a little misunderstood, only, by people who do not see your generosity."

Grace began to feel concerned she might not break free. Ever. "I'm delighted, Mr. Hofer." She squirmed. "Only—"

"Ah, but I am embarrassing you! You are modest!"

"That is not a quality I've had the pleasure of having ascribed to me. However, I'm so pleased that you—"

"See? You are even modest now!" Chuckling, Hofer embraced her again. Over his shoulder, Grace glimpsed several customers pointing and nudging each other. A few grinned. "Thank you, thank you," Hofer said. "If there is ever anything I can do for you, you only have to ask. Jedediah Hofer is at your service."

"That's very kind of you, Mr. Hofer." Torn, Grace hesitated. But if a woman were to be practical... "As it happens, I could use a bit of castor oil and some tea," she proclaimed, hoping her nose wouldn't become permanently crooked from being compacted against Hofer's suit coat. She wiggled it experimentally. "I'm going through both at a fearsome rate. If it's not too much trouble, that is."

"Ah! For you, nothing is too much trouble!"

He released her, sweeping aside other customers with his beefy arms as he led her into the mercantile. Grace followed in his wake, the smells of pickles and rolled calico and wood smoke reaching her instantly. There was nothing homier than a properly run mercantile. She savored the entire enterprise.

Twenty productive minutes later, Grace emerged with her satchel filled to overflowing. The bargains she'd made would keep her supplied with restorative tea for the entire week.

"Thank you!" she called, clutching everything to her middle. "Thank you, Mr. Hofer. You're very kind."

Four pounds of tea and a whole gallon of castor oil.

Jack would be very pleased.

With that thought in mind, Grace journeyed home next. She kept her steps brisk so as to not leave Jack alone for too much longer. Harry had assured her that he looked in on Jack during those times when Grace had errands or work to attend to, but ever since the time she had returned to find them both throwing dice with Daniel, she tried not to linger with her duties.

At the Crabtree household, after a welcoming hug from her mother and a plateful of Cook's best whole-flour Grahamite biscuits with jam, Grace got directly to the point of her visit.

"Your recuperative tea is working wonders," she said pensively, "but I'm wondering if there's something more I could be doing. I have cleaned everything just as you suggested—"

"Pleasant surroundings do enhance healing," Mama agreed.

"—and it was awfully sloppy in there, believe you me!" Grace elaborated, picturing the scene. "Leftover whiskey bottles, piles of cigarillos—which were most peculiar, given that Mr. Murphy does not partake in them—boots and jackets everywhere. It was quite a chore."

Her mama only smiled indulgently. "To think that you never cared much for housework," she commented.

"I've organized everything, too. Alphabetically in the case of the foodstuffs and by color and purpose in the case of the clothing and other items." Grace doled out a small grin. "Mr. Murphy proclaims he can't find a thing anymore. But I know he'll comprehend my classification system with some teaching."

Fiona Crabtree nodded. "Alphabetical, you say? Well, I would expect nothing less of you."

Heartened somewhat, Grace nodded. "I've also made sure that Jack—I mean, Mr. Murphy, of course—keeps himself well bathed with strong soap. And neatly combed and barbered, too."

"That sounds very…civilized."

"Thank you." Grace tilted her head to the side, momentarily silent as she recalled the kerfuffle between her and Jack when she'd attempted to wield his straight razor on him herself. Even now she felt downright astounded at the strength he'd mustered. Most men would not have been so robust while laid low with a head injury. Clearly, Jack was exceptional.

"I've supervised his meals and his liquor intake, allowing only small sips of watered brandy occasionally. And I've kept him warm with myriad blankets at all times." Grace leaned toward her mother, concerned all over again. "He insists they make him sweat," she confided. "Does that mean he's fevered?"

Her mama considered it, looking unconcerned. "Probably not," she said as she perused the biscuit plate. "Not given the other symptoms you described to me yesterday. And the day before. And earlier this week as well."

Too worried to be mollified or concerned with that reminder of her multiple visits, Grace shook her head. "I'm afraid Mr. Murphy won't allow evidence of any weakness to reach me."

"Hmm," Mama mused. "Imagine that sort of stubbornness…"

"Exactly." Grace nodded more vigorously, feeling understood at last. "Also he seems to go out of his way to be contrary. Do you know, he even refused to eat the barley broth I made him?"

At this, her mama froze with her hand partway to a biscuit. She withdrew and stared at Grace. "You made?"

Grace nodded. "I read the recipe in a nutritional pamphlet from the library of the Social Equality Sisterhood. It was a very nourishing combination of turnips and rutabagas and chicken broth, coupled with pearled barley and four pounds of onions."

Her mama widened her eyes. "Four pounds? Goodness!"

"Yes, I cried a river while chopping," Grace recalled. But next she remembered her worry over Jack and rushed to the real reason for her visit. "But nothing is working! I fear my Mr. Murphy will never recover—"

"Your Mr. Murphy?" Again came that knowing smile.

Grace couldn't counter it. "And it will be all my fault for failing to teach him to sled properly on that first run. If only I had exerted my will just a bit more forcefully—"

Her mama appeared to stifle a guffaw.

"—perhaps he would never have been hurt at all!"

Desperately, Grace stared down at her clasped hands. The truth was, she did not know what else to do. She was not by nature a particularly nurturing individual, she feared, and for the first time she felt the lack of that quality.

Women were supposed to be caring and helpful, weren't they? Able to conjure failsafe remedies and kind encouragement and hand-sewn sickroom samplers at a moment's notice, complete with coordinating linens and perhaps a flowered tea cosy.

"I do not," she admitted gravely, "even know how to begin knitting a tea cosy." She did not glance up. "I am...a failure."

For a moment, the only sounds in the parlor were the ticking of the grandfather clock in the corner, the thump and crackle of a log falling into the fire and the distant bustling of Cook preparing lunch in the kitchen. Miserably, Grace waited.

"Oh, Grace," Mama told her quietly. "You are not a failure. No one who loves as deeply as you do could ever be considered a failure at anything." She paused, undoubtedly regarding her in that gentle way she had. "Do you know how rare that is?"

"You don't understand. I'm not helping him!"

Undaunted by that confession, her mama continued. "I

should have known it from the moment you sent that news-boy here for the makings of my special tea." Placidly, she poured more coffee for them both. "You are smitten, Grace. More than that, you are in love with Mr. Murphy. No, don't bother denying it. There's no other reason you would be here right now."

"If you'd only tell me what to do——"

"Why, follow your heart, of course. That usually does the trick." This time, Fiona did choose that biscuit she'd been eye-ing. Leisurely, she applied some jam. "You'll find that——"

"I mean about Jack," Grace interrupted. She felt near to gritting her teeth with frustration. Why would her mama ram-ble on about love and hearts when there were practical concerns to be worked out? "Please, Mama. I'm desperate for your help."

"Which is why I know for certain you do not need it."

Thoroughly baffled, Grace shook her head. "The world has gone mad," she announced. "Jack is delirious, Jedediah Hofer has gone round the bend and both Sarah and Molly give me silly looks when they see me. What is wrong with everyone?"

"Grace." Mama set down her plate, regarding her seri-ously. "Let me ask you one thing, and maybe you will see what I mean." Delicately, she paused, her gaze roving over Grace's face. "How many times have you felt moved to ask me for help?"

"Er…" Grace deliberated. "Umm…I know there must have been several times. When I was small, perhaps, or——"

"The last time you asked me for help," Mama informed her placidly, "was when you were twelve years old and asked me to devise a dress pattern for bloomers."

Grace remembered. She hadn't possessed the patience or skill for seamstress's work, but had dearly coveted her own version of the scandalous garment. "You refused. Likely be-cause you knew I would never be seen in a proper dress again."

"That's right. You would have worn those bloomers—scandalous or not—until they fell off you in rags." Mama gave her a fond smile. "Since then, you haven't asked me for a single piece of advice or help, Grace, no matter how strenuous or challenging the task before you." Momentarily—astonishingly—she seemed almost proud. "Even when you were tossed into Sheriff Caffey's jail, you never wanted us notified. It was a sore challenge to your papa, believe me. Especially that first time."

"He came to collect me, all the same."

"And I'm going to help you now, all the same." Mama gave Grace's hand an affectionate squeeze, then straightened to her usual regal stature. "Love is not bloomers, and you are not the same person you were at twelve. So I hope you'll have a mite more patience when I suggest this to you."

"I will." Fervently, Grace nodded, feeling hopeful. She respected her mama's judgment. She knew she would be grateful for whatever morsel of advice her mama had now. In all eagerness, Grace asked, "What should I do?"

"Stop trying to change Mr. Murphy." Mama stirred her coffee. "A man is who he is, and that's all there is to it. You have to take him as he comes and be happy for it."

Grace stared. A moment passed, ripe with incredulity.

"That's your advice?"

Her mama nodded. "I hope you'll consider it."

"That's truly your advice?"

"It truly is. Believe me, Grace. It only sounds simple. At times I'm sorely challenged to follow it myself."

This time, Grace did gnash her teeth. She could not believe this was what came of asking for help. Nonsensical advice and impractical suggestions, when what she truly needed were clever strategies and prudent measures. No wonder she had avoided it.

It was at that moment, as her teeth ground together and her mama regarded her patiently, that Grace realized the truth.

Perhaps she had overestimated her own ability to handle Jack Murphy, she thought in alarm. Perhaps she had bitten off more than she could chew. Perhaps she never should have agreed to care for him. Perhaps she never should have kissed him.

No, she decided. She couldn't regret the kissing.

She couldn't quite regret the caring either.

What was she going to do?

All amuddle, Grace stood and said her goodbyes to her mother. There would be no further help to be found here. But before she left…

"If you think of any other advice," she said urgently, "please be sure to let me know."

Despite the way she'd initially discounted it, Grace recalled her mama's advice a few days later when she discovered something very unexpected beneath the bar in Jack's saloon.

She understood what her mother had been trying to say, of course. Naturally it was better to accept people as they were. That was exactly the consideration Grace wished the people of Morrow Creek would extend to her more often. But surely, had Fiona understood the potential inherent in the things Grace stumbled onto—and what they implied about Jack Murphy—she would have thought differently. Wouldn't she?

Astonished at her findings, Grace sneaked a quick glance around the saloon. It was dark and shuttered, unlit except by the single oil lamp she'd carried from Jack's quarters in the back room. She'd only meant to grab some brandy for a nightcap with Jack—a watered nightcap, of course—but instead she'd found this. An entire sheaf of papers, jutting from a cubby between the bar cloths and the extra tequila, just begging to be found.

Biting her lip, Grace looked over her shoulder. She listened. No rumblings came from Jack's rooms. She'd left him grumpily perusing a Jane Austen novel, which she'd brought with a mind toward continuing her broad-mindedness scheme but which she had employed as an ordinary diversion instead.

Poor Jack seemed woefully bored of late, resentful of being kept still and hungry for the outdoors. He'd certainly told her often enough that he wished he were "out hunting bear" or "climbing a blasted mountain" instead of being cooped up.

The remembrance of that made her smile. She could not quite picture Jack cornering a black bear or scaling the territory's northern peaks, but she had admired the winning way he flexed his muscles while describing those things. She had been most impressed with his imitation of a fierce hunter, too.

Confident he was still comfortably settled and usefully occupied with his reading, Grace again spread her hands over the papers she'd found. She held her breath, studying them. The first was a beautiful drawing, technical in nature, depicting what seemed to be a mechanical device for pouring whiskey.

The drawing held all sorts of numbered parts and diagrams. It included meticulously detailed views of the device's workings from both sides, the front and the back. As much as she looked, Grace could detect neither a trademark symbol nor a patent notice. The image did not include a company letterhead or even the designer's signature at its bottom.

Mystified but intrigued, Grace turned over the sheet to reveal the next page. It contained another drawing, this one of a device that seemed—to her untrained eyes—to be intended for use in a lumber mill such as Marcus's. It featured pulleys and wheels and long-bladed saws in an intricate combination, along with the same multiple views the first drawing had shown.

Clearly, Grace reasoned, Jack possessed an admiration

and an eye for art—one that had gone heretofore unde-
tected. Otherwise why would he have saved these very inventive drawings? Most likely, they'd been left behind by a
visitor to his saloon, and Jack hadn't been able to throw
them out.

Wiser now in the ways of Jack Murphy, Grace gave a perceptive glance to his bawdy over-the-bar oil painting. She
suddenly comprehended that frolicking water nymph for the
ploy she truly was—an attempt to hide Jack's cultured side.

Smiling, Grace nodded. She couldn't say she felt entirely
surprised. She examined the water nymph again, satisfied
with her conclusions. She'd known all along there was more
to Jack than could be seen at first glance. Doubtless that explained why she pondered him so often herself…and why she
found him so very fascinating, too.

The next drawing was of something familiar—a single fas-
tener for a pair of men's braces. Instantly, Grace could see it
was cleverly designed, its features making it more durable
and functional than most. It looked to be convertible, too, although she couldn't quite make out—no matter how she
turned the drawing—exactly how such a marvel would work.
Something about its design niggled at her….

Pondering the matter, Grace glanced up, wishing she had
someone to share her findings with. The saloon lay silent
though, as it always did on Sundays. Even Harry was not in
his usual place behind the bar. She would have liked to ask
him about the drawings. They really were extraordinary.
She'd only seen their like in books, never in person.

No wonder Jack had thought so highly of them. Appreciation of artistic talent was something the two of them had in
common.

Carefully, Grace rerolled the papers. Then she collected a
bottle of brandy and a pair of glasses, and headed back to

Jack's rooms. This time, she might add a bit less water to Jack's nightcap…and learn a few more things in the process.

Deeply embroiled in the adventures of Elizabeth Bennet and Fitzwilliam Darcy, Jack didn't realize Grace had returned until she clunked two heavy-bottomed glasses on the table beside him and added a bottle of his best brandy.

Instantly, he schooled himself into a deep frown and aimed his displeasure at his book, making his forehead wrinkle beneath its wrapping of unneeded bandages. Moving his lips silently, Jack pretended to struggle over the next passage—one he particularly liked under ordinary circumstances.

It would not do for Grace to realize as much, however. Jack still had his nonprofessorial western persona to maintain. For the sake of hiding his past, he had to appear rugged, rough and completely uninterested in things like literature—especially literature about men and women falling in love.

"Enjoying your book?" Grace asked cheerfully.

Jack grunted. He decided he might never surrender that useful all-purpose reply. It had proven far too handy to be laid aside.

After dashing to the kitchen for water, Grace drew a chair closer to the fire. Purposefully, she slid it nearer to him. As usual, she fussed over the maneuver, making sure the chair was evenly aligned and plumped before turning to the brandy.

Glasses and bottle clinked. Shortly, the liquor's heady aroma wafted across the pages Jack still pretended to ponder. With Grace in the room, he could scarcely read at all. If he did, he inevitably became pulled into the story and was completely unable to maintain his pretense of reluctance.

Once or twice, Grace had even caught him chuckling over a particularly witty passage. Her sharp-eyed glance had been a warning he'd tried to heed ever since.

There was a rustling, then Grace sat. For a few moments

they remained in place, Jack concentrating on moving his lips as absurdly as possible while reading—and sometimes grumbling—Grace waiting, plainly, for him to reach a stopping point. He could almost feel her impatience, buzzing from her chair to his like one of her damned dark-hooded, red-backed Juncos.

"Jack?"

"Hmm."

"There's something I want to ask you about."

He closed his book, then lay it aside with a fairly good approximation of relief. "If it's another vocabulary quiz, Grace, I've had enough. It's late." Also he meant to devote the rest of the evening to uncovering her romantic inclinations, a task he'd only accomplished a little of. "Why don't we—"

"No, it's about these," Grace interrupted.

Her face shining in the firelight, she lifted a bundle from her lap. She leaned forward, alert with interest and curiosity…and a determination Jack recognized all too well.

Then he glimpsed the papers she held, and everything changed. The firelight brightened, the glass in his hand chilled, his breath stopped. For an instant, it was all Jack could do not to bolt from his chair and snatch them away.

"What about those?" he managed.

"Well, I found them by accident behind the bar, and I was wondering… Did a drummer leave them at the saloon by mistake? Or some other traveler? An inventor perchance?"

Uncomfortably, Jack remained silent.

"I can certainly see why you kept them," Grace nattered on, gesturing, "but they look valuable to me. Someone is probably missing them. Perhaps I should post a notice in the *Pioneer Press?* I'm sure Mr. Walsh would agree that…"

She went on, but Jack could hardly listen. His whole body tautened as he clenched his brandy more tightly. Visions of his past unraveling in the pages of the town newspaper swirled before him. Remembrances of his very public debacle in Boston assaulted him, too. Before, publicity had cost him his reputation and livelihood alike. This time…

"Why would you do that?" he demanded.

Obviously taken aback at his abrupt tone, Grace hesitated. Her gaze darted from his brandy to his abandoned book. Then, evidently deciding he must still be grouchy from his enforced literature appreciation session, she brightened.

"In case we could return these drawings to their proper owner, of course. In certain instances, Papa even has the capacity to wire notices to other newspapers all across the territory. The country even. I'm sure he'd give permission to do so." She glanced at the papers. "These are extraordinary."

At her praise, the tightness in Jack's chest eased a fraction. His past faded by degrees.

"Are they?" He made himself suck down the remaining half of his brandy. Its warmth spread through him. "Extraordinary?"

"Of course!" Grace shook her head as though unable to believe he'd find them otherwise. "Here, look at the detail. The richness of scale and quality. The surety of the strokes." She beamed at the whole lot like a proud explorer. "Whoever drew these will certainly want them back."

Warmed by more than his liquor now, Jack gazed at her in wonderment. This complicated things greatly, he realized. But somehow, he couldn't find it in himself to be sorry. Not while Grace held his schematics in her careful fingers…not while she regarded the lot of them with such awe in her expression. Not even the widow Marjorie Lancaster, his most ardent supporter in Boston, had viewed his work with so much admiration.

A part of him felt glad Grace had found them.

Those drawings, it occurred to him with a surge of pleasure, were among the most genuine parts of him she'd seen.

"I haven't examined them all yet," Grace was saying, deftly laying aside the first two schematics. "I wanted to bring them back here where the light was better." She bent her head over the next paper to be uncovered. "Ooh, look. This one is—"

She paused, her finger hovering over the paper. Her gaze skated from the drawing depicted there to his face, then back again. Her cheeks pinkened prettily.

"But this—" Looking confounded, Grace stared again. "I don't understand. This bustle contraption with the lifting mechanism attached...the model for it looks somewhat—" Gamely, Grace tried again. "Well, I know it sounds absurd, especially since she's holding a spyglass, but she almost seems—"

"It's you." Jack finished his brandy. He lifted the bottle and pointed it toward Grace. "Shall we have another?"

Chapter Thirteen

If not for the caution Jack had learned during his first hard-scrabble days in the territory, he would have grinned unabashedly at the look on Grace's face. For once, he had surprised her. Doing so felt better than...

Well, better than playacting at being incapacitated for the sake of staying next to her did, that was for certain.

She stared at the drawing. "It's me?"

"Yes." Hell, he might as well come out with it all. He'd come this far. "When I had the idea for the noiseless bustle buckler," Jack explained, "meant for use by female ornithologists in the field who did not want to scare away...oh, let's just say the dark-hooded, red-backed Junco, for example's sake, you seemed a natural model."

Grace's gaze met his. She seemed wholly unable to speak. Her brow furrowed in consternation. "But this model—" she gestured to the paper "—is beautiful."

Jack shrugged. "So?"

"So you are teasing me." But her eyes said she hoped he wasn't.

"Believe what you want." Jack spread his arms, experiencing a certain reckless freedom now that one of his secrets was out. "I know you will, no matter what I say."

"Of course I will. But—but—"

He rose, gulped the remainder of his brandy, then set the glass aside. He scooped up the telltale drawings. "But you were never meant to find these. They're a diversion, nothing more."

The moment the papers left her lap, Grace recovered. She bolted upright, her gaze fastened on the bundle.

"I've seen you scribbling before." She all but pounced on him as she considered everything she'd learned. "I thought you were wasting time, the way you're prone to do!"

Jack arched his brow. "Wasting time?"

"You must admit, you enjoy far too much leisure as it is." Grace watched with plain dismay as he rerolled the drawings. "Your whole life—your livelihood!—is devoted to pleasure. And you enjoy it far too much for a man of your position."

"My position?"

"And your potential."

"Potential?"

She paid his questions no mind at all, so fixed was she on the papers in his hand. "What are you planning to do with those?" Grace demanded.

This time, Jack couldn't hide his grin—but he could turn away before she saw it. "Find a better hiding place."

"No!" Grace followed him, clutching at his sleeve. "Wait. I haven't even seen them all yet."

"That's just as well."

"Please!" Impatience blanketed the word. "You can't seriously think to keep those from me. After all this time, I have learned that you have a talent—an artistic talent just waiting to be nurtured—and you're going to hide it?"

Thoughtfully, Jack gazed at the rolled papers in his hand. "Looks that way. Yep."

She trailed him all the way to the kitchen table, heedless of the determined manner his boots rang across the floorboards. As pleased as Jack was by her interest, he had to be resolute. Nothing good could come of Grace knowing about his drawings—especially given her original intentions to publicize them in her father's newspaper. The less she saw of them, the better.

What he'd said was true, Jack reflected. Those drawings—and the inventions they depicted—were only a diversion. They could be nothing more, not after everything that had happened in Boston. He had tried to resist drafting them. But he'd failed.

No matter how hard he'd strived to leave all his past behind him—giving away his fine suits, hiding his books, grunting and simplifying his speech—Jack had proven woefully unable to do one thing: quiet his mind.

It chattered at him night and day, tossing out notions for new inventions and improvements on the things he worked with and myriad wild ideas. It harped especially strongly whenever someone he knew encountered a problem and confided it in him—hence the schematics for an automatic log-splitting device for Marcus's lumber mill and the silent bustle buckler for Grace's ornithology club members, among others.

At first Jack had endeavored to ignore those urgings. But, like his pestering attraction toward Grace Crabtree, they had proven too fierce to be denied. So he had scribbled a few of them during slow times at the saloon, or late at night when he couldn't sleep, and stuffed them all away in his cubbyhole. He'd never intended anyone to find them.

He might have known Grace would have.

Stubbornly beside him, she tried to wrest his arm downward, making the sheaf of papers rattle. "Just let me see them all first. I want to tell you if they're any good."

Jack almost took the bait. Instantly, indignation rose in him. Of course they were good. He might be a western man now, but once he'd been a very successful—no. He had to re-main firm.

"The few I saw looked brilliant," Grace coaxed as though sensing his indecision. "I had no idea you had such raw talent."

Raw? Incredulous, Jack hesitated further. He cast Grace a measuring look, taking in her blooming cheeks, her bright eyes, her barely parted mouth. He remembered his plans for the night.

He decided to continue them.

"I'll let you have another look," he conceded, twisting his arm to hold his drawings behind his back. "If you can remem-ber you want to view them at all…after this kiss."

Her eyes widened. She recognized his challenge then.

"All right," Grace bargained after a minute. "But you'll have to tell me why I'm pictured in one of those drawings, too. In detail. And don't tell me it was because I was beauti-ful," she scoffed, "because I'm too sensible to believe it."

An urge to argue struck him. Jack tightened his mouth against it. He did find her beautiful, in person and in ink. But there was no sense saying so. His hand-drawn rendition of Grace, outfitted in his noiseless bustle buckler, rose in his mind. He'd drawn her as the model because…because…

Damn it. Just because she'd been in his thoughts.

And often was. More than he was willing to admit.

And had been, for a far longer time than he'd say.

Not that those details would matter. Grace would never have a chance to learn them once he started kissing her again.

Assured, Jack nodded. "Done. Now let's get you settled."

He set aside his rolled drawings to a nearby kitchen shelf, noting Grace's yearning glance toward them. *Extraordinary,* she'd called them. *Brilliant.* However unwittingly, Grace had admired the real him. The secret, wholly authentic him. For that, he decided, she deserved an especially worthy kiss.

"What are you waiting for?" she prodded.

He grinned. "Eager, are you?"

"Impatient," she countered smartly. "Our nightly political discussion awaits, you know, just as it does every evening. I'd hate to see us miss such a lively experience, given how much it's broadened your outlook already."

"I'll try to keep this lively then," he promised. "Maybe it will prove a fair substitute."

Jack found himself smiling, anticipating, even as he slid his hand to Grace's cheek and stepped nearer. Her skirts brushed his knees, sober today in shades of brown and white, like cream poured into coffee. He tilted her face up, gazing into her eyes.

What he saw there spurred him further. Jack would swear his heart opened wide in that moment, however poetic and unlikely it sounded. "Ah." He paused. "This is lively already, I'd say."

Grace's expression agreed. She leaned closer.

It was time. Jack's mouth touched hers, and all the floorboards rocked. Sucking in her breath, her fragrance, her spirit, he spread his feet wide for balance.

Something about Grace set him akilter every time, making her the only solid thing in a world turned dizzying. Her warmth slid over him. Her hands touched his shoulders as she strove to tiptoe higher…nearer. Their kiss ended too soon.

Her dark gaze met his. She seemed bedazzled for a moment. She smiled. "Now may I see your drawings?"

Jack shook his head. He refused to believe he was the only one affected by their kisses. He could not be. Not while Grace looked at him that way…not while she clutched at him so eagerly. He slid his hands to her waist, enjoying its subtle curve beneath his fingers.

"I'm not done yet," he told her.

"Oh." The firelight shimmered over her face, wrapping them both in a sultry glow. It made Grace look lovely, even as she furrowed her brow. "Perhaps we should enlist some parameters then. Exactly how many kisses do you intend to trade for a viewing of your drawings?" she asked. "Because I feel I could safely withstand—I mean, one or two seems more than fair."

"I'm not interested in parameters."

"Hmm. Well, if you're curious, a parameter is defined as a fact or circumstance intended to restrict—"

"I know what it means." Jack tightened his grasp and lifted her, setting her neatly atop the kitchen table. She squealed, but he paid no mind. "There," he said in his gruffest voice. "That's better. Now I can reach you properly." He grinned. "Without your man-shoes, you're just not as tall."

Grace scoffed, her eyes wide. "This won't do! You—your—" She gaped as he stepped even closer, directly between her skirt-covered knees. She appeared to muster a stern expression. "You have an unfair advantage."

"I never said this would be fair." Jack kissed her again.

This time, he coaxed open her mouth immediately, hungry for a deeper taste. Grace obliged despite everything, her hands closing around his ears. She tugged at his lobes, holding him steadily to her. It was an unusual approach, but effective.

"Why are you grinning?" she demanded, peering at him.

"Because you kiss the same way you do everything else." He hugged her closer, his arms firm around her waist. "Bossily."

For an instant, Grace looked offended. Then she smiled in an utterly brash manner. "I daresay you can withstand that."

"You'd better believe I can."

Jack kissed her again, pouring all his feelings—all his need—into giving Grace pleasure. He swallowed her breathy cries, welcomed the helpless squeeze of her knees against his hips, stroked her hair. All he wanted, all he needed, was to stay here exactly like this.

With Grace. Together.

Encouraged by her smiles, her whispered compliments, her free response, Jack pressed nearer. The table edge pushed at his thighs; a nearby peach tin rolled and thumped to the floor. Neither of them cared. He lost himself in Grace again and again, bracing his palm flat against the tabletop to support both of them. With a glance to Grace's flushed face and closed eyes, he brought his mouth to her arched neck and kissed her there, too.

"Mmm. Delicious." He smiled as she fluttered her eyelashes, then fisted her hand in his shirt to hold him close. He nuzzled her again, thoroughly enjoying himself. "You taste—" Jack sampled again, her smooth skin touching his tongue "—like everything I've ever wanted. Ah, Grace. You're remarkable."

Moaning sweetly, she trailed her hands upward. Her touch on his chest, his shoulders, was like a blessing. Jack could scarcely believe he found himself here…with Grace. Eagerly, she grabbed a fistful of his hair, tugging passionately.

"Oh, Jack! I don't—oh, my." She sighed, tipping her head back with abandon. She wiggled, making the kitchen table creak beneath her. "Please, you really ought to—I mean—"

He'd never known her to be at a loss for words. That she was right now gave Jack a fierce sense of protectiveness. Even gratitude. He doubted anyone had gotten this close to Grace before…and he knew no one had gotten this close to him.

"Ought to what?" he urged. The inquiry required all his effort. He only wanted to kiss her more thoroughly, to touch her everywhere, to forget every contention that had ever lain between them and savor this moment instead. Jack slipped his hand to her high-buttoned shirtwaist collar. Deftly, unable to help himself, he slid the top button free. "Tell me, Grace. Tell me."

Another button came free. Then a third. Jack regarded the bare skin he'd revealed with reverence—and desire. He spread the gap wider, then kissed her there, making her gasp.

"Ought to do something about all this." Impatiently, Grace wriggled on the table, her body arching upward to meet his. "I'm not sure—perhaps you're not kissing me properly." Her breath panted across his neck as she twisted his hair harder. "I feel as though there really ought to be more, Jack."

He smiled manfully. "There is. I promise."

"Oh." Her hand roved higher, doubtless ruffling his hair beyond recognition. "Then I insist you should—"

All at once she stopped. Her eyelids popped open with almost comic suddenness. Tentatively, she probed at his head.

"Should do what?" Jack asked, feeling equally needful. He knew there was something about this kissing business he ought to have remembered, some purpose to it he'd set out with. But he couldn't quite recall what it was. Also he seemed to remember having begun this evening with a plan of some sort, but that was lost to him, too. "Do what, Grace? What do you want?"

Something was wrong. Grace had quit squirming, quit sighing, quit tossing her head back like the sauciest of coquettes. As much as Jack missed those things, he missed knowing she was with him—truly with him—even more.

Confused, he squeezed her.

"You must still be delirious," she announced, her appalled gaze going straight to his. She snatched her fingers away from his bandages, obviously having just encountered them again. "You don't know what you're doing."

"I know what I'm doing. I intend to do much more of it."

He met her dubious look with a confident one of his own.

Jack meant every word. He wanted to revel in the togetherness he felt with Grace. Wanted to indulge in all his old fancies of having her in his arms, eager and ready and wanting him in return. He wanted to kiss her till she gazed at him with stars in her eyes and a smile on her lips and announced that he was the man she needed—exactly as he was.

Or pretended not to be. Damnation, this was a muddle.

"No." Grace shook her head. "I'm afraid I can't allow that." Astonishingly, she hoisted her fabric-frothed skirts and wiggled backward. She slid from the table to the floor beside him in one adroit move. "I will not have you risk your health with this…this overexertion, Jack. I will not. What kind of caretaker would I be then?"

Jack tried a rascally grin. "Every man's favorite kind?"

For an instant, Grace almost seemed persuaded by his smile.

But then—disappointingly—she brushed her hands together.

"You need more tea," she announced with vigor. "I will brew a pot for you right now. With extra castor oil!"

Then, leaving Jack gawking in her wake, Grace bustled to the cast-iron stove and proceeded to do exactly that.

Over the next few days, Grace noticed, Jack achieved a near-miraculous recovery. He even sent for Doctor Finney and convinced the old sawbones to remove his bandages. To her surprise, Jack's head had seemed as good as new afterward, looking as handsome and undented as it ever had.

Jack winked. "I guess I'll try sledding again."

"Not unless you let me steer!" Grace replied.

Then, while he and the doctor finalized their arrangements, she scurried to alphabetize Jack's incoming post and her own by return address. But although Grace sat firmly at the makeshift desk she'd arranged, she was scarcely able to read the writing on the envelopes for the relieved tears in her eyes.

Privately, Grace credited Jack's mended condition to the healing power of love—and a great deal of fortifying tea, which she'd been pouring down his gullet by the potfull ever since their rousing encounter atop the kitchen table. Publicly, she merely explained that Mr. Murphy was "improving by the day," which neatly allowed her to carry on seeing him.

It was gratifying to know that she hadn't lost her knack for obtaining what she wanted…no matter how addled she felt these days whenever Jack smiled at her or touched her hand.

"Then your plan is working?" Molly asked as the three sisters strolled to the Crabtree household the next week for a family visit. "Mr. Murphy is becoming more liberal-minded?"

Sarah perked up interestedly. "I might have known you could do it," she said, kicking her boots at the slush. "Is Mr. Murphy prepared to move his saloon to another property already then?"

"Well…we have not come quite so far as that," Grace demurred. "Soon, perhaps. I remain confident."

Despite her efforts, she couldn't quite say Jack had yet become a radical, fully tamed freethinker. And he certainly hadn't volunteered to move his saloon. Although he had gazed at her in a near-poetic fashion while they'd kissed that night. To Grace that counted nearly as well.

"Watch out, Molly." Grace caught her sister's arm, helping her over a patch of icy street. "You should be more careful."

Both her sisters stared at her, Molly with her hand cradled protectively over her abdomen. Sarah smiled.

"What?" Grace demanded, noticing their foolish expressions. "That's my little niece or nephew Molly's carrying. I don't want her to slip and fall. In fact, someone ought to sawdust these passageways regularly." She glanced about the busy street and false-front buildings, rallying her most indignant rabble-rouser's voice. "Doesn't anyone care about the rights of expectant mothers? If women had the vote, I expect they would make such safety procedures mandatory!"

Now Sarah and Molly looked relieved.

"I'll speak to Marcus straightaway," Molly said, moving onward, "about donating some sawdust from his lumber mill."

"And I'll notify Daniel the minute I get home about your impending nuptials," Sarah said, straight-faced as she walked, too. "No doubt you and Mr. Murphy will be inviting the whole family. Once you both stop being so stubborn, that is."

Grace gave her a withering look. "Very funny."

"You can't fool us," Sarah insisted. "You've become downright sentimental, Grace. Ever since you fell in loooove." Skipping ahead, Sarah cast a grinning glance over her shoulder. "Next thing you know, you'll be sewing your own wedding dress."

"Sewing?" Appalled, Grace chased after. "Take that back!"

"I won't." Sarah laughed, throwing her scarf. "It's true."

Several steps behind them, Molly sighed. "Don't run!" she admonished. "Behave yourselves!"

It was an excellent imitation of their girlhood days... until Grace heard one final decree. Just as she rounded the corner, Molly called after them, laughter ringing in her voice.

"Don't be silly, Sarah. You know Grace won't have time to sew a dress," she said, finally joining in. "She'll be too busy embroidering every bit of her trousseau!"

Alarmed by her sisters' teasing, Grace immediately and diligently resumed several of her least conventional activities.

Rather than embroider, she oiled bicycle parts with the members of the Morrow Creek Bicycling Association. Rather than sew her own wedding dress—as Molly and Sarah so aughingly predicted—she lugged home books from the library of the Social Equality Sisterhood and read each one straight through. Rather than bow to traditionalism or sentimentality, she wore all her most radical reformer's hats, one after the other.

And rather than dreamily contemplate the excellence of Jack Murphy's kisses, Grace devoted herself to perfecting her snowshoeing skills. It was a meager substitute, she knew. But her newfound absentmindedness would stand no chance when stacked against strict hours of practice, she reasoned.

So each afternoon, Grace trod a path outside of town. Through the wind-scoured ponderosa pines, over the hills and along the iced-over pond she went, her woven snowshoes clomping, till she panted for breath and even her eyelashes felt frozen.

Unfortunately, her practice did not lessen the urge she felt to sigh over Jack Murphy's smile, his eyes or his shoulders. It did, however, leave Grace little time to indulge overmuch in such things. For that she felt grateful.

Until, that is, the day she arrived to find the Irish rascal himself standing on her familiar trail, waiting with a pair of sporting implements slung over his brawny shoulder.

"You," he announced, "are being foolish."

"Of course I'm not." It never occurred to Grace to claim anything less. "Everyone knows that vigorous activity is the best remedy for daydreaming. Therefore I was simply—"

His smile quirked. "I meant that you should have company on these excursions of yours. It's not safe for a woman alone."

"Oh. Of course." Caught off balance by Jack's unexpected appearance and by the fact that she'd very nearly admitted to mooning over him, Grace adjusted her hat. "But it's perfectly safe for me. You needn't worry." She mustered a smile, hoping to hide her discomfiture at being discovered in so private

a place. "Good day, Mr. Murphy. I'll let you get on with you
business."

She moved sideways, gesturing as though to dismiss the
both. Then Grace waited, afraid that if he stood there muc
longer she might do something truly foolish…such as sig
over how handsome Jack appeared in his coat and fla
brimmed hat.

He didn't so much as step aside at her motion, not for th
sake of business nor gentlemanly courtesy. Instead he eye
her bundled-up form, her snowshoes and the woods surround
ing them.

My, his eyes were blue today….

"I've come to invite you ice-skating," he said.

She goggled. "Ice-skating?"

"I know you don't have blades, so I brought these." An
other grin as Jack lofted pair of weather-beaten iron blade
"The same size as mine, the better to fit on your man-shoes.

She frowned at her feet. "But I'm already snowshoeing.

"Easily remedied."

Taking her arm, he led her to a nearby log. With scarcel
a moment to examine her snowshoe fittings, Jack unbuck
led them.

"You're very adept with your hands," she observed.

His next smile, wicked and knowing alike, weakened he
knees. It was fortunate she was already sitting, Grace decide
although she couldn't quite recall how she'd come to be i
such a compliant position. It was very unlike her.

Before she'd quite reasoned it out sufficiently, Jack ha
outfitted her with one pair of the skates he'd brought. Admir
ingly, she wiggled her foot, turning it to test the weight of th
blades and the snugness of their leather straps.

"From Daniel's smithy," Jack told her, watching.

He checked her skates' fit, then nodded in satisfaction. Sh

ould scarcely recall seeing him so assured, so tall, so un-
bashedly masculine. Perhaps the effect owed itself to the
outdoors, Grace mused. That or her own susceptibility.

Their kisses had changed things, after all.

Dreamily, she watched as Jack took his place beside her
on the log. His legs flexed as he lifted them to attach blades
to each big boot. His fingers worked with fascinating dexterity.

He stood, then nodded to the pond just distant. "Let's go."

At once, the reality of her situation descended. "Oh, no,
thank you," Grace blabbered, reaching with awkward hands
to wrangle with her borrowed skates. She spied her snowshoes propped against the log's edge. How had they gotten
here? "I really must get back to my snowshoeing practice.
You see, my club is relying on me to lead our next trek, and
I should—"

"You don't know how to ice skate, do you?"

He sounded amused by the realization. Ignoring his
crossed arms and shrewd look, Grace attempted to remove
her skates.

"As it happens," she informed him, "I don't need to
now. After all, Morrow Creek has no women's ice-skating
association."

"You've never started one?"

"No, because I can't—" Skate. She refused to admit as
much. It went against every part of her. "Can't abide skating."

She felt Jack's contemplative gaze on her, even as she continued to wrestle with her skate fittings. Suddenly, he took her
arms and hoisted her to her feet. Grace wobbled mightily, clutching his coat for balance. When she finally glanced up, his face
loomed, rugged and familiar and disconcertingly appealing.

He held her arms securely. "Let me teach you."

Goodness, but his grasp was strong. His voice had turned
luring, too, his brogue deepening on those few words alone.

Grace gulped. "Thank you, but I'm very happy snowshoe ing."

"Take my hand. We'll step to the ice's edge together."

"Mr. Murphy, I try not to make a fool of myself."

"It's only me," he said inanely, then stepped outward a pace. Stranded at the very edge of his grasp, Grace wavered. Her ankles felt as unsteady as her fluttering heart suddenly did.

Jack let go.

Grace wobbled, watching in disbelief as he took another pace away from her. How could he leave her stuck this way?

From the edge of the ice, Jack regarded her. Tenderness suffused his expression. Certainty, too. "You'll like it."

Indeed she would not! She'd found the only man in all of Morrow Creek who dared naysay her, Grace fumed. She balled her gloved fists, glaring at him. This was ridiculous, equipping her with ice skates and then leaving her to maneu ver in them alone.

She would make a cake of herself for certain.

If Jack had not been so charming, in fact, she'd never have allowed events to progress this far, Grace assured herself.

"Try it. I won't believe you can't ice-skate till I see it with my own eyes." Jack pushed sideways, moving on the ice in a single powerful motion. It was galling. "I'll help you."

All of her rebelled at the notion. Except…

Except she did wish she could skate like that. A women's ice-skating association might be just the thing for next year.

With trepidation, Grace examined the slick surface. "I pre fer snowshoeing." Something else caught her eye. A shovel propped on a nearby tree trunk. "Did you shovel this pond?"

Seeming abashed, Jack peered at his upturned blade.

"Did you shovel this pond for me?" she persisted.

"You'll never know," he relented grudgingly, "if you don't come out here with me."

The gruffness in his tone made her smile.

"I think you shoveled this pond for me," Grace announced.

He didn't deny it. "I'll hold on to you the whole time." Again Jack reached out his arm for her. Holding it outstretched, he skated to the very edge of the pond. "I'll keep you safe."

Somehow the rebuttal Grace might ordinarily have made caught in her throat. As odd as it seemed, she believed that Jack would keep her safe…that he would protect her and stay beside her, for as long as she would allow.

"Don't move," she commanded. "I'm coming."

The few steps required to reach him took forever. Grace concentrated on the forward progress of her feet, listening as her blades punched through the snow. One more. Nearly there…

Then Jack's brawny arms enfolded her. So did the scents of fresh air, damp wool and—oddly—tobacco. Warmth passed from him to her, making her cheeks tingle. Stubbornly, Grace clung to him as little as she dared. Letting go altogether felt impossible.

"I'm as wobbly as a newborn foal," she complained.

"All you need is practice." Jack nudged her chin with his thumb, bringing her face to meet his. "The first few steps are the hardest. Now lean into me and push with your right foot."

The moment he shifted position, Grace's balance deserted her. She flailed madly, only to find that Jack still held her securely with his hands on her upper arms. He'd only given her a bit of room to maneuver and was—aggravatingly enough—skating backward while he guided her. Pursing her lips, she pushed off.

He nodded. "Now the next foot. Follow me."

"No." But Grace did it all the same. She clutched Jack's shoulders, her whole body stiff. But then… "Look! I glided!"

Jack only nodded. "Keep going. You're doing fine."

"I'm doing wondrously!" She could scarcely believe her own agility. She concentrated on Jack's movements, rapidly learning to discern which way she was supposed to move next. "I can feel your shoulders bunch up, then you lean back a bit—"

Fascinated by the wonderful flex and tug of his muscles, Grace forgot what she was saying. For a saloonkeeper, she decided, Jack Murphy boasted an unusual quantity of brawn.

He caught her ogling and laughed outright.

Affronted, Grace walloped him with her scarf.

"Careful," he warned, giving her arm a teasing squeeze. "Reformer's garb like yours has been known to injure a man."

"Not a big, strong man like you," she argued.

"Ah, Grace." Guiding them both across the ice, Jack cupped her cheek in his hand. He gazed at her, finally releasing a sigh. "When it comes to you, I'm not so very strong after all."

His admission moved her. Especially given, as it was, while the wind tossed their coats and the snowy trees slipped past and Jack's very strength in keeping them both upright proved him wrong in his claim. He was strong, Grace realized.

He was strong and brave and powerful enough to risk shoveling an entire pond for a woman who might easily have been too obstinate to appreciate the gesture. To try something new.

To try and falter and, in the end, do everything but swoon.

"Let's go around another time," Grace said.

Jack peered at her. "Another ladies' club brewing?"

"Mmm. Perhaps," was all she said. Because if things went well, Grace dared to hope, she might not need so many clubs in her future. But not even a certain Irish rogue's kiss could have made her admit such a girlish wish aloud.

Chapter Fourteen

~~~~~~~~~~~~~~~~~~~~~~

After her skating lesson with Jack, Grace found herself enjoying the rest of February in a way she never had before. The weather was wintry, as usual, the winds blustery and cold, but the sun came out every day all the same—as it often did in the territory—and so did Jack. To see her.

Now when they passed on the street, they shared a secret smile and sometimes brushed gloved hands together in hello. When they emerged from their shared building at the same time—as they were magically wont to do—they stopped to talk and laugh and steal a kiss in the shadow of the stairs. When they heard each other moving about late at night, practicing their individual duties, they often quit those tasks altogether…and met for a heady conversation instead.

"Hmm." Jack paused in the passageway between his saloon and his living space one afternoon, looking Grace up and down. He seemed especially handsome in his shirtsleeves and vest, all dark-haired and broad-shouldered and smiling at her in that unique way he had. "Grace, I didn't expect to see you here."

"Oh, no?" Demurely, Grace produced a note from the pocket

of her dress—an ordinary one, not chosen for its practicality and utility but instead for the way Jack had once said it made her eyes look pretty. "Then I suppose this note is a code. Tell me, Jack. Where it says *meet me at four,* does that mean—"

"It means I'm glad you came," he said and kissed her.

Exactly as she'd known he would.

He surprised her in other ways though. Jack's vocabulary improved steadily, augmented with words Grace could not remember having taught him—but which she must have, she reasoned. His demeanor progressed rapidly, featuring more talking—but with a quantity of grunting nonetheless.

His views on subjects ranging from literature to science to history astounded her—but whenever she pressed him on them, Jack merely blinked as though taken aback to hear himself expressing such notions…then pulled her near for another seductive kiss.

It was as if he could not get enough of them.

Which, Grace had to admit, did not bother her as much as perhaps it ought to have, given her avowed intellectual stance.

But then…several things changed for her during those weeks, and her analytical outlook was the least of them. Somehow, Jack learned that she enjoyed Molly's cinnamon buns. He arranged to have a whole dozen delivered to her as a gift, wrapped in a vivid blue bow and sprinkled with extra sugar.

"Mmm." Grace sucked cinnamon from her fingertip, heartily enjoying her second bun. She scooted closer to Jack on the newly shoveled steps leading to her meeting rooms, regarding him with evident fondness. "Delicious. I can't imagine how you knew I enjoyed these so much." She paused. "Aren't you having one?"

"Maybe when I'm done watching you have yours."

"Oh?" She nudged the box across her lap in open invitation. "But you look awfully hungry to me."

Jack raised an eyebrow. "I am. But not for sweets."

Then he pulled her closer and kissed her, right there in broad daylight. His touch melted the sugar on her lips. Licking them eagerly afterward, Grace was abashed to find Jack watching her with an even more devilish expression.

"Next time," he promised, "two dozen cinnamon buns."

Grace only smiled and devoured another bite.

Not that Jack's new thoughtfulness was confined to treats alone. He also learned that she enjoyed attending the spelling bees and recitals down at Sarah's schoolhouse, and waylaid her one evening when Grace had walked only halfway there.

"A spelling bee is better shared," he announced in cocksure tones, giving her a wink. He took her arm and escorted her through the snow, cheerfully ignoring Grace's astonished look.

The two of them scrunched onto short benches at the back of the schoolhouse like overgrown children. Jack left his arm chivalrously around her shoulders, provoking more than one whisper from the townspeople nearby—and a few approving nods as well. Grace couldn't help but snuggle closer, feeling wanted and appreciated for herself at long last…and less like an overlooked spinster than ever she'd dreamed.

There was something marvelous about having someone special to share things with, Grace thought happily, watching Jack applaud a particularly spectacular effort at the word *quixotic*. Someone special like Jack, who truly understood her and did not find her peculiar because of her interests or her passions.

"I'll bet you were the best speller in all the territory when you were a girl," he judged, leaning near to whisper in her ear during a break in the spelling bee. "I can picture it now. I'll bet you beat everyone plumb easily."

"Of course I did. But it wasn't easy."

Jack nodded, his dark hair tickling her cheek. "I reckon so," he agreed. "Nothing worth having is ever easy."

Then he straightened to watch Eli and several of his schoolmates square off in the next spelling round, looking the perfect gentleman all the while…and oblivious as ever to Grace's pleased contemplation.

There was more to Jack Murphy, she realized, than even she had hoped. More than sparkling eyes and rugged features and a manner as charming as the most blarney-tongued Irishman.

There was kindness. And intelligence. And trust.

Even if Jack could not hide anything to save his soul, Grace recalled with a private smile. It had taken her only a matter of minutes to locate his drawings after Jack had stashed them away that night. She had very much enjoyed perusing those sketches at her leisure later, feeling proud all over again at his level of artistic skill and inventiveness. Not that he would discuss as much with her. Every time Grace broached the subject, Jack grunted his fiercest and swept her off her feet, off to some new adventure or joke or indulgent variety of kissing.

They were alike in surprising ways, the two of them. The fun they both had in attending the spelling bee—and the cider-fueled social afterward—did more than prove it. As did their private ice-skating party a few days later, the intimate poetry reading they conducted next and the sleigh ride they enjoyed.

But she and Jack were different in important other ways, and Grace would never have expected to enjoy those differences quite so much. Jack was stronger than she was, for instance, as evidenced by the burly way he helped crowbar open the hidey-hole where Grace had stowed her contraband baseballs, allowing her to hoard a few stragglers till springtime.

"Interesting tactic," was all he said of her strategy.

He was also funnier than her, and Grace couldn't help laughing at all of his jokes. Who would have expected taciturn Jack Murphy to make the adventures of a dancing frog sound so terribly, madly funny? Not Grace, that was for certain.

She'd only quit chuckling for an instant when she caught Jack smiling at her, his eyes sparkling. "You look beautiful when you laugh," he said, his tone serious.

"Nonsense." She swiped a wayward tear, knowing she must be red-faced and scrunch-nosed and possibly in need of a hankie. "I am many things, but beautiful is assuredly not—"

"You are." He stopped her with a kiss, even though they'd only met for a moment on his snowy saloon steps. Ostensibly they were exchanging neighborly pleasantries. In truth they hadn't been able to resist lingering. Jack leaned on his shovel with no pretense at all of working. "You're beautiful to me."

And Grace had only blushed all the hotter, surprised to find the snowbanks not melting all around them from his warmth.

All that month long, she found herself rushing through her days, dreaming about when she could next be with Jack. His new attentiveness thrilled her; his insight into what she found appealing made her marvel. He even indulged her admittedly unusual interest in all things scientific, when Grace knew perfectly well a brawny, plainspoken man like him probably cared little about new discoveries and spectacular improvements.

But they shared them together all the same.

"Now this is unexpected." Jack handed her the stereoscope, offering her another turn with the viewing device at Jedediah Hofer's mercantile. Usually such things were kept under lock and key. Somehow—undoubtedly though sheer deviltry—Jack had finagled a way to get access for himself and Grace. "You—the redoubtable Grace Crabtree—enjoying an activity that's strictly leisurely."

"My goodness. Redoubtable?" Pleased by his progress, she glanced up. She grasped the device carefully by its handle so that the stereograph card attached to it wouldn't wobble while they completed the transfer. "I'm impressed."

"It means formidable," Jack supplied with a naughty grin as his fingers brushed hers. "Also extraordinary. Just in case you're wondering."

"Yes, I know." Unable to help herself, Grace smiled at him. How could she not, when Jack regarded her so very tenderly, as though she were…precious? "And I'll thank you to quit looking at me as though—" she leaned nearer, feeling scandalized "—as though you would like to kiss me right here!"

"I would," he said bluntly. "Let's. Put that down."

Grace knew she reddened all the way to her toes.

"And besides all that, I'll have you know this device is highly educational, not strictly leisurely." Feeling giddy at Jack's continued sultry perusal, Grace affected her best instructive tone. "The stereoscope is a great invention, one I have the utmost respect and gratitude for."

Demonstrating, she raised it with a flourish.

A slightly wobbly, flustered flourish.

He gave a grunt. "A great invention, you say? I reckon that explains why you squealed with delight when you saw it," Jack guessed, his features deadpan but somehow teasing all the same. "Why you jumped up and down with glee."

"Yes. Well." Doing her best to muster a bit of dignity— however belatedly—Grace peered through the stereoscope's viewfinder. Like magic, a view of a New York City street greeted her, full of tall buildings and myriad traveling buggies. "It just so happens that I often find myself unable to contain my enthusiasm lately…when it comes to certain things at least."

Like you. She dared to glance at Jack as she said it. His gruff nod was all the agreement Grace required. Even the mercantile storeroom seemed romantic when he gazed at her that way, she realized delightedly. All she wanted now was more time with him, alone like this.

"Are there more images?" she inquired.

Obligingly, he reached into the box of stereoscopic cards. After a short perusal, Jack selected one and inserted it into the device's holder with ease. "Try this one. It's a good view."

"For a saloonkeeper," she remarked, watching closely as he surrendered control of the stereoscope to her again, "you seem awfully familiar with scientific devices."

He shrugged. "I've always been good with my hands."

"But the way you handle mechanical things is—"

"Look." Jack tapped the stereoscope. "You'll see."

Giving up on her questions for now, Grace raised the viewer. "Oh, did you see this? Look, Jack!" Unable to keep the excitement from her voice, Grace tugged his sleeve with her free hand. "It's Paris! And the buildings almost seem to jump out at you. It's just as though you're strolling the Champs-Elysées."

She passed the stereoscope, watching as he enjoyed a turn, too. "I've seen ordinary pictures in books of course," she chattered on, "but none of them could compare with that." Struck with an idea, Grace turned toward the box of cards, which they'd propped on a nearby pile of flour sacks. "Let's see what else we have here...."

"You've barely seen this one and you already want more?"

"Naturally." Eagerly, Grace thumbed through the ordered cards, examining their labels one by one. She seized one, its side-by-side pictures looking unremarkable as they were. Once viewed through the stereoscope though, they would form one dazzling three-dimensional image. "Let's try this one!"

"Yes, ma'am." Grinning, Jack held out his hand.

"Oh, I'm sure I can manage." Biting her lip, Grace cautiously removed the stereograph of Paris. She mimicked all the movements she'd watched Jack perform, then stepped back with a flourish. "Voilà. This time you go first."

For a moment, he only went on smiling at her. "You are a capable woman, Grace. I'm impressed."

She blushed with contentment. "Go on. Look."

He did, allowing her an unhindered view of his chest and muscular arms as he lifted the stereoscope. She studied him with unabashed longing, wondering how she had found herself in such good fortune. After all this time, she'd found a man who understood and admired her. It felt almost too good to be true.

Suddenly, Jack stiffened. He thrust the stereoscope away. "I just remembered. I have an appointment."

Confused, Grace stared at him. "An appointment? But when you spirited me away from the *Pioneer Press* offices this morning, you said we had all day."

"I was wrong." Grimly, he packed up the cards they'd scattered while viewing. "You can stay. I'll speak to Hofer."

"No, I—" Grace didn't understand. What had happened? "It won't be the same without you. I'll just have one final look."

Jack crossed his arms. "Do what you want."

Frowning, Grace lifted the stereoscope. "Oh, it's Boston! I've never been, but I've heard it's lovely."

Jack grabbed his coat and hers from the storeroom peg, then carried both across the dimness. For some time he stood beside her, his shoulders broad and rigid beneath his shirt, holding her heavy wool and scarf at the ready. She glanced at him, recognizing impatience in the set of his mouth.

"Very well. I'm finished." Reluctantly, Grace put away the viewing device. She shrugged into her coat and wrapped her scarf tightly. "Will you escort me back to the *Press?*"

"I'm late already," Jack said, his face stony. "I'm sorry."

For the first time in weeks, they parted on the steps of Jedediah Hofer's mercantile and went their separate ways.

* * *

Grinning at the raucous music from the saloon piano, Jack slid a whiskey across the bar in a practiced arc. It came to a stop in front of the folded arms and slumped shoulders of a stranger who looked vaguely familiar. His youthful face was smudged with weariness, his whole demeanor downtrodden.

Probably a drummer, Jack decided, to judge by the citified but shabby clothes on him. Or a down-on-his-luck miner, chased from his claim by the weather. Lately, warm winds had blown down the mountains outside Morrow Creek, turning all the surrounding countryside to an enormous soup of mud and snowmelt, fooling the oak trees into believing spring was near. Their branches sported buds far too early, ready to unfurl, not knowing they'd only been lulled by the fickleness of nature.

"Much obliged," the stranger mumbled. He closed his eyes, quaffed back all his whiskey, then shuddered. "One more, sir."

Shaking his head, Jack served up another Old Orchard. He didn't linger though, not wanting to be too accessible. A man like that was bound and determined to drink himself to a stupor. Jack would rather allow the poor lunk time to sober a bit.

"He'll clean out his pockets at that rate," Marcus observed. Sympathetically, he frowned at the stranger. "It's not natural to spend that much money with your eyes closed."

Beside him, Daniel chuckled. "That's female trouble right there." He aimed his chin toward the stranger, then finished a quantity of his own lager. He exhaled with pleasure. "Not that I've ever had any female trouble myself, mind you."

"Course not." Gratified by his friends' company, Jack spread his arms along his glossy bar. It felt uniquely good to be there, ensconced behind the workings of his own business again. It had taken him a long while to build up his saloon.

He was proud of it. "Only for some reason, I can't get any more dance-hall ladies in here," he complained good-naturedly, aiming a deadeye glance at the blacksmith. "Whenever I ask, they all say they're not coming within two feet of that scoundrelly Daniel McCabe. Or some such."

Daniel choked on his lager. His brows lowered. "Don't say any of that twaddle when Sarah's nearby. She's tetchy about my 'amorous' past already. She'll take a frying pan to my skull."

"Ha. Nothing like a reformed bachelor to keep us all in line." Marcus spared a second pitying glance for the stranger, then regarded his friends with sure wisdom. "There but for the grace of God we all go." He sighed. "I'm just hopeful that Molly's new mania for orderliness is temporary—because of the baby coming and all. Yesterday she made me go back to the mill six times for 'prettier' boards to make the cradle with! I can't think what's next."

"Ah." Jack nodded, selecting a cloth to clean glasses with. "That explains why you're here, Copeland, spending money you usually hoard. Buying sarsaparilla."

Daniel made a face. "Prissy drink."

"You're afraid to go home," Jack concluded.

"The hell I am!" Marcus protested, looking aggrieved. "I only came by because Molly wants to know why Murphy here—" he nodded at Jack, making sure Daniel was paying attention "—hasn't been spooning with Grace anymore. That's all."

This time it was Jack's turn to blanch. His hand stilled on the glass he was wiping. He remembered that stereoscopic image of Boston, its familiar sights looking real enough to touch…real enough to reach all the way to the territory and wreck his second chance at things. It hadn't been Grace's fault, but he hadn't wanted to face her inevitable questions either.

Daniel perked up. He slapped on an inquiring expression, which looked damned foolish on his huge, masculine face.

"Tell us, Jack. Why haven't you been spooning with Grace?"

"Shut up, the both of you. I'm working."

To prove it, Jack gazed over the bar, making sure his rowdy evening business was still underway. No one appeared to need anything, but the place wasn't as crowded as he would have liked either.

He suffered the aftereffects of Grace's troublemaking visits even now, he noted with a hitch to his breath. Customers chose to drink elsewhere rather than risk a run-in with the most rabble-rousing suffragette of Morrow Creek.

But across the saloon, a few brave patrons huddled around the Faro table, hooting over a wager that was underway. And two cowboys drank near the window, so there was hope for a turnaround still. Harry played the piano, indulging a table of merchants with his until-now undiscovered skill at bawdy ballads and rousing polkas.

"What happens with me and Grace," Jack informed Marcus and Daniel in even tones, returning to the more important matter at hand, "is none of your damned business."

His friends pretended astonishment.

"It's not?" they asked each other. They guffawed.

"Drink up or get out. I've got paying customers to serve."

"We pay!" Marcus objected. He probably knew exactly how much he paid, down to the last penny. He'd become a little less tight since his marriage to Molly, but he would never be altogether loose with his coin. "Give me another sarsaparilla."

"Another lager, too," Daniel added.

The stranger down the bar raised his head. "A whiskey!"

Jack served up all the drinks, affecting gruffness. At least his knack for sliding a glass down the slick bar hadn't deserted him. He'd been away from his saloon too often these past weeks…although he couldn't strictly say he regretted it.

With every inch of him, he didn't.

Which was worrisome in the extreme. He hadn't even found Grace a husband for all his trouble.

Daniel tasted his lager, smacking foam from his lips. "Grace is a good woman." He slapped his hand on the bar, typically unreserved. "You're a good man, Murphy. But I'm here to tell you, if you're just diddling with my sister-in-law—"

"You'll have us to answer to," Marcus vowed.

Jack stared at them in disbelief. They only gazed back. Belligerently. "Oh, hell," he complained. "You're serious?"

They nodded, Marcus going so far as narrowing his eyes.

"You can't shake loose from a Crabtree woman," he opined after taking another swig of sarsaparilla. "So don't even try."

Daniel agreed. "We've already stood in your shoes, Murphy. Just go along peacefully, and you'll be fine."

Jack couldn't believe what he was hearing. "You two are threatening me? Damnation. What happened to loyalty?"

"Loyalty," Daniel said, "can't keep a man warm at night."

"You'll need us later," Marcus added. "Believe me."

But before Jack could answer that befuddling claim, the piano music stopped. Harry nudged his chin toward the door.

"Looks like somebody's here to see you, Murphy."

Grace. She was all Jack could think of.

First she'd sent her damned turncoat cronies—Marcus and Daniel—to drink his liquor and lecture him on loyalty and women and long nights needing warming up, he figured. Now she'd come herself, ready to take advantage of his weakened state.

Jack might have known she wouldn't hang on to his "appointment" excuse for long. It had been all he could think of with that stereoscopic image of Boston in his head.

"Barkeep!" The stranger raised his scrawny arm. "One ore whiskey!" Then he slumped in a snoring pile on the bar.

"Boss!" Harry yelled. "Look there!"

"Well, Murphy?" Daniel demanded amid the ruckus. He med a serious look at Jack. "What will it be?"

"What do you say?" Marcus pressed on. "About Grace?"

Hell. This night was too much on him.

"It's none of your damned business," Jack said.

Then, throwing down his towel, he left Harry in charge and ent outside to meet his fate. There was no coming up with way this night could possibly get any worse.

Chapter Fifteen

Except it did.

Jack stepped outdoors, not bothering with his coat and ha[t] and found himself confronted not with Grace Crabtree de[?] manding answers about Boston and their current lack [of] "spooning," but with Jedediah Hofer, the mercantile owne[r] The big Swede stood bundled outside the saloon, his deliv[?] ery wagon waiting on its runners at the hitching post. H[is] team of bays snorted and blew, their hooves and harnesse[s] loud in the deepening twilight.

Beyond him, people went about their business, riding pa[st] through the slush. Two men talked outside the news dep[ot] across the street, one of them carrying a copy of the *Pionee[r] Press*. Two ladies waved to Jack politely, then entered th[e] milliner's.

"Evening, Hofer." Jack offered a handshake, surprised [to] see the man so late in the day. "That my delivery?"

"Yessir. It's all there, crated and ready. Just like you o[r-] dered." Hofer shuffled, looking unhappy. "I wasn't going [to] bring it over at all, only you said you might pay some mo[re] on your account this time."

Damnation. Too late, Jack remembered he no longer had the ready payment Hofer spoke of. He'd sent the money to Nealie and Corinne to pay for emergency railroad tickets when his sisters had missed their connection and wired him for help. For Jack, family came first. Business obligations followed close behind.

"I have been paying on my account." That much was true, however much he still owed. "It's wintertime. Business is slow."

The mercantile owner made a noncommittal sound.

Hell. This would be harder than he'd thought. "Once I get the Excelsior Performing Troupe in my place," Jack promised with a genial lilt to his brogue, "I'll have the money to pay in full. Plus extra orders to boot."

Unmoved by Jack's Irish conviviality, Hofer squinted inside the saloon. "I still see men drinking. You still need whiskey."

A nod. "And you've still got my standing order in your wagon, too. I'll take it round back at the alley, as usual."

"No, sir. Can't do that."

Jack lowered his brows, inwardly cursing the ongoing problem of Grace and her do-gooders scaring men away from his saloon. Her shenanigans had bruised his finances for certain. More to his discomfiture, he couldn't seem to get her safely married either. But in the meantime...

"Course you can, Hofer. Let's go. I'll help you unload."

Hofer removed his hat. In the lamplight from the saloon window, he looked twice as fretful. He shook his head.

"You've been a good customer, Murphy, ever since you came to the territory. We both know it. I'd like to keep supplying you. But buying all this on account—" Hofer gestured helplessly toward the piled crates waiting in his wagon bed. "I'm a businessman! You can't expect me to oblige you forever."

Fortunately, that was exactly what the mercantile owner

had done until now. For that show of faith, Jack felt beyond
grateful. But he wasn't a man who took advantage—or who
viewed his obligations lightly. He met Hofer's worried gaze
head-on.

"My credit is good," Jack assured him. "I found a way to
pay last year, didn't I?"

Grudgingly, Hofer nodded.

"The farmers drink on trade this time of year, you know
that. They won't have coin till spring. I can't very well deny
them a snort of Old Orchard to keep them warm, especially
when they're townsfolk. I could pay you in full now if you'd
take preserved peaches or eggs by the basket—"

Hofer frowned. "I've got accounts, too. They pester me for
payment! Eggs would be fine by me, but I need more to—"

Mystifyingly, he broke off. With a sudden broad smile,
Hofer gestured toward the boardwalk. He'd clearly forgotten
Jack altogether in his haste to welcome someone.

"Miss Crabtree," Hofer called. "This is a pleasure!"

Jack stiffened. Having Grace witness this entanglement
was the last thing he needed. On the verge of offering Hofer
a partial payment, something to tide him over awhile longer,
Jack held his ground instead.

"Hello, Mr. Hofer." Grace strode to meet the merchant,
holding a satchel in one hand and what looked to be a pair of
letters in the other. "What brings you out this evening?"

"Well—" Hofer glanced from Grace to Jack, then back
again. A curious expression crossed his face. "Just a delivery."

"I see. I came to share some important news with Mr.
Murphy," she confided. Her eyes widened when she glimpsed
him in the shadows. "But that can certainly wait till you're
finished with your business. Do go on, won't you?"

Jack frowned. He didn't want his dealings to become public, especially when it came to Grace. He tried to telegraph

as much to Hofer with a vociferous grunt. But the man merely gazed as though bedazzled by Grace's presence…and she, for her part, simply smiled at them both in an encouraging fashion.

"Please," she coaxed. "Do proceed as you were. Don't pay me any mind at all."

"Well, er…" Hofer turned his hat in his hands, clearly caught in a dilemma of some kind. "The fact of the matter is—"

There was nothing for it. Jack stepped up. "We can do this another time, Hofer," he said roughly. "Thanks kindly, but I'll wait for my delivery when terms are settled between us."

To his surprise, Hofer shook his head. "No, I deliver to you right now. I just decided this moment. Six crates on account, with money off for delivering them so late today."

Flabbergasted, Jack stared at him.

Grace had no such reservations. "Why, that sounds excellent, Mr. Hofer!" She beamed. "You're very generous."

The man all but blushed. "I'll just get started, *ja?*"

Jack decided he was in no position to argue his good fortune, no matter how inexplicable. While Grace watched with evident satisfaction, he helped Hofer unload the packed crates.

Whiskey and mescal bottles clinked against one another, their crates bearing Spanish names of Mexican towns Jack had never seen. Hofer labored red-faced and stammering beside Jack, stealing frequent glances at Grace all the while. He lingered on the stoop with the final box to inquire after her health and the letters she held.

He nodded toward them. "Good news, *ja?*"

"Yes, very good news!" She bounced on tiptoes, fairly crackling with suppressed excitement. "Very exciting, too."

Jack puzzled over that, but only for a minute. Right now he had more pressing concerns to deal with. He stepped nearer to Hofer so they could speak privately.

"Thank you, Hofer," he said, grateful for the man's change of heart. "I'll be around your place later to settle up."

Hofer regarded him with a nod. "Don't wait too long."

Jack agreed. For a moment, Hofer squinted at the crates of liquor as though wondering how they'd traversed from his wagon to Jack's saloon. Then the mercantile owner shook his head.

"Evening, Murphy. Miss Crabtree."

Grace bade him goodbye with a wave of her letters.

The mercantile owner plunked his hat on his head, then climbed into position on his delivery wagon. With an unaccountably fond parting glance at Grace, he drove away.

Jack dragged in a deep breath, relieved to have things settled for now. A quick glimpse inside told him Harry had things in order behind the bar. Marcus and Daniel rolled dice, their drinks at their elbows. The stranger slumped, probably still snoring. Someone had put a bucket on his head—his patrons' idea of a joke.

A breeze stirred the fragrance of castile soap and starch surrounding Grace, reminding Jack she still waited for him.

Ordinarily, the sight of her would have put him in fine spirits. But tonight…tonight, the way things were going, he reasoned her visit could only bode ill.

"All right." He faced her. "What's next?"

"Well." Grace felt her smile widen now that she held Jack's full attention at last. "I'm afraid I was frightfully rude to poor Mr. Hofer just then, being so reticent about my letters and all, but I wanted you to be the first to know my exiting news."

She touched his arm, her whole heart filled to overflowing. It was wonderful to feel this way, eager to share her happenings with someone other than her family.

But Jack only waited, his face partly in shadow. Behind

him, the saloon carried on in all its boisterousness, doubtless earning him bundles of profits. Everything seemed taken care of in his absence, at least for the moment, so Grace forged onward.

"I wasn't coming inside this time," she assured him with a nod toward the noisy saloon. "Nor intruding at all. I promise I wasn't. But this simply couldn't wait until morning, so—"

At Jack's continued silence, Grace hesitated. She'd never seen him appear quite so…burdened before. Not even when he'd set aside the stereoscope the other day. Although his outlook would undoubtedly improve with the news she brought.

"I'll just come to the point, shall I?" Deciding to delay her own thrilling news for the moment, Grace chose one of the letters from her hand. "Perhaps this will make you smile."

Jack took the mail by rote, his face impassive.

"Look at the return address," she urged, crowding closer to peer past his shoulder and burly arm. "The Excelsior Performing Troupe in Chicago. Isn't that the one you've contacted?"

Jack turned over the letter, his fingers blunt-tipped and shadowed by the lamplight behind him.

"Our mail got mixed up together," Grace explained, gazing at his profile. "When I was fetching both. I'm sorry it's taken me so long to get it to you, but I've been preoccupied."

She smiled, knowing she'd been preoccupied with Jack and all the enjoyable things they'd done together.

"Go ahead," she prodded. "Open it!"

Jack did. Grace watched him eagerly, recalling the times they'd talked about the troupe. Jack had been reluctant to disclose many details, but she knew some such companies included musicians and performers and renowned stage actors. Jack's interest in hiring the troupe was further proof, Grace reasoned, that her improving influence had taken hold at last.

He had broadened his ambitions, dared to invite the arts and culture to his saloon for the betterment of all Morrow Creek.

"Well?" She nudged him, helpless to hold back a smile. "Will you be bringing some culture to Morrow Creek at last?"

His gaze slid to hers. Held. "You could say that."

"Excellent!" Grace beamed. "I told you taking an interest in 'highbrow pursuits' would be good for you. Didn't I?"

Typically, Jack only grunted.

He gazed inside his saloon. In a lesser man, his peculiar expression might have been ascribed to worry. But Jack, Grace knew, was far too confident for ordinary troubles to touch him. Weren't their lively weeks together evidence of that? She'd never had a finer time in her life—not even while bicycling.

"You'll have plenty of time to prepare for the troupe's arrival, too, because I'll be busy with a project of my own." She withdrew her second letter and fluttered it toward him. "Look!"

Jack shoved his letter in his trouser pocket. With what seemed to be a considerable effort, he smiled. "What is it?"

"Heddy Neibermayer!" Grace shouted, wholly unable to contain her glee. Several heads turned from inside the saloon, but she didn't care a whit. "She's coming to Morrow Creek! In a few weeks at least. And my chapter of the Social Equality Sisterhood will be hosting her! Isn't that magnificent?"

Astonishingly, Jack didn't grasp the wondrous implications of her news right away. He lowered his shoulders. "Heddy who?"

"Neibermayer. You must have heard of her. *Women and Suffrage* is her most famous work, but far from her only accomplishment." Awestruck, Grace admired the elegant penmanship and fine paper in Jack's hand, both of them worthy of framing. She could scarcely believe Heddy Neibermayer had answered her letters at last. "She's my idol, Jack. A speaker, an author and an activist of the highest caliber."

"This paragon of accomplishment," Jack began, earning an even wider smile for his use of vocabulary. "She's coming here?"

"She and all her retinue!" Grace enthused, squeezing his arm with delight. "They've agreed to a speaking engagement as a part of their westward touring commitments. You wouldn't believe the accomplished women who travel with Heddy Neibermayer, Jack. Reformers and protesters and artists—and the usual hangers-on, of course, but that's to be expected. Everyone wants to bask in the company of greatness."

Jack's eyebrow quirked. "Greatness?"

"Yes! And the accompanying merchandise fair, too, of course. I've been trying to convince Heddy Neibermayer to visit Morrow Creek for ages." Hastily, Grace sucked in a deep breath. "I've written every month for years, keeping Heddy informed about all my activities and everything my various clubs and ladies' organizations have accomplished. I knew that eventually she would realize Morrow Creek is worthy of a visit."

"Indeed it is," Jack agreed, a hint of irony in his brogue. "I would offer them all a place to stay, if I had the boardinghouse rooms I wanted."

He nodded upstairs, where lamplight still blazed from her meeting rooms. For an instant, Grace hesitated. This wasn't the time for their old disagreement to reappear. And yet…

"Don't be silly!" Laughing, she gave him a playful whack to his arm. She plucked her prized letter from his grasp, then carefully folded it. "Heddy Neibermayer and her retinue would hardly consent to stay at a saloon boardinghouse." She rolled her eyes at the very notion. "Very good, Jack. That almost beats out your dancing frog joke."

Jack grunted. She couldn't discern a thing from such a nonsensical sound, so she didn't even try.

"As you can see, this is a dream come true!" Grace said instead. "We'll have a parade, naturally, and a suffrage rally... possibly a reading from Heddy Neibermayer's latest book. There'll be speeches, and of course a tremendous gathering at the train station to greet everyone." Grace frowned as a new thought struck her. "Do you suppose Jedediah Hofer stocks bunting at the mercantile? Oh I wish I'd asked him about it! We'll need a great deal of it."

"I have no doubt you'll procure yards and yards of it. But I don't want to talk about Jedediah Hofer." Jack took her arm, gently steering her around the corner to the stairs. He stopped in the nook beside the rain barrel, his eyes troubled.

"I have work to do, Grace. But before I go..."

His mouth touched hers, sweetly and softly. He cradled her cheek in his palm, his fingers warm despite the chill in the air. Grace leaned daringly against him, unable to resist.

"This night could not get any better," she told him.

"Funny, I was thinking something similar earlier."

Jack smiled as he said it. But his worrisome tone belied his words altogether. Uneasy, Grace brought her hand to his chest. She sandwiched her letter between Jack's warmth and her own gloved hand, keeping it secure.

"Don't worry about this, Jack. I've already decided to suspend my literature club until after Heddy's visit, and my women's choral group has had all the practice it needs for now." She straightened her spine, trying hard not to sag under the sudden weight of her new responsibilities. "I so want to make a favorable impression upon Heddy Neibermayer," she confessed. "But in the spirit of our new...togetherness, I'll try not to affect your saloon overmuch in the process."

Her compromise left him less impressed than she'd hoped. Jack didn't say a word in reply, not even to argue the point.

Eyeing his frown, Grace gazed up at him with concern. This was more than unfamiliarity with one of the most famous females in all the United States, she realized. More than the strain of his own performing-troupe preparations to manage.

"What's the matter, Jack? I can tell there's something—" His gruff reply was immediate.

"I'm all bereft at the notion of having no more suffragette caterwauling, that's all." He offered a dazzling smile—one that didn't fool her in the least. "What will my patrons do without your choral group to serenade them once a week?"

Grace sighed. Clearly he intended not to bend, even for her. "I suppose they'll manage somehow. As will we. In the meantime, if I don't see you quite as often—"

"All for the sake of a few uppity bluestockings and some humorless Heddy-ites—"

"—I want you to know—" Grace gulped, struggling for a variety of courage she'd never before tried to muster. She stroked his chest with her fingertips, lost in memories for a moment. "This has been my favorite February of all. With you."

Jack's smile touched her, genuine at last. He kissed her again, lingeringly. "The month isn't over with yet."

And with those encouraging words, Grace found the strength to tackle her newfound challenge head-on. When she finished preparing for Heddy Neibermayer and her retinue, Morrow Creek would not know what hit it.

At least one other person in Morrow Creek was suitably impressed with Grace's accomplishment. The day after Grace confided her news in Jack, she sat at her typesetter's desk at the *Pioneer Press*, grinning over Thomas Walsh's ebullient expression.

"Good gracious! Heddy Neibermayer herself? That's quite a triumph, Miss Crabtree. Quite a triumph." He adjusted his spectacles as though scarcely able to believe it, blinking at her. "Naturally you'll request an exclusive interview for the newspaper, won't you? It will be the jewel in the crown of our little broadsheet!"

"I will," she promised. "In the meantime...you'll grant us the use of the printing press? We'll need to produce handbills and flyers and the like, quite independent of the regular run."

"Certainly, certainly." He sighed, shaking his head. "A tremendous achievement indeed. I'm very proud to know you."

Grace flushed and hastened to lay out the first flyer.

Lizzie's response was similar. "Oh, my! That's wonderful news, Grace!" Her newly wedded friend hugged her, rosy with contentment. "What can I do to help?"

"Hmm. Well, you could sew a suffrage flag or two...?"

"I'll do my best," Lizzie promised. "I need to prove my homemaking skills to Alonzo anyway. He's still recovering from my first attempt at succotash last week."

Grace gave her a consoling pat. And a grin. "There is always tinned beef if you're desperate. The modern age is gradually coming around to women's rescue, you know."

Lizzie poured them more tea, her expression thoughtful. "Although I do have to wonder... What will Heddy Neibermayer think of your friendship with Mr. Murphy? After all, he is a saloon owner, and you said some of the women in her retinue are temperance advocates. Aside from which, he is a bit rough."

"He is." For a moment, Grace lost herself in remembering Jack's masculine demeanor, his big hands, his hearty laugh. "But there's much more to him than that! He has unknown talents."

Lizzie bit her lip, seeming unconvinced.

For an instant, Grace worried, too. What would Heddy say? Grace had set out to achieve great things in Morrow Creek…and had wound up smitten with one of the brawniest men in town instead. Then the most brilliant idea occurred to her.

"I'm sorry, but I have to hurry away." Grace hugged her friend. "I'll be back tomorrow with the patterns for the flags!"

In the meantime, Grace had a new challenge to meet—making sure Heddy Neibermayer knew exactly how unique Jack Murphy was…and exactly how right Grace was to admire him.

In fact, she decided as she carefully folded a select few of his drawings and sealed them for mailing, with the correct evidence, Heddy would be sure to see that Grace had improved more than the quality of women's lives in Morrow Creek. She'd improved her very own rough-and-ready saloonkeeper, too. And she couldn't wait for Heddy and her entire retinue to see and admire Jack's talents for themselves.

All those next few weeks, Jack stole every moment with Grace he could. He waylaid her on her way upstairs, recognizing her footsteps in the wee hours as readily as his own and hurrying to meet her. He bowed to her requests to invent things—special fatigue-fighting paintbrushes for parade banners, unique fasteners for hoisting bunting, even weight-bearing designs for wearable placards and advertisements—and grinned with pleasure over the effusive way Grace received every one.

"Oh, Jack! This is spectacular!" She threw her arms around him, treating him to an impulsive kiss. "Thank you. You are a true genius, to be sure, to have created all these things."

She gazed at his designs, evident awe in her expression.

"Don't tell anyone," he warned.

Grace scoffed. "Why wouldn't you want everyone in the world to know you can do this? You're wonderful."

"Don't tell anyone that either."

She smiled, then wrapped her arms around his middle. Her smile bedazzled him. "I don't care how fearsome you look," she declared. "Because I know the real Jack Murphy."

And when she proved it by hugging him even closer, then pressing her mouth against his with all the ardor of a recently enlivened spinster, Jack couldn't find the heart to disagree.

Grace was right, he thought as he caught her head in his hand, unraveling her prissy knotted hair with every urgent caress. Right to be cocksure in their affection for one another. Right to know he wanted her…and would refuse her nothing.

With the promise of the Excelsior Performing Troupe's impending arrival as a guarantee, Jack managed to secure more liquor deliveries from Jedediah Hofer. With the assurance of a crowd-drawing spectacle in hand, he risked all the rest of his meager funds, working hard every day to enlarge his saloon's stage, tune his piano and print handbills.

With Grace's promises ringing in his ears, he even believed that the two of them had finally reached a workable compromise—a middle ground where her suffrage activities didn't impinge on his successful saloon running, and his unruly patrons didn't deter her ladies from their meetings and preparations.

It seemed too good to be true, Jack knew, but all the evidence pointed to it as fact. He and Grace seemed to have reached an accord. However unlikely that would have seemed to him a few months ago, Jack dared to hope it would last.

The weeks whisked past, bringing even more frenzied activity from Grace. The snow melted, seducing the scrub oaks into giving up their furled leaves. All the ponderosa pines straightened, too, free of their winter coats. The whole mountain turned green with saplings and bright with sunshine. But indoors Grace raced to and fro, thundering upstairs to her meeting rooms with ever more bunting and canvas and paint.

"Wait," Jack called. "I have something for you."

She stopped, her man-shoes skidding. Jack smiled at them, feeling inexplicably charitable toward their clunky soles. He watched as they trod briskly downward again. Grace's face, flushed and harried, appeared over the edge of the stair rail.

"What is it?" she asked. "Heddy Neibermayer is arriving in two days' time, Jack. I don't have a moment to spare."

"Hmm. You'll have to come closer to claim it."

Grace held her burdens—a bundle of printed programs, an assortment of flags and a gaudy pile of fabric—and duly clattered lower. Not even her dowdy reformer's dress could staunch his happiness at seeing her. It felt years since they'd been alone together...ages since they'd kissed.

"Very well. I'm ready," she announced. "What is it?"

She fidgeted. Worry emanated from her, along with the harsh scents of paint and paste. Up close, Jack realized, Grace seemed beyond frazzled. Even her hair looked tightly strung, bundled as hastily as everything else she touched these days.

This endeavor was harder on her than he'd known.

"Oh, Jack. It's a kiss, isn't it? I recognize that look in your eyes." She puffed out her cheeks, plainly overwhelmed. "That sounds lovely, honestly it does. But it's getting late, and everyone else has gone home to their families, and I've the parade to organize and the banners still aren't finished and the podium for the suffrage rally still hasn't been—"

"It's not a kiss." Making a lie of that claim, Jack kissed her all the same. He could not resist—he was a man, after all. And it proved a failsafe way to make her stop babbling long enough to breathe. Deftly, he removed all the items from

Grace's arms and assumed their jumbled heft himself. "I'm helping you with all this. You're not doing it alone."

"No, Jack. I won't—"

"I'm not leaving until everything's done and ready," he said. "Come upstairs. We've got rabble-rousing to do."

Chapter Sixteen

$$\mathcal{C}\!\!\sim\!\!\mathcal{O}\!\!\sim\!\!\mathcal{O}\!\!\sim\!\!\mathcal{O}$$

Much later, exhausted but relieved, Grace stood in the center of her primary meeting room and surveyed the remarkable progress she and Jack had made.

All around her rested parade signs and placards and suffrage banners. A beautifully embellished lectern and podium waited near the window, ready to be toted to the rally. On the tables nearby, assorted Wild West souvenirs lay higgledy-piggledy, set for Heddy Neibermayer and her retinue.

"What do you think?" Jack asked.

She turned to find him at the opposite end of the room, standing near her rumpled cot. Grace had never moved it, finding it useful to store bunting and paintbrushes and advertising flyers. When viewed in juxtaposition with Jack's height and breadth, her makeshift bed looked spindly indeed.

In the lamplight, Jack's dark hair gleamed. His shoulders straightened. He'd cast aside his brocade vest with typical carelessness some time ago and now held its replacement— an enormous suffrage flag—over his chest with both broad hands.

Grace smiled at his earnest expression. "I think not many

men would work so diligently on behalf of female suffrage and women's deserved equality."

He made a mischievous face. "About the flag."

"Oh, that." Pretending to notice it for the first time, Grace strode nearer. She traced the length of fabric Jack held against him, enjoying the solid warmth of his chest against her fingertips. "On you, this suffrage flag looks surprisingly masculine. I wonder if we should redesign it?"

Jack's mouth pressed together. With a firm nod, he agreed. "I'll paint another one. Pink this time."

Smiling, Grace stopped him in midturn. "I'm joking. It looks superb. You make a marvelous model, too."

His cheeks turned ruddy. "Someone had to do it, else this overlong thing would drag on the floor."

He undraped his flag, then folded it with nimble movements. He set it aside with the others they'd already finished.

Grace no longer wondered at his mechanical agility, having seen Jack perform nothing less than miracles with his creations for her over the last few weeks. She felt very grateful for his help…and very interested in the muscles that pulled and flexed so intriguingly beneath his plain white shirt right now.

Jack turned. "What's wrong? You look strange."

"I was merely thinking…" Blushing, she set aside her musings. "You are nearly a suffragist now yourself, I'd say."

He grunted. This time, she found the sound charming.

"I may order you about all the time," Grace continued, teasing him. "It certainly proved an effective tactic today."

Jack merely nodded. "Everything is done here. I reckon you're ready for Humorless Heddy and her bluestocking band."

"Jack!"

"I'll say what I want. I'm helping you, not them." He sauntered nearer, then took her hands. He clasped them in his own, twining their fingers together. He studied them. "Most people could not have organized such a shindig as this, Grace. I'm proud of you."

At his kind words, Grace felt warm all over. She had never in her life blushed so often as she had in Jack's company. Somehow, he brought out the girlishness in her. It should have felt ridiculous in a veritable spinster such as herself.

Instead it felt…good. It felt right.

"Thank you for helping me." Fatigued to her toes, she stretched upward for a brief kiss. She wriggled her hands free and gestured expansively at the disarray surrounding them. "I don't know what I would have done without you tonight."

His smile flashed. "If you need more, I am at your command."

"Hmm." Emboldened by the notion, Grace pretended to consider it. "My command? Why, that's all I've ever asked, all along." She found herself smiling back at him, unable to resist.

"Only you cannot command more modeling of suffrage flags from me," Jack stipulated, running a hand through his already disordered hair. It stood appealingly rumpled. "I feel my manliness in dire danger if I perform another pirouette."

This time, Grace laughed aloud. He looked disgruntled, abashed…and wholly, unreservedly hers. At least for tonight.

"Well, I wouldn't want to waste my opportunity," she said, studying him. Jack's shirt lay flat against his throat, casually unbuttoned to display a few tantalizing inches of sun-browned skin. His twin braces teased her gaze lower. His trousers fit him with blatant masculinity in places she'd never before dared to look. "I think you should kiss me immediately," she managed. "Strictly as a celebration of our progress, of course."

Silence descended. Then… "No."

Startled, Grace glanced up. Jack's expression looked solemn, his eyes dark in the lamplight. The room was dim, she realized in a rush. Sometime while they'd worked, the night had swept in, leaving stars hanging outside her window. It was a view she'd never shared with anyone, much less a man like Jack.

Suddenly, Grace felt aware of her position.

And all the possibilities it implied.

"I don't need an excuse to kiss you," Jack said. "Nor a celebration. But if you keep looking at me that way…" His dark gaze met hers as though reading every secret. "I should leave."

"Nonsense." Grace crossed the span of floorboards dividing them, her heart pounding with every step. She wasn't a girl, to be swept away foolishly. But when Jack looked at her that way…somehow, she felt as though she were.

She felt swept away and secure at the very same time.

"Don't leave." Grace framed his face in her hands. His day's growth of beard rasped against her palms. She smiled, loving that proof of their new intimacy. "Stay awhile."

"Grace, we've—"

She shushed him with a kiss. "You have to do it." A smile of recognition shimmered between them. "I command you."

Jack closed his eyes like a man summoning courage. Or maybe a man resisting temptation. Grace fancied it was the latter.

He opened his eyes, and she glimpsed stunning honesty within their depths. "I've wanted you all along," he said.

Entirely unable to speak, Grace felt her mouth drop open.

"I want you now," he added.

Questions whirled through her mind, racing with instant rebuttals and arguments and all her usual staunch disavowals. But this time Grace could muster none of them. Her wit deserted her while looking into Jack's raw expression.

"I think I'll want you always." His hand rose to hers, flattening it against his cheek with fervor. His gaze held hers, braver by far than Grace's could ever be. "I know I will."

She gaped, her heart hammering. Hopefulness surged.

Jack's mouth quirked. "It's your turn to talk."

Grace blinked, roused by the husky, needful tone of his voice. Jack's rugged face veered into view, waiting. A million denials imposed themselves on her, borne of a lifetime of never needing anyone...never allowing herself to need anyone.

Much less needing someone to love.

"I want you, too, Jack." The words emerged in a rush. Grace felt she might hold them in forever, but they refused to be unsaid. "I didn't know how—I've never—but I love you and I—"

His smile was dazzling. He pulled her to him for a kiss as heartfelt as any they'd ever shared. Their noses collided, then angled sideways; their breaths hitched and held and finally tangled. Caught up in the urgent press of Jack's mouth, Jack's hands, Jack's need, it was all Grace could do to hang on to him...to tell him, with this kiss at least, all the things she'd been unable to voice just a moment ago.

"Usually I'm so good with words," she babbled when they parted, her whole body tingling with giddiness. "If only I—"

His next kiss cut off her speech, splendidly and wonderfully. Not minding a bit, befuddled but elated, Grace shoved herself closer. She kissed him back with all her heart.

"I'm certain I could explain," she gasped between kisses. Jack tipped her head back, his mouth traveling unerringly to all the places she loved but hadn't known it till now. "If only my heart would quit pounding, perhaps my mind would—"

Jack squeezed her. She stopped on a squeal of pleasure, squirming with all the agility her bicycling and snowshoeing had earned her to get closer. Closer. Jack slid his hand lower, holding her around her middle, cradling her as though he simply could not hold her tightly enough, and Grace found the sensation remarkable. She wanted more and more and more…

"Perhaps you have the right of it." He paused and smiled more widely, his entire demeanor wicked. Scandalously so. "This is a celebration after all."

He proved it with more kisses, this time to her neck, her throat…the delectable, previously untouched spot revealed by her unbuttoned dress. She couldn't remember when he'd begun loosening it, but the feat, once accomplished, felt perfect. Jack worked diligently at her remaining buttons, his agile fingers making a short task of freeing her.

As though she could feel any freer than this.

Laughing, weeping, Grace nodded. "It feels it. It feels like a celebration. Oh, Jack…"

"We were foolish." He tucked his hand over her hammering heart, palming her with reverence. His expression fraught with wonder, he gazed at all he'd revealed. Her bare skin, her bosom—pushed to their limits by her corset—her helpless need. "We were foolish to wait," he said.

"To deny." Willing, thrilled and far too inexpert for her own liking, Grace dared to grab Jack's clothes, too. She bit her lip and wrested with his shirt buttons. She caught his surprised look and widened her eyes. "What is good for you to do is just as good for me to do." She gestured to his top few buttons, already freed. "Given my inexperience, I would say I am very skilled at this. Wouldn't you?"

"Very, very skilled," Jack agreed. With his eyes shining in clear approval, he cupped her chin in his hand and kissed her again. "Don't stop or I'll begin to doubt your sincerity."

"Never." Grace set to her undertaking again, only to find herself tipped backward a moment later. She fell, shrieking.

They landed together atop her crowded cot, its blankets kew and its pillows fluffing around them. Sprawled igno- y beneath Jack, Grace squirmed. "Now I can't reach your ttons."

"I'll take care of everything," he promised. "Even you."

For once, Grace didn't disagree. Jack's care and concern ere too obvious to argue with—as was his sincerity, when thumbed away a few more buttons and spread apart her ess. For a long moment, he was silent as he looked his fill.

"You are beautiful, Grace," he said. "Beautiful."

And just then, Grace believed him.

She wanted to blush beneath his admiration. Strangely, she d not possess that much modesty—probably because she pidly became engrossed in her own discoveries. Holding ck's shirt wide, Grace admired the broad span of hair- rinkled chest she'd uncovered. He looked even better than e'd imagined, fit and strong and sun browned. With a help- ss sound of appreciation, she flattened her palms against ck's bare skin.

"I might have known you would be bold in this, too." He asped his hand over hers, his fingers stroking. "Oh, Grace. ly Grace. You are wondrous."

Grace smiled at his praise. She was bold, but whether be- ause of her nature or her feelings for him, she couldn't say. eneath her hand, Jack felt hot and hard and wonderful—so fferent from her, but so right.

Closing his eyes, swallowing hard, Jack tautened above her s she touched him. He liked this, she realized. He did. The nowledge gratified her beyond all expectation. Fondly, Grace queezed his shoulders with both hands, exploring further.

"You are spectacular also," she observed seriously. "I find ou most handsome, Jack. And extremely perfect otherwise."

He opened his eyes to see her smile.

"There is no one like you, Grace."

His tender touch roused her all over. Quickly, it turned pas
sionate, too. Again and again he stroked her, leaving Grace
breathless and wanton and eager to shove the bunting from
the cot, the forgotten paintbrushes from beneath their shoul
ders, the whole world aside for this magical night.

In the lamplight, Jack lowered himself over her, kissing
her in ways more pleasurable than she'd ever dreamed. She
clutched him to her as though she would never let him go.
His hand slid from her knee upward, claiming parts of her no
man ever had, and Grace welcomed him eagerly. Her skirts
bunched. Her whole body arched upward, wanting to be
closer still.

"Even dress-reform clothes aren't sufficient for this," she
complained breathlessly, wriggling to be free. She shoved at
her skirts. "Whoever devised such items should be—"

"Don't worry," Jack said, just as breathless as she. His
smile warmed her through. "We can do it together."

In a heartbeat, Grace was naked. Jack dropped her corsetry
and chemise to the floor beside her dress and the oversize bro
gan shoes she'd kicked off, leaving Grace to marvel at him.

"You are excellent at that!" she said. "I had no idea."

He gave a modest shrug. "I am inspired by you."

They came together again, Jack with his shirt hanging
from his shoulders, Grace with her whole self revealed to
him. The sheeting lay soft beneath them. Outside, the stars
shone down, making the night as miraculous as any she'd ever
imagined.

"But this is not fair," Grace said, twisting a few moments
later to gaze into Jack's face. He looked handsome enough to
make her want to sigh…rascally enough to make her want to
kiss him all the more. "I am wearing nothing, while you—"

He bolted upright. In a trice, his clothes were shed.

Grace sat up, insatiably and unabashedly curious. In the flickering lamplight, Jack's body was splendid, his torso lean but ridged with muscle, his arms as strong as ever. His hips were fascinating and his legs powerful, covered with more muscle and manly dark hairs. In between all that…

"You are larger than I thought," she observed. "More finely shaped, too." Candidly, she peered nearer. "Yes, I approve."

His smile delighted her. His embrace, when next he joined her atop their skewed blankets and rickety cot, made her heart feel overflowing with tenderness. Jack spread himself beside her. Gently, he leaned closer to kiss her, his hand on her hip.

"That's a good thing," he said, his brogue deep and beloved. "For I feel every kind of naked in front of you."

She gazed into his eyes, seeing the truth there.

"Then we are equal," she told him, and kissed him again.

With Jack there was no hiding. No feeling peculiar or lacking or unwanted. There was only love…love and needing.

On a moan, Jack kissed her more deeply, his hand delving into her hair to loosen its pins. They pinged to the mattress beneath them, as liberated as Grace herself felt, scattering all around. For once, she didn't care about the disarray.

There was something momentous in this night—something special in the way Jack had come to her aid, leaving his saloon to Harry's supervision without hesitation. Jack cared for her, Grace realized, just as she did him. As she gazed at him in wonder, memorizing the angles of his face and the tenor of his whispered words, she knew she would never forget whatever happened between them next. Nor ever regret it.

Feeling on the brink of something new…something marvelous and extraordinary and necessary, Grace drew in a deep breath. Her chest expanded to meet Jack's, causing a riot of pleasurable sensations. Instantly, his hands closed on her

breasts. His mouth came next, leaving her writhing beneath
his gentle kisses, his sweet words, his promises of what was
to come.

"All that?" she managed, tingling all over with expectation and newness. She could scarcely believe she found herself here, now, needing and wanting and... Grace hesitated.
"Jack, I'm not entirely sure I'll be satisfactory in this. I
haven't any expertise at all. I'm generally quite adept at
things, but... I would not want you to be disappointed."

Worriedly, she studied him, taking in his strong nose,
his disheveled hair, his kind eyes. A man like Jack was rare
indeed.

He tipped up her chin and kissed her. "All I want is to be
with you. If you would rather stop—"

"Oh, no! I find myself quite eager to continue. It's only—"

His grin broadened. "Listen to this. Listen carefully and believe me when I say you have nothing to worry about. Here."

As though in demonstration, Jack drew his hand from her
hip to her breast. He cupped her there, sweetly, offering her
to his mouth for another kiss, making Grace gasp and twist
and clutch his arm. With a heartfelt glance to her face, Jack
slid his fingers further with maddening surety, with impossible slowness, along a matching path to her other side.

"Do you hear that?" he asked, his expression intent.

Grace squirmed. "You didn't say anything," she pointed out.

"Mmm." His eyebrows rose. "Listen more closely then."

Keeping his gaze locked with hers, Jack trailed his hand
down the middle of her chest, barely brushing her breasts. His
expression reverent and his breath held, he slipped his fingers lower, past her rib cage, over her belly, lower still...

A tremor shook her. Wild with it, Grace felt her eyes
widen, even as she held Jack's gaze. She grasped his shoulder, helpless to do more than breathe and feel and listen.

"With every touch," he said earnestly, not stopping—never stopping, "I'm telling you I love you."

"Oh, Jack! I—" Grace quivered, yearning to believe him.

"I love you, Grace." He swallowed her cries with a lingering kiss, keeping her safe and whole while the world turned dizzying around her. "I'll tell you again and again."

And for all the rest of that night, Jack did. He held her and showed her, and tutored her in his love in ways Grace had never envisioned...but cherished all the more.

There was more to Jack than manliness and clever drawings and whiskey, she learned. There was gentle surety and unbelievable strength, and as Grace trembled beneath him again and again, devoutly giving as much to him as he did her, she learned that there was more to her than she'd believed, as well.

There was vulnerability in her. And laughter. And love. So much more love than she'd known lay inside her, just waiting for Jack's kiss, Jack's jokes, Jack's love to awaken it. Holding him close, lying drowsily in his arms, Grace knew she was forever changed by that night. She could not be anything but glad.

She'd left her old self behind, she realized, with her eyes newly opened to all the possibilities of love and loving and needing. And giving, too. Nothing in her life had prepared her for it, but that made it all the more special.

"Thank you, Jack." Snuggled up beside him, wrapped in their blankets—and possibly the leftover bunting but not caring a whit—Grace laid her head on his chest. She sighed contentedly. "Thank you."

He gave a rumbling sigh of his own, then tightened his arm around her shoulders. Being with him this way felt perfect. It felt right and good and utterly indispensable. Grace felt her whole heart open, ready to embrace whatever came next.

"Thank you?" Jack nuzzled her enticingly. "For what?"

Grace gazed up at his profile, knowing she would remember it forever. "For giving me the rest of myself."

"Ah." She would never have thought to see a man so rugged as Jack seem quite so moved. He looked at her for a long moment, his face a study in caring…in protectiveness.

"Then we are even," he said, and his smile lit the night.

Jack awakened slowly, lulled by the distant jangle of wagon fittings, the clip-clop of horse traffic and the faint murmuring of faraway voices. Morrow Creek had risen before him, he realized—an event fairly unprecedented since he'd come to town. Usually, Jack was up with the sun, doing whatever he could to maintain or build or grow his saloon.

And his new life besides.

But today everything was different. Blinking at the rafters overhead, Jack smiled broadly. His body felt sorely used, his left arm completely benumbed. His toes hung over the mattress, which was miserably cramped and lumpy besides. A powerful thirst bedeviled him, and he felt fairly certain he would benefit from a particularly hearty breakfast to regain his vigor. But all those things paled beside the woman who slept alongside him.

Grace. Foolishly enamored by her, Jack turned his head. Her slumbering profile met him, partly obscured by her pillow and a wayward scrap of suffrage flag trimmings. She looked beautiful. Her cheeks were pink, her brow smooth, her mouth tempting. Her hair tumbled over his chest, brown and lustrous.

He'd never seen it loose before last night. Now he never wanted to see it any other way. With her hair unbound and her eyes passion-filled, Grace had seemed all the more herself—freed of every scrap of convention and open to him in a way she'd never been before. The things they'd shared humbled him. To be a part of such feelings...Jack had never experienced its like.

Awash in remembrance, he ignored his squashed arm and gazed at her all the longer. Tenderness suffused him. Her freckled nose? Perfection. Her stubborn chin, her wayward arms, her teardrop breasts? Ideal. The way she crowded him on their narrow mattress, uninhibitedly draping one lithe leg over his thigh? Everything he wanted. Satisfied, Jack thumbed a strand of hair from her face, lingering over her soft skin.

If this was rabble-rousing, he wanted more every day.

But only if he had Grace for company.

With a mighty groan, Jack stretched himself out. Grace roused only a little, snuffling closer to him. Doubtless she would drool on his chest, cramp his hips still further, leave his arm asleep till it dropped clean off. But Jack couldn't seem to muster the will to care. He grinned and slipped his free hand to her shoulder, then swept his fingers along the curve of her back. He would wake her in the most pleasurable way possible.

Soon, surely. But first another besotted look. While Grace slept and could not object nor claim he was being foolish.

Jack lost track of how long he watched her...how long he stroked her, enjoying the smooth warmth of her skin and the luscious curve of her hip. Her bare buttocks fit his palm exactly, offering further proof of their rightness for one another. Grace had glimpsed almost all of the real him, Jack realized, and she loved him. She loved him. Beyond everything else, that meant more than he could say—him, a man of words.

If the real him were known, at least.

Grace's eyes fluttered open. Groggily, she blinked. She stretched. Her lips puckered and smacked as though seeking another kiss. Jack obliged, his lack of peppermint tooth powder be damned. He wove his fingers into her hair, holding her carefully to him.

Grace moaned. Sweetly, she kissed him, her arms moving unerringly to pull him closer. Her fingers spread over his back, clinging tight, assuring him of the rightness of their being together...the completeness of the tender feelings Jack felt.

When he ended their kiss, she smiled. She looked lovely.

"You are a rowdy awakener," Grace said. "I approve."

"I'm glad." Naked, Jack rolled nearer, feeling wholly united and not the least bit sated—not now that Grace had cast him that seductive look. Their bodies pressed closer, sharing warmth and love. "For I've no intention of letting you leave."

They kissed again, heedless of the sunshine outside the window, the passersby on the street below, the day meandering past without them. All of that felt decidedly remote. For once, Jack decided, his saloon could open very, very late. Being with Grace felt more intoxicating than any liquor could anyway.

"Anyone would think you're at home here." Looking equally blissful, Grace gestured to the cluttered space around them. "Surrounded by suffrage accoutrements and paint and the like."

"I want to be wherever you are."

She issued a fond sound, bringing her palm to his cheek. "And I want to be with you." Grace hesitated, but only for an instant. "Do you think we dare be together? Truly? The whole of Morrow Creek will likely believe we've gone mad."

"I don't care," Jack said. "I—"

A strange sound reached him, making him pause. He angled his head sideways, listening. Shuffling came from the street outside, calling to mind—curiously enough—dozens of stamping feet. There was a rumbling, too—distinguishable as voices, but he couldn't make out the words. If he hadn't known better, Jack would have sworn that the surprised citizenry of Morrow Creek had gathered outside Grace's window already.

The notion made him grin.

"They will applaud our charitable ways toward one another," he predicted, shoving the blankets lower to reveal the curve of Grace's hip. His attention caught, he stroked her there. "We have certainly found a compromise between us."

Despite his best attempts at diversion, Grace cocked her head, too. "Do you hear that?"

Her body tensed beneath his fingertips. Reluctantly, Jack listened again. Now it sounded as though a hundred people turned the pages of a book, creating a peculiar ruffling. There were more footsteps. Another clanging wagon. He glanced to the window and glimpsed a sheet of paper, rising on a puff of dust and drifting all the way to Grace's second-floor meeting rooms.

Grace kicked aside the sheets. "I'd better go see—"

"No, I will." Offering her his most promise-laden wink, Jack disentangled himself. Carelessly nude, he strode to the window. The shutters were still flung wide, the glass the only barrier between him and the outside. "Then I'll—"

At the sight that greeted him, Jack stared in disbelief.

A whole crowd of people truly had gathered outside, downstairs at the steps to his saloon. Women of all shapes and sizes and ages chattered avidly to one another, their heads craning to see if the place had opened.

At the edges of the group, a few men loitered, their grins wide as they examined something. More papers, Jack discerned, like the one that had wafted upward on the breeze. They seemed to be printed pages, torn from somewhere and then brandished like the most hilarious of jokes. Frowning, Jack squinted.

Grace joined him at the window, wrapped in the blanket with her hair tumbled. At the sight outside, her smile faltered.

"I wonder what's happening." She peered. "There are nearly as many people down there now as gathered at the train station when that circus passed through town last year."

Jack nodded. The merest hint of an unusual event was enough to draw a crowd in Morrow Creek, so hungry were the residents for gossip and entertainment. It wasn't often anything lively enough happened to cause such a stir.

"What are those papers?" Grace asked. "They look—"

She ended on a gasp. Wordlessly she pointed, even as the ruckus outside grew louder. More people joined the group, several striding from the direction of the Lorndorff hotel.

Jack looked. A powerfully built woman strode between the assemblage, clad in reformer's clothes with a badge pinned to her chest. Her gray hat was massive, her hair a matching color, her parasol an efficient instrument to prod slowpokes. The group parted to allow her passage, several women ducking their heads.

"It's Heddy Neibermayer," Grace said. "She's early!"

Four familiar women parted from the group, all of them dark-haired but with wildly varying dress. They clustered around Heddy, obviously explaining something in eager terms. They waved those peculiar papers, but Heddy didn't linger to confer.

She marched directly to the saloon doorway.

Her firm knock echoed all the way upstairs.

"Jack Murphy, come out at once!" came her gravelly voice.

Behind her, the women in the crowd cheered.

"We have not come all this way for you to ignore us!"

With a dreadful jolt, Jack realized what those papers were. They were catalog images of his newfangled corsetry creations. He'd thought—he'd hoped—never to see them again.

"We have money!" cried one of the ladies, holding a coin.

"We want fittings!" yelled another. "A personal one for me!"

"An autograph!" shouted a third, earning herself a bushel full of giggles from the women around her. "Come out!"

Downstairs, Heddy Neibermayer rapped soundly again. Beside Jack, Grace froze.

"Mr. Murphy!" Heddy exclaimed. "Do stop cowering. We're only a handful of women. We're nothing to fear, and we present an excellent opportunity for commerce regarding your designs."

"Yeah, Murphy," came an amused masculine voice. "Come meet your lady admirers."

From the crowd, Thomas Walsh stepped forward, wearing his bowler hat and glasses, his notebook in hand. "Mr. Murphy," he called, cupping one hand around his mouth. "If I might have a word about this startling development—"

Jack couldn't speak. Couldn't move. How could this be?

He cast a bewildered glance to Grace, who'd drawn away from the window. She gazed back at him, clutching her blanket.

"Well, this is good news," she announced astoundingly. "Now everyone knows you're more than a saloonkeeper. More than a—"

"More than a saloonkeeper?" he echoed. Her vaguely guilty expression made his belly tighten. He didn't understand what was going on—what had caused the uproar outside—but all at once, Jack felt dismally certain Grace had had a hand in it.

"Well, you're also an artist, aren't you?" She clutched her blanket, her eyes wide. She sounded skittish…but proud. "An inventor, a creator, a designer of wonderful drawings and schematics. I'll admit this is more than I counted on though."

"More than you counted on?" More shouting reached him from outside, but Jack couldn't listen. All his thoughts were filled with Grace—with Grace and the realization that his past had, unbelievably, come home to roost in Morrow Creek. Complete with newspaper reportage and multiple overbold women. Damnation. It was all he could do to keep a level head. "You did this?"

She raised her chin, confirming his worst fears.

"I only sent a few of your drawings to Heddy," Grace explained. "Just so she could see how very talented you are, Jack. Just so she could see why I'm proud of you."

Heedless of her pleading tone, hearing only that he had—once again—trusted someone in error, Jack clenched his fists.

He cast another beleaguered look at the ruckus outside. Women clamored for his novel undergarments exactly as stridently as they had in Boston. Perhaps worse. Men yelled slurs about his "seamstressing." The whole occurrence was a nightmare.

"I couldn't have known this would happen!" Grace waved her arm toward the window. "Jack, I—I don't understand. It was only a few drawings. I still don't know where all those papers—"

"You wanted this." Even as he said it, Jack realized the horrible logic of it. "You wanted to make me as ready a joke here as I was in Boston, and when you found those drawings—"

"In Boston?" Grace touched his arm. "No, I don't even—"

"You wanted to have your way at any cost. Even this." Bitterly, Jack grabbed his britches. He tugged them on, then reached for the rest of his clothes with jagged movements. "I should have known. I should have known the renowned Grace Crabtree would not accept defeat, nor share this space forever."

"Of course I'm sharing! I don't know what you mean." Grace pursued him, watching as he dressed. Her panicky look did not fool him. "Tell me what happened in Boston. Maybe I'll—" She paused. "Why are you talking that way?

Of a sudden, you bandy about words like *renowned?* You sound like a stranger."

Jack felt like one, too. He could not look at her any longer. Instead he snatched his shoe. He shoved it on, but only partway. "Damnation! This one is yours," he growled.

He hurled it. It bounced from the wall, making Grace jump.

"What is wrong with you?" She waved her palm to the window, the gesture sharp and urgent. "What do they all want?"

Jack couldn't believe she would pretend not to know.

"They want to make a laughingstock of me, too," he said as the clamor outside continued. It seemed a hundred years since he'd awakened so happily, but in truth only minutes had passed.

"Jack," Grace urged. "Please wait. Don't behave this way."

He paused. "You can meet my sisters. You wanted that, I think." He offered a humorless grin. "They are the four who waylaid your idol, Heddy. You'll have a great deal in common."

For a moment, Grace honestly seemed hopeful. She stopped chasing him long enough to smile. "They are here?"

"I don't know how, but yes." Jack shoved his hand through his hair, then straightened. He released a gusty breath, listening to the hubbub outside. He could scarcely accept that his disastrous past was being repeated here, in Morrow Creek. Here, in his new life. "You can bring them apple fritters and ask them how they ruined my reputation the first time."

Grace looked appalled. "You don't mean that."

"I do."

Heartsick and distraught, prodded by even more pounding from Heddy Neibermayer, Jack girded his strength. There was nothing for it but to accept things as they were. To clear up this damnable mess and get on with whatever came next.

Likely it would be his leaving town. He didn't see how he could continue business here, with his saloon a gathering place for an entire horde of demanding women and himself a joke.

"I do mean it." He turned to face Grace at last. He kept his fists clenched, his shoulders rigid. "Just as I mean this: Our battle is finished. You've won, Grace."

"Not if you're leaving, I haven't!" She rushed to him, her face pale and her hair tangled. Her eyes were enormous, wet with sudden tears. "I was done fighting with you! This—this doesn't have to mean anything. Not to us. I'll set it right, if that's what you want. I know—I know now that I should have asked you first. I should not have sent those drawings, only—"

With difficulty, Jack looked away. "Leave me be. Don't come to my saloon—for as long as I still own it. Don't come to my quarters, don't approach me on the street, don't talk to me."

"What?" Grace stared, unmoving. "What do you mean?"

"This was a mistake."

She raised her chin. "Of course it wasn't."

Against all his intentions, her stout declaration almost made Jack smile. It was so like Grace to not give an inch—to fight to the finish for whatever she wanted.

Unfortunately, she hadn't really wanted him.

He motioned outside. "I have things to take care of."

"Wait." Grace stepped nearer. "Last night…" She twisted her hands. "Last night you said you would want me always."

Her beseeching look snared him. For the merest instant, Jack allowed himself to drink in the sight of her, to remember all the ways they'd been happy together…to imagine all the ways they might have been happier still. He could not say he didn't love her. But he refused to say he did.

"Goodbye, Grace," he said instead.

Then he went to meet his fate without looking back.

* * *

Alone, Grace stared at the door of her meeting room.

Outside, the tumult caused by Heddy Neibermayer and her retinue—and, seemingly, most of the people in town—reached a higher pitch, complete with a rousing chant. There was no one like an experienced suffragist to stir up a crowd, she mused. Evidently Heddy was even more capable than Grace had imagined.

Thoroughly chilled, she grasped her blanket with numb fingers. All of her felt benumbed in fact, heartily willing to deny everything that had just happened. Jack's accusations, his dawning look of betrayal, his raspy goodbye. Grace still didn't understand any of it. She'd only wanted to help him. To prove to everyone how very far Jack had come under her tutelage.

To demonstrate just one of the reasons she loved him.

Our battle is finished. You've won, he'd said. But just then, Grace could not grasp how. After years of refusing to admit how much loving someone would mean to her, now she finally had…and just as quickly, she had lost him. She'd lost Jack.

Grace refused to accept it. Defiantly, she stared at the work they'd accomplished. She gazed at the cot they'd shared, still rumpled with the aftermath of their night together. She recalled the look in Jack's eyes as he'd held her close. It could not be that those things had ended.

She would not allow them to be ended.

With her heart in her throat, she scrambled into her clothes. She raked her hair into its knot, shoving in pins willy-nilly. She scrubbed her face, sucked in a deep breath and readied herself for the battle to come.

Anything worth having is worth fighting for, Grace always said. Now she felt battered, it was true. Confused and bereft and alone. But the time had finally come, she decided, to prove that Jack Murphy—that the love they'd shared—was infinitely worth the struggle. She would find the truth, she would learn all its facets, then she would deal with the matter accordingly.

Now more than ever, no one stopped a Crabtree woman.

Chapter Seventeen

Everywhere Jack went, things were equally disastrous.

"Sewed up any pretties?" his patrons asked him, laughing.

"Mebbe you oughtta make them corsets a mite bigger," a cowboy remarked, elbowing his friend, "so's you can wear 'em yourself."

"I ain't never seen me a sissified barkeep afore," said another, chortling as he hefted his ale. "You wear pantalets?"

Even O'Neil had his fun when Jack ventured into the butcher's shop two days after the whole debacle struck.

"I wouldn't mind all those ladies comin' round me all trussed up in their unmentionables." O'Neil leered. "Hell, I might even take up fashion likewise. Only I can't make me a straight stitch to save my life." The man held up his raw-boned hands. "Maybe you ought to give me embroidery lessons, Murphy."

Laughter echoed through the shop. "Yeah, Murphy," another man shouted. "Tell us, so's we can have women clamoring, too."

Jack only shouldered his way outside, guffaws trailing him.

It was bad enough to have lost Grace, but to have become the town joke, too? That was more than he could stand.

Since word had gotten round about his scandalous past, mothers looked askance at him in the street, then whispered to their curious children. Men tipped their hats with mocking grins. More than one bold female offered her services as his real-life fitting form. A few timid ladies even stopped him in secret, casting furtive glances before confiding in him.

"Bless you," one said, squeezing his hand. "Before I found your corsetry, I was squashed fair past breathing all the time!"

"Your designs are a godsend," said another. "I fully intend to buy two more corsets—one to send to my sister in Landslide!"

But despite Jack's grudging nods in reply to that praise, he could not feel happy for what his meddlesome sisters persisted in calling his "proudest achievement."

"You see?" Corinne, the eldest, nudged him. She offered a wise nod toward his departing admirers, having waylaid him—along with the rest of the brood—on his way from the Lorndorff Hotel. "You have done a great service to women everywhere."

"We're simply making sure women everywhere know about it," Glenna added with her toothy grin. "It's been so exciting!"

"Traveling around with Heddy and her retinue, seeing all the cities and towns and people." Arleen sighed, hugging herself in the dreamy way she had. "One time a writer from a newspaper interviewed us, Jack! We could be as famous as you in the end!"

"Don't scowl that way, Jack." His sister Nealie gave him a no-nonsense look. "It's not healthful for your facial muscles. Besides, you know we're right. Everyone in Morrow Creek may have mistaken you for an ordinary barkeep—for a time—but the truth was bound to come out eventually."

"Nobody asks questions in the territory," Jack argued.

"Well, they should," Corinne said firmly. "Inquisitiveness makes life so much more invigorating."

She sounded exactly like Grace. Jack began to believe his

secret past really had been doomed to haunt his future—at least from the moment Grace had trod downstairs in her dress-reform hat and starchy clothes to meet him, her new co-tenant.

"You're scowling again," Nealie noted in a singsong voice.

"Leave him alone." Arleen grabbed his arm, giving him a squeeze. "Haven't you all heard the teasing Jack has endured?"

"Well, if he hadn't deceived everyone," Corinne argued, "then he wouldn't have to endure any teasing, now would—"

"I've made amends, damn it!" Jack interrupted.

His sisters gasped. Nealie tsk-tsked. "Language, Jack."

He didn't care. He hadn't set out to deceive anyone—only to leave his problematic past behind. Now that it had caught up with him anyway, Jack had tolerated the joking, the name-calling and the whispering. He'd let all the townspeople have their fun and, where appropriate, he'd even apologized—however gruffly—to those who were upset. He had made amends, and he didn't want a pile of lecturing on top of that humbling task.

"It's just as I was saying before," Arleen chattered blithely, offering him another consoling squeeze. "You can't hide your talents under a bushel forever. You're far too brilliant for that, Jack."

"That's right, far too brilliant," Glenna agreed. "Why, we've scarcely been able to keep up with the corset orders!"

"They're ever so popular," Arleen added, her skirts swirling girlishly. "The catalog printing has paid for itself twice over already, and we've hired three seamstresses in Boston. Yours is a veritable enterprise, Jack! Just like the famous Bloomingdale Brothers emporium in New York City."

Hell. They'd been busier than he'd known. Wanting to deny that fact, Jack only frowned more deeply and strode onward. All his sisters trotted in his wake, chattering in unison.

Almost since they'd stepped off the train, they hadn't left him alone. He could scarcely keep up with the hullabaloo they engendered.

"We would garner even more orders," Nealie said, "if you would put on a suit though. You used to look so nice in Boston."

Fisting his hands at the sides of his plain trousers, Jack kept going. Stoically. He swore not to recall traveling this same stretch of road with Grace…and failed.

"It wouldn't hurt if you'd speak at the rally, too," Nealie continued. "I realize we set out—the four of us—to remedy the trouble we caused you back home, but with a little cooperation—"

"I'm not going to the damned rally," he interrupted.

Grace would be there. Jack knew he couldn't bear it.

"Jack! Once again, that language is uncalled for."

"Don't pester him, Nealie," Corinne commanded loudly. They all trod past Nickerson's Book Depot and News Emporium in a colorful group of ribbons and lace—and one fierce scowl. "Can't you see he's still lovesick over that Miss Crabtree?"

Abruptly, silence fell. Jack stopped.

He rounded on them. "Where did you hear that?"

All four of his sisters shut their mouths. Defiantly.

"Now you decide to quit prattling? Out with it."

Arleen glanced at Glenna, her mouth quirked. "See?" she whispered, gesturing to Jack. "He does love her, else he wouldn't be so ferocious about hearing her name."

"Arleen—" Jack began warningly.

"You owe me your purple ribbons, Glenna," Arleen added in a hasty undertone. "You promised."

Glenna disagreed. Arleen poked her.

Catching the gist of their bickering, Jack stared in disbelief at his sisters. "You wagered on me?"

"Well…it's a long time between rallies, Jack."

"To be honest, we learned everything you've been up to within a day of arriving in town. Possibly less." Corinne sighed. "You've never been very mysterious, you know."

Affronted, Jack folded his arms. "I am completely mysterious," he informed them. "Or was—until you came here with your suffragette friends."

Nealie cleared her throat. "Actually, Jack, the respectful term is suffragist, properly referring to persons of either gender who advocate—"

"You? Mysterious?" Corinne chuckled. "Come now, Jack."

"I said if he married her, you won our bet," Glenna argued, speaking over both Nealie and Corinne. "So there."

"Pining over her is good enough," Arleen insisted, shaking her head. "He's clearly smitten. Anyone can see it. I do win!"

"Stop it, all of you." Jack glared at his sisters, each of them unrepentant. "Can't you leave well enough alone? Ever?"

His sisters, properly shushed, looked at one other.

He could see they were befuddled by the question.

"Never mind." Squaring his shoulders, Jack glanced toward his saloon. Remarkably, patronage had increased, partially in anticipation of the Excelsior Performing Troupe's debut tonight.

To his chagrin, however, a quantity of his newest customers had been women looking for corsets or other unmentionables from him. Assured by Grace's letters to Heddy Neibermayer, they all believed him to be enlightened. "I have work to do."

"Yes, Jack," Arleen said piously.

Glenna widened her eyes. "We're sorry, Jack."

Jack wasn't fool enough to believe their ladled-on naiveté for a minute. He hesitated. "What mischief are you up to now?"

Corinne waved him away. "Nothing you should worry about."

"Everything will be fine," Nealie assured him.

Casting them a suspicious look, Jack wavered.

Then he realized the truth. No trouble his sisters could wrangle during their short time in town could compare with the misery of missing Grace. Despite that she'd revealed his secret, purposely betrayed him and brought on all kinds of aggravation on him in the process, he did miss her. Idiotically, he missed the nearby clomp of her man-shoes, too.

Knowing he was daft for certain, Jack said his goodbyes, then turned on his heel and headed for his saloon.

Beneath a gnarled oak at the town square, Grace glanced at the reformers and suffragists who ambled between the assembled tents. This was a fine spring day for a rally, and the equality march she and Heddy had led this morning had been excellent. But despite the crisp snap of the flags in the breeze, the vinegary tang of Doctor Winstetter's Female Remedy samples from the booth nearby and the arrival of her bicycling club members, Grace could not find herself cheered in the least.

She missed Jack. That was all there was to be said. And no matter how hard she tried, she could not repair the trouble between them. It was downright vexing. He veered away when he saw her coming, left his saloon to Harry during the hours Grace could visit, abandoned his entire routine of errands and mail fetching…all to avoid her, she felt sure.

He would never forgive her. That much seemed plain.

Grace tried all her usual tactics in response, hoping to move past her lovelorn feelings. She lost herself in marches and speeches and rabble-rousing. She listened to Heddy's lectures and applauded with due vigor. She even launched a protest and got herself hoisted off to Sheriff Caffey's jailhouse for what she'd hoped would be a distracting few hours' incarceration.

It had not worked. There'd been no solace to be found.

But just when Grace had decided to abandon her quest to reach Jack, to accept her fate and live without him, he was suddenly everywhere she looked. His image appeared on several banners at the rally. His catalogs piled inside numerous tents. His fame and achievements taunted her from every direction, reminding Grace that she hadn't really known him at all.

In every tent, during every march, Grace's suffragist friends were aflutter with breathless discussion of "Professor Jack Murphy" and his "miraculous female inventions."

Even her family wasn't immune. Her mama applauded Jack's innovativeness, not the least bothered by the fact that he'd hidden part of his past life in Boston. Her papa nodded in agreement. Molly pronounced it "pure fate" that Grace had become smitten with an intellectual man, however much he grunted and served up whiskey.

And Sarah…Grace shuddered to remember that.

"Is it true," her sister inquired in all eagerness, "that Mr. Murphy's corsetry designs can make a grown man weep with longing? Is it?"

"I would not know," Grace announced, then hastened away.

But she had almost yearned to find out—with Jack himself—and that was worst of all. She didn't even approve of corsets, newfangled ones or not! Now Grace hadn't the scarcest idea what to do with herself. She tromped the grounds of the suffrage rally, nodding to friends and traveling vendors and members of her newly approved female baseball team, feeling despondent.

She should have known not to open herself to love and all its fancies, she reminded herself. Apparently, love was the only thing in the world not moved by strict effort. She was better off without it. Grateful to be without it, Grace assured herself. In fact, if she ever felt inclined toward love again, she would heartily pinch herself until sanity returned.

"Grace Crabtree?" someone asked. "Are you Miss Crabtree?"

Reluctantly, Grace roused herself from her visions of pinching and pinching every time she saw Jack. She turned to face four bright-eyed women. "Yes? I am Miss Crabtree."

They glanced at each other. Nodded. "We should have known," one said, nonsensically. "You look exactly right for him."

"For whom?"

"For our brother, of course." One woman stepped forward and took Grace's elbow. Her smile was as warm as Molly's ovens, and her manner nearly as brisk as Grace's. "I am Corinne, and this is Nealie, Glenna and Arleen. We are the Murphy sisters."

They all beamed as though this were good news.

"Oh, dear." Grace balked. "This is awkward. I should not—"

"Come with us," said another sister—Nealie, Grace recalled. Purposefully, she took Grace's other elbow. "We have a great deal to accomplish, and not much time to do it in."

"Especially given Jack's muleheadedness," Glenna advised.

"And his determination not to let us help," Arleen added.

All four of them laughed uproariously at that.

"I am finished with Jack Murphy," Grace said. "Don't—"

"See? She is just as stubborn as he is!" Corinne's smile widened even further. She nodded at her three sisters, then waved toward Grace. "And obviously just as miserable."

They gave her commiserating looks.

Grace hesitated, her heart pounding. "Jack is miserable?"

"Without you?" Glenna nodded vigorously.

"Only until we women take charge," Nealie assured her.

"It's simply the way of things," Arleen added.

Hmm. Grace quite liked the way the Murphy sisters viewed things. They were very practical. For the first time in days, she felt hopefulness soak all through her like sunshine on the springtime soil.

"I would like to know about his life in Boston," Grace admitted. "And about what happened there."

"Easily done," Corinne said. "Come right this way."

Alone in his saloon, Jack wandered between the tables. He righted those that had been upended, then snatched empty bottles and added them to the armload he already carried.

Last night, the whole place had been packed as a pickle barrel, filled with patrons eager to see the Excelsior Performing Troupe. Grace's suppositions of culture aside, the retinue had included more than one bawdy dance-hall girl, two jugglers and one magician. Hardly refined, but very profitable.

Even if Jack had had to endure numerous ribald jests about underwear while his customers paid their admissions. Nowadays, those jokes seemed more friendly in nature than he'd first supposed though…and it felt strangely liberating to have his secret in the open, too. Not that Jack would admit it.

Scowling, he left the liquor bottles on the bar. Harry would be here soon to help clean up, open the saloon and prepare for the troupe's second night performing. In the meantime, Jack needed to do all manner of restocking.

He bent to the crate of tequila he'd brought from the back and plucked two bottles free. By rote, he carried them behind the bar, treading slowly. If last night was any indication, he had finally achieved the successful saloon he'd long worked for. He'd earned enough to pay Jedediah Hofer in full, to square up his other accounts and even to expand sooner than he'd thought.

Right now, though, Jack felt anything but pleased.

Behind him, the doors creaked. A shaft of light fell over the bottles in Jack's hand, alerting him to a visitor.

"Saloon's closed." Grouchily, he turned. "Come back later."

Adam Crabtree planted his feet, his usually jolly demeanor anything but this morning. "If I do that, I will not have done my utmost. And that is not like a Crabtree at all."

Jack wanted to groan. Evidently doggedness ran in the family as much as freethinking did. He nodded. "Crabtree."

"Murphy." Adam gave him a shrewd look. "I don't care if you're closed. I'm here to talk about my daughter."

Grace. Jack could not speak. He shelved two more bottles.

"I can see you're feeling uncommunicative," Adam said, untroubled by that fact. "Very well. I'll get straight to the heart of things, shall I? Then I can go back to my peaceable retirement, and you can go back to being obstinate."

Against his will, Jack smiled. Appalled, he sobered before turning to the crate to fetch another pair of tequila bottles.

"I have to tell you," Adam announced, striding across the saloon floor like a practiced orator, "I am most displeased with the way this matchup has turned out. Or not turned out, as the case may be." He wagged his finger at Jack, his whole manner blustery behind his spectacles and graying hair. "I'll admit— with no undue modesty, mind you—that I am quite skilled at these matters. It didn't seem possible that two such brash, bookish, unnaturally muleheaded individuals as yourselves wouldn't suit one another, so quite understandably I assumed—"

"Matchup?" Jack asked. "What matchup?"

Adam gave him a warmhearted, almost commiserating smile. "Between you and Grace, of course. Why else would I be here?"

Wholly confused, Jack stared at him. "I don't know."

"It took me months to find you," Adam mused. "I must have perused hundreds of applicants for this building. My land agent was pushed near to fisticuffs several times, he was so frustrated with me. But I insisted on waiting till I was sure."

This made no sense at all. "Sure of what?"

"Why, that I'd found the right man for my Grace. And when I met you at last, I knew you were the one for certain."

On that bewildering note, Adam strode across the saloon, studying the place as though seeing it for the first time. It occurred to Jack that perhaps he was. Crabtree did not attend meetings of the Morrow Creek Men's Club here, nor indulge in whiskey like most men in town. He was an anomaly.

A meddling, matchmaking, property-owning anomaly.

Jack stared in disbelief, realizing the truth with a jolt.

Adam sensed exactly the moment when he did.

"That was a near thing," he observed, chuckling. "If you hadn't cottoned on by now, Murphy, I would have had to revise my entire opinion of your intellect. Very good. Excellent."

"You own this property," Jack said.

"Indeed I do. Bought it with the first profits from the *Pioneer Press* and held on to it until the time was right."

"But your land agent." Jack marveled over it all, the pieces dropping into place like parts of the puzzles Grace had claimed her father loved so well. "Your lease demands. Your—"

"All necessary, I'm afraid." Adam shook his head. "My daughter is too savvy otherwise. Grace doesn't know the whole story, you see." The man eyed Jack's drooping bottles. "You might want to put those down. No profits in spilled tequila."

Awkwardly, Jack did. "You set us up," he declared.

"Yes, and I'm not sorry either. Sometimes people require a certain nudge in order to do the right thing, I've found."

"I see where Grace gets her meddling streak."

"Perhaps." Adam's face glowed with affection. "Of all my

daughters, Grace is most like me, I'll admit. But the fact remains—enough is enough." His expression hardened as he wheeled around, suddenly the staunch businessman. "I've heard how you and Grace are avoiding one another, and I've had my fill. I'm fit to turn you both out if you can't cooperate for a change."

Instantly, Jack objected. "Grace will be forlorn!"

A telling twinkle entered Adam's eyes. "Ah. Interesting, that you thought of Grace's well-being before your own."

Disgruntled, Jack frowned. But before he could refute that outrageous claim, Adam strode to the bar. He studied Colleen's painting, nodded, then addressed Jack with satisfaction.

"But since Grace is *already* forlorn," Adam pointed out, "and since her broken heart is likely to blame for it, my reapportioning your shared property can hardly injure her much more, can it? A clean break would be best." He paused. "However, I'll hear your arguments to keep your share intact if you wish."

Jack met the man's ostensibly cheerful expression with a fierce one of his own. He thought of Grace, turned out of her meeting rooms. Thought of her without her clubs and activities and nook for hiding contraband baseballs. Thought of her alone.

"Let Grace have the upstairs." He frowned. "I'll leave."

Aggravatingly, Adam smiled. "Perhaps you should think about why you made that offer, Murphy. Think about why you withstood all those seamstress jokes. Why you owned up to your past at all." He gave Jack a measuring look. "I have a feeling packing up and pulling foot for someplace new won't look quite the same to you after that."

Then he tipped his hat and took himself away, leaving Jack with a scowl as wide as the new saloon stage he'd constructed—and a lion's share of food for thought in the bargain.

* * *

For the first time in all her years of rabble-rousing, Grace missed a protest march that day. Instead of carrying a banner and agitating for women's rightful equality, she sat enraptured at the square while Corinne and Nealie and Glenna and Arleen told her all there was to know about their brother, Jack.

They spoke of his fine work at Boston College. His long history of inventing things. His abiding care for his family, and the scandal that had chased him from home. All of it.

Rapidly, from that conversation onward, Grace found herself welcomed into the chaotic fold that was the Murphy family. It was wondrous and lively. Even though Jack himself had not come round—not even two days after her enlightening talk with his sisters—Grace could not help but feel a little better.

No wonder Jack had reacted so strongly to her publicizing his drawings, Grace realized. No wonder he had felt betrayed when all the scandalous doings he'd left behind had turned up again at Grace's unwitting instigation. Likely she would have felt the same if their situations had been reversed.

"All I needed was the proper information," she proclaimed to her father a day later, breakfasting with him before the final engagement of Heddy Neibermayer's speaking tour. "The correct and complete information. If I had known about Jack's past, I would never have called attention to those drawings."

"Of course you would have, Grace." Her papa munched his toasted Graham-flour bread, his eyes mischievous and somehow wise behind his spectacles. "You wouldn't have been able to help yourself. You were born to meddle and manage and interfere."

"Papa!"

"What?" He blinked. "I mean that in the most loving manner possible." He patted her hand fondly. "You have always been boundlessly aware of your own opinions, from the day you first wailed out your displeasure at having been born so abruptly. You haven't stopped stirring up a fuss for a minute since." He smiled. "It's one of your most endearing qualities."

"Endearing?" Grace frowned.

"To those of us who love you," he specified, spying the jam. He helped himself to more. "Which is how I knew, if I were ever to match you up with someone suitable—as I so love to do, being singularly meddlesome myself—I would have to be clever."

Grace stilled, no longer enjoying her oatmeal. "Match me up with someone?" Thoughts of the whispered-about matchmaker of Morrow Creek swirled through her mind, making her distinctly uneasy. All this time, she'd thought she was immune to the family legacy. Now it seemed… "Papa, tell me you didn't!"

"I did. You and Jack Murphy were an ideal match," her father informed her, his chin jutting in stubborn likeness to her own. "Pairing you with him was an excellent idea. My only mistake was in underestimating your identical obduracy."

Grace groaned, long familiar with her papa's…unusual tendencies toward romance. He'd done this before. But she'd never expected to find herself at the wrong end of his meddling.

"You promised you would leave me alone!" she reminded him, wadding up her napkin in frustration. "You promised you would not interfere with my life, because I am the eldest, and—"

His warmhearted smile stopped her. "Dear girl. A promise is nothing compared with making sure you're happy. I'm a father! My whole purpose is to raise daughters who are secure and loved."

Still… Grace could not believe it. "But to match me with a man? With Jack Murphy?" She waved her arm, aghast at the very notion. "As though I were a silly skirt with no sense at all? With no mind of my own to handle my own affairs?"

Her papa regarded her calmly. He pushed away his plate, then laid his hand gently on her forearm. His beloved face was sincere and serious and terribly, wonderfully, honest.

"It is because you have a mind of your own that I was compelled to intervene," he said kindly, shaking his head. "Else see the daughter I love trapped in a solitude she'd never admit—nor ever be able to solve on her own."

Stricken, Grace gazed at him. She opened her mouth, instantly prepared to deny it…but in the end she could not.

Her papa was right, she knew. Without being forced to deal with the man she fancied, without having Jack Murphy situated so vexingly downstairs, Grace might never have broken free of her lonesome routine. She might never have touched real happiness, nor ever understood what it meant to truly love someone.

To truly be loved in return.

"Don't be angry with me." Her papa's voice was quiet among the china and toast. "I only meant the best for you."

"I'm not angry. I—" Another thought struck Grace. "Is this why you refused me the editorship of the newspaper?" she asked, distraught. "Because you wanted me to be matched instead?"

"No. Not at all." As though that were patently obvious, her papa patted her arm. "I did that because the *Pioneer Press* really did require an experienced editor. And because you never truly wanted to have that job yourself."

"Papa! Anything an experienced man can do, I can do."

"That's true." Blithely, he crunched more toast. "But you didn't want to be editor. You wanted me to be proud of you."

She shook her head. "They were the same thing."

"They were not." His smile was sunny—and understanding. "It's not what you do that makes me proud, Grace. It's who you are, both inside and out. So long as you are yourself—truly yourself—I'm beyond proud of you. Always and forever."

Grace's eyes filled with tears. She simply couldn't help it. "You are? You're proud of me?"

"Endlessly proud," her papa assured her. His startled gaze met hers. "You didn't realize that already?"

Grace could not speak. She felt too astonished.

"Well. All talk of pride aside," Papa blustered, "I still insist you are doing yourself a disservice by giving up on love so easily. Poor Mr. Murphy is bereft, you know."

And with that reminder—and an extra helping of toast with jam—Grace knew exactly what her next mission had to be.

Chapter Eighteen

With a mixture of pride and dismay, Jack gazed at his saloon's packed tables and full bar. Men stood between both, hefting whiskeys or lagers, and they lingered at the billiard tables, too. Even the skinniest drinker in Morrow Creek could not have found room to bend an elbow at his place today.

"It looks as if Heddy Neibermayer is good for business," Marcus observed, setting down his sarsaparilla. "There's hardly a man in town who isn't hiding out in here."

"Hiding out? Pshaw." With a blustery exhalation, Daniel waved to a friend in the crowd. His brawny reach almost upended a nearby cowboy. "There's not a man alive who's afraid of a bunch of tiny little women. Not me, that's for sure."

Jack smiled. "I'll be certain to let Sarah know that."

Daniel's horrified look made him laugh.

"You can't." Marcus shrugged. "Sarah's getting ready for that closing rally today, just like Molly is."

The rally. Jack knew Grace would be there, too. But after...

"There won't be any livin' with 'em," opined a banker who stood within spitting distance, rolling his eyes, "now that those suffragettes have all our women het up over 'equality.'"

"A man just can't reason with them," said another. "Last night, my wife made me wash my own dinner dishes! Said I ate the blasted food happily enough, and I might as well wash up, too."

The men beside him grumbled. More grousing was heard.

"Ah, but the ladies at Miss Adelaide's place have got them corsets you made now, Murphy," a miner volunteered with an eager grin. "The sight of them 'most makes it all worthwhile."

"That's for certain!" O'Neil raised his mescal.

"Three cheers for Murphy's underwear!" someone yelled.

Bedlam erupted. Men from every side of the saloon hoisted their drinks, sloshing ale and tequila with good-natured yells.

All was forgiven, it seemed to Jack—secret past and all. At the realization, a curious sense of relief struck him. Even Jedediah Hofer—recently paid a bonus for his kind business terms—genially raised a glass in salute.

Daniel joined in. Then, seeing his friends watching, he lowered his drink. He winked. "There's something special about those unmentionables, all right."

"So, Murphy." Marcus addressed Jack with an interested gleam in his eyes. "I guess you've gone from seamstress to savior in a matter of days. And you've given every man in town a sanctuary to hide from the suffragettes in, too." His satisfied smile flashed. "How does it feel to turn from sissy to hero?"

Jack scowled. "Shut up and drink, Copeland. Else I'm giving your place to someone who spends more money."

"I want to know, too," Daniel butted in, edging closer. "What miracle are you going to work next, Professor?"

Professor. The designation had rapidly become his nickname. Jack decided he didn't mind the sound of it so very much after all. He spread his hands along the bar. "Well, as soon as Harry gets here, I've got something special in mind."

"Something to do with Grace," Marcus crowed. "I knew it!"

"I didn't say that," Jack countered—not entirely convincingly, he felt sure. "I didn't say a thing about Grace."

But she had been all he'd thought about for days.

"We figured you'd come round eventually." Daniel whacked the bar, making drinks totter. "Just like us. If two of us are going to be hog-tied to uppity Crabtree women, we might as well all three of us be."

"Damned straight." Marcus took a celebratory sarsaparilla swig. "What's your plan?" he asked, always eager for strategy.

"Tell us," Daniel urged. "You're sure to need our advice."

Jack rolled his eyes, then slapped down his bar cloth.

"It's true. You will need help." Marcus offered a solemn look, untroubled by the raucous saloongoers all around him. "You shouldn't go off half-cocked, especially with Heddy Neibermayer and her retinue in town. Their opinions matter to Grace."

"She's likely to turn you down flat just to save face," Daniel opined. He caught Jack's aggrieved look and raised his hands in apology. "Can't argue with a woman. The last thing Grace Crabtree is going to do is accept your proposal—"

"Who says I'm going to propose to her?" Jack protested, appalled to be caught in such a sentimental wallow.

"—with a whole caboodle of lady reformers around."

Wisely, Marcus nodded. "Daniel is right. Wait till Grace is alone, Jack. You'll have your best chance with her then."

"You two are daft. Grace isn't like that," Jack disagreed. But as he considered matters further, the certainty he'd awakened with this morning—the certainty engendered by his visit with Adam Crabtree and his own damnable loneliness—slowly seeped away. Jack felt the blood drain from his face. "Although she does put a lot of store in what Humorless Heddy says...."

Alarmed for certain now, he gave Daniel and Marcus a wide-eyed look. They nodded somberly. "You don't get many chances with women. They're funny that way," Daniel said. "Tetchy."

The cowboy leaned in. "All I can say is, don't wear your trail boots with cow patties on 'em." He gave a sage wink.

Fraught with uncertainty, Jack stared back. But before he could so much as answer the cowboy, a strange sound reached him from outside. It sounded like many feet tramping in the street. Like chanting and rabble-rousing and marching. Like trouble.

He glanced to the doorway and glimpsed dust rising.

"Damnation. Is there a protest outside my saloon?"

His patrons heard it, too. One by one, they quit laughing and drinking and clanking billiards. The faro table fell silent. The dice stopped clattering. Whiskeys went slack in several hands as every head turned to the saloon's entryway.

He'd waited too long, Jack realized. Grace had gotten fed up and hurt and knee-deep in frustration and had taken out her dissatisfaction the best way she knew how. By leading a whole cadre of uppity women against his saloon. Or him. Or both.

She probably meant to shutter him for good, he realized, with an entire contingent of troublesome females at her command.

Swallowing hard, Jack steeled his courage. He fisted his hands. Then he headed for his saloon doors, ready to defend everything that truly mattered.

It would not be easy, he reasoned as he heard the chanting grow louder. It would not be pretty, nor done the fancy way he'd hoped. But it would be done, and that was all that counted in the end.

With the saloon hushed behind him, Jack straightened his shoulders. Outside, all was in a ruckus. Inside, everyone held their whiskey-soaked breaths, waiting as he crossed the floor.

He pushed open the doors. Every chair scraped as men rushed to follow him, crowding behind in a tobacco-stinking clump.

Jack stepped onto the stoop. Sunlight blinded him. He shielded his eyes, ready to confront the trouble head-on.

It was even worse than he'd thought. Women crowded every inch in front of his saloon. More marched from either side, some ladies he recognized and some he didn't—doubtless Heddy's reformers. Many of Morrow Creek's finest women had come, too.

In astonishment, Jack gaped at the placards they wore, the signs they held aloft. He spied a pair of dance-hall girls from the Excelsior Performing Troupe, then a lady juggler, then his four sisters, gaily waving from behind their banner.

Grace stepped from among the crowd, and the sight of her made his breath stop. Dressed in her usual commonsense garb, her hair up high, she held a gaudy sign firmly in hand. It did not—as Jack had feared—proclaim his uselessness to the entire world.

Instead, in enormous letters, it read…

GRACE CRABTREE LOVES JACK MURPHY.

Disbelieving, he blinked. Grace's sign remained, held in a grip as steadfast as the gaze she fixed him with next. Her face flushed with love and trust and truthfulness, and Jack felt humbled by the realization of what he was seeing.

Grace. Beautiful, proud, maddening Grace. His Grace. If she would dare to declare her feelings this way, in front of her suffragette idol and all her friends—in front of his sisters and hers—then surely there was a chance she meant it.

GRACE CRABTREE LOVES JACK MURPHY.

Every sign read the same, Jack realized in a daze. Somehow, Grace had marshaled all her reformer friends, all the members of her clubs and teams, nearly every female in town, just to say…

GRACE CRABTREE LOVES JACK MURPHY.

"I reckon she means it," Daniel said from behind him.

"What are you waiting for?" Marcus poked him. "Go!"

The damned fools sounded nearly as choked up as Jack felt. Any minute now, they'd start blubbering. So would he. Casting them a helpless look, Jack stepped forward.

Grace met him halfway, her eager strides biting through the dusty street. Her gaze never left his. Jack welcomed the telling thump of her man-shoes all the same. He grasped her free hand, and knew that touching her again was all he'd wanted.

"I'm sorry, Jack." The words came in a rush, husky and heartfelt. "I'm sorry I hurt you, sorry I doubted you—sorry I didn't make sure to stand by you when you needed me most."

He could only gaze at her, awestruck, taking in the beloved angles of her face, the familiar sprinkle of freckles on her nose, the telltale and hopelessly endearing tilt of her chin. Grace meant what she said. She meant it, and because of that, Jack knew he couldn't wait any longer.

"Grace, listen—"

"Please say you'll accept my apology," she hurried on, giving his hand an impassioned squeeze. Her homemade sign wobbled, then straightened against the vivid sky. "Please say you'll give me another try, Jack. If I have to ask you every day, you know I will. You know I possess the fortitude, when I really, truly want something, to try and try—"

"Grace." Jack shook his head. "You're not—"

"I've always said that anything worth having is worth fighting for. Haven't I?" Her gaze beseeched him. Her speech rambled on, scarcely leaving a word edgewise for Jack. "You are worth having, and so is the love we shared. I won't give up! I know now—thanks to my sisters and yours, thanks to Papa and my mother—that the important thing is being who we are. I couldn't improve on you if I tried, Jack. I thought I was, only...only all I was really doing is loving you. Just as you are."

He stood there, buffeted by her rush of words, waiting for Grace to say her piece. It was important that she speak freely, Jack told himself, before he turned loose all the explanations, the apologies, he held so tightly inside him. Grace needed to know he understood—and forgave. Wholly.

Instead Grace flung her sign-holding arm outward. "Say something!" she demanded, tears in her eyes. "Grunt at least!"

The women nearby pressed nearer. The men inside did, too.

But somehow Jack couldn't do a thing but smile. His heart simply felt that full. So he contented himself with squeezing her hand once more, loving her courage and strength. "Grace—"

"I know we still have problems to overcome," Grace rushed onward, jittery even in her clodhopper shoes. The pink in her cheeks heightened further. "They can't all be shoehorned away, all neat and tidy just because we say so. But I know we can do it, Jack! If you'll only forgive me, and—"

"I forgive you, Grace." Happiness burbled up and threatened to cut off his words. Determined, he kept on. "I'm sorry, too. Sorry I didn't tell you everything. Please—" His voice broke, causing him to try again. "Say you forgive me."

Her eyes widened. "Oh, Jack! Oh course I forgive you!"

"Because if you do," he continued doggedly, "I feel certain there's no problem too big for us to tackle together."

"Do you mean that? Do you?" Grace pushed even nearer, her sign now threatening to conk him on the noggin. At his nod, her relief was evident. "Because there's another matter we should discuss straightaway, and I know I can't wait, because I love you so much, and I've already wasted so much time, and as often as a certain saloonkeeper—"

The women behind her beamed. A few lofted their signs.

"—has been pestering me to sample the 'glories' of marriage, I've decided there's only one sure way to—"

Damnation, Jack realized. He was about to have his marriage proposal wrestled right out from beneath him. His free-thinking reformer of a woman was about to lead his proposal herself.

"Stop." Jack could scarcely form the word, so overwhelmed did he feel in that moment, with his palms sweating and his head swimming and his heart pounding and nearly all of Morrow Creek scrutinizing his every move. "Just wait a minute."

Grace's eyes widened. Biting her lip, she waited.

"I may not be the roughest man in the territory," Jack said. "I may not be the most rugged either. But I do know that I love you, Grace. And I won't have my marriage proposal sneaked out from under me."

He tried to muster a fierce look—and knew he only succeeded in squeezing her hand still harder. Love caught his breath and made his heart hammer, and there was only one way to move forward. Still holding her hand, Jack dropped to one knee.

Grace gasped, her eyes shimmering with new tears.

"That is why," Jack told her hoarsely, "you will stand silent while I tell you I love you. I love you, Grace, with all my heart and soul and every single breath I'll take."

Women nearby swooned. Grace only nodded.

"And that is why," he continued, "you will wait patiently while I explain all the ways I missed you, and plan never to miss you again for as long as I live. Without you," Jack said in plain truth, "I feel only half a man, needing all the time."

This time, his saloon patrons sighed, the sound deep and soulful. A few men sniffled. But Grace only nodded.

"And that is why," Jack said finally, as sternly as he could, "you will nod agreeably when I say that you must marry me soon, before I lose all hope of happiness altogether."

Grace nodded with a vigor that astonished everyone. The tears in her eyes overflowed, dampening her cheeks, but she looked beautiful to Jack all the same.

"It's only with you," he said, his knee fixed in the dusty street, "that I am truly myself, Grace. I was a fool not to realize it before. I am a saloonkeeper and an inventor, a man who loves good lager and science alike. Thanks to you, I'm whole again. And I don't want another day without you by my side."

Hastily, Grace shoved her sign away. As befit any proper lady suffragist, she fell to her knees right beside him in the street, then flung her arms around him. "I'll marry you, Jack. I could not possibly love you more. Yes," she said urgently, holding his face in both hands. "Yes, yes, yes!"

Overcome with joy, Jack drew her close and kissed her. Rowdy applause filled the saloon behind them. Raucous feminine cheering overflowed the street. But all Jack's thoughts were for Grace…for the woman in his arms and in his heart.

Hardly able to keep from bawling himself, Jack ended their kiss. He drew back and regarded Grace with all the gratitude of a man who'd nearly lost everything—but had somehow found it again. He pressed his forehead to hers, gazing into her eyes.

"Thank you," he whispered. "For not giving up. For loving me still. Most of all…for being yourself."

"Thank you." Grace grinned. "For loving me anyway."

They stood, laughing, Grace wiping away happy tears. Jack clasped her hand and raised their joined arms aloft.

"Who wants to go to a wedding?" he yelled.

The whole assembly cheered, Heddy Neibermayer and all. Men surged forward to offer congratulations, sham commiseration and hearty slaps on the back. Women rushed closer, aflutter with talk of wedding planning and flowers and dresses.

Grace's whole face shone as she turned to Jack. "See? Isn't this marvelous? With all this help and a bit of orderly cooperation—"

"Courtesy of you, I'm sure." Jack smiled.

"We ought to have no trouble at all with planning a wedding, bringing our families together, finding a way to share our building space and everything else."

Gladly, he held her close. "Well…I didn't want to say so before," he admitted, spying his sisters, "but we might have an easier time of that last than we thought. It seems I'm quite a bit wealthier than I planned on, thanks to a certain quartet of meddlesome women who've sold my designs far and wide."

Corinne reached him. "Pshaw, Jack! We only wanted to help."

His other three sisters nodded, utterly unrepentant.

"So I figure I'll have plenty of money to build my boardinghouse rooms and a finer meeting space for you besides."

Grace leaped at the notion. "Jack! That's wonderful."

Her family crowded around, Adam and Fiona looking on with evident satisfaction. Marcus and Molly gazed in delight, and Daniel and Sarah nodded in certainty. Jack grinned at them all.

"Exactly how much money?" Grace nudged him, fairly rising on tiptoes in eagerness. "Enough to finance a mayoral campaign, I wonder? Because I have a few definite ideas about how things ought to be run in Morrow Creek, and there's no reason that I can see why a woman shouldn't run for public office."

She beamed, positively alight with the idea.

"Oh, Grace," Adam Crabtree warned. "That's quite ambitious."

"Yes, that's too much," her sisters echoed. "Even for you."

But Grace remained perfectly sure, Jack could see—as sure as she'd ever been about their loving one another. So he only wrapped his arms around her and surrendered to the inevitable.

"If there's not enough money for that now, there will be with my next designs," he promised. "Anything for you."

"Excellent!" Grace kissed him. "As it happens, I quite like this corsetry of yours, you know." She gave a saucy wink. "I hear your scandalous designs make grown men weep with longing."

"And love," Jack corrected. "Never forget that."

Then, united by that love, they joined hands and went to raise a toast—to rabble-rousing and stubbornness and rascally men who grunted when no words would do…and to planning the biggest, rowdiest wedding that Morrow Creek had ever seen.

* * * * *

New York Times *bestselling author Linda Lael Miller is back with a new romance featuring the heartwarming McKettrick family from Silhouette Special Edition.*

SIERRA'S HOMECOMING
by Linda Lael Miller

*On sale December 2006,
wherever books are sold.*

Turn the page for a sneak preview!

Soft, smoky music poured into the room.

The next thing she knew, Sierra was in Travis's arms, close against that chest she'd admired earlier, and they were slow dancing.

Why didn't she pull away?

"Relax," he said. His breath was warm in her hair.

She giggled, more nervous than amused. What was the matter with her? She was attracted to Travis, had been from the first, and he was clearly attracted to her. They were both adults. Why not enjoy a little slow dancing in a ranch-house kitchen?

Because slow dancing led to other things. She took a step back and felt the counter flush against her lower back. Travis naturally came with her, since they were holding hands and he had one arm around her waist.

Simple physics.

Then he kissed her.

Physics again—this time, not so simple.

"Yikes," she said, when their mouths parted.

He grinned. "Nobody's ever said that after I kissed them."

She felt the heat and substance of his body pressed against hers. "It's going to happen, isn't it?" she heard herself whisper.

"Yep," Travis answered.

"But not tonight," Sierra said on a sigh.

"Probably not," Travis agreed.

"When, then?"

He chuckled, gave her a slow, nibbling kiss. "Tomorrow morning," he said. "After you drop Liam off at school."

"Isn't that…a little…soon?"

"Not soon enough," Travis answered, his voice husky. "Not nearly soon enough."

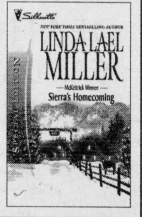

Silhouette
SPECIAL EDITION™

Silhouette Special Edition brings you a
heartwarming new story from the *New York Times*
bestselling author of *McKettrick's Choice*

LINDA LAEL MILLER

Sierra's Homecoming

Sierra's Homecoming
follows the parallel lives
of two McKettrick women,
living their lives in the
same house but
generations apart,
each with a special son
and an unlikely new
romance.

December 2006

REQUEST YOUR FREE BOOKS!

 Harlequin® Historical
Historical Romantic Adventure!

2 FREE NOVELS PLUS 2
FREE GIFTS!

USA TODAY bestselling author

BARBARA McCAULEY

continues her award-winning series

SECRETS!

**A NEW BLACKHAWK FAMILY
HAS BEEN DISCOVERED…
AND THE SCANDALS ARE SET TO FLY!**

She touched him once and now
Alaina Blackhawk is certain horse rancher
DJ Bradshaw will be her first lover. But will
the millionaire Texan allow her to leave
once he makes her his own?

Blackhawk's Bond

On sale December 2006 (SD #1766)

Available at your favorite retail outlet.

Harlequin® Historical
Historical Romantic Adventure!

Loyalty...or love?

LORD GREVILLE'S CAPTIVE
Nicola Cornick

He had previously come to Grafton Manor to be betrothed to the beautiful Lady Anne—but that promise was broken with the onset of the English Civil War. Now Lord Greville has returned as an enemy, besieging the manor and holding its lady prisoner.

His devotion to his cause is swayed by his desire for Anne—he will have the lady, and her heart.

Yet Anne has a secret that must be kept from him at all costs....

On sale December 2006.
Available wherever Harlequin books are sold.